Scare Yourself
to Sleep

For Tom, Molly and Alice
RI

For Andrew
MK

First published in Great Britain by Ragged Bears in 1988
First published in paperback by Collins in 1993
This edition first published in 1997
Collins is an imprint of HarperCollins *Publishers* Ltd
77-85 Fulham Palace Road, Hammersmith, London, W6 8JB

3 5 7 9 8 6 4 2

Text copyright © Rose Impey 1988
Illustrations copyright © Moira Kemp 1988
Insides designed by Herman Lelie
Produced by Mathew Price Ltd
The Old Glove Factory Ltd
Bristol Road
Sherborne
Dorset
DT9 4HP

ISBN 0 00 674852 X

The author asserts the moral right to be identified as the author of the work.

Printed in Singapore

Scare Yourself
to Sleep

Rose Impey
Illustrated by Moira Kemp

Collins
An Imprint of HarperCollins*Publishers*

When my cousin comes to stay
we sleep in a tent
at the bottom
of the garden.
We don't let my brother in.
He'd spoil everything.

We love it
just the two of us
lying there
side by side
talking.

We tell each other jokes
very quietly
because we don't want anyone
to know we're there.

We know Simon is there
outside the tent
trying to listen
so we whisper.
We don't want him
spoiling everything.

Soon it starts to get dark.
The shadows rise
and outside it grows
quiet and still.
Then me and my cousin
always play the same game.
We call it
'Scare yourself to sleep.'

First I whisper to her,
'Are you scared?'
'No,' she says, 'are you?'
'No,' I say, 'but I bet
I could scare you.'
'Go on then,' she says.
'Right,' I say
and I tell her all about
The Dustbin Demons.

They are the gangs
of evil little goblins
who live
under the rubbish
in the bottom
of dustbins.

Each night
just as the moon comes up
they throw back the dustbin lid
with a clatter
ready to go on the prowl.

They fling
all the rotten food
up in the air
then out they crawl
climbing over one another
in their hurry to be off.
They swarm around the garden
until they find
some helpless creature
foolish enough
to be out alone.

Then they carry it off
struggling and squealing
back to their smelly den
never to be seen again.

My cousin is very quiet.
She wriggles down
into her sleeping bag.
I smile to myself.
That scared her.

Suddenly there is a
CRASH!
It sounds like a dustbin lid
banging and clattering
on the garden path.
Our hearts are thumping.

Then we hear, 'Gottya. Heeheehee.'

'Oh, Simon, go away.
You are stupid,' we say.
'You didn't scare us.'
But we move our sleeping bags
a little closer together
just in case.

Next she tells me about
The Flying Cat.
It creeps along
on its soft padded paws
pretending to be
any ordinary cat.
But at the stroke of
midnight it sprouts
wings and flies up
into the air,
a giant furry moth
that miaows.

'Never sleep with your tent open,'
she warns me, 'because
when The Flying Cat
finds its prey
it swoops down
and lands on it.

It sinks its claws
and its razor-sharp teeth
into its victim
and sucks its blood.
Slurp . . . Slurp . . . Slurp.'

We both shiver
and hold hands.
She doesn't like cats
and I don't like moths.

Just then something
blunders into the tent
flapping its wings.
'Miaow . . . miaow,' it says.
We hug each other.
We don't make a sound.
'Miaow . . . miaow . . .
slurp . . . slurp,' it says.

'Look, Simon,' we say,
'just go away, will you.
You aren't funny.'
We lie there quiet for a moment
ignoring him.
At last I say, 'That's nothing.
Wait till you hear about
The Tree Creeper.

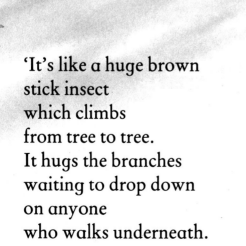

'It's like a huge brown
stick insect
which climbs
from tree to tree.
It hugs the branches
waiting to drop down
on anyone
who walks underneath.

'Never pitch your tent
under a tree,' I warn her,
'because if you do
in the middle of the night
The Tree Creeper
will drop down
and crawl inside
and crush you
in its stick-like arms.
Crunch! Crunch!'

Neither of us
likes that story.
I don't know where
I got such a horrid idea from.
We reach out
and hold hands.

Suddenly there is a
BANG!
as if half a tree
has landed
on top of the tent.

We scream
and hide our eyes.
We hear, 'Crunch, crunch, crunch.'
Then a silly laugh.

'Simon, you are stupid,' we say.
'You spoil everything.
Go away.'
Now my cousin
is very quiet.

I begin to think
perhaps I have won.
But then she says to me,
'You don't know about
The Invisible Man, do you?

'He can walk through walls
and see through doors.
He could pass through this tent
like a beam of light.
He could be standing there
by your side
and you wouldn't even see him.
You'd just feel him
breathing on you.

'It doesn't matter where
you pitch your tent,' she tells me.
'The Invisible Man
would get you.
Nothing could keep him out.'

Now it is really dark.
There isn't a sound.
I am lying here
wide awake
thinking about this monster
that is coming to get me
that I won't even
be able to see.

I grab my cousin's arm.
'What does he do?' I say,
'if he gets you?'
She yawns.
'He dissolves you,' she says,
'so you're invisible too.'
'And then what?' I say.
There is no answer.
'THEN WHAT HAPPENS?'

But my cousin has gone to sleep.
I can hear her
breathing through her mouth
as if she has
a peg on her nose.

Now I start to hear
other sounds.
It's raining,
hitting the tent
tap . . . tap . . . tap.
But I begin to think
it's The Invisible Man's footsteps.
He's coming to get me.
Tap, tap, tap, tap.

Then I hear the wind
blowing against the tent.
But I think
it is The Invisible Man,
breathing heavily
panting
as he comes closer,
ready to dissolve me.

I slide down
into my sleeping bag
and hide.

Now I can hear a ripping sound.
Someone is trying to get in.

I reach out for my torch
and switch it on
in time to see
the zip burst open
and a horrible face
appear in the gap.

'Can I come in?' says Simon.
'It's raining out here
and I'm getting wet.'
I take a deep breath.
'Oh, Simon, you are stupid,' I say.
But I don't send him away.

He slides down
between me and my cousin
and we start to giggle.
Then I remember the picnic
we brought with us.
'Are you hungry?' I say.
Simon grins.

We sit up
in the torchlight
side by side
just the two of us
eating our midnight feast.
We whisper
so we don't wake my cousin.
That would spoil everything.

In the morning
when she asks me
who ate her food
I shall tell her
it must have been
The Invisible Man.

SUNITA'S SECRET

SECRET

NARINDER DHAMI

CORGI YEARLING BOOKS

SUNITA'S SECRET
A CORGI YEARLING BOOK 978 0 440 86629 9 (from January 2007)
0 440 86629 4

Published in Great Britain by Corgi Yearling,
an imprint of Random House Children's Books

This edition published 2006

1 3 5 7 9 10 8 6 4 2

Copyright © Narinder Dhami, 2006

The right of Narinder Dhami to be identified as the author of this work has
been asserted in accordance with the Copyright, Designs and Patents Act 1988.

Papers used by Random House Children's Books are natural, recyclable products
made from wood grown in sustainable forests. The manufacturing processes
conform to the environmental regulations of the country of origin.

Typeset in Palatino by Palimpsest Book Production Limited,
Polmont, Stirlingshire

Corgi Yearling Books are published by Random House Children's Books,
61–63 Uxbridge Road, London W5 5SA,
a division of The Random House Group Ltd,
in Australia by Random House Australia (Pty) Ltd,
20 Alfred Street, Milsons Point, Sydney, NSW 2061, Australia,
in New Zealand by Random House New Zealand Ltd,
18 Poland Road, Glenfield, Auckland 10, New Zealand,
and in South Africa by Random House (Pty) Ltd,
Isle of Houghton, Corner Boundary Road & Carse O'Gowrie,
Houghton 2198, South Africa

THE RANDOM HOUSE GROUP Limited Reg. No. 954009
www.kidsatrandomhouse.co.uk

A CIP catalogue record for this book is available from the British Library.

Printed and bound in Great Britain by
Cox & Wyman Ltd, Reading, Berkshire

CHAPTER 1

It's my birthday. My dad does something over the top, even for him, and takes us all on holiday to the Bahamas. I spend my birthday swimming in warm waters with dolphins and tiny, electric-coloured fish, and later, a waitress from the posh hotel brings an enormous birthday cake with pink icing down to the beach. Dad lights the candles under the stars, and everyone sings 'Happy Birthday' to me . . .

No.

It's my birthday and I'm half asleep and I'm remembering *last* year. No Bahamas, no dolphins, no posh hotel, no pink birthday cake this year.

This year was different. My birthday began with a kick in the backside and hot, sticky little fingers clamped around my neck.

'It's your birthday, Sunita!' yelled Debbie, her mouth cupped around my ear. 'Wake up! Happy birthday!'

'Oh, I'm sorry,' I yawned, surfacing reluctantly

from my beautiful half-dream. 'I'm afraid I didn't quite hear that.'

'IT'S YOUR BIRTHDAY!' Debbie roared even more loudly, yanking the duvet off my shoulders. She's only five. Sarcasm goes way over her head.

'Mum told us not to wake you up yet,' said Davey, bouncing painfully up and down on my legs. 'But we didn't take any notice.'

'What a surprise,' I said, trying to push them off the bed. But they clung onto me determinedly like two baby monkeys.

'We haven't got you a present,' Davey said. 'Debbie saved you one of her sweets, but she'd already sucked it.' He pulled a face. 'Eurgh! She's disgusting!'

'Well, where is it then?' I asked Debbie. 'Hand it over.'

Debbie looked disgruntled. 'I dropped it on the floor and Davey picked it up and ate it. But I *would* have given it to you.'

'Well,' I said, 'it's the thought that counts.'

'You're *twenty-eight*, Sunita.' Davey poked my kneecap through the duvet. 'That's *old*.'

'Actually, I'm twelve,' I replied.

'That's even older,' Debbie said wisely.

I didn't bother to put them right, as today I felt a hundred and twenty-eight at the very least.

The door opened very quietly and Mum crept

2

in carrying a cup of tea. She came to a full stop when she saw the twins curled up on my bed.

'I told you two demons not to wake Sunita up,' Mum said, looking harassed. Her short cropped hair stuck up all around her face in a kind of halo. 'Happy birthday, love.'

The day Mum decided she didn't have the time or the money to look after her long, long black hair any more was one of the worst days. I know it was silly, after everything that's happened, but when she chopped it off in front of the mirror and we picked up the swinging, glossy locks and put them in the bin, it felt as if someone had died.

'Sunita was awake,' Davey said angelically.

'Wide awake,' added Debbie.

'You little liars,' I said indignantly. 'I was not wide awake. I was remembering my birthday last year—'

I almost bit the end of my tongue off trying to swallow my words.

'Were you thinking about Dad?' Davey wanted to know.

There was the usual frozen silence. Mum and I did not look at each other.

'Not really,' I mumbled.

'Don't talk about Dad.' Debbie gave her twin a poke. 'Mum doesn't like it.'

'I didn't talk about him,' Davey roared, grabbing

her bouncy little ponytail and tugging it. 'I just said his name.'

'Dad's not his name,' bellowed Debbie, expertly trapping Davey in a headlock. 'His name's Sohan Singh Anand. It said so on the radio.'

They tumbled to the floor, where they began to wrestle like two cute but vicious bear cubs. I leaned over and pulled Davey out of the tangle of arms and legs, and Mum scooped up Debbie.

'Come on, you two,' Mum said, hauling Debbie over to the door. 'Time to get ready for school.'

School. I knew there was something I'd forgotten. My heart floundered and lurched inside me.

'School!' Davey said with deep disgust. 'I don't want to go to a new school. I liked the old one.'

It was how I felt myself.

'We can't go back to the old one.' Debbie hesitated, then added in a whisper, 'Because of *you-know-who*.'

'Who?' Davey asked, looking blank.

This time Mum and I *did* look at each other. We almost smiled.

'Twins, I don't mind you talking about your dad,' Mum said quietly. 'Now come along and get ready for school.'

'I don't want to go,' Davey grumbled. 'And if anyone's horrible to me at this new school, I'm going to smack them.'

4

'And I'll pinch them,' Debbie added.

'You know, that is not the best way to make friends,' Mum said sternly, herding them out of the door like a sheepdog.

My tiny bedroom seemed too quiet and empty without them. I opened the curtains, picked up the cup of tea and reached for my dressing gown, all without getting out of bed. The room was so small, there wasn't space to swing a mouse. A cat wouldn't have had a chance.

All the rooms in this terraced house were tiny. I tried not to remember our old home because it hurt so much. My big, sunny bedroom, painted sunshine yellow; the billowing white curtains around the window seat; the TV, computer and DVD player in the corner; even my silly telephone shaped like a pink heart. It had all gone and it was never coming back. Well, I still had the phone, but there was no way Mum could afford to pay the bills. It was shoved under my bed, collecting dust.

Don't think about it.

I put on my dressing gown and two steps later I was out on the landing on the way to the bathroom.

Last year, even after the trip to the Bahamas, I'd still had a birthday party at home. All my friends had come: Kareena, Lucy, Daisy and Rekha. When she saw the presents and the cake and the firework display in the field behind our house,

5

Kareena said that I was the luckiest girl in the world, and that Britney Spears had nothing on me. I hadn't seen Kareena or Lucy or Daisy for months now, although Rekha had sneaked over to say goodbye the day we moved. I wonder if her mum ever found out. She would have gone mad at Rekha if she did.

I knew I wouldn't get a present this year because Mum couldn't afford it. I didn't care. I was worrying about starting at Coppergate School, wondering if anyone would recognize me. But the pictures that had been printed in the newspapers were about four or five years old. I was only seven or eight in those photos, and the twins were babies.

I stared at myself in the bathroom mirror and told myself I did look different. My face was thinner and my hair was longer. Probably, no one would recognize me. After all, ten long months had passed. But occasionally the story and photo popped up again in the newspapers, usually when the police were appealing for new leads. It had even been on TV, on *Crimewatch*, just a couple of months ago.

Most of the teachers would know about me, of course. But the headteacher, Mrs Bright, had promised my mum that no one else would be told.

Maybe I should go in disguise, I thought. I scraped my black hair into a ponytail, but I didn't

like the way my ears stuck out. Then I spread a thin layer of white toothpaste across my upper lip like a moustache. That made me laugh.

I'm wasting time.

I washed, cleaned my teeth and hummed a tune to pretend everything was fine. That I wasn't starting at a new school in the middle of term, when everyone else in my class would already know each other, meaning that I would stand out like a fish on a bicycle.

'It's simple,' I told myself as I wandered slowly back to my bedroom. 'Just keep your head down, stay in the background and nobody will notice you.'

The old Sunita wasn't a stay-in-the-background kind of person. I liked to talk, I liked to be noticed. At my old school I'd been the editor of the school newspaper, and I'd started a campaign against bullying. My teacher, Mr Harris, told me that bullies stood no chance against me and my big mouth.

The new Sunita was different; *had* to be different. I would have to keep my head down. The trouble was, I hadn't worked out yet how I could stay in the background, keep my head down and still make friends. But I was thinking – maybe it was easier not to make friends at all?

I hummed louder as I opened my bedroom door. Did I need any friends? I had enough to do at

home, helping Mum look after the twins. She was finding it tough without Dominique, the au pair. The twins were like tornadoes, destroying everything in their path. Anyway, I had no money so I wouldn't be going out shopping or to the cinema or to have a burger. And I would have to keep secrets, watch what I said, to make sure that nothing about Dad slipped out. *Honestly*, friends were something I could really do without—

I came to a stop in the doorway. Someone had been busy while I was in the bathroom. My bed had been made. My school uniform – second-hand, of course, not new – had been laid out neatly on the bed, and my old school shoes stood on the rug, polished like glass. Debbie's favourite cuddly blue elephant, Lollipop, sat on my pillow. A tiny vase of flowers had been placed on the windowsill, and next to it was a small parcel wrapped in silver foil. I opened it and a sparkly pink pencil case fell out.

I did just about manage not to disgrace myself and bawl my eyes out.

Mum was laying the table in the kitchen and the twins were getting under her feet, when I went downstairs. I'd put on my Coppergate uniform (blue and brown, an evil colour combination) and had my new pencil case in my hand. The twins started giggling as soon as they saw me.

'It wasn't us,' Debbie said immediately.

8

'So did Lollipop walk into my room and jump up onto my pillow all by himself?' I asked, tweaking her ponytail.

Debbie looked a bit anxious. 'He's only for you to borrow,' she explained. 'I expect he'll want to come back to my bedroom tonight.'

'Did you see the flowers?' Davey wanted to know. 'I didn't *steal* them from Mrs Brodie's garden. They were growing under our fence.'

'They're lovely,' I said. 'And so is this.' I held up the pencil case. 'Thanks, Mum. But how did you afford—?'

Mum held up her hand. She was flipping through a cookery book, a never-say-die look on her face. 'We're having a proper breakfast for a change,' she announced. 'No Coco Pops in front of the TV. Today we're having pancakes.'

The twins cheered.

'Dominique used to make pancakes for us,' said Debbie.

'With raisins, lemon and chocolate sauce,' added Davey.

'Thank you, Jamie Oliver,' said Mum. 'These will just be regular pancakes.'

'What are pancakes made of?' I asked.

Mum screwed up her nose. 'Ooh, don't tell me,' she groaned, 'I know this.' She thought for a moment. 'Batter! That's it, isn't it?'

'And what's in batter?'

Mum looked blank. 'I have absolutely no idea.'

'Flour, milk and eggs,' Debbie said.

'Butter and salt,' said Davey. 'And you have to flip them in the air three times, or they don't taste as good. Dominique used to say that.'

'Mum,' I began, 'juice and toast will do just fine—'

'Nonsense,' Mum said robustly, getting out the frying pan.

'Surely we don't have any flour?' I argued. Mum had never cooked anything in her life before, as far as I was aware.

'I bought some,' Mum said triumphantly, rooting in the cupboard. 'I thought I might make you a birthday cake.'

The twins hooted with laughter, and I looked worried.

'Oh, relax, Sunita,' Mum went on as the twins began fencing with their forks. 'All right, maybe a cake was a bit ambitious. But how hard can a few pancakes be?'

Ten minutes later she was standing on a stool, giggling hysterically and trying to peel a pancake off the kitchen ceiling. I was laughing so much myself, I had juice coming out of my nose. Meanwhile, the twins were poking at their pancakes with suspicious faces.

'Mine's all rubbery, like jelly,' Debbie grumbled.

'So is mine.' Davey picked up the pancake and put it on his head. 'I can use it as an umbrella if it rains.'

'Oh, stop it, you two.' Mum scraped the last bit off with a spatula, and climbed down. I hadn't seen her laugh so much for ages. I had actually forgotten what she looked like when she was happy. 'Anyone for toast?' She glanced at the clock. 'We've just got time.'

My stomach lurched. That new-school feeling again.

'I haven't,' I said, stuffing the pencil case into my bag. 'I'll miss the bus if I don't go now.'

'Oh.' Mum stared pleadingly at me. 'I thought we'd all go together.'

'What?' I tried not to sound horrified. 'But that means you'll get to the twins' new school really early.'

'Doesn't matter.' Mum, in her turn, was trying not to sound too needy. 'I have to go in and speak to their teacher anyway.'

We couldn't look each other in the eye, because we knew exactly what the other was thinking.

If we go out together, there's more chance of us being recognized . . .

I don't want to go out at all, but I feel safer if we're all together . . .

11

'All right,' I mumbled.

We'd been in the house for a week, but we'd hardly set foot outside. Now we would have to go out almost every day. I wasn't sure how to cope.

'Sunita, check and see if any of the neighbours are around,' Mum said in a low voice as she manhandled the twins into their coats.

I opened the front door a crack and peered out. On one side, Mrs Brodie's curtains were still drawn. Mr Chan's windows were open, but I couldn't see him.

'All clear,' I whispered.

'If any of them come out to speak to us, I'll attack them with my Spiderman web gun,' Davey announced, waving it threateningly.

'Give that to me at once,' Mum said. 'You're not taking it to school.' She tried to wrestle the gun from his grip. 'I can just see you tying your teacher up in a spider's web. Davinder, give that to me *now*.'

We had to wait for Davey to stop bawling before we could leave, otherwise the neighbours might have heard us and rushed out to say hello. They might be nice and understanding and friendly, but they might not. We didn't want to run the risk. After all, they were strangers who didn't know us. Why should they be understanding? People we'd been friends with for ages wouldn't speak to us after what happened.

When we finally made it out of the house, the postman was coming down the other side of the street. I tried not to stare at him. I wasn't expecting any birthday cards, of course. It would be silly, with almost all of our relatives not speaking to us for one reason or another. Besides, there was only one person I hoped would send me a card. And how likely was that? Not likely at all. I didn't know where he was, or if he'd remember. Even if he was alive.

Mum and the twins walked me to the bus stop. We took a short cut which led us through a small estate of very big, luxurious houses that reminded me of our old place. None of us said much then, even the twins, who had been chattering non-stop since we left home.

As we got closer to the bus stop, I became more and more edgy because there were too many Coppergate pupils milling around the streets. They all looked confident and relaxed and happy. I envied them.

'I'll be fine on my own from here,' I said, too brightly.

'Yes, OK,' my mum replied in a fake cheerful voice. I willed her not to cry. 'Say goodbye to Sunita, twins.'

The twins were poking each other with twigs they'd picked up along the way. Now, with one of

their lightning changes of mood, they both dropped the twigs and stared at me with enormous, sad, chocolate-brown eyes. Their bottom lips trembled.

'Don't want to say goodbye,' Debbie sniffled. 'I love you, Sunita.' She flung her arms around my legs.

'Me too,' Davey whimpered, hugging my knees. 'I love you too, Sunita.'

Oh, no. Please, no. Now everyone was staring at us and some of the kids were pointing and laughing.

'I love you too,' I whispered, trying to prise their fingers off my legs. 'Now let go.'

'I love you the most, Sunita,' Debbie announced loudly, tightening her grip. 'I love you loads more than Davey.'

'You do not!' Davey wailed. 'I love Sunita more than I love Spiderman, so there!'

Debbie pinched him and Davey stepped on her toes, so luckily normal service was resumed as quickly as possible. My cheeks burning with embarrassment, I hurried to hide behind the bus shelter as Mum dragged the twins off down the street. I could hear laughter, and assumed it was because of me. I felt wretched.

I didn't come out until I heard the bus rumbling along the street. Then I sidled over to join the end

of the queue. It wasn't a queue, though, more a test of the survival of the fittest. There was a stampede as everyone surged towards the bus in one huge, seething crowd.

'Get back!' the driver roared, his face red with fury as fifteen people tried to squeeze through the open doors at once. 'Get back, I say!'

I stood just behind a little group of four girls, waiting my turn. I didn't mean to listen to what they were saying, but it was impossible not to. I imagine people three streets away could hear them perfectly.

'*Oh*, my *God*! You are just *s-o-o-o* lucky, Celina Patel!' one of them, the curly-haired redhead, shrieked at the top of her voice. 'I absolutely and totally *hate* you!'

The girl called Celina shrugged and laughed. She was pretty. Her glossy, dead straight, dark hair was cut short at the front so that it hugged her cheekbones, and then it flipped out at the sides. Quite unusually for an Indian girl, she had green eyes. Everything about her looked expensive. The thin gold hoops in her ears, the leather designer bag, the Nike trainers which I recognized as a limited edition.

'Some of us have it and some of us don't, I guess, Danielle,' she said in a mock-American drawl. 'I was just lucky my birthday was during half-term.'

'Yes, but *Florida*!' Danielle wailed enviously as we shuffled closer to the bus. 'My mum and dad took me to Alton Towers for my birthday surprise last year. How gross is that?'

The other three girls squealed piercingly with horror.

'Don't you dare tell the story of how your brother was sick when you went on Nemesis,' Celina giggled, flicking her flippy hair over her shoulders.

'What story?' asked the tiny, doll-like blonde, wearing too much make-up, who was standing next to her.

Celina rolled her eyes and shook her head. 'Honestly, Chloe, you *so* don't want to hear that story.'

'Oh, I do,' Chloe insisted. She looked as if she could barely lift her eyelashes under the weight of mascara. 'Tell me.'

'If you tell that story again, I'll be sick myself, I swear,' the fourth girl said melodramatically, putting her hand over her mouth. She was tall and slim, but not as pretty as Celina.

'Don't listen then, Jyoti.' Danielle turned to Chloe. 'Well, I was on Nemesis with my mum and Adam, and he felt *really* sick. But he had nothing to be sick in, of course. Except—'

Celina and Jyoti both screamed and put their hands over their ears.

'What?' Chloe asked eagerly.

'Let's just say my mum's Chanel handbag has never been the same since,' Danielle giggled.

'OK.' Chloe looked puzzled. 'So what happened?'

Celina, Jyoti and Danielle squealed with laughter.

'Oh, Chloe, you're such a no-brain.' Celina flapped her hand dismissively at Chloe, showing off her manicured nails painted with pale pink, sparkly gloss. 'Don't you get it?'

Chloe frowned, concentrating hard. 'Dani's brother was sick on Nemesis, but I still don't see what her mum's handbag has to do with it— Oh!' She clapped her hands to her face. 'That's disgusting! What did you tell me that for?'

'I think she's finally got it,' Celina said. 'Clo, you're never going to make Prime Minister.'

'I don't want to be Prime Minister,' replied Chloe, playing with her silver necklace. 'But I'd love to be on *Big Brother*.'

Chloe was obviously a complete airhead, and her friends didn't seem a whole lot better. But, standing silently behind them, I was envious. They had each other, and they *belonged*. It had been that way for me, once, with Kareena, Lucy, Rekha and Daisy. Being on my own felt cold and lonely.

We moved closer to the bus. Suddenly, and unexpectedly, the girl called Celina swung round and looked me straight in the face. She took me

by surprise so I didn't smile at her or say hello. Neither did she. She stared at me for a second or two, then turned back to her friends.

I don't know why, but my heart was thumping like a drum after that. I got myself onto the bus, and sat as far away from them as I could.

'Hey!'

I almost leaped out of the open window in fright as someone behind me yelled out at the top of their voice.

'Hey, Williams!'

I sagged with relief as I realized that the boy in the seat behind wasn't talking to me. I could just see him out of the corner of my eye. He had dark hair, stiff with gel, which stood up in short spikes all over his head. He was good-looking, and oh, did he know it. That type. He was staring over my head at a plump boy waddling down the aisle between the seats. This one was *not* good-looking.

'Have you paid for two seats, Williams?' he went on. Everyone around me sniggered.

'N-no, Jack,' the boy stammered, looking up nervously from beneath his pudding-bowl fringe.

'You'd better stand then, fatso,' Jack said. There was that supremely confident edge to his voice which only really good-looking boys ever have. 'Why should your big butt take up two seats?'

The boy tried to smile, didn't succeed and

obediently stood there, chewing his lip. I stared out of the grimy window as we moved off and the plump boy lurched from side to side. That was *so* not going to happen to me. There was no way I was going to end up a victim.

I had been told to go straight to the school office when I arrived. It was a relief. The enormous playground was crammed with pupils chattering away; it brought home to me the fact that I didn't know a single soul. The school wasn't warm and welcoming either. It was a modern, angular building, made of glass and steel, and every door looked the same. I walked right around the whole building twice, looking vainly for the school office. I didn't like to ask.

As I rounded a corner of the building for the fourth time, starting to feel all hot and bothered, I bumped straight into three girls. Beautiful and glamorous, even in the hideous blue and brown uniform, they looked like Bollywood film stars – big dark eyes, glossy hair and lots of attitude. I stared at them, open-mouthed.

'Hello-o-o?' said one, rather crossly. 'How about an apology here? You know, *I'm sorry for bumping into you* – something along those lines?'

'Jazz!' The oldest girl elbowed her in the ribs, then swiftly looked me up and down. 'You're new, aren't you?'

I nodded dumbly, wondering if all the girls in the school were going to be as gorgeous and sophisticated and confident as these three, and Celina and her friends.

'Don't tell me' – the third girl, tall and with the longest legs I'd ever seen, smiled at me – 'you're looking for the office, right?' She pointed high above my head. I looked up and saw a large sign that read SCHOOL OFFICE with an arrow pointing to a nearby door.

'Thank you,' I said shyly.

'They really ought to move that sign down about two metres,' the girl called Jazz grumbled. 'It's way too high for most of us normal-sized people. Only vertically abnormal people like Amber can see it.'

Amber raised her eyebrows at me. 'Don't mind my sister,' she said. 'She's even grumpier than usual because she's sleep-deprived. Our uncle and aunt, who live next door to us, have just had a baby.'

'Babies!' Jazz groaned. 'Babies are so over-rated. All they do is eat, sleep, poo and wake innocent people in the night with their howling. Change bedrooms with me, Geena?'

'No chance,' the oldest girl retorted.

'Amber?'

'I'll see you in court first.'

I would have liked to know more, but the three girls moved away, still arguing. I watched them go, feeling a little sad that they were all older than me and so wouldn't be in my class. But it was wonderful to have a conversation like a normal person. They were the first Coppergate pupils I'd spoken to so far. And, most important of all, they had showed no sign of recognizing me.

Mrs Bright, the headteacher, was like the school, modern and angular and streamlined, with a precisely cut blonde bob sawn off with perfect symmetry all around her face and a spotless cream tweed suit. I was shown into her office, which was the size of a large classroom, by the secretary, Mrs Capstick, and I think it took me at least five awkward minutes to walk from the door to Mrs Bright's desk. She sat watching me from start to finish with a piercing blue gaze that did nothing to put me at ease. When I eventually reached her desk, I half expected a trapdoor to open in the floor and send me plunging into a dark dungeon.

'Sunita.' Her face did soften a little then. 'Welcome to Coppergate School. We're very pleased to have you with us.'

She spoke very smoothly, and smiled, but I got the impression she wasn't *that* pleased. Mum had told me that Mrs Bright was new to the school herself. She'd only started a few months ago, and she

21

probably had big plans to make her mark there. I felt I was a small but annoying spanner in her works. Or maybe I was being over-sensitive. It's hard for me to be sure these days.

'You're in class Seven B,' she went on briskly, not waiting for me to speak, which was lucky because I couldn't think of anything to say. 'Your class teacher is Mr Arora. He's also head of the lower school, so if you have any problems settling in, go straight to him.'

She cleared her throat. 'Mr Arora, of course, knows all about—' She paused.

I waited with interest. How would she refer to what had happened?

'The unfortunate incident with your father,' she went on smoothly. 'But only the senior teachers have been told. We have kept it on a strictly need-to-know basis.'

I felt I was expected to say something here, so I said the safest thing I could think of, which was 'Thank you'.

Mrs Bright nodded and smiled. 'Off you go then,' she said, quite kindly this time. 'Just remember that you're lucky to have a place at Coppergate. It's a wonderful school.'

Her tone implied *And I'm going to make it even better*.

I wondered if I should curtsy my way out of the

room, but decided it probably wasn't necessary. A few moments later I was back out in the playground, having been given directions to my classroom by Mrs Capstick. It seemed to involve a lot of stairs and right turns. I hoped I could find it.

By now I was breathing a little more easily. My worst fear, that everyone would recognize me straight away, hadn't happened. That alone made me feel better.

Trying to remember what Mrs Capstick had told me, I made my way over to the lower school entrance. Celina Patel and her friends were leaning against the wall, chatting, and Chloe was staring into a make-up mirror, brushing on yet more lip gloss.

Celina saw me and waved in a friendly way. I was so shocked, I didn't wave back. I looked over my shoulder. She couldn't really be waving at me . . .

'Yes, you.' Celina laughed and pointed at me. 'Hi there. You're new, aren't you?'

'What's your name?' asked the other Indian girl. I'd forgotten her name. Jyoti, I thought.

'Which class are you in?' That was Danielle.

'What's your favourite lip gloss?' asked Chloe, still squinting at herself in the tiny mirror.

I felt overwhelmed by their interest. Should I be friendly or not? It took me two seconds to make up my mind.

'Sunita.' I smiled at them. 'I'm in Mr Arora's class.'

'Oh, fab!' Celina looked pleased. 'The same as us. You can sit at our table if you like.'

'I can?' This was wildly unbelievable. How wonderful. 'Thank you.'

'It's a funny time to start a new school, just after half-term,' Danielle said curiously, after they had all introduced themselves.

I'd already worked out what I was going to say. 'Well, we were moving house and it took longer than we expected. I should have started at the beginning of term really.'

They looked sympathetic.

'Oh, it's horrible coming to a new school, isn't it?' said Chloe, who was now brushing her hair. 'I remember when I started at Coppergate in September, I had a big spot on my nose the first day. I felt *terrible*.'

'Really?' I said, secretly thinking that if that was the worst that had ever happened to her, wasn't she the lucky one?

'She kept her hand over her face all day, and Mr Arora told her off because he couldn't hear what she was saying,' Danielle said with a grin.

We laughed. Cautiously, I began to feel my way towards being – well, maybe not happy, but *comfortable*. I was with people who liked me, or at

least were going to give me a chance to see if they liked me. Maybe I could belong here, after all.

'Oh!' A loud shriek from Celina made us all jump.

'What is it, Cee?' Chloe enquired, putting her mirror away.

'I remember now!' Celina was staring at me triumphantly, her kitten-green eyes narrowing. I felt a flicker of fear pass through me. 'I *thought* I'd seen you before. You're the girl whose dad stole all that money!'

CHAPTER 2

Of course, we didn't know Dad was stealing money. Even Mum didn't know.

Dad was an accountant. He never read books, he wasn't interested in stories, but he could do maths like lightning in his head. My favourite thing when I was little was to sit on his knee and ask him impossible sums. 'Dad, what's 4,678 times 91?' Dad would work it out in his head, and then I would check it on the calculator. He was never wrong. Anyway, that's how I remember it.

We lived in a nice but ordinary sort of house, and Mum didn't have to work, which was lucky because the twins were a full-time job from the day they were born. But then a few years ago Dad was made a partner in his firm. Suddenly we seemed to have lots of money. We moved to a bigger house with six bedrooms and a conservatory and a swimming pool in the garden, and Mum got her own BMW to sit on the huge drive

next to Dad's Mercedes. We had a cleaner, a gardener and an au pair. Dad even talked about sending me to a private school, but I didn't want to leave my friends.

By the time everything came crashing down around our ears, Dad had already disappeared. The first we knew, Mum got a phone call from one of the other partners, Mr Deol. He told Mum that Dad had been stealing their clients' money from the firm for the last three years. Thousands, he said.

Then the police arrived, but Dad had already packed his things and gone. He didn't tell me where he was going. He didn't tell Mum. We still don't know where he is, or even if he's alive.

I don't have to describe how we felt. Can you imagine? Maybe you can't. Nobody can really understand until it happens to them. I can hardly believe it myself. I loved my dad, I still love my dad. But what he did makes me feel sick and angry inside.

The newspapers wouldn't have been so interested if the firm's clients hadn't included a reasonably famous pop singer, and a sort-of-well-known actress who took her clothes off in films a lot. The next day Dad was all over the national papers, and so were we. Somehow the press had got hold of the photo of us that Dad kept on his desk at work. I don't know how.

Mum was in shock, but she did her best to keep everything going. There wasn't much she could do, though. We had to sell the big house and the two cars and everything else except what we needed to survive. Mum paid as much money as she could back to the firm. We didn't know the reasonably famous rock star and the sort-of-well-known actress who removed her clothes regularly, but some of the other clients whom Dad stole from were family friends. Used to be, anyway.

After ten terrible months we just about had enough money left to buy a little house, miles away from where it happened, and try to start again.

That didn't seem likely now.

Chloe, Danielle and Jyoti were staring from me to Celina with huge eyes.

'What do you mean, Cee?' Danielle asked, looking confused.

'What money?' Jyoti wanted to know.

I don't know why, but I felt quite calm. I met Celina's smug, green-eyed gaze head-on. She had known who I was all along, I think. She'd recognized me in the bus queue. But she'd kept the knowledge to herself so that she could make a big impression when she chose to reveal it.

'*You* know.' Celina shrugged her slim shoulders

elegantly. 'That accountant guy who stole money from Guy Kingsmith and Kara LePage.' She put her head on one side, looking at me as if I'd just crawled out of the sewers. '*She's* his daughter.'

'Oh, my God!' Jyoti and Danielle screamed in unison while Chloe looked blank and said plaintively, 'I still don't know what you're talking about.'

Heads were starting to turn around us, and people were looking. I realized then that keeping in the background wasn't going to be an option any more. New meek and mild Sunita wasn't going to be any help at all. Only old Sunita could get me out of this situation with any dignity.

'Yeah, well done.' I shrugged, managing to look almost as casual as Celina. 'You win first prize.'

'Oh!' Chloe clapped a hand to her mouth. 'I remember now. Your dad stole loads of money!'

'Brilliant.' I gave her a slow handclap. 'That loud, creaking sound I just heard must have been your brain finally getting into gear.'

'Don't talk to Chloe like that,' Celina said sharply. She raised her voice so that everyone around us could hear perfectly. '*Her* dad's not a dirty thief.'

'Oh dear,' I said in a mocking tone. 'Does that mean you don't want to sit with me in class, after all? I'm utterly heartbroken.'

Without giving them a chance to reply, I turned and strolled off through the whispering crowd. Their eyes were out on stalks. I marched into school, not knowing where I was going, not caring. Then, when I was out of sight of everyone, my knees finally gave way and I slumped against a wall. I was shivering violently. What I had been dreading had actually happened. Now I had to deal with it. Not for the first time, I thought how unfair it was that my dad had done something wrong and the rest of the family had to suffer for it . . .

The morning bell shrilled out right above my head, jarring my nerves even more. Taking a deep breath, telling myself to stay calm, I set myself the task of finding my way to the Year 7 classrooms.

I found 7B more by luck than anything else, having had to walk around half the school and brave the stares and whispered comments of the people I met along the way. Someone called out something, I didn't hear what, and everyone around me sniggered. I was a kind of celebrity, I thought grimly. How amusing.

The Year 7 cloakrooms were at the end of the corridor. I fixed my eyes at a point above everyone's heads, and went to hang my jacket up.

'Don't leave anything in your coat pockets, girls.' Jack, the boy from the bus, was leaning

against the cloakroom wall, one hand in his pocket, the other arm draped casually round Celina's shoulders. 'It might get nicked.'

I could feel my face start to burn. Celina, Danielle and Jyoti tittered. Only Chloe looked blank.

'I thought her dad was the thief,' she said. 'Not her.'

'That's the first sensible thing you've said all morning.' I had to struggle to stop my voice from shaking. 'You're not as stupid as you look.'

'Hey, girls, we've got a smartass here.' Jack narrowed his eyes to slits. 'Shall we show her what we think of smartass thieves?'

He took a step towards me and tried to grab my sleeve, but I jumped backwards out of his reach.

'Keep away from me,' I said, and this time my voice did shake.

'What's going on here?'

The voice from behind took us all by surprise. A teacher stood there, frowning at us. I'm guessing it was a teacher, although he was as a pale as a ghost and had huge dark circles under his eyes. Actually, he looked like an addict from one of those posters that try to put you off doing drugs.

'Didn't you hear the second bell?' he went on, putting his hand to his mouth to cover an enormous

yawn. I swear I heard his jaw crack. 'Into class right away.'

'Sorry, Mr Arora,' Celina said sweetly. She and her friends slipped out of the cloakroom, followed by Jack, who gave me a look that I knew meant trouble ahead.

Mr Arora looked at me, blinked a few times and seemed to be trying to re-focus his eyes. 'And you must be Sunita,' he said at last, as if he'd just hooked my name out of the depths of his memory with some effort. 'Welcome to Coppergate.'

'Thank you,' I mumbled. I wondered if I should tell Mr Arora that my secret was out, but what could he do about it? He looked as if he was having enough trouble staying upright.

Mr Arora showed me to the classroom, and as soon as we walked in, there was a wave of excited whispering. I knew I was going to have to get used to it. Mr Arora didn't even notice – he was yawning four times in succession without a break.

'Let's find you somewhere to sit,' he said, gazing listlessly around the room.

I could see a few empty chairs. One was at the table where Celina and her fellow witches were sitting. As Celina caught my eye, she deliberately lifted her bag from the floor and placed it on the spare chair. A tiny smile played around the corners of her mouth.

There was an empty seat next to the boy Jack had teased on the bus, the fat one. I didn't want to sit there. I might as well put a sign round my neck reading VICTIM.

'She can sit with me, sir.'

A girl on the other side of the room was calling and waving her hand in the air. I felt ridiculously grateful that someone wanted me, but shocked when I saw that this girl had a large purple stain covering half of the left side of her face. She looked as if someone had thrown violet ink at her. I couldn't help staring.

'Thank you, Zara.' Mr Arora, moving as if he was weary to his bones, seated himself on his chair. 'I have a timetable for you somewhere, Sunita.' He made a half-hearted attempt to search his chaotic desk, but quickly gave up. 'I'll find it in a minute. Go and sit down.'

There was nothing to do but go over to the girl with the purple face. I tried not to look at her, but it was difficult. My eyes were drawn helplessly to the stain.

'It's all right,' Zara said as I sat down. 'It isn't catching.'

'Sorry?' I muttered, pretending lamely that I didn't know what she meant.

'This.' Zara pointed at her face. 'It's a birthmark, that's all. Nothing to be scared of.' She stared

aggressively at me. 'Although I must admit that when I go trick or treating, I do tend to freak people out.'

'Oh.' I cleared my throat. 'Right.'

'That was a joke,' Zara said dryly.

'Oh.' I tried to stretch my lips into a smile. 'Sorry.'

'So.' Zara raised her eyebrows at me. 'How does everyone know about your dad?'

'Do you mind?' I snapped. 'I'd rather not talk about it.'

'Well, everyone else is talking about it, dumbo,' Zara replied rudely. 'I just thought it would be interesting to hear your version.'

At that moment Mr Arora, with many coughs and yawns, began to take the register, so I was saved the trouble of replying. I turned in my chair so that I had my back to Zara. It was clear that she and I were not going to get along, and it had nothing to do with the birthmark on her face.

Unluckily, when Mr Arora eventually found my timetable, it turned out that Zara and I were going to be in the same classes for almost all our subjects, so she was allocated the role of my minder.

'That was embarrassing, wasn't it?' Zara remarked as she marched me down the corridor for our first lesson. 'All those people staring at you

in assembly. I thought their eyes were going to pop out.'

'Shut up,' I muttered.

'Don't be so touchy,' Zara said with a shrug. 'I know what it's like. People stare at *me* all the time.' She pointed to her face.

'It's not the same thing at all,' I retorted. 'You could cover that up if you wanted to.'

Zara stared scornfully at me. 'What with? A mask?'

'Well,' I said through gritted teeth, 'you know . . .'

'With make-up, you mean?' Zara asked in a prickly tone. 'Maybe I don't *want* to cover it up.'

'What do you mean?' I asked, amazed. 'Of course you want to cover it up. Nobody would want to walk around looking like—' I stopped talking and tried to pull my foot out of my mouth.

'Looking like a freak, you mean?' Zara glared at me. 'What do *you* know about it?'

'Oh, go away and leave me alone,' I said rudely, wondering how I'd got into this discussion in the first place.

'Nothing would give me greater pleasure.' Zara actually poked her tongue out at me. 'But we're in the same French class now, so I can't.'

We stomped towards the language room in bitter silence. Most of the class was already there, lined

35

up outside the door. My heart sank to see that Celina, Danielle and Jack were in my French set, as well as some kids from the other Year 7 classes, who were gawping at me as if I had two heads. Most of them began sniggering as Jack moved out of the line and launched into a gangsta rap which had been number one in the charts a few months ago. It was about a guy who robbed a bank and died in a shoot-out with the police. Celina was giggling the loudest.

'Ignore him,' Zara said unexpectedly. 'Jack Browning looks gorgeous, but he's a bone-headed idiot. A cruel trick of Mother Nature's, I'm afraid.'

I closed my fingers into fists and began to recite the seven times table in my head. It was a good way of shutting out everything around me.

'Henry!' Jack moved along to the boy in front of Zara and me, and slapped him on the back. It was the overweight boy from the bus. 'How're you doing, mate?'

'I-I'm all right,' the boy stammered, looking surprised.

'You know what, Henry, my old chum?' I was distracted by 7 x 9, but Jack's oily grin suggested a piranha about to pounce on a small and help-less fish. 'You and that new girl should really get together. You're both a pair of useless losers.'

With one swift movement he gave Henry a huge

shove, which sent him staggering backwards right into me. His weight crushed me against the wall, knocking almost all the breath out of my body.

'Get off me!' I gasped, trying to push him away.

Jack and the others were screeching with laughter. Red with mortification, Henry regained his balance and stared at me anxiously.

'I'm really sorry,' he mumbled. 'Are you all right?'

'Ooh, I think I can smell romance in the air,' Celina giggled. 'Henry and Sunita, you make a lovely couple.'

'Yeah,' Jack sneered. 'Nobody else likes them so they deserve each other.'

'Surely you're talking about you and Celina?' I said, although I was fully aware that it would have been better if I'd kept quiet.

Only a couple of people dared to laugh. One of them was Zara.

'You cheeky—!' Celina bit back the insult she was about to add, as a teacher hurried past. 'I've got *lots* of friends and everyone likes me!'

'You call that bunch of shrieking, airhead drama queens you hang around with *friends*?' I asked coolly.

'Oi!' Now Danielle was muscling in on the argument. 'I am *not* an airhead!'

'Oh, of course you are,' I retorted. 'Your mate

Chloe's got so much air between her ears, I'm surprised she doesn't float upwards like a balloon.'

This time more people laughed, and Celina pouted angrily.

'Calm down, Cee.' Jack put his hands on his hips and grinned tauntingly at me. 'We'll be the ones who are laughing our heads off when her dad's caught and gets thrown in jail.'

I felt the colour drain from my face, I couldn't help it. Jack knew he'd got to me. He smirked and pushed his way to the top of the line as the French teacher finally appeared and let us into the room. Of course, in my head I knew what would happen when – if – the police caught up with Dad. But – Dad. Jail. They were words I couldn't get my head around in the same sentence.

Later, much later, it was finally lunch time. As I dragged myself out into the playground after double maths, I felt exhausted. I was finding it hard to handle the constant staring, pointing, gossiping, whispering, laughing . . .

'It'll get better, you know.'

Zara had followed me over to the bench where I was slumped in a self-pitying daze. I didn't even bother to answer her.

'It will,' she insisted. 'They'll get fed up soon, and they'll start talking about something else. They went on and on about my birthmark at the

beginning of term, but it stopped after a while.' She tilted her head to one side and looked at me speculatively. 'Everyone's saying it was Celina who blew your cover. Was it?'

'I don't want to talk about it,' I snapped.

'Her mum's one of the school governors.' Zara sat down on the bench next to me. 'She probably knows about you, and told Celina.'

'Thanks, Sherlock,' I muttered.

'And Celina's dad has just become the town's mayor,' Zara went on. 'She's acting like he's been crowned king, the way she goes on about it.'

I sighed deeply. 'Look, I know where the canteen is, and what time I need to go in to lunch. Now, I'm not being rude, but do you mind just going away, please?'

Zara ignored me. 'I've been thinking it over, and I've got a proposition to put to you,' she announced briskly. 'A business proposition.'

I stared blankly at her. 'Pardon?'

'Look, you haven't got any friends, and you aren't likely to make any at this rate,' she went on.

'Has anyone ever told you you're a little ray of sunshine?' I asked wearily. 'Nope. Thought not.'

'And *I* haven't made any friends since I started at Coppergate in September,' Zara went on. 'No one wants to know me, obviously, because of my birthmark.'

'Here's a thought,' I said spiritedly. 'Have you ever considered that it might be because you're aggressive and bad-tempered and hard to get along with, and not because of your birthmark at all?'

'Nonsense,' Zara retorted. 'I had friends at primary school.' I looked disbelieving, but she swept on regardless. 'Anyway, I think it would be good for both of us if we at least *pretended* to be friends.'

'Why?' I asked.

'Oh, it would be purely a business arrangement,' Zara said airily. 'Just to save us from embarrassment in all those awkward little school situations. You know, when the teacher says find a partner; when we go on trips and have to sit next to someone on the coach. That sort of stuff.'

I stared at her. 'I don't think it would work,' I said. 'We don't like each other.'

'Oh, that's not important,' Zara said, waving her hand dismissively. 'We'd have to have some ground rules, though. Like I wouldn't ask you about your dad, and you wouldn't mention my birthmark, that kind of thing.'

I wasn't listening because I'd realized that someone was edging their way towards us, taking in every word we were saying. It was Henry Williams, looking red and sheepish, but determined.

'What do *you* want?' Zara asked in a scary voice.

Henry blushed harder, fixed his eyes on me and began to stammer and stutter. 'I-I-I just wanted to say sorry, about what happened before,' he finally got out.

'Forget it,' I said. 'It wasn't your fault.'

Henry nodded, but seemed strangely reluctant to go away. For the first time I took a good look at him. He had ordinary blond hair and ordinary blue eyes and a pleasant but ordinary face. Sadly, the only unusual thing about him was his weight.

'Well, goodbye then,' Zara said pointedly.

'I heard what you were saying,' Henry gabbled. 'About not having any friends, I mean . . .'

'What's it to you?' demanded Zara.

'Well . . .' Henry looked scared to death, but soldiered manfully on. 'I haven't really made any friends since September either. And I was thinking . . . Maybe we could all be friends.' The words came out in a rush. 'Maybe we could be a *gang*.'

Zara immediately jumped up and stood in front of me, blocking Henry's path.

'Forget it,' she informed him haughtily. 'I saw her first. If anyone's going to be friends with her, it's me. Go find your own friend.'

'Stop it.' I got to my feet. 'I don't want to be friends with either of you. In fact' – I shrugged –

'why don't you be friends with each other? I'll take my chances on my own, thanks.'

I did not add that I knew if I hung around with Zara or Henry or, worse, both of them, I would definitely be seen as a loser. There would be no way back then.

'I know what you're thinking,' Zara called after me as I walked off. 'And you're already seen as a loser anyway, so join the club.' I glanced back in time to see her turn on Henry. 'What did you have to interfere for? I was *that* close to getting her to agree.'

The day moved slowly and painfully on. Now, as well as the staring, whispering and pointing, I had to put up with Zara bending my ear about the advantages of a business-like friendship and Henry staring at me with sad, puppy-dog eyes. When I finally got out of school at three thirty, I felt something like I imagine a captive animal feels on being released back into the wild.

I ran for the first bus, got a seat at the front and was home in half an hour. I had to bolt for the front door when I saw Mrs Brodie, our neighbour, arriving home from the opposite direction. Luckily she was still too far away for me to have to say anything. I managed a nervous wave and then shot inside before she got any closer. I slammed the door behind me. I was safe.

'Sanctuary,' I whispered to myself, then smiled. I was being as melodramatic as Celina and her friends. But it was how I felt.

I could hear shouts and screams from the back garden, where Mum was playing with the twins. I was about to go and say hello, when I noticed a small pile of letters next to the telephone. My heart began to flutter hopefully. I grabbed them and leafed through. There were bills, quite a few of them. And two birthday cards. My hopes soared briefly, then fell like a stone.

There was a card from Auntie Babita, my mum's sister. She was the only person from my mum's family who still talked to us. Everyone else was too offended that Mum hadn't divorced Dad after what he'd done. The other, lilac-coloured, envelope was from Dad's parents in Chicago, where they lived with Dad's brother. The police thought that Dad might have gone to hide out in the States with them, but it wasn't very likely. Babaji and Biji were shocked and distressed by what Dad had done, and they were old and frail. I couldn't imagine Dad involving them. But then, I couldn't imagine him stealing thousands of pounds of other people's money.

'Sunita?' Mum was coming down the hall towards me. 'I didn't expect you home yet.'

'You'd better get the twins in,' I said. 'Mrs Brodie's just come home.'

'In a minute.' Mum stared at me and I slowly registered the paleness of her face and the tension crackling through her whole body. She was holding something behind her back.

'What is it?' I asked, suddenly trembling all over.

Mum held out a pink envelope. 'I hid it,' she said, her voice quivering. 'I didn't want the twins to see it.'

I took the envelope from her. I instantly recognized the handwriting on the front.

It was my dad's.

CHAPTER 3

I stood looking down at the envelope without moving.

'Why didn't you open it?' I whispered.

'It's addressed to you – of course I wouldn't open it,' Mum said too quickly. 'Oh, all right. I thought about it. Lots of times. I even put the kettle on twice to steam it open.'

The letter had been posted in India. India was one of the places the police thought Dad might be hiding, but that didn't mean anything. He could have posted the card to India and someone else could have posted it there for him. A relative, maybe.

'How does he know where we are?' I could hardly speak, and had to force the words out. My voice sounded like someone else's.

Mum's dark eyes looked huge in her thin face. 'I don't know, Sunita.'

I turned the envelope over in my hands. Wherever my dad was, he'd touched this piece of

paper. It was the only contact we'd had for months.

'But you didn't open it.'

'No.' Mum shook her head. 'I was scared.'

I chewed my bottom lip. 'So am I.'

'Oh, Sunita.' She put her arm round my shoulders. 'We'll open it together.'

I put my thumb under the flap and carefully slit the envelope open. Ripping it carelessly felt wrong.

My fingers were shaking so much, I couldn't get the card out. Mum put her hand over mine and helped me.

The card had a pink, glittery cat on the front holding a cake with candles. Across the top it read, *To my daughter*. Inside it said, *Hope you have a lovely day!* And underneath, *Dad xxx*. Nothing else. It was a huge anticlimax.

'Is that it?' My voice cracked.

Mum swallowed audibly. 'At least we know he's alive.'

'*Hope you have a lovely day*,' I read out. 'Well, that's not very likely, is it? In the circumstances.'

Mum hugged me, and we stood there silently for a while. We drew apart when Debbie came charging in from the garden.

'Mum, can we have another pancake?' she panted. 'Davey threw the last one too high, and it got stuck in the tree.'

I slid the card behind me out of sight. Questions were teeming in my head about Dad, the card – everything – but I needed to be on my own to think it through. I managed to smile at Debbie. 'What are you two up to?' My voice wasn't normal, but it was a good try.

'Mum gave us the leftover pancakes to play with.' Debbie beamed at me. 'They make great frisbees.'

Mum forced a laugh. 'At least they're good for something,' she said. 'Go and tell Davey it's time to come in now.'

'Oh, *M-u-u-um*.' Debbie pouted.

'Mrs Brodie's home,' said Mum sternly. 'Remember what I told you?'

'Ooh!' Debbie's big brown eyes almost popped out of her head. 'Will she *really* put a spell on us and turn us into frogs?'

I raised my eyebrows at Mum, who looked sheepish.

'Yes, she will,' she muttered. 'Now go and get Davey in.'

'I don't care if Mrs Brodie turns Davey into a frog,' Debbie said sulkily. 'He's horrible. He tried to put a pancake down my knickers.'

'Debbie! Get Davey in right now!' Mum made a dash at her and, with a squeal, Debbie ran off towards the back door.

'Nice one, Mum,' I said, following her into the kitchen. 'Give the kids nightmares by telling them the neighbour's a witch.'

'It's the only way I can get them to come in—' Mum began defensively.

The doorbell rang, loudly and shrilly.

Mum and I froze, literally froze, right where we were standing. I couldn't even take a breath.

'Who – who's that?' I mouthed at Mum. Memories of endless police visits and journalists knocking at the door and trying to peer into our front windows rushed through my head. The card in my hand seemed to grow hot and burn my skin. I felt like a criminal.

'I don't know.' Mum stared helplessly at me. 'Shall I answer it?'

'No!'

We huddled round the kitchen door, which was slightly ajar, and peered through the narrow gap. We could see a blurry shape in a red coat through the glass rectangle in the front door.

'It looks like Mrs Brodie,' I whispered.

'Oh.' Just one word, and Mum sounded guilty. I stared accusingly at her.

'Well,' she whispered, fidgeting from one foot to the other, 'it was raining, really hard. Her washing was outside, and I knew she'd gone out. And there's that gap in the fence between our gardens, so . . .'

I groaned. 'You went next door and took Mrs Brodie's washing down?'

Mum nodded, biting her lip. 'I put it in her shed, out of the rain. I didn't think she'd guess it was me. It could have been one of the other neighbours, after all. Her side gate's never locked.'

I couldn't help smiling. Although Mum very definitely wanted to be left alone at the moment, she couldn't help being friendly and helping people out because that was just the way she was. And it was going to be difficult keeping ourselves to ourselves for ever. We were living in a narrow street, crammed with little terraced houses. I wondered how long it would take before she gave in and started getting to know people.

The doorbell rang again.

'Keep quiet and she'll go away,' Mum hissed desperately.

'MUM! DEBBIE PUT A SNAIL IN MY EAR!'

Two pairs of small feet thundered into the kitchen.

'I DID NOT PUT IT IN YOUR EAR, YOU FIBBER!' Debbie bellowed, her round face as red as a tomato. 'I JUST PUT IT NEXT TO YOUR EAR, SO YOU COULD HEAR WHAT IT WAS SAYING!'

Mum and I each clapped a hand over the mouth nearest to us. The twins squirmed and wriggled, but we held onto them until Mrs Brodie had gone.

'Now,' Mum said at last, releasing Davey. 'I want you twins to go and watch TV quietly, because I'm going to be very busy for the next hour or two. I'm making a special birthday tea for Sunita.'

'Will we be able to eat it?' Debbie asked, solemn-faced.

'I think so,' Mum said with a smile. 'I'll make some sandwiches, and we have cakes, *which*' – she held up her hand as both twins opened their mouths – 'I bought at the supermarket.'

Debbie and Davey clapped and cheered.

'I'll get on with my homework then.' I was longing to be on my own.

Upstairs in my tiny cupboard of a bedroom, I stood the card on the windowsill. Then I sat and stared at it as if it might contain a secret message or some sort of code. Of course, it didn't. I supposed that Mum would have to tell the police about the card. They'd said they wanted to know if we received any messages from Dad. Not that this would tell them very much.

Hope you have a lovely day. How? How could I have a lovely day?

As I'd done countless times before, I wondered where Dad was. India, America, England? Somewhere else? I imagined him hiding in a secret compartment in a house, and never coming out, like Anne Frank. Or if he wasn't in hiding, was he

in disguise? Would I even recognize him if I passed him in the street?

The biggest question of all was, of course, if he was ever coming back.

I didn't know.

There are 365 days in a year, fifty-two and a bit weeks, five days of school a week minus holidays. It worked out to – oh, days and days and days when I had no choice but to grit my teeth and go to school. I hadn't told Mum yet that my secret was out. She had enough to worry about. I was hoping, as Zara had said, that people would get used to me being around. I just had to give them time.

But I knew that Celina and her gang of drama queens (including Jack Browning) didn't have any intention of letting me off the hook. It was partly my own fault for making serious enemies of them. I knew I should have kept my big mouth shut.

I don't suppose they were waiting for me on purpose when I arrived at school the next day, but they were grouped casually around the gates, chatting, and there was no way of avoiding them except to climb over a two-metre-high fence. I went for the cool option and walked past them, narrowly avoiding Jack's foot, stuck out deliberately to trip me up.

'There's a totally gross smell around here,' purred Celina, holding a finger under her nose. 'Has anyone else noticed?'

'Yeah, smells like a dirty thief to me,' Jack agreed.

'Oh dear, no marks for originality,' I yawned, strolling by. 'Keep trying.'

Celina just smiled, cat-like, confident that she could get under my skin. 'I'm going to ask my dad to complain to Mrs Bright. We shouldn't have to go to school with the daughter of a criminal.'

'Celina's dad's the mayor,' Chloe chimed in haughtily.

'Well, fancy that!' I oozed sarcasm. 'I am incredibly impressed. No, *really*.'

Celina shrugged. She was determined not to let me get under *her* skin. 'My dad's been elected mayor because he's an honest, upstanding member of the community,' she drawled, running a hand through her glossy hair. 'Something you and your dad would know nothing about.'

'Are you saying I'm not honest?' I should have left it, I know. But something inside me couldn't.

'Well, *duh*.' Celina rolled her eyes expressively at me. 'I know it was your dad who stole the money, but you must have known what was going on. You and your mum.'

'Yeah, you must have all been in it together,' Danielle added spitefully.

My hands bunched into fists. I knew I should walk away, I knew they were only trying to wind me up, but the injustice made me flame with anger.

'My mum and I had no idea,' I said in a shaking voice, wondering if Mrs Bright would suspend me if I grabbed Celina and the grinning Jack by the neck and banged their heads together.

There was a chorus of jeers which infuriated me even more.

'Yeah, right!' Jack sneered. 'You ought to get done for – what d'they call it? Receiving stolen goods.' He puffed himself up like a peacock. 'Yeah, that's it.'

A red mist danced in front of my eyes. What I was going to do next would definitely have got me suspended, maybe even expelled. But nothing happened because right then Mr Arora shambled through from the teachers' car park, clutching an untidy pile of folders and exercise books. His eyes looked crusted with sleep, as if he could barely keep them open. He was followed by the three golden and glamorous girls I'd met yesterday, while looking for the school office.

The tall girl, Amber, caught my eye and smiled. 'All right?' she said casually, and walked on.

Just *that* was enough to stop me in my tracks. It was more than being nice to me, it was treating

me like a normal person. It reminded me that if I wanted to fit in, I had to get on with it.

I pulled myself together with an effort. Ignoring Celina and Jack and their taunts, I turned away and walked into school. *I would not let them beat me.*

I was still congratulating myself when I came face to face with a second problem. Zara Kennedy and Henry Williams were both lurking at the classroom door, pretending not to be looking out for me.

'Hi, Sunita,' Zara called. 'You're sitting next to me again today, aren't you?' She shot Henry a poisonous stare.

'Th-th-there's a seat by me too,' Henry said nervously, keeping his distance from Zara. 'If you're interested.'

'She's not,' snapped Zara, trying to shove him out of the way. Being small and weedy, she looked like a mouse trying to shift an elephant. 'Didn't you hear what I said? She's sitting next to *me*.'

'I-I just thought she might like a change of scenery,' stammered Henry, who looked terrified but was no way giving in.

I felt my brief good mood melting away in an instant. 'Stop!' I raised my hand. 'Do either of you two *know* how people actually make friends? They get together because they *both* want to, and

because they've got things in common.' I looked from one to the other. 'Spot the difference?'

'Help!' Zara raised her arms and waved them in the air. 'Save me from the huge rush of people who want to be your friends! I'm getting trampled!' She dropped her arms and looked pointedly round. 'Spot the difference?'

'Both of you, just stop hassling me, OK?' I said crossly, and flounced into the room. I was annoyed only because Zara was right. While I had no friends, I would always be the odd one out. On the other hand, I didn't want to be *one* of the odd ones. I did not want to hang out with losers. I would only give in if I was desperate, and I hadn't got there yet . . .

I longed to sit somewhere else, other than next to Zara, but thought that I'd better ask Mr Arora first. However, when he trudged in yawning, as usual, he looked so depressed, I decided against it.

'What's the matter with Mr Arora?' I asked Zara. I didn't want to talk to her, but curiosity got the better of me. 'Every day he looks half dead.'

Zara glanced smugly at Henry, who was observing us closely. 'His wife's just had a baby,' she replied. 'I suppose it keeps them awake at night, crying. He actually fell asleep in a maths class just before half-term.'

'Oh.' I looked at Mr Arora with sympathy.

Memories of the newborn twins roaring in chorus came flooding back to me.

'He's married to the auntie of those Dhillon sisters,' Zara went on, eager to keep me in conversation. 'You must have seen them and if you haven't yet, you will. Geena, Amber and Jazz. Apparently they're known as the Bindi Babes. They think they're so *great*.'

Things clicked into place.

'Well, maybe they are,' I said sharply, remembering how one of them had stopped me from, at the very least, killing Celina and Jack that very morning.

Zara shrugged. 'All right, all right, don't get your knickers in a twist.' She grinned at me, and for the first time I noticed that her eyes were a deep sea-green, fringed with long, sweeping lashes. 'Look how we're talking! Like friends, wouldn't you say?'

'Forget it,' I said, taking a book from my bag. I fixed my eyes firmly to the first page, ignoring both Henry's hopeful stares and Zara's loud tutting in my ear. I would find some 'normal' friends, I told myself, if it killed me.

But Zara and Henry were not giving up. Unluckily, they were in all the same sets as me that day, and every lesson became a test of strength, courage and wits as they battled to win

the seat next to me. They each had their own advantages. Zara was quick and light on her feet, while Henry had the bulk to block her path. Zara won out in English, by grabbing my arm and yanking me into the seat next to her, narrowly avoiding dislocating my shoulder. But Henry triumphed in the battle of German conversation by getting into the room first and asking the teacher if he could partner me at the computer.

'Isn't it funny how losers tend to stick together?' Celina said lightly as we queued for lunch at the canteen doors. She was ahead of me, but I could hear her perfectly. I knew I was meant to.

Chloe, Danielle and Jyoti sniggered. Henry, who was trying to edge in next to me, blushed. Zara, who was glued to my other side, shrugged.

'And isn't it funny how nasty, small-minded airheads tend to stick together too?' she said thoughtfully.

Celina, Jyoti and Danielle scowled, while Chloe asked plaintively, 'Who's she talking about?'

Exactly what I didn't want to happen *was* happening before my very eyes. I was being identified with the losers. Quickly I tried to wriggle out of the queue and get away from my 'friends', but it was impossible.

'Will you two stop squashing me?' I hissed at Henry and Zara. 'I feel like the meat in a sandwich.'

They ignored me and pressed closer.

'Sit by me on the bus tonight,' Zara urged.

'No, sit by me,' Henry said breathlessly. 'I'll carry your bag for you. You can make it as heavy as you like. I don't even mind if you put that big atlas in.'

I groaned, knowing that they were going to duel their way across the canteen to get a seat next to me. It would be forks at twenty paces. How could I get away from them?

As it turned out, Jack Browning did me a favour. He 'accidentally' knocked into me as we stood at the serving hatch, spilling my cheese omelette, chips and peas onto the floor. By the time I had helped a cross dinner lady clear up, and collected a second plate of food, Zara and Henry were already seated at another table. I ate up and got out of there as fast as I could.

My plan was to disappear round the side of the school towards the playing field, where there were several useful trees to hide behind. But when I glanced round, I saw Henry tracking me furtively across the playground. I stopped and groaned.

'Look, I can't put this politely,' I said. 'Go away.'

Henry flushed with distress. 'I just wanted to make sure you were OK.'

'Why shouldn't I be?' I snapped. I did feel guilty,

though. It was like being angry with an overgrown puppy.

'I saw what Jack did,' Henry began.

'Yes, well, it gave me an excuse to get away from you and Zara,' I said rudely. 'Where is Zara, anyway?'

Henry's round face broke into a rare smile. 'One of the dinner ladies asked her to wipe our table. Zara said no, so now she's got to wipe every table in the canteen.'

That made me smile too, I admit. 'She'll be in a great mood this afternoon then.'

'Does that mean you'll sit next to me for French and science?' Henry asked hopefully.

'No!' I clutched at my hair. 'Please, please go away and find someone else to be friends with, Henry.'

Henry stared down at his feet. 'No one wants to be friends with me,' he mumbled. 'Because I'm fat.'

'Oh, nonsense,' I said briskly. 'Are you saying that fat – er – large people don't have any friends? That's rubbish.'

Henry raised his eyes and stared at me. 'Well, why don't *you* want to be friends with me then?'

I couldn't answer. It wasn't Henry's size so much as the fact that his bulk *and* his gentle nature made him a perfect victim. He had latched onto me

because I stood up for myself. I didn't have the energy or the inclination to stand up for *him* too, and I would have to, if we became friends. Well, that's the kind of friend I was, anyway.

'Look, Henry,' I said, neatly sidestepping his question, 'maybe you're a bit too shy and quiet. Don't let people like Jack boss you around. Try to stand up for yourself.'

'I can't,' Henry mumbled glumly. 'I'm useless. That's what my mum says, and she's right.'

I groaned silently. I was *so* not the person to deal with somebody else's self-esteem issues, or whatever they call it on those chat shows. So I was actually pleased to see Zara exit the canteen at that very moment and rush across the playground towards us, her face red with rage.

'Here's Zara,' I said, and whisked myself away out of sight while Henry turned round, looking petrified. I rounded the corner and hid behind a convenient wall. As long as I kept on the move, I could avoid my wannabe 'friends'.

Home time, and I was exhausted. Zara and Henry were sapping what little energy I had left with their constant stalking. But I was saved from the bloody battle of the bus seat by Mr Arora, who managed to gather together enough energy to ask to speak to me at the end of the day. I watched with relief as Henry and Zara trudged reluctantly

out into the playground, and then I returned to classroom 7B. I waited for fifteen minutes, wondering if Mr Arora had forgotten that he'd asked me to wait, but eventually he arrived, clutching a mug of black coffee. I wondered if he'd been having a nap in the staff room.

'Sunita, thank you for waiting,' Mr Arora said, slumping down in his chair. The caffeine obviously hadn't kicked in yet. 'The reason I wanted to talk to you is to check that you're all right. I'm worried about you because I've noticed that everyone seems to have found out about your – er – background.'

I stared at him. I didn't think he'd noticed *anything*. 'Yes, sir.'

Maybe I sounded just a teensy bit disbelieving, because he looked slightly sheepish.

'To be honest, I didn't actually notice myself . . .' Mr Arora cleared his throat. 'I was told, by my nieces. I think you've met them. Geena, Amber and Jazz . . .'

He took a huge gulp of coffee and blinked several times. I waited for him to prop his eyelids open with his fingers, but even he seemed to feel that would be a step too far. 'Well, anyway, I just wanted to make sure that things weren't too difficult for you. Obviously this wasn't what we were expecting, but I'm sure that things will settle down

if we give it time, and that you'll be accepted at Coppergate on your own merits.'

I hesitated. I wondered whether to tell on Celina and Jack, who were making my life miserable and would certainly continue to do so. But Mr Arora looked so exhausted, I just didn't want to add to his problems. Anyway, it would be telling tales.

'I'm all right, sir.'

'I'm glad to hear it.' Mr Arora's face contorted this way and that as he tried to stifle a yawn. 'And remember, you can always come to me if you need any help.'

I escaped. I just managed to catch the last school bus, which was lucky because I had no way of letting Mum know I would be late. My tiny, sleek, silver mobile phone was a thing of the past.

I was so late, I took the short cut, even though I didn't much enjoy walking past those big, posh houses. They reminded me too much of what we'd lost. As I hurried along the pavement, I saw Chloe Maynard come out of one of them. Her house had landscaped gardens, a large, separate granny annexe at the side and two double garages. She didn't see me. She crossed the road and went up the driveway of the opposite house, her skinny hipbones jutting sideways out of her designer jeans. Her crop top showed off her flat stomach, so flat it was almost inside out, and she

carried a denim jacket, even though it was freezing.

The house opposite was bigger and more luxurious in every way, with a sweeping, paved drive. There was a silver Mercedes parked outside the front door. Chloe knocked, and Celina Patel opened it. I could not stop myself staring.

Celina wore a denim miniskirt, high-heeled black boots and a fluffy, white fake-fur jacket. I think it was fake. She was followed outside by a man, tall and well-built, in a dark grey suit. I supposed it was Celina's dad, although he wasn't wearing his mayoral robes and gold chain. They were joined by a glamorous, sophisticated woman in a pink sari and pointed shoes, the exact same colour. She wore a lot of diamond jewellery.

My footsteps had unconsciously slowed as I watched. But then Celina saw me. She immediately whispered to her mum and dad, who stared at me openly and curiously. Blushing, I walked faster as they all climbed into the Mercedes. Celina's dad held the door open for her and patted her shoulder as she got in. A moment later the car swept past me.

I felt angry. Celina's mum, the school governor, had possibly given away my secret to Celina. She shouldn't have done that. I felt jealous. Celina wasn't one of the nicest people in the world (what

an understatement), but her dad loved her, and he was there for her. I felt sad. My dad loved me, but he wasn't here.

But that only made me more determined. I was going to stay at Coppergate and find proper friends and shut Celina and Jack up by making people forget what my dad had done, and like me for myself.

I changed my mind, though, when Mr Arora's wallet went missing.

CHAPTER 4

I had made it through to Friday afternoon, the end of the first week. I was proud of myself. I had fought the continual attempts of Celina and her gang of drama queens to needle me. And I think people were beginning to get used to me, just a little. All right, some of them were still making pointed comments about fugitives and thieves and jail when I passed by. But I thought I could cope . . .

I hadn't made any friends, though. No one except Zara and Henry showed any interest in getting to know me at all. Although I was still telling both of them to leave me alone, secretly I was beginning to get used to them hanging around. After all, some days I wouldn't have spoken to anyone except teachers, if I hadn't had Zara and Henry to argue with. I did start to wonder if I should just give in and be mates with them.

And then . . .

'Where's my wallet?' Mr Arora had wandered

into the classroom after lunch, dropped the register on his desk and slumped in his seat. Now he sat up as if he'd been shot in the back. 'I left it right here.'

Everyone glanced up, including me. Mr Arora, looking more wide-awake than I'd seen him so far, began to rifle through the haphazard and chaotic contents of his desk. Bits of paper went flying, followed by paperclips, folders and small lumps of Blu-tac.

'It was here,' he wailed. 'And now it's gone.'

I didn't notice immediately that some of the class were staring at me. Then, slowly, I became aware of people looking. Jack, Celina, Jyoti, Danielle and Chloe, of course, but others too. Whispering, nodding, pointing . . . I felt the colour drain from my face. Surely, *surely* they couldn't be so stupid as to think I would steal something? Because my dad was a thief, why did that mean I was one too? I wanted to shout my innocence out loud, but my throat had closed up.

'Are you sure you left it there, sir?' Zara said suddenly. 'Maybe it's in the staff room.'

'Or maybe somebody took it,' Celina remarked casually.

There was a murmur of agreement and all eyes were on me. I felt as if someone had stabbed me in the heart.

'That's ridiculous,' Zara said loudly, glaring at Celina. 'I don't think *anyone* in this class would take something that belonged to Mr Arora.'

I couldn't believe that she was standing up for me after the way I'd pushed her aside.

'I'll help you look, sir,' said Henry. Pink in the face, he was already out of his chair and lumbering to the front of the room before Mr Arora could say anything.

'Careful!' shrieked Celina as Henry brushed past her table, knocking books and papers and everything else to the floor.

'Ow!' yelled Jack as Chloe's make-up bag landed on his toe.

'Be careful,' Mr Arora said nervously as Henry began pulling at piles of folders and exercise books. As the whole lot cascaded to the ground, half the class shot out of their seats to help. Not me. I was rigid in my chair. Thoughts rushed through my head at the speed of sound. Would this happen *every* time something went missing? I couldn't stand it. I would have to leave. I would tell Mum tonight that I had to start over somewhere else—

'Sir,' Zara called over the noise. 'Are you sure you didn't put the wallet in your pocket?'

Mr Arora thrust his hands into his jacket pockets. Then a sheepish smile spread across his face. He

pulled out a black leather wallet and waved it in the air.

'Well done, Zara,' he said with a sigh of relief. 'My wife would have killed me if I'd lost all my money.'

I was saved. But I couldn't stop shaking. I still felt sick as the bell pealed out for afternoon lessons. I might have guessed that Celina and Jack and their friends would make the most of the situation, but *everyone* in the class thought I might have taken Mr Arora's wallet; thought that I might be a thief, although I'd never actually stolen anything in my life.

Not everyone, though. I swallowed down the hard lump in my throat, and turned to Zara.

'Thanks.'

'What for?' Zara picked up her bag as the other kids milled over to the door.

'Sticking up for me.' I swallowed again. 'You didn't have to.'

Zara shrugged. 'I knew you didn't do it,' she replied. 'I'd have done the same for anyone who was innocent.'

Innocent. What a lovely word. So much better than *guilty*.

'You couldn't know that,' I said curiously.

Zara snorted with derision. 'Of course I knew,' she scoffed. 'You'd have to be stupid to do that. And you're not stupid. Annoying yes, stupid no.'

'Thanks,' I said again.

Henry was pushing his way against the tide of the crowd towards us.

'Are you all right, Sunita?' he asked anxiously.

Someone else who thought I was innocent. I smiled at him.

'I'm fine.' It was so comforting to have people who were on my side. I knew I might regret it later, but right there and then I made an instant decision, and pushed away all thoughts of consequences. 'You know what? Let's all three of us sit together this afternoon.' I looked at Zara. 'OK with you?'

Zara frowned, her head on one side. 'Does this mean we're all friends then?' she asked tartly, as Henry beamed. 'You do know that three is a very awkward number.'

'For a business arrangement, maybe,' I replied. 'But not if you're *real* friends.'

Henry looked thrilled, and even Zara's eyes lit up. Maybe they weren't the friends I would have chosen. No *maybe* about it: they definitely *weren't* the friends I would have chosen. But they were the friends I'd got. And you know, *friend* is an even more beautiful word than *innocent*.

I was singing to myself as I walked home from the bus stop after school. When was the last time I'd

felt even a tiny bit happy? Months ago. I couldn't remember.

Henry, Zara and I had sat together on the bus. It was a bit of a squeeze because Henry took up so much room, but we managed. Celina and her witches, and Jack, of course, were ready with their insults, but it didn't matter. I'd forgotten how it felt to be one of a group instead of on your own. The solid bulk of Henry on one side of me and the sparky presence of Zara on the other were surprisingly comforting.

As I walked towards our house, I was surprised to see Mum dart out through Mr Chan's garden gate next door. She glanced fearfully up and down the road and then ducked down onto her hands and knees. She seemed to be clearing something from Mr Chan's hedge.

'Mum, what are you doing?' I asked, coming up behind her.

Mum gave a little scream and leaped to her feet. I was even more surprised to see the twins charge out through Mr Chan's gate and launch themselves at me. They held bunches of red, gold and yellow leaves in their mittened hands.

'Sunita!' Davey roared, head-butting me in the tummy. 'Look! We've been cleaning up Mr Chan's garden!'

'We've picked up all the litter stuck in Mrs

70

Brodie's hedge,' Debbie added. '*And* the other neighbours too.'

I glanced at Mum, who slowly turned pink. 'Have you tidied the whole street?' I asked, amused.

'Well, I was just cleaning all the leaves and litter out of our own front garden,' Mum said defensively. 'And you know how frail Mr Chan is. I thought we could give him a hand.'

'So you've spoken to him?' I asked, my eyes wide.

Mum looked slightly sheepish. 'No, it's his day for the community centre. He doesn't get back till five.'

'And Mrs Brodie?'

Mum stared down at her feet like a naughty schoolgirl. 'I think she's gone away for the weekend,' she mumbled. 'I saw her getting in her car with a suitcase.'

I couldn't help smiling. 'So you thought you'd sneak around doing good deeds while the neighbours were away. Who do you think you are, Superman?'

The twins hooted with laughter.

'No, Supermum,' Debbie giggled.

'Mum, you need a costume to be a proper superhero,' Davey declared. 'I'll lend you my Spiderman suit.'

'Thank you,' said Mum. 'But don't you think it might be a bit big for me?'

Debbie and Davey clutched at each other, helpless with giggles. It was good to see.

Too quickly, we were under siege again.

'Oh, no,' Mum whispered, her face changing. 'Here comes that woman who lives next door to Mrs Brodie. Inside, kids, right away.'

We didn't know the names of our other neighbours, although we knew them all by sight. It helped when you were desperate to avoid them. As the woman hurried up the road, pushing her baby in a buggy, we dumped the black sacks of rubbish in the bin and disappeared indoors.

'I know we're going to have to get used to meeting people sometime,' Mum said to me as the twins charged into the living room to argue over the TV remote control. 'But I just don't feel ready for it yet.'

I didn't know what to say. I still hadn't told Mum that our secret was out at school. I couldn't decide which was worse – being on tenterhooks in case anyone found out who you were, or having to put up with hurtful comments from people who did know. It was a tough one.

'How's school?' Mum asked me, almost reading my mind. I followed her into the kitchen, glad she had her back to me.

'All right.'

'Have you made any friends?'

This, at least, I could answer truthfully.

'Yes, two. Zara and Henry.'

'A boy?' Mum said teasingly. 'Is he good-looking?'

'You're joking!' I replied. 'But he seems nice.'

Mum still had her back to me as she filled the kettle at the sink.

'Sunita, the police came today.'

'What?' My stomach began to churn. 'Why? They haven't found—?'

'No. Not that.' Mum turned round to face me. 'They knew it was your birthday and wanted to see if your dad had been in touch.' She bit her lip. 'They took the card away. I'm sorry, Sunita.'

'They shouldn't have done that,' I said in a wobbly voice. 'It was mine.'

'They promised you'd get it back,' said Mum, stroking my hair from my face.

'Mum?' I'd never voiced this fear openly before, but it seemed the right moment to bring it up. 'What if Dad never comes home?'

'I've thought about that too.' Mum sighed deeply. 'I suppose we have to get on and make ourselves a new life without him.' She tried to smile, but I could see a faint glimmer of tears in her eyes. 'Listen to me, pretending to be all brave,

when I can't even bring myself to say hello to the neighbours.'

'You *are* brave,' I said. 'And the neighbours will love you when they realize you've been doing all these nice things for them.'

Mum didn't look very convinced and, as usual, we spent the whole weekend in the house. This was partly to avoid meeting anyone, but also because we didn't have any money to do anything else. Being cooped up in a small space for two days and three nights with Debbie and Davey was a horrifying experience. We did make a mad dash to the park on Saturday evening as it was getting dark, just so the twins could run around yelling and hitting each other with twigs. But other than that we stayed inside. Monday morning, and I almost couldn't wait to get to school. But Mum was looking pale and wrecked, and I wanted to cheer her up.

'Listen, you two monkeys.' I cornered Davey and Debbie on the landing while Mum was downstairs making breakfast. 'We're going to do something nice for Mum today before we go to school. A lovely, secret surprise, just like she's been doing for the neighbours.'

'Ooh, what?' Debbie demanded.

'We're going to tidy your pit of a bedroom,' I replied, trying to push the door open wider, but

a red felt-tip pen was stuck underneath, wedging the door in position.

Davey's face fell. 'That's not a lovely surprise,' he scoffed.

'Yes, it is.' I kicked the felt-tip pen away, grabbed one arm each and pulled them into the room. 'Mum will be ever so pleased. Trust me.'

'But tidying up is really hard, and we're only little,' Debbie said glumly.

I gazed hopelessly around the room, which was not much bigger than mine. Nothing which should be put away had been put away. The floor was heaped with clothes, books, pens, toys and bits of jigsaw. The wardrobe doors were open and more clothes were spilling out. Even the bunk beds were covered with stuff.

'How did you two get to sleep last night?' I asked.

'I just lay on top of it,' replied Davey.

I groaned. 'OK, listen to me,' I said sternly. 'We're going to tidy up, just like Mary Poppins and Michael and Jane do in the film.'

'You mean we click our fingers and everything will tidy up like magic?' asked Debbie, her eyes wide.

'No, I've got a much better idea,' I said. 'We'll *pick* everything up. Debbie, you collect the clothes, and, Davey, you put the toys away.'

'How is that better than magic?' Davey grumbled, kicking at a battered fire engine.

'Because Mum will know that we worked hard to help her,' I said sternly. 'And she'll be proud of us. Isn't that better than doing everything by magic?'

'No,' muttered the twins sulkily.

'All right, I'll give you each a KitKat,' I offered.

'Four-finger, not two-finger,' Debbie bargained.

'Done,' I agreed. 'But don't say anything to Mum. It's meant to be a surprise.'

The twins did keep quiet, amazingly, and Mum didn't guess what we were up to, so when I went off to school that morning, I was smiling. Mum would find out later, when she got back from taking the twins to school, that their room was tidy for once. I imagined her opening the door and seeing what we'd done. I could picture the look of delight on her face. It was a good feeling. I decided there and then that every day I'd do something secret to make Mum smile.

Just for a change, I took a different route to the bus stop. Well, not just for the change. I didn't want to walk past the big houses and run the risk of bumping into Celina and Chloe on their way to the bus, which would certainly wipe the smile off my face. Today I was happy. I wanted to keep hold of the feeling for as long as I could.

Instead of the short cut, I followed the road round, into a street of big, old Victorian houses. At the corner, though, I came to a dead stop. The red door of a house not far from me had just opened. Henry came out.

I didn't know he lived here, I thought.

Henry didn't see me. I was just about to call his name, when a woman appeared on the doorstep. Henry's mum? But she was tiny, bony, bird-like. She was hardly taller than I was.

'Now do try to choose the healthy option for lunch, Henry.' Mrs Williams began fiddling with Henry's hair and brushing fluff from his coat. Henry stood there obediently. I watched, fascinated. He had his back to me, but I could see that his shoulders were rigid with tension. 'And we'll have a nice salad for tea tonight.'

At this moment the blue front door of the next house opened, and another completely unexpected ingredient was thrown into the dramatic mix. Jack Browning came out. He looked handsome and stylish even in uniform, his tie knotted loosely around his neck, white shirt collar open.

'Hi, Mrs Williams,' he called, raising a hand. 'Hiya, Henry.'

My jaw dropped. Jack's open, honest smile and friendly manner was staggering, considering I knew very well how he treated Henry at school.

'Good morning, Jack.' Mrs Williams beamed at him and gave him a little wave. Did she really not know what he was like?

Jack sauntered down the path and out onto the street. He saw me straight away and, as he walked past, he tried to barge into my shoulder. But I'd already guessed his intention, and stepped aside.

'Hey, loser,' he said out of the corner of his mouth, and strolled away with a grin.

'Sunita!'

Henry had come to the gate and was waving at me. His mum was right behind him, checking me over with sharp blue eyes and an over-bright smile. She was even tinier close up. I was sure I could probably fit my hands around her waist.

'Mum, this is my friend Sunita,' said Henry. He sounded quite proud, which touched me a little.

'I'm very pleased to meet you, Sunita.' Mrs Williams gave me her dainty hand, a collection of bones and rings, to shake. 'What a pretty girl you are. Lovely and slim too. I expect you always choose the healthy lunch option at school, don't you?'

'Mum!' Henry groaned, flushing bright red. 'We've got to go. We'll be late.'

I didn't get a chance to say anything to Mrs Williams before Henry hustled me away, down the street. We were silent for a moment or two. My

head was swimming with so many questions, but where did I start?

'I didn't know you lived next door to Jack Browning, Henry.' That seemed like quite a good place to begin.

'Unfortunately,' Henry said with a heavy sigh.

'Your mum seems—' I stopped. *Nice* didn't seem the right word. 'Well, she seems to worry about you a lot.'

'Yes.' Henry sighed even harder. He stopped abruptly and pointed at a newsagent's shop across the street. 'I just have to pop in there for a minute. I won't be long.'

I stood there waiting. For some reason I felt vaguely worried about Henry, although I couldn't really say why. When he came back, he was carrying a plastic bag.

'Do you want something?' he asked, opening the bag wide so that I could see into it. It was full of chocolate bars and crisps.

I shook my head.

Henry took out a Flake and ate it in four bites before we'd walked to the end of the street.

'How did you get on with that English home-work?' he asked, starting on a bag of Doritos.

We talked about homework all the way to the bus stop, while Henry ate his way through half the contents of the carrier bag. We'd missed the

first bus, and had to wait for the second. By the time we got to school, Henry only had half a packet of Rolos left.

Zara was waiting for us in the playground.

'You two are a bit late,' Zara remarked. 'I thought you weren't coming.' Without ceremony she leaned over, took the Rolos from Henry and helped herself to one.

'I would have offered them to you,' Henry protested, the tips of his ears turning pink.

Zara shrugged. 'I didn't want to take the risk,' she replied, handing the packet back to him. 'So, what did you two do at the weekend?'

It was possibly the worst question she could have come up with.

Immediately I felt and looked rather flustered. 'Nothing much,' I mumbled. 'Nothing at all.'

Zara pounced like a cat on a mouse. 'Now why should such a simple question cause you so much anxiety?' she said thoughtfully.

'Zara!' Henry muttered, looking embarrassed.

'I'm not anxious,' I said with as much dignity as I could scrape together. 'We just didn't do anything much, that's all.'

'Surely you're not all lurking at home because you're scared to go out after what your dad did?' Zara went on, raising her eyebrows.

I felt angry with her for hitting the nail on the

head so accurately. 'You don't know what it's like,' I snapped. 'People can be so horrible. We just want to be left alone.'

'Well, I think you should stand up for yourselves,' Zara said robustly. 'After all, you and your mum and your brother and sister haven't done anything wrong.'

'It's not as easy as that,' I muttered.

'Can you – well – I mean, do you have any idea where your dad might be?' asked Henry haltingly.

I hesitated. I wasn't at all sure that I wanted to talk about my dad, even to my new friends.

'Don't answer if you don't want to,' Henry added, seeing the look on my face.

'It's all right,' I said, making a snap decision. 'We don't know where he is. Neither do the police.'

'What was he like?' Zara said curiously.

'He's not dead!' I snapped.

'Sorry.' For once, Zara didn't take offence. 'What *is* he like?'

I thought for a moment. 'He's kind,' I said. 'Funny. He'd do anything to make us laugh. He looked after us.' I didn't say it, but I knew that a big part of why Dad took the money was for us, the family. That didn't make it right, but it was the way things were.

'He sounds nice,' Henry remarked, popping a Rolo into his mouth.

Zara took the packet of sweets from him again, and offered me one.

'How old are your brother and sister, and what are their names?'

I was grateful to her for changing the subject. I told them a bit about the twins, which made them laugh.

'Have you two got any brothers and sisters?' I asked.

Henry looked suddenly gloomy as he shook his head. 'Just me.'

Zara's face closed in on itself as she replied, 'Two younger brothers and two younger sisters.'

I was astonished. 'You've got *four* brothers and sisters?' I said. She'd never mentioned them.

'Sure.' Zara shrugged. 'My parents had me, and then they wanted to see if they could have a baby with a normal face. So they had four more. Luckily, none of them have got a birthmark.'

I knew Zara well enough by now to understand that she sometimes said things just to shock. But this time I *was* shocked.

'You don't mean that.'

'Oh, I do,' Zara replied calmly. 'They're ashamed of me, my mum and dad.'

'I don't believe you.' I looked to Henry to back me up, but he was staring down at his trainers.

'They are,' Zara insisted. 'I overheard them

talking once, and my mum said she wished I didn't have the birthmark.' Her voice quivered very slightly.

'But what did you expect her to say?' I asked, puzzled. 'That she was *pleased* you had it?'

Zara stuck her bottom lip out rebelliously. 'It shouldn't matter,' she snapped. 'It shouldn't make any difference.'

'I bet it doesn't,' I argued. 'I'm sure your mum and dad love you just the same.'

'So why do they keep telling me I can have laser treatment to get rid of it when I'm older?' Zara demanded.

I rolled my eyes in annoyance. 'They're just trying to be helpful,' I replied. 'But you're so damn prickly, it's like trying to help a hedgehog!' I did not add that it would be just like Zara not to have the treatment, so she could irritate everybody all the more.

Zara pulled a face at me, and I decided it was better to shut up. I did feel angry with her, though. She was lucky enough to have her mum and dad around, and all she could worry about was something I was sure wasn't true.

'*My* mum's ashamed of *me*.'

Henry spoke in such a low voice, we only just caught the words.

'Why?' Zara asked bluntly. 'Because you're fat?'

'I'm not really fat,' Henry began earnestly. 'I'm just big-boned—'

'Henry, your bones would have to be the size of a dinosaur's, in that case,' Zara broke in. 'Face it, you're fat.'

'Zara!' I exclaimed in horror.

'Well, he is,' Zara retorted. 'And you know why? He eats too much. Chocolate every morning, and chips every day for lunch.'

'I'm sure your mum's not ashamed of you, Henry.' I glared pointedly at Zara to shut her up. 'From what I saw today, I think she's just worried about you.'

'She *is* ashamed,' Henry insisted glumly. 'She wishes I was like Jack Browning.'

'He lives next door to you, doesn't he?' Zara raised her eyebrows. 'Doesn't she know what he's *really* like?'

Henry shook his head. 'Mum thinks he's great,' he mumbled. 'She's always going on about him.'

'You mean you haven't even told her that he bullies you?' I asked.

'You should put her straight,' said Zara tartly.

Henry didn't look that convinced. 'And you know what?' he went on gloomily, 'Mum wants me to go to Fat Camp next summer.'

'Fat Camp?' Zara frowned. 'What's that?'

'It's for kids to lose weight.' Henry sighed, a

sigh that seemed to come from the depths of his supposedly bigger-than-average bones. 'They make you diet and run around and exercise.'

'It sounds just what you need—' Zara began, but stopped when I elbowed her discreetly in the ribs.

'Look, tell your mum you really don't want to go,' I said helpfully. 'She won't force you.'

Henry looked unconvinced. 'She will. She wants me to be skinny just like her.'

I looked from one to the other in silence. And I thought I had problems with *my* parents. I was sure I had the worst deal of the three of us – although I'm not boasting about it – but I felt sorry for Zara and Henry. Are there any normal parents, anywhere?

'Well, you know what you have to do to get on better with your mum,' Zara said briskly. 'Stop eating junk, run around a bit more and lose some weight.'

'And what are *you* going to do to get on better with *yours*?' snapped Henry, quite rudely, for him.

Zara's eyes darkened, and she drew her brows down.

'Can we check that maths homework together?' I broke in hastily as she opened her mouth. 'I'm not sure I did mine right.'

Zara started muttering under her breath, but she

did open her bag. So did Henry. With a silent sigh of relief, I did the same. My friends were turning out to be a bit more complicated than I'd been expecting.

I was surprised to see a folded piece of paper sitting on top of my books inside my bag. I picked it up, opened it out.

Sunita, whatever happens with your dad, we'll be OK, the note read. *I just wanted you to know that. Have a good day at school, Mum xxx*. She'd drawn a smiley face at the bottom.

'Are you all right?' Zara asked, flipping through her maths book. 'You look like you're going to cry.'

'I'm fine.' I so wanted to believe Mum, but it was difficult. I was glad she was trying, though. If we were going to do this at all, we had to do it together.

Henry, Zara and I were deep into comparing the answers to our sums, when shrill screams from nearby interrupted us.

'Ooh, it's gorgeous, Celina!'

'Can I try it on?'

'Oh!' Zara said grumpily, covering her ears. 'Screaming drama queen alert.'

Celina, surrounded by her gang of shrieking harpies, threw us a superior stare. She was holding out one of her slim wrists so that her friends could

admire the heavy silver bracelet of linked, cut-out hearts she was wearing. Flashes of pinpoint sparkles glinted off it in the pale autumn sunshine like laser beams.

'Those aren't *real* diamonds?' breathed Danielle reverently.

Celina shrugged. 'They're only tiny,' she said. 'You need a microscope to see them.'

'But diamonds!' Danielle groaned.

'Ooh, look!' Chloe squealed. 'There's one set in each of the hearts. It's *gorgeous*.'

'Celina Patel, if you aren't just the luckiest girl alive,' Jyoti said with deep envy. 'I thought your mum wouldn't allow you to wear it to school.'

Celina winked at them. 'She doesn't know,' she explained smugly. 'I sneaked out with it when she was in the shower this morning.'

'Oh no,' I muttered, putting my head in my hands. 'Please, please, *please* don't let Celina lose that bracelet or I'll be arrested.' I was half joking for Henry and Zara's benefit, but I was serious too. The memory of Mr Arora's wallet was still fresh in my mind.

'Yes, the mayor would make sure you were given life imprisonment,' Zara added with a grin.

Celina didn't hear what she said, but she saw us smiling. Maybe what she did next was because she couldn't stand the sight. Anyway, sliding the

admittedly beautiful bracelet up and down her wrist with her other hand, she turned to face me.

'My dad says he knows where your dad is,' she called casually.

If she wanted to stop me smiling, she succeeded. If she wanted to jolt me up, she did, like an electric shock. I jumped to my feet, overturning my maths book into a puddle. Henry rushed to fish it out, while I fronted Celina.

'What are you talking about?' I demanded.

Celina shrugged, half smiling. Her favourite thing, I was beginning to realize, was playing people like instruments. Starting soft and quiet and *adagio*, and then winding them up for a big crescendo.

'Well, he doesn't *know*, as such,' she purred. 'But he can guess.'

'And what does he guess?'

'Let's see . . .' Celina tapped her chin with one pearly pink fingernail, enjoying making me sweat. 'My dad says that there's only one place any sensible person would choose. Any sensible *Indian* person. And that's India.'

I took a deep breath as I remembered the birthday card. I had to fight to keep my face from betraying the fact that it was possible Celina's dad was right.

'I mean, it's the perfect place to lose yourself if

you're on the run, isn't it?' Celina went on. 'After all, there are over a billion people there . . .'

She stopped as she caught the expression on my face. I knew I looked guilty, despite my best efforts.

Celina broke into peals of giggles. 'Ooh, you know something, don't you, Sunita?' she declared. 'My dad's right. He *is* in India, isn't he?'

Her friends started to laugh.

'You should go to the police, Cee,' said Danielle.

'Oh, yes,' Jyoti agreed with a snigger. 'There might be a reward!'

'Sunita, let's go in,' Zara said urgently as the bell rang.

'Here's your maths book,' Henry added, holding it out to me.

I ignored them, fixing my burning gaze on Celina. I knew she was half joking to wind me up, and I knew the police were already considering India as one of Dad's hiding places. But I had truly had enough.

'I'll talk to my dad tonight,' Celina said, flipping her hair back. 'Maybe he *should* go to the police and suggest it. After all, it would be the right thing to do—'

She didn't get any further. I flew at her and gave her a shove.

'Mind my bracelet!' Celina screamed as she staggered backwards.

'Yes, mind her bracelet!' the witches chorused. They gasped with horror as Celina didn't manage to regain her balance, but carried on falling, falling, falling until she landed smack on her bottom in a puddle.

'This is not good enough, Sunita.' Mrs Bright speared me with her blue-eyed stare as I stood silent but unrepentant in front of her. 'Whatever Celina Patel is alleged to have said, I cannot condone this kind of behaviour.'

'Sorry,' I muttered. But, you know, I wasn't.

Mrs Bright was not deceived. 'I would normally expect Mr Arora to deal with incidents like this,' she went on frostily, 'but in the circumstances I felt it was better to speak to you myself.' She didn't say what those circumstances were, so I didn't know whether it was because Mr Arora was too sleep-deprived to punish me properly, or whether my crime of attacking the mayor's daughter was so heinous, only Mrs Bright could handle it.

'I understand that it must be very frustrating for you that the news about your father has leaked out,' Mrs Bright went on, and she did look more sympathetic. 'But now that it has, it's up to you how you deal with it.'

'Yes, Mrs Bright.' I knew she was right. I'd let

my feelings get the better of me, and now Celina would never leave me alone.

'Look on this as a character-building exercise, Sunita,' Mrs Bright urged. She got up from her chair, walked round the desk and put a hand on my shoulder. 'If you can get through this, you'll learn a valuable lesson in life.'

I nodded. 'I'm sorry,' I said again, and this time I sounded a bit more sincere.

Mrs Bright looked satisfied. 'You will write a one-thousand-word essay entitled *Why Violence Is Never the Solution to a Problem*, and hand it in to Mr Arora tomorrow.'

'Is that it?' I blurted out – then I could have kicked myself. 'I mean, all right.' I'd been expecting detentions for a week. After all, Celina had screamed loud enough to wake the dead.

'And, Sunita' – Mrs Bright raised her voice to stop me as I turned to leave – 'if you really feel that things have become too difficult here, there is always the option of transferring to a different school.'

I wondered if I was imagining that she sounded faintly hopeful.

'I'll be fine, Mrs Bright,' I replied. I was determined that I *would* be fine. My mum had had to fight for a place at Coppergate for me. I wasn't going to let her down; that was my part of the deal.

Henry and Zara were lurking at the other end of the corridor, pretending to read the sports noticeboard, when I left Mrs Bright's office. They rushed towards me, and I told them what had happened.

'That Celina,' Zara grumbled, knitting her dark brows together in a ferocious frown. 'This is all her fault.'

'No, it's my fault too, for letting her wind me up,' I said. 'But not any more.'

'It's not fair,' Henry chimed in. 'Celina shouldn't be able to say things like that to you, and get away with it.'

'Maybe she won't,' Zara muttered. 'I'm thinking . . . revenge!'

'Revenge?' Henry and I repeated. We exchanged a worried look. Zara was, we thought, pretty much capable of anything.

'Yes.' Zara stroked her chin thoughtfully. 'I have a plan.'

'Zara, will you stop acting like a villain in a Bond movie?' I broke in. 'To be honest, I think it would be best if I just kept away from Celina from now on.'

'Ah, but that's the beauty of my plan.' Zara grinned. 'We take our revenge secretly. No one knows it's us.'

'That's a good idea, actually,' Henry said

eagerly. 'Celina irritates loads of people, so it could be anybody.'

'We could have a secret society to get revenge on people who annoy us,' Zara went on, getting all fired up. 'Not just Celina, but anyone. I've got quite a few people on my list.'

'Me too,' Henry agreed, looking excited. 'You know, we could have calling cards. When we've taken our revenge on someone, we could leave a tastefully designed card behind. I could print them out on my computer.'

'You have just been punished by the Masters of Revenge,' Zara suggested. *'Next time you'd better be more careful.'*

I laughed. Zara and Henry stared at me. I stopped laughing.

'You're serious?'

'Absolutely.' Zara nodded.

'Oh, yes,' said Henry.

I blinked. The idea of getting my own back on Celina was enormously tempting. But was it worth the risk?

'I'll think about it,' I said.

We left it at that, and the day began. Of course, Jack, Celina and her friends weren't going to let me forget what I had done. There were many loud comments about the damage to Celina's designer coat, and how the daughters of thieves shouldn't

be allowed to associate with 'normal' people. But I closed my mouth and stopped my ears and tried hard not to get drawn into it. If I was tempted to speak, I thought of Mum and how disappointed she would be if I had to change schools. That was enough.

I'd had enough excitement for one day, but there was so much more to come. At lunch time Henry and I were out in the playground waiting for Zara. She'd popped back to our classroom after the last lesson to collect her gloves. Henry and I were chatting, our breaths steaming in the cold air, him trying to convince me the secret revenge society idea was a goer, when Zara suddenly erupted out of school like a genie from a bottle.

'You'll never believe this!' she gasped. The purple birthmark looked even more startling because her face was so pale. 'Celina lent her diamond bracelet to Chloe, and the airhead's only gone and lost it!'

'No!' I felt literally sick, and my stomach heaved. 'How do you know?'

'They're weeping and wailing outside our classroom.' Zara plonked herself down on the bench next to me. 'Celina's in hysterics, and Chloe's not far behind. She's hyperventilating like mad.'

For a moment I couldn't breathe myself. 'This

is just what Celina wanted,' I said shakily. 'She'll blame me, you'll see. She'll say I stole it.'

But Zara shook her head. 'I don't think so,' she said, patting my arm. 'Chloe reckons she lost it while she was in lessons this morning.'

'You're not in any of Chloe's sets, Sunita,' Henry added quickly. 'You haven't been near her all morning, so Celina can't possibly blame you.'

That did not really help. I could have spent the morning on Mars, and Celina would still say I was a thief. She could twist things. My heart pitter-pattered as Celina, Chloe, Jyoti and Danielle came out of school, all talking at once. A distraught Chloe was sobbing loudly, while Jyoti and Danielle had their arms round Celina's shoulders. She was sniffing and dabbing at her eyes with a tissue.

'How could you be so careless, Chloe?' she wailed. 'You knew how much that bracelet meant to me! It was a birthday present from my gran!'

'S-s-s-orr-eee!' Chloe hiccupped. Her running mascara made her look like an anorexic panda. 'It was an acc-acc-acc-accident! You know how thin my wrists are – it must have slipped off without me noticing.'

'You should have been more careful!' Celina wept, clutching at Danielle and Jyoti for support. 'Oh, God, my mother's going to *kill* me!'

Now this might just be me – and you know that Celina and I aren't exactly the best of chums – but I did get the teensiest-tiniest impression that Celina was kind of *enjoying* the melodrama of the situation just a little bit.

'Hey, nobody died, you know,' Zara called.

I elbowed her in the ribs, but luckily Celina and Chloe were wailing so loudly, they didn't hear.

'I really don't want to hang around waiting for Celina to start accusing me,' I muttered. 'Let's go somewhere else.'

'We've got half an hour before our lunch sitting,' Henry said, glancing at his watch.

'I know the perfect place,' Zara said. 'Follow me.'

Obediently Henry and I went after her, but we were shocked when she opened the door and marched into school.

'We're not allowed inside at lunch times,' Henry said nervously.

'This is foolproof,' Zara said with confidence. 'Trust me.'

She led us to our classroom, ushered us inside and closed the door. It was quiet, peaceful and, best of all, Celina-free.

'What if Mr Arora comes in for something?' I asked.

Zara shrugged. 'We just tell him we offered to

stay in and tidy the bookshelves, and he said yes,' she replied, a wicked glint in her eyes. 'He's such a zombie, he won't remember.'

'I like it,' I said with a smile.

'Maybe we'd better go and sit by the bookshelves just in case.' Henry still sounded nervous. 'Then it looks like we're tidying.'

Zara tutted loudly as she followed Henry across the room. 'Henry, you don't have to do everything by the rules, you know,' she said tartly. 'Have you ever tried living dangerously?'

'I ate a chilli once,' Henry retorted, and looked quite cross when Zara and I giggled. 'Maybe we'd better do a bit of tidying, just in case—' He stopped, bent over, peered closely at the floor. 'What's that shiny thing?'

I bent over too, saw it, but couldn't speak.

'Celina's bracelet,' Zara said with enormous satisfaction. 'Well, well, well.'

She hooked the bracelet with her little finger, and lifted it up. It hung there like a glittering silver snake, and we all stared at it as if it was an unexploded bomb. Which, in a kind of a way, it was.

'It's the perfect, *perfect* moment for revenge,' Zara whispered, laying the bracelet on the nearest table. 'What shall we do?'

Smash it up? Dip it in paint? Dunk it in water? What?

'We could leave an anonymous note for Celina,' Henry said breathlessly. 'We could demand a ransom.'

I reached out and touched the beautiful bracelet with the tip of my forefinger. I made a decision.

'You two go outside,' I said in a low voice. 'Leave this to me.'

Zara looked disappointed. 'But—'

'I mean it,' I said with determination. 'This is between me and Celina.'

'What are you going to do, Sunita?' breathed Henry, his eyes round as round could be.

'Just go,' I said.

I waited, not moving, until Zara and Henry had reluctantly left the classroom. I sounded so confident, so sure, that they must have thought I knew exactly what I was going to do. But I didn't. I had a choice, of course I did, but what would I choose?

For the first time I realized that my dad must have thought about stealing that money before he did it. There must have been a split-second when he had that choice – to take the money or not to take the money. He made his decision, and then he had to live with it. I would have to do the same.

I reached out and picked up Celina's bracelet.

CHAPTER 5

A few moments later I stepped out into the playground. The low-lying November sunshine hit me directly in the eyes, and I blinked.

'What did you do?'

Zara and Henry instantly surrounded me, their faces full of questions.

'Tell us!' Zara demanded.

I shrugged. 'You'll have to wait and see,' I replied.

'No!' Zara wailed. 'You can't do this, Sunita!'

'It must be something big,' Henry speculated.

'You'll never, ever guess,' I replied confidently. Henry and Zara looked thrilled.

'When will we find out?' Zara breathed.

'Before afternoon lessons,' I said. 'Let's go to lunch.'

Celina, Chloe and the others were nowhere to be seen as we queued up outside the canteen. We found out later that one of the dinner supervisors had felt sorry for the hysterical Celina, and

had allowed them to have an early lunch with the Year 9s.

'Typical Celina,' Zara sniffed. 'Trust her to get everything she can out of the situation.'

I did not answer. I was wondering about Celina's reaction when she found out what I'd done with her bracelet. I was already feeling slightly sick inside, trying to decide if it had, in fact, been the right thing.

'Can't you just give us a clue?' Zara pleaded as, at last, the bell rang for afternoon lessons.

I shook my head. 'You've only got a few minutes to wait now,' I replied. I hadn't eaten much lunch, but I felt like I was going to be violently sick.

'It must be something *really* big,' Henry said excitedly.

I swallowed. 'Believe me, you won't be expecting this,' I assured him as we pushed our way into school with everyone else.

We were coming down the Year 7 corridor when I saw, ahead of me, that Celina was already at her locker, collecting the books she needed for afternoon lessons. I took a breath. Any minute now . . .

'Oh, my *God*!'

Chloe, Danielle and Jyoti, who were standing alongside her, turned.

'What is it?' asked Danielle.

'My bracelet!' Celina screamed joyfully. 'It's here, in my locker!'

'What?' Chloe almost collapsed with the emotion of the situation.

'Here! It's here!' Celina waved the bracelet in the air. 'You must have put it back in my locker, Chloe, you idiot!'

'But I didn't,' Chloe said earnestly. 'I know I didn't.'

I had come to a full stop in the corridor when Celina screamed. Zara and Henry had stopped too, and I was fully aware that their eyes were fixed on me in bewilderment.

'Well, who did then?' Jyoti asked. 'Maybe somebody found it and put it there.'

'Check it over, Cee,' Danielle said urgently. 'Make sure it's not damaged.'

I heard Zara and Henry's sharp intake of breath as Celina looked the bracelet over carefully.

'It's perfectly fine!' She beamed. 'Nothing wrong with it at all.' She snapped the clasp open, and fastened the bracelet to her wrist. 'I tell you what,' she declared, glowing with relief, 'I'm not taking this off again until I get home tonight!'

'But where did it come from?' asked Chloe, puzzled. 'How did it get there?'

I didn't hear any more. Zara grabbed my arm

in a vice-like grip and hustled me round the corner out of sight. The door to the girls' toilets was open, and she dragged me inside and slammed it shut behind us.

'What's going on?' she demanded, her eyes spitting green sparks.

'Hello?' Henry called plaintively from outside. 'I can't come in there, you know.'

'Calm down, Zara,' I said, attempting to take control of the situation. 'I gave Celina her bracelet back, that's all.'

'I *know* that!' Zara squealed, dancing up and down in frustration like a demented pixie. 'But why? *Why?*'

This was where it all got very tricky to explain.

'I just wanted . . . to do the right thing,' I said lamely.

Zara looked more than frustrated now. She looked furious. 'But this is *Celina*!' she spluttered. 'What about everything she's said and done to you? Why are you being nice to her? What about our secret revenge society?'

'If you let Sunita get a word in, she'll tell us,' Henry called through the door.

'Go on then,' Zara snapped, planting her hands on her hips. I would not have been surprised to see steam coming out of not only her ears, but everywhere.

'It's quite difficult to explain,' I mumbled, staring down at my feet. 'But it's nothing to do with Celina, really—'

'How can it not be anything to do with Celina?' Zara growled.

'Zara!' invisible Henry said crossly.

'It's about *me*,' I went on, fumbling for the words I needed. '*I'm* not a bad person, whatever my dad's done. Doing the right thing makes me feel better.' I stared defiantly at Zara. 'And I *do* feel better.'

'I can see that,' Zara retorted. 'You've got this silly little smile on your face. And I can tell you, it's *really* annoying me.'

'Look, I know it doesn't make sense,' I said, 'but what I've done makes me feel generous. It makes me happy that I didn't do something mean. I don't want to do bad things, even to Celina. I want to like myself again.'

'You'd have felt a lot better if you'd made Celina's life hell,' Zara retorted, reaching for the door handle. I could see she was still furious. 'Or at the very least, you could have *given* the bracelet back to her and made her feel awful for the way she's treated you.'

'Look, it doesn't matter if Celina knows it was me who returned the bracelet or not,' I went on hesitantly. 'It's about me and the way I feel. My mum can't speak to our neighbours yet, but she's

secretly been doing little things for them, and that makes her feel better—'

'Oh, so now you're doing the same,' Zara jeered, wrenching the door open. 'I'll have to call you Saint Sunita from now on.' She pushed her way past Henry and stomped off round the corner.

I sighed. I was no saint, far from it. At the moment I was feeling a bit of a fool. But inside me there was still a small secret glow. *I'd done the right thing*.

'I suppose you think the same?' I asked.

Henry shrugged. 'Not really,' he said carefully. 'It was brave of you to give the bracelet back.'

'Do you get why I did it?' I asked.

Henry nodded. 'I think so. Because of what your dad did, you kind of feel like you've got to prove that you're a good person. No—' He stopped for a moment, thinking. 'You feel like you've got to be even *better* than that.'

Henry had understood exactly what I'd been trying to say. Suddenly I felt enormously fond of him. 'Thanks,' I said, touching his arm. 'You're a good friend.'

'We'd better get to class.' Henry spoke very matter of factly, but I could tell he was pleased. 'Do you want me to talk to Zara?'

'I don't think Zara will be talking to either of us,' I predicted.

As I'd imagined, Zara was sitting at our table, tight-lipped, when we walked into class. On the other side of the room Celina, surrounded by Jyoti, Danielle and Chloe, was still rejoicing over the recovery of her bracelet and waving her wrist around to show it off.

Zara raised her eyebrows at me. *See what you've done?* her look said. She didn't speak to me for the rest of afternoon lessons.

But apart from Zara sulking, everything seemed better. Different. I felt as if, suddenly, I could breathe again. I'm not sure I felt totally happy, but I didn't feel totally miserable either. Life suddenly appeared to be a little worthwhile after all.

'Are we still friends?' I asked Zara bluntly as Henry and I followed her out of school at the end of the day. 'If not, tell me now.'

'I suppose we are,' Zara snapped, not looking at me. 'No one else would put up with your ridiculous behaviour.'

'Look who's talking,' Henry remarked, then his mouth fell open at his own bravery. I laughed and even Zara's lips twitched slightly.

'All right,' she snapped. 'I'm still your friend. Even though you're obviously raving mad. But I just don't get it.'

'All right.' I thought for a minute. 'Forget Celina.

Imagine doing a secret good deed for one of your friends. Henry here, for instance.'

Zara raised her eyebrows. 'What, if he loses his bracelet, you mean?'

Henry chuckled.

'No, of course not.' I punched Zara lightly on the arm. 'Something else. Say you knew Henry was worrying about his science project, and you wanted to help him out. You could slip some notes secretly into his locker.'

'Or I could just give them to him,' Zara pointed out tartly.

'Sure you could.' I shrugged. 'But this is much more fun. Imagine how pleased Henry would be. And that would make *you* happy too.'

For the first time since that afternoon, Zara looked a bit uncertain. 'All right,' she admitted, 'I can see the point of that, doing things for people you like. But *Celina*—'

She gritted her teeth as, just then, Celina barged her way past us, flirting outrageously with Jack Browning, fluttering her eyelashes and waving her braceleted wrist under our noses.

'That makes it even better in a way,' I said, with a grin. 'Just imagine her face if she knew it was me!'

Zara frowned darkly. She opened her mouth, almost certainly to say something cutting, but a shout from the gates interrupted us.

'Zara!'

The three of us turned. A battered old camper van, painted shocking pink, had drawn up to the kerb. A man with shaggy black hair was driving, and a woman sat next to him. What seemed like hundreds of children were hanging out of the windows, waving at us.

'Zara! *Zara!*'

Henry and I turned to stare at her. Zara blushed to the roots of her hair.

'Who are they?' Henry asked.

'I have no idea,' Zara snapped, ignoring the hollering children completely.

'That's your mum and dad, and your brothers and sisters,' I guessed.

The man, Zara's dad, climbed out of the van and came over to us. He had the same sea-green eyes and long, feathery eyelashes as Zara.

'Hi, sweetheart,' he said, his eyes flicking over me and Henry. 'Are these your friends?'

Zara ignored the question. 'What are you all doing here?' she snapped, making it sound like an accusation.

'Ah, well.' Mr Kennedy cleared his throat, looking quite shockingly nervous. 'We have to go into town to get some new shoes for Brad.' He stared anxiously at Zara. 'Is that OK with you?'

I couldn't stop myself from glancing at Henry. He looked back at me, equally stunned.

Zara sighed loudly. 'I suppose so,' she said coolly. She turned to Henry and me. 'See you tomorrow.'

Henry and I moved reluctantly away, but not before we'd seen Zara's mum hop out of the front seat. She wore the same anxious expression as her husband.

'You can sit here, darling,' she said to Zara, ushering her into the van before squeezing herself, folded double, into the back with the other children.

'Well!' Henry breathed as they drove away, the exhaust banging loudly. 'Who do you reckon is the boss in *that* house?'

'I think that's obvious,' I replied. Zara seemed to have her parents under her thumb so firmly, they were walking on eggshells around her. After meeting Henry's mum that morning, I was beginning to realize that I wasn't the only person in the world who had problems.

But today, for once, those problems weren't lying on my shoulders like a dead weight. It was hard to explain, even to Zara and Henry, but I felt as if I'd won an Olympic marathon and got a gold medal. How many people, if asked, would guess that I'd take the revenge option? That I'd destroy

Celina's bracelet because of the way she'd treated me? Maybe even keep the beautiful bracelet for myself?

But I hadn't. I hadn't done any of those things. I'd faced temptation, and I'd won. I was a better person than that. If I told Mum, I knew she'd be proud of me, and that gave me the warmest glow of happiness inside.

I bounced up the street towards our house, not caring for once if I met any of our neighbours. Mum and the twins were watching TV, and I greeted them energetically.

'Why don't we go out for a walk?' I suggested, after recovering from the twins' greeting, which was a complicated ritual but generally consisted of wrestling me down onto the sofa and hitting me with cushions.

Mum's eyes automatically turned to the window. 'It's not quite dark yet—' she began.

'I thought we could go and enrol at the library in the shopping precinct,' I broke in. 'If we wait any longer, it'll be closed.'

It was mean of me to ask Mum in front of the twins, I know, but I was relying on them to back me up. They didn't disappoint.

'Yeah, the library!' Davey roared. 'Let's go, Mum!'

'Please, please, please,' added Debbie, bouncing up and down and making the floor vibrate.

Mum looked anguished. I felt bad about forcing her into the situation, but we had to get used to going outside. We couldn't hide for ever. Now, while I felt so happy and confident, was the time to begin getting used to our new life. Who knows how I'd feel tomorrow?

'All right,' she said without any enthusiasm. 'Get your coats and boots, twins.'

'I really think this is a good idea, Mum,' I said quietly as the twins tumbled out of the room.

She sighed. 'I know you're right, Sunita. It's just that—' She stopped. 'Anyway, I do owe you one.'

'What for?'

Mum smiled. 'Do you really expect me to believe that the twins tidied their bedroom all by themselves this morning? Thanks, love.'

'I don't know what you mean,' I said cheerfully.

We set off for the library. Mum looked nervous at first, but as we walked on, and the darker it became, the more she relaxed.

Outside the library, though, she stopped. I knew why. Light was blazing from every window of the building.

'Sunita,' she whispered anxiously, 'it's so *bright* in there.'

'Well, you can't expect people to choose their books in the dark,' I pointed out. 'Come on. If anyone stares at us, we'll pull faces at them.'

Davey and Debbie cheered. We all linked hands and advanced towards the sliding glass doors.

Although I was talking the talk, I was still secretly very nervous, and my heart was hammering in my ears. The library was busy. There was a long queue at the counter, and there were people seated at every one of the long bank of computers along the opposite wall.

'I'll get some registration forms,' Mum whispered, glancing warily from side to side. 'Sunita, you take the twins to the children's section.'

I herded the twins across the library, leaving Mum to join the queue at the counter, her eyes fixed firmly on the floor. As I realized with dismay that the children's area was packed with mums and kids, I gave myself a silent lecture. *We're not criminals. We haven't done anything wrong. We've got every right to be here. Anyway, no one's going to take any notice of us.*

I was almost right. Nobody took any notice of us until the twins began arguing over a book about dinosaurs. By the time I'd refereed the dispute (luckily, before any blows had been struck), we were getting a few curious stares. But I told myself that was just because of the twins. Nothing else.

When Mum eventually joined us, she was smiling.

'The ladies at the counter were so nice, Sunita,'

she whispered, her face glowing with relief. 'We can borrow books right away.'

Something had changed, I realized, as we marched up to the counter to check out our books. This time Mum wasn't looking down at the floor, and neither was I. Maybe some of those people in the library had recognized us. Maybe they hadn't. But whether we made ourselves miserable about it or not was down to us. I think Mum was coming to the same conclusion.

We skipped down the library steps, Debbie and Davey singing a song about the alphabet they'd learned at school. Everything was going so well, it was a shock to hear a voice say, 'Mrs Anand?'

Although it was dark, I guessed that all the colour had drained from Mum's face. I know, because it was the same for me. We turned round, dreading what we would see. Police? Journalists?

A short, round-faced young woman with blonde curls stood there, smiling at us. She had a pink-cheeked, sleepy baby in a buggy, and a pretty little girl with the same blonde curls was holding her hand.

'Megan!' Debbie and Davey screeched, launching themselves at the girl like rockets.

'Oh, hello,' Mum said in a shaky voice.

'Sunita, Megan's my *bestest* friend at school,' Debbie announced, grabbing her in a vice-like hug.

'And she's my girlfriend,' Davey added, planting a big wet kiss on Megan's rosy cheek. 'She likes me better than Debbie, don't you, Megan?'

Megan giggled, and wisely said nothing.

'I'm Jan Rice, Megan's mum.' Mrs Rice smiled at us. 'I've been wanting to invite you round for coffee, but you always seem in such a rush whenever I see you at the school.'

Mum glanced at me. I raised my eyebrows just a little, and nodded gently.

'Oh.' Mum made a huge effort. 'Coffee would be lovely. Thank you.'

'Bring the twins as well,' Mrs Rice said. 'Megan would love them to see them anytime.'

'We can play in the Wendy house my dad built for me,' Megan added.

'You're lucky,' Davey said enviously. 'We haven't got a dad.'

Mum and I glanced at each other in utter horror.

'Yes, we have, stupid.' Debbie poked him in the arm. 'We just don't know where he is, that's all.'

'Why?' Megan asked curiously.

I could feel Mum trembling at my side.

'Megan.' Mrs Rice laid a hand on top of her daughter's curls. 'You know we talked about this before. Some children don't have their mummies and daddies living in the same house, and it's rude to ask too many questions.' She looked at Mum,

113

and her eyes were full of sympathy. 'Please come and have coffee with me sometime. Will you?'

'Well, all right,' Mum replied. But I could feel her still shaking beside me.

Debbie and Davey had to be physically removed from Megan before we could say goodbye and leave. As the twins ran on ahead of us, I turned to Mum.

'She knew, didn't she?'

'I think so,' Mum said. Her voice sounded thick, as if she had a cold.

'Mum, are you crying?' I peered anxiously up into her face.

'It's silly, I know.' Mum wiped her wet face. 'But when someone's nice to me . . .' She shook her head.

'You *will* go and have coffee with Mrs Rice?' I asked.

'I think so.' Mum straightened her shoulders. 'No, I will. Promise.'

I slipped my hand through her arm, smiling. Three milestones in one day. Celina's bracelet. The library. Mrs Rice. I had a feeling things were, slowly, going to get better.

At school, we were supposed to lock our lockers, but no one ever did. Although the school was brand new, the lockers took a lot of abuse. Locks

114

were broken, kids regularly lost their keys and, even if they did have keys, quite often people forgot to use them. Apparently one of the top priorities in Mrs Bright's school manifesto was to sort out the unsatisfactory lockers situation. Until then, though, most of us just followed the unofficial line, which was not to leave anything valuable in them.

I had a plan. I'd left early for school this morning, even before Mum and the twins were up, and I'd loaded the washing machine and laid the table for breakfast before I left. Mum would be pleased. I'd slipped into school early and illegally, and now I was making my way stealthily to the Year 7 lockers. I stopped next to Zara's, which was two down from mine. I knew the lock on hers was broken, and that she'd complained bitterly about it to Mr Arora about five hundred times. Of course, it went in one of his ears and out of the other.

I opened Zara's locker, which was obsessively tidy – books stacked in order of size and thickness in neat piles – unlike mine and Henry's, which were chaos. I placed a Twix and an apple on top of Zara's maths book, and smiled to myself. I just wanted to let her know that there were no hard feelings about yesterday.

As I closed the locker door, I heard the sound

of soft footsteps. I panicked and whisked myself round the end of the lockers, flattening myself against the wall.

Zara tiptoed round the corner.

'What are you doing here?' I asked, stepping into view.

Zara gave a little shriek. 'I've just been to the toilet,' she snapped. 'Is that a crime?'

'Yes, if it's before the morning bell,' I replied.

'Well, what are *you* doing here then?' Zara demanded.

'I – er – I just wanted to put some books in my locker,' I said quickly. 'My bag's really heavy.'

I opened the door of my locker, not expecting to see what I saw. The tangled mess of textbooks and papers and pens had been cleared up, the books stacked in order of size and thickness in neat piles.

'Zara!'

'What?'

I spun round, a big grin on my face. 'You tidied my locker!'

'Who says it was me?' Zara snapped, her brows drawn down like a ferocious bulldog.

I couldn't stop smirking, even though Zara was glaring at me. 'Well, thanks anyway.'

'No point in thanking *me*,' Zara growled, yanking the door of her own locker open. Her face

was a picture as she saw the chocolate bar and apple perched neatly on top of her books.

'Did you put those there?' she spluttered.

'Who, me?' I asked innocently. 'Why would I do a thing like that?'

'How childish!' Zara sniffed. But I noticed that she slipped the apple and the chocolate into her bag.

'Your parents seem nice,' I said casually as we walked back to the playground.

'Oh, so you saw that in all of thirty seconds last night, did you?' Zara snapped, biting my head off as she always did when things got personal.

'I'm very observant,' I retorted. 'Since when were you crowned queen of the Kennedy household?'

For once, Zara was utterly speechless.

'Only I could see that your mum and dad were terrified of upsetting you,' I went on boldly. Now I'd started, I might as well finish. 'Why is that?'

I wondered if I'd gone too far. Zara looked as if she didn't know whether to hit me or not. Then, amazingly, she shrugged and looked sheepishly at me.

'Because of this, I suppose.' She pointed at the birthmark on her face.

'Oh.'

I didn't say anything more. We were silent as we went outside, but I just couldn't stop breaking

into smiles. The weather was cold and grey and very November-like, but there was sunshine inside me. I was remembering how it felt to be happy, and I liked it.

We made our way over to Henry, who was sitting on our favourite bench. We shouted. He ignored us. We waved. He didn't wave back. He looked stunned and dazed, as if he'd just had some terrifically good, or some terribly bad news.

'You do realize that we've been calling you for the last five minutes,' I said, tapping his arm as Zara and I reached the bench. 'Ignoring Zara is not a very wise move.'

'Oh.' Henry's stare was glazed. Then he focused on us, and managed a small smile. 'Sorry.'

'No chocolate bars today?' Zara asked pointedly.

Henry shook his head. 'I forgot to stop at the shop.'

'Funny.' Zara squinted up at the sky. 'I don't notice any pigs flying past.'

'Henry?' I was beginning to feel a little nervous. 'Are you all right?'

'I'm fine.' With a startling change of mood, Henry jumped to his feet and threw his arms open wide. 'Never better.'

'Now you're scaring me,' Zara said with a frown. 'What's going on?'

'It was Sunita.' The words tumbled out of

Henry in an unstoppable stream. 'I thought about what she said, and I decided to do a secret good deed for my mum. So I sneaked out into the garden early this morning and swept up all the fallen leaves she's been moaning about. She's been nagging my dad to do it for ages, and he hasn't.'

'And?' I asked eagerly.

Henry's pale blue eyes were saucer-like with amazement. 'She loved it! She guessed it was me, even though I didn't say anything. And you know what? She couldn't stop talking about it all through breakfast. We didn't even argue about what I ate, like we usually do.'

'Saint Sunita strikes again,' Zara scoffed.

'Don't listen to her.' I grinned at Henry. 'I'm glad your mum was pleased.'

'Me too,' Henry agreed. Then he frowned. 'The trouble is, clearing up the leaves took me so long I only had time for a quick bowl of cornflakes. And then I was thinking so hard about what happened, I forgot to stop at the shop for chocolate.' He looked hopefully from me to Zara. 'Have you got anything to eat?'

'Zara's got a Twix and an apple she might share with you,' I remarked. 'Someone left them in her locker.'

'Oh, a secret admirer?' Henry asked.

'As if!' Zara snorted. 'Here.' She pulled out the apple and handed it to Henry. 'Your need is greater than mine.'

Henry looked disappointed, but he was too polite to ask for the Twix, so he dutifully bit into the apple.

'I still think that this secret good deeds stuff isn't all it's cracked up to be,' Zara grumbled, perching on the bench arm. 'I mean, where's the fun in being nice to people if they can't show you their undying gratitude because they don't know who you are?'

'But that *is* the fun of it,' I said earnestly. 'Them not knowing. And even if they guess, they still love the surprise. And *you* get the fun of surprising them. It's a win-win situation.' I grinned teasingly at her. 'Come on, admit it. Didn't it make you feel good this morning when I saw my locker?'

'That wasn't me,' Zara snapped, trying not to blush and failing.

'My mum guessed it was me who'd swept up the leaves, and she was still thrilled,' Henry agreed. 'She didn't even sigh when I put sugar on my cereal, like she usually does.'

'Oh, hurrah,' Zara said with a sniff. 'Domestic harmony at last in the Williams household.' Her gaze shifted to a point beyond my shoulder. 'Hello, here comes trouble.'

I didn't turn round. 'Celina?'

Zara nodded.

'Pretend you're a duck, Sunita,' Henry said solemnly, 'And that everything Celina says is just water off your back.'

Zara and I grinned. I mentally squared my shoulders and breathed in deeply through my nose as Celina stopped purposefully in front of us.

'I'm surprised you've got the nerve to show your face today,' she said with a curl of her perfectly glossed lips. 'My dad's going to complain to Mrs Bright about you attacking me.'

'Quack quack,' I replied. Zara and Henry burst out laughing.

'I beg your pardon?' Celina snapped.

'Private joke,' I said airily. 'Now, don't let us keep you. I'm sure you have many more people to annoy before the morning bell.'

I picked up my bag and sauntered away, followed by Zara and Henry.

'There they go,' Celina called spitefully after us. 'Losers United.'

Zara spun round slowly. 'Celina,' she said in a dangerously quiet voice, 'have you ever considered how lucky you were to get that bracelet back yesterday?'

Celina stared blankly at her. 'What do you mean?'

'Well, if it wasn't any of your friends who found it and put it in your locker, then who was it?' Zara went on silkily. 'Maybe you should start being nicer to everyone. If someone can do a secret good deed for you, they might also do a secret *bad* deed. If you annoy them, I mean.'

Celina looked quite startled. With a wide smile, Zara turned and hurried after Henry and me.

'That shook her up a bit, didn't it?' Zara said with satisfaction. 'She might think twice about being so vile from now on.'

'I think I've just seen that flying pig you mentioned earlier,' I said with a grin. I felt elated. It's a great word. I don't think I'd ever felt so *elated* in my whole life. I'd walked away from Celina and her insults, I'd turned the other cheek and not let her get to me. It felt so good.

What happened next was something I wasn't expecting. We went into school when the bell rang. I was sitting in the cloakroom trying to re-tie my trainers, but I'd managed to tangle one of my laces into a complicated knot. Zara and Henry had gone on into class ahead of me, and so had almost everyone else. The corridor was quiet, so I couldn't help overhearing voices. I recognized them as Layla Bishop and Kavita Sharma, who were in my class.

'That stupid idiot, Jack Browning!' Layla fumed.

She added a few more choice and unrepeatable words. 'Look at my maths book. The cover's torn right across.'

'How did it happen?' asked Kavita.

'He wanted me to show him last night's homework, and I wouldn't.' I heard Layla wrench open her locker, throw the book into it and slam it violently shut. 'He tried to grab the book off me, and he tore it . . .'

Their footsteps receded into the distance, Layla still grumbling.

I don't know why I did what I did.

I came out of the cloakroom, and the corridor was deserted. I went over to Layla's locker and opened it. The maths book with the torn cover lay on top.

I had a glue pen in my bag. I took it out and stuck the two halves of the cover neatly together. Then I popped the book back into Layla's locker and went into class.

'Where have you been all this time?' Zara pounced on me instantly. 'And what are you smiling about?'

I was saved from a reply because at that moment Mr Arora stumbled in sleepily to take the register. I couldn't really understand why I'd repaired Layla's book for her. She'd never been particularly nice to me, although she'd never been nasty either.

It just made me feel *great* to do something secret, something good . . .

And it didn't stop there either. Now that my eyes were opened, there were lots of secret good deeds that could be done around the school. Tidying lockers. Returning lost property. Cleaning graffiti off tables. Repairing damaged files, folders, books, papers, equipment, PE kit. Leaving a couple of sweets in the locker of someone who was having a bad day. My eyes were dazzled by all the small, secret things I could do to make people, including myself, feel better. By the end of the day I had five or six little secrets to feel good about.

'This is so weird,' Layla Bishop muttered as she stood by her locker, holding her maths book. A few doors down, I grinned to myself. 'Am I going mad, Kavita?'

'No, the cover was definitely ripped,' Kavita asserted. 'I told you that at lunch time.'

'I know. I've spent all afternoon wondering who repaired it.' Layla peered more closely at the book. 'They've done a good job too.'

Someone tapped me on the shoulder. It was Zara, accompanied by Henry.

'Ready to go?' she asked.

'Sure,' I replied. I followed Zara and Henry out, leaving Layla and Kavita staring at the maths book with puzzled faces.

'Right.' Zara grabbed my arm as we walked out into the playground. 'What have you been up to?'

'I don't know what you mean,' I said, attempting surprise mixed with innocence.

'Don't give me that.' Zara stared aggressively at me. 'I know someone repaired Layla Bishop's maths book. And Callum McKenna in Seven D said he found a bag of sweets in his locker.'

'Is he the boy who set fire to his sleeve in chemistry class?' Henry asked with interest.

'The very same,' Zara replied. She eyeballed me sternly. 'I've been keeping my eyes and ears open today, Sunita Anand. I know you've been flitting around Coppergate like a good fairy, waving your magic wand and doing good deeds.'

I sighed. 'All right. It was me, I admit it.'

Henry grinned.

'But why?' Zara wailed.

'Surely you know the answer to that by now?' I replied.

'All right,' Zara snapped. 'I don't mind you doing secret good deeds for me and Henry. It's all these other idiots I object to. I mean, I overheard Danny Armitage saying that someone had washed his muddy football and put it back in his locker. How stupid is that?'

I stared at Zara. 'I didn't wash any football.'

'Er – that was me,' Henry said sheepishly.

I burst out laughing as Zara spun round to face him.

'You as well!' she spluttered. 'Well, that's *too* much, it really is! You can both stop this nonsense right now!'

'But we enjoy it,' Henry and I said together, and we beamed at each other.

'Oh, now I've heard everything!' Zara snorted, stomping off towards the bus stop.

'She'll come round,' said Henry with a grin.

'And even if she doesn't, we're not going to stop, are we?' I asked.

'No way!' Henry replied. 'I've already got three lined up for tomorrow.'

I was feeling so joyful that it seemed things couldn't get any better. I was wrong. As I marched up the street towards our house, singing to myself, I saw Mum and the twins walking towards me from the opposite direction. This was more than unusual. It was unheard of. They were usually home an hour or more before me.

'Sunita!' Davey waved at me. 'We've been to Megan's house for tea!'

'You have?' My eyes went instantly to Mum's face. She looked happier and less tense than I'd seen her in a long while. 'Did you have a good time?'

'Lovely,' Mum replied. I could see she meant it. 'And the twins were very good, for once.'

'We're always good,' Debbie said indignantly.

'Of course you are,' I agreed.

Debbie nudged Davey viciously in the side with her elbow. 'Race you to the front door!' she yelled. 'Last one there is a big fat pig!'

'Jan was so kind,' Mum went on as the twins flung open the gate and disappeared into our garden. 'She didn't ask me about your dad at all. I'd forgotten how nice it feels just to sit and chat like a normal person.'

'We *are* normal people,' I said firmly. 'Well, except for Davey and Debbie maybe.'

Mum laughed. But the smile was soon wiped off her face when we heard Davey yell, 'Mum, there's something funny on our doormat!'

Mum and I both broke into a run, heading for our gate. Davey and Debbie were crouched over a small cardboard box on the mat. It wasn't taped down. The flaps were loose. There was no address on it.

'What do you think it is, Sunita?' Mum whispered. I knew she was thinking the same thing as me: that it might be something to do with Dad.

'There's only one way to find out,' I said. 'Stand back, kids.'

I peeled back the flaps and looked inside. The box held a large, round cake tin with a picture of Edinburgh Castle on the lid.

'I don't think it's an unexploded bomb,' I remarked, taking the lid off. We could smell ginger and lemon and walnuts. We all peered into the tin. There sat a large, golden-brown cake.

'Oh, my goodness,' Mum breathed. 'Who on earth has left that there?'

'It's got to be one of the neighbours,' I said. 'Mrs Brodie? She must have guessed it was you who's been doing all those good deeds.'

'How kind.' Mum's eyes were a bit teary again.

'Mum, don't start crying,' I said, smiling to stop myself doing exactly the same thing.

I'd realized something amazing. That while doing secret good deeds made you feel great, having someone secretly do something kind and generous for you was just as wonderful.

'Everyone in Year Seven is talking about us,' Henry informed me with satisfaction. 'But, of course, they don't know it's *us*.'

It was lunch time, the end of the week. Despite Zara's sarcastic jibes, Henry and I had continued to do secret good deeds for our fellow Year 7 pupils every single day. At first it seemed as if no one had noticed. But gradually we'd heard people start asking their friends if they knew anything about the lost property returned to them, the possessions cleaned or repaired, the hidden treats in their

tidied lockers. As Henry and I did more and more good deeds, more and more people became interested and intrigued, and, suddenly, everyone was talking about it. Yesterday I'd overheard Layla Bishop, Kavita Sharma and Bronagh Kelly discussing who could be responsible. But no one had any idea it was me and Henry.

'I love doing the good deeds,' Henry went on, beaming with delight. 'It's the best thing *ever*.'

'By the way, how are you getting on with your mum?' I asked. Reports from the Williams household had been good too, for the last few days.

'*Loads* better,' Henry replied enthusiastically. 'I do things for her all the time. This morning I put all the washing in the machine before she got up.'

'Great.' I looked closely at Henry. I thought he looked just a tiny bit lighter than a couple of weeks ago. He seemed to have lost one of his chins. But maybe it was all in my mind, so I said nothing.

'Sunita, I forgot to tell you something,' Henry went on, looking at me a bit anxiously. 'Do you remember last week when Mr Arora sent me to the office with a note?'

'No,' I said. 'Why, is it important?'

Henry shook his head. 'Not really. It was just that – well, you know Dean Ashton in Year Nine?'

'No.' I groaned. 'Henry, will you please get to the point?'

'Dean's got those flash Predator football boots like David Beckham—'

'Henry!' I pretended to grab him around the throat.

'OK, OK.' Henry fended me off. 'Well, when I was on my way to the office, I saw his boots lying in the Year Nine cloakroom. I knew they were his because they had his name in . . .' He stared guiltily at me. 'So I put them back in his locker. Just in case they got lost or stolen. I know we were only supposed to be doing the secret good deeds for Year Seven, but—'

'Well, I'm shocked.' I stared sternly at him. 'I shall certainly never speak to you again.'

'Oh.' Henry smiled at me. 'For a minute there I thought you were serious.'

'I actually think it's a great idea,' I went on eagerly. 'Why shouldn't we branch out into the rest of the school?'

Henry frowned thoughtfully. 'No one notices us around the Year Seven corridor, but it would be different in the upper school. Still, I reckon we could do it.'

'Let's,' I agreed. 'Even if it only winds Zara up, that'll be something!'

'Talking of Zara, she's been a long time, hasn't she?' Henry glanced at his watch. 'I thought she was only popping inside to get her chewing gum.'

'Really?' I said disbelievingly. 'I think it's time we sorted out Madame Zara once and for all.'

'What do you mean?' Henry followed me as I headed into school, keeping a sharp lookout for any roving teachers.

'Well, someone's been keeping my locker tidy all week,' I replied. 'And if it's not you—'

'It isn't,' Henry broke in.

'Then there's only one other person it can be.' I stopped at the corner and peered round the wall into the Year 7 corridor. 'Aha! Caught red-handed!'

Zara had her head inside Henry's locker. She was tidying manically, screwing up bits of rubbish and tossing them into the wastepaper basket at her side. She was so intent on her work, she didn't hear us walk up behind her.

'Having fun?' I asked.

Zara almost leaped out of her skin. She blushed redder than I'd ever seen her blush before.

'Thanks, Zara.' Henry beamed as he peered into his locker. 'It looks great.'

'Don't thank me,' Zara snapped. 'I only did it because it was so messy, it was getting on my nerves.'

'Yeah, right,' Henry chuckled. 'You're just as much into the good deeds as me and Sunita. You don't want to admit it, that's all.'

'Maybe you should try it out at home, Zara,' I remarked. 'It's doing wonders for Henry and his mum.'

Zara did not reply but, if anything, she turned even redder.

'You already have!' I gasped in amazement.

'Tell all,' Henry demanded.

'Why do you two have to make such a big deal out of everything?' Zara muttered. 'All right, I did some stuff around the house for my mum. So what?'

'Was she pleased?' Henry asked eagerly.

Zara sniffed. 'She didn't even notice!' she snapped. 'Well, that's not surprising really, considering the madhouse we live in.' And she turned away as if she wanted the conversation to end right there.

'But she *did* notice eventually?' I persisted.

Zara nodded impatiently.

'And was she pleased?' Henry asked again.

Realizing we weren't about to let her off the hook, Zara lowered her eyes. 'She cried,' she admitted, looking more uncomfortable than I'd ever seen her look before.

Henry and I were both silent. I couldn't imagine that Zara was the easiest person to live with, and from the few things she'd said before, and what we'd seen when her parents picked her up that

day, I knew that life at her home wasn't great. Now she seemed just a little ashamed of how she'd been behaving before, and I wondered if this could be a tiny turning point.

'Well, now that we've all finished polishing our haloes, we'd better go outside before a teacher catches us,' Zara snapped, stomping off down the corridor.

Henry and I followed. I wondered if there could be anything more amazing than sarcastic and prickly Zara getting into the secret good deeds. But there was.

We were in the classroom after lunch, waiting for Mr Arora. Like he always did, Jack Browning was taking 50p bets on how late Mr Arora would be for registration. Sometimes he was only a minute or two before the bell for lessons, and he had to take the register at breakneck speed. Celina was painting Chloe's nails. Danielle and Jyoti were flicking through magazines. Zara, Henry and I were chatting.

Suddenly a great shriek rent the air.

'Oh, for God's sake!' Celina snapped, just catching the bottle of nail varnish before it tipped over. 'What did you do *that* for, Kavita?'

Kavita Sharma was standing by her chair in the middle of the classroom, her face flushed. She was clutching an MP3 player to her chest.

'Someone's fixed it!' she spluttered.

'What are you talking about?' Layla Bishop asked.

'My MP3 player!' Kavita waved it at her. 'It wasn't working so I left it in my bag – and now it's working! Someone repaired it!'

'Like my maths book,' added Layla.

'The mystery do-gooder strikes again,' said one of the boys, Charles Bolton. There was a buzz of excited chatter as everyone began talking and speculating at once.

'Well done, Sunita,' Henry whispered in my ear. 'I didn't know you were a techno kid.'

'It wasn't me,' I whispered back. 'I thought it was *you*.'

Henry shook his head. We both turned and looked at Zara.

'Oh, get real,' Zara snorted. 'I wouldn't know where to start.'

I clapped my hand to my mouth. 'Oh!'

'What is it, Sunita?' Henry asked.

'Don't you see?' My voice was trembling so much, I could hardly get the words out at all. 'If it wasn't one of us, then it must have been someone else.'

Zara and Henry looked blank.

'Brilliantly deduced, Sherlock,' Zara said. 'Here, have a medal.'

'No, no, no!' I whispered. 'Don't you under-stand? It means that *other people* have begun doing secret good deeds too! Henry, Zara, I think we've started something . . .'

CHAPTER 6

'So what's the story with all these secret good deeds?'

I stopped in my tracks. I tiptoed into the Year 7 cloakroom, and flattened myself against the wall out of sight. I didn't make a habit of listening to teachers' conversations. But this I had to hear.

'The kids in my Spanish classes haven't stopped talking about it for the last week,' Mr Hernandez went on. 'And my Year Eight form think it's the best thing since sliced bread. I haven't seen them so excited since I tripped and head-butted the whiteboard.'

'I know,' replied Mr Lucas. 'My Year Tens don't think it's cool to get excited about anything, but this has really got them going.'

'Have you noticed that there's a different atmosphere around the school these days?' Mr Hernandez went on. 'It's happier, somehow.'

'Well, anything that keeps the kids happy makes our lives easier,' Mr Lucas said. 'Shame

they can't start doing secret good deeds for the teachers . . .'

Their voices died away down the corridor.

'Your wish is my command,' I murmured. I stepped out of my hiding place and hurried towards our classroom. It was the end of the day, and most people had already left. Zara and Henry were waiting for me out in the play-ground, but there was something important I had to do first . . .

The last two and a half weeks had been mental. I was right. Henry, Zara and I weren't the only ones doing the good deeds now. More and more Year 7 kids were joining in every day. So Henry and I had begun spreading our secret good deeds around the school. The first thing I did was to leave a pretty mauve gel pen, which I'd only used once, in Amber Dhillon's locker.

It was amazing to see how quickly everyone became involved as a wave of good deeds began to sweep across the school. Wherever you went, people were talking about what had been done for them, and who could have done it. I had never seen anything like it. Something amazing had happened to me too. When I lost the folder with my English project inside it, someone had found it and secretly put it back in my locker. Dizzy with relief, I tried to thank first Zara, and then

Henry, but they both insisted that it wasn't them. Then, slowly, I realized that *someone else* had done a good deed, just for me. The thought made my heart sing.

The good deeds were gathering force and getting bigger and stronger every single day, and it made me feel wonderful, I had to admit. I'd started this. Me. No one else. It didn't matter that Celina and the others still took every opportunity going to have a dig at me, make snidey little comments. They couldn't stop me feeling happy, knowing that I'd started something amazing. I was sure Mum would be proud of me, although I hadn't told her yet. It was her birthday in a few weeks' time and I knew I didn't have the money to buy her a proper present, so I thought I'd tell her all about it then. It would a special kind of gift.

I was about to turn into the classroom when I heard footsteps coming from the other direction. Mr Arora? I whisked the book I was holding behind my back, just as Amber Dhillon came round the corner.

'Oh, hi, Sunita,' she said, 'I was just looking for my uncle – you know, Mr Arora. You haven't seen him, have you?'

'I think he went to the staff room,' I replied as casually as I could, still keeping the book out of sight.

Amber sighed. 'That means he's fallen asleep again. He's supposed to be taking us home.'

'Is your auntie's baby still keeping you awake?' I asked with sympathy.

'Tell me about it.' Amber rolled her eyes. 'I mean, we only live next door, for goodness' sake, and *we* hardly get a wink of sleep. Little Simi has got the Dhillon lungs, all right.' She smiled at me. 'See you later.'

I watched her safely out of sight round the corner, and then went into the deserted classroom. I cleared a space on Mr Arora's desk and laid the book down, right at the front where he couldn't miss it. It was more than a book really. There was a pocket at the back of it which held two CDs. The book was called *Stop the Screaming and Start Sleeping!*

One of Mum's friends had bought it for her just after she'd had the twins. It was full of hints and tips about getting your baby to sleep, as well as CDs of soothing music. It had helped. After a couple of weeks the twins had started sleeping, and I'd stopped yawning my way through the day at school. I was hoping it would do the same for Mr Arora and his wife.

I slipped out of the classroom and headed for the playground, where Henry and Zara were waiting for me.

'Mission accomplished,' I said, taking my bag from Zara. 'I hope it works.'

'I think secret good deeds for the teachers are a great idea,' Henry said enthusiastically.

Zara groaned. 'Do we have to?'

'No, we don't have to,' Henry replied sternly. 'We *want* to. That's the difference.'

'Oh, you two are a pain in the backside,' Zara muttered. But I noticed she didn't say she wasn't going to join in.

'Shall we run for the next bus?' Henry suggested, picking up his bag. 'I want to get the potatoes peeled for dinner before my mum comes home from work.'

'Nice one, Henry.' I grinned, slapping him on the back. Zara just sniffed.

A loud bang from behind made us all jump. We turned to see the Kennedys' bright pink camper van drawing up at the kerb.

'Oh, for God's sake!' Zara muttered grumpily.

Zara's mum was driving, and the kids were stuffed in the back as usual. She leaned over and stuck her head out of the passenger window.

'Hi, love,' she called. 'I thought we'd go straight to Gran and Gramps' place from school. We've got lots to do, so it's best to make an early start.'

I glanced at Zara. To my surprise, she was bright red.

'Lots to do?' I asked, raising my eyebrows.

'Don't start,' Zara snapped. She glared at her mum. 'I need to go home and change.'

'I've brought some clothes for you to change into,' her mum replied. 'Come on, Zara, it was *your* idea to decorate Gran and Gramps' living room while they're on holiday. *A secret good deed*, you said, *and a lovely surprise for them when they get back.*'

Henry and I slowly turned to stare at Zara. How we managed to keep our faces straight, I don't know.

'All right, all right, all right!' Zara muttered, avoiding our gaze as she stomped over to the van and climbed in.

'Bye then, Zara,' Henry called. 'Have a *good* evening!'

'Don't do anything we wouldn't do,' I added.

We burst out laughing as the camper van moved off, and Zara shot us a poisonous look.

'I always knew she was up for it!' Henry chortled. 'All that sarcasm is just a load of hot air.'

'Wait till tomorrow,' I said with a grin. 'We're never going to let her forget *this*—'

I broke off. A woman holding two children by the hand was walking down the road towards the school. It looked like Mum and the twins, but, of course, it couldn't be.

It was.

'Can we run for the bus?' Henry was hopping anxiously from foot to foot. 'I really want to get home before my mum.'

'You go.' Mum and the twins *here*? 'I've – er – got something to do first.'

'See you.' Henry flapped his hand at me and shot off towards the bus stop. He seemed to be a lot lighter on his feet these days.

'Sunita! Sunita!'

The twins had spotted me, and were pulling Mum along like two puppies on leads. I ran towards them. My school bag was heavy on my shoulder, but my heart was as light as a feather.

'What are you doing here?' I asked as the twins flung themselves at me.

'We went to Best Burgers with Megan and her mum,' Debbie yelled excitedly. 'Then we came to meet you.'

'Yeah, and we've got you a present, Sunita.' Davey pulled his hand out of his pocket and solemnly presented me with a sachet of tomato ketchup.

'Thank you,' I said. 'I'll have it with my dinner tonight.' I glanced at my mum. She looked completely relaxed, even with people milling up and down the main road around us. 'Did you have a good time?'

Mum smiled. 'We did. It was a shame you

couldn't come too, though. Was that your friend Henry we saw running for the bus?'

I nodded. 'That's him.'

'Funny,' Mum went on as we walked along, 'I got the impression from you that he was quite a lot bigger.'

'He used to be,' I replied. 'But I think he might be losing a bit of weight.'

'Mum, why can't *we* get the bus home?' Debbie asked grumpily. 'I don't like walking.'

'Sorry, honey.' Mum shook her head. 'I used up all our money in the burger bar.' She turned to me. 'Even then we had to share fries and a milkshake. It was a bit embarrassing, Sunita.'

'I bet Mrs Rice didn't mind,' I said.

'Oh, she was lovely,' said Mum. 'She bought me a cup of coffee. But we can't carry on like this. I'm going to have to get some extra money, one way or another.'

Davey stopped in the middle of the pavement, scowling. 'I can't make my feet work any more,' he pouted. 'They're too tired.'

'Come on,' Mum said encouragingly, taking his hand. 'Let's sing all our favourite songs, and we'll be home before you know it.'

We sang our way home. It was a long walk, and even Mum and I were feeling the strain when we finally reached our street.

'Wouldn't it be great if there was another cake on the doormat?' Debbie asked wistfully, as we walked towards the house.

There wasn't a cake. Not today. But there *was* something else.

We all stopped at the gate and stared.

'Oh, my goodness,' Mum said faintly.

Mrs Brodie, our next-door neighbour, was perched on our doorstep. She was warmly wrapped up in coat, scarf, gloves and boots, and there was a flask and a half-eaten packet of biscuits on the ground beside her. She was knitting something in dark blue wool.

'It's the witch!' Debbie whispered, clutching my hand tighter.

Mum and I blushed.

'Don't worry, my dear,' Mrs Brodie replied. She had a rich, rounded, Scottish voice which seemed to roll off her tongue like cream. 'I only use my powers for good.' She got to her feet, rolled up her knitting and put it in her bag. 'Well, I'm pleased to meet you at last. We seem to keep missing each other, so I decided to camp out and wait for you. I hope you don't mind.'

'Not at all,' Mum managed to say.

Mrs Brodie came towards us and shook hands, first with Mum, then with me, while the twins hid behind us and peered cautiously at her. Tall

and thin, Mrs Brodie looked as if she didn't have a spare ounce of fat anywhere. Her eyes were a very bright, clear blue, the kind that search right into you.

'Well, now,' she said thoughtfully, 'Someone has been doing some lovely, secret things for me over the last few weeks. I think it's the fairies, myself.'

Giggles came from behind me and Mum.

'Perhaps it's the pixies,' Mrs Brodie went on. 'Or the leprechauns.'

'It wasn't the leppery corns,' Debbie chuckled, peeking out from behind me. 'It was us.'

'You!' Mrs Brodie bent down until she was at the twins' level. 'Are you sure you're not pixies in disguise?'

'No, but I've got a Spiderman costume,' Davey added, edging out from behind Mum.

'Will you show it to me?' Mrs Brodie asked.

Davey nodded. Mum and I watched in amazement as first Davey, then Debbie slipped their hands into Mrs Brodie's.

'Would you like to come in for a cup of tea, Mrs Brodie?' Mum said, glancing at me. We were both smiling.

'Oh, do please call me Susan.' Mrs Brodie smiled herself, broadly. 'I was hoping you might say that. I've a home-made chocolate cake in my bag.'

'Did you make the other cake?' Debbie asked, wide-eyed. 'Was it magic?'

'I mixed a lot of good luck into it for you,' Mrs Brodie replied solemnly.

'Maybe Dad will come home then,' said Davey.

'Maybe he will.' Mrs Brodie glanced over the twins' heads and nodded kindly at Mum and me.

We went inside with our new friend. When just one or two people are mean and spiteful to you, you can sometimes forget how kind and generous almost everyone else can be.

How good did I feel?

I can't describe it. School was *buzzing*. Wherever Henry, Zara and I went, we heard people discussing the latest good deeds. From snooty Year 12s and 13s, who thought they were a cut above the rest of us because they didn't have to wear uniform, right down to the tiniest Year 7 pupil, everyone was involved. If they weren't doing good deeds themselves, other people were doing it for them. Or they were, at the very least, *discussing* the good deeds. Teachers were talking about how they'd found their desks tidied and their whiteboards cleaned and the bookshelves put into alphabetical order and their car windscreens wiped. It was the nicest kind of epidemic.

However, there were some people who didn't

quite get the idea behind the secret good deeds. You might be able to take a guess who they are.

'Someone's put this beautiful new lipstick in my locker!' Chloe Maynard screeched, prancing into the classroom one morning the following week. Everyone looked round, including me, Zara and Henry. Chloe was glowing like she'd won the lottery. 'Isn't it *gorgeous*?'

'A lipstick?' Zara sniffed. 'Like she really needs *that*. It's a pity someone didn't leave a brain in her locker instead.'

Celina, Danielle and Jyoti gathered around Chloe, ooh-ing and ah-ing.

'Can you guess who left it there?' Celina asked with a knowing smirk.

'No, I haven't got a clue!' announced Chloe.

'She never spoke a truer word,' Zara said tartly.

Celina giggled. 'It was me, Chloe, you idiot!'

'You!' Chloe shrieked. 'Oh, Cee! Thanks ever so much!'

'I think the idea of *secret* good deeds has gone right over Celina's head,' whispered Henry.

I glanced over at Celina and Chloe, who had thrown their arms around each other dramatically, and grinned. 'No, do you think so?'

'What're you laughing at?' Jack Browning had suddenly appeared at my elbow. I jumped, not realizing he had been so close.

'Nothing,' I said, staring him straight in the eye.

'You were laughing at Celina and Chloe.' Jack was frightening close up because he was so tall. I tried not to let my eyes drop. 'What have *you* got to laugh about?'

'We were just chatting,' Henry said bravely, but squeakily.

'Yes, so why don't you go away as quickly as you can?' Zara said with a yawn.

'Shut up, beetroot head.' Jack's gaze was still locked on mine. With one swift move of his hand he grabbed my hair and yanked it back. I cried out in surprise and pain. 'Now say sorry to Cee and Clo.'

'Jack Browning!'

The words curled across the classroom like the crack of a whiplash. Mr Arora stood in the doorway, holding the register. His brows were drawn down, and there was an expression on his face I'd never seen before. He looked fierce.

Jack immediately let go of my hair, flushing bright red.

'Go and sit down, Jack,' Mr Arora said coldly, his voice cutting through the shocked silence. 'You will report for detention at lunch time every day this week.'

'But, sir—' Jack began.

'Sit down.'

Everyone in the classroom jumped at Mr Arora's tone.

'Are you all right, Sunita?' he asked in a gentler voice.

I nodded dumbly. We all stared as Mr Arora strode to his seat, sat down and snapped the register open. There was something different about him. He still looked pale and a little tired, but the dark circles under his eyes were gone. I wondered if the book and CDs had helped.

'Serves that idiot Jack Browning right,' Zara said with satisfaction as we lined up for assembly. 'He's got away with murder since term began.'

'Not any more,' Henry said, also with deep satisfaction. Jack was slumped in his seat, glaring at me. Celina and her friends were also giving me black looks.

I didn't say anything as we walked down the corridor to the hall. We weren't supposed to talk on the way to and from assembly, but that wasn't the reason why I was quiet. I was listening. As classes converged on the hall from every direction, all around me was a tidal wave of secret good deeds.

'Somebody tidied my locker.'

'Someone found my purse and put it on my chair.'

'I don't know who it was, but somebody hid a copy of that CD I couldn't afford in my locker.'

'I thought my Game Boy was broken, but now it's been fixed.'

'Someone helped me with my maths homework.'

I felt as buoyant as if I was being lifted up and carried along on a wave of good will. As our class filed into the hall, I overheard Mrs Parkinson and Mrs Holland speculating about who had tidied up the English cupboard. Mr Hernandez was practically dancing around the hall with glee, telling Mrs Kirke how someone had cleaned the mud off his car bumper. I tried not to smile too widely. As Mrs Bright marched into the hall, blonde bob swinging purposefully, I wondered what she thought of it all.

To my surprise, I found out at the end of assembly. After discussing arrangements for the Christmas Fair, which was coming up in a few weeks, Mrs Bright changed tack abruptly.

'Finally, I wish to speak to you about a matter which has been brought to my attention over the last few weeks,' she said briskly. 'It concerns these "secret good deeds" which appear to be happening all over the school.'

A rustle of excited interest rippled around the hall, teachers and pupils alike. I sat up straighter and glanced from Henry to Zara, who were on either side of me.

'While I applaud the sentiment behind these

good deeds,' Mrs Bright went on, 'I feel that, on health and safety grounds, we cannot have people sneaking around the school doing things secretly, even when they are doing kindnesses for others. So my message to you is' – she cleared her throat, looking slightly embarrassed as the rest of us looked extremely confused – 'keep doing good deeds, but do not be sneaky about it.'

There was a murmur of puzzled dissatisfaction as Mrs Bright swept out of the hall.

'So what does that mean?' Henry wanted to know. 'Are we allowed to carry on doing them or not?'

'As long as we don't do it secretly, apparently,' Zara said scornfully. 'But that's the fun part.'

Henry and I turned to stare at her.

'All right, I admit it,' Zara said irritably. 'You've converted me. Just don't go on about it.'

I had to admit that I felt a tiny bit deflated. I thought Mrs Bright would be pleased, but she didn't seem completely sure it was a good thing.

I'm happy to say that everyone else did, though. No one took the slightest notice of Mrs Bright. We all carried on 'sneaking' around the school doing more good deeds. And when I counted up all the ones I'd heard about at the end of the day, it was the most yet.

That evening, as I walked home from the bus stop

with Henry, I wondered what Mrs Bright would think if she knew that I was the person who'd started it all. Me, the daughter of a thief . . .

'Why don't you come in, Sunita,' Henry suggested as we neared his house. 'We could do our homework together. And you could stay for tea.' He grinned at me. 'We're having a nice healthy salad.'

I laughed, shaking my head. 'Thanks, but not tonight. I'd have to ask my mum first.'

'All right.' Henry waved and turned through the gate. I carried on down the street. But before I'd gone two steps, I saw the Williamses' front door fly open.

'There you are, darling!' Henry's mum was beaming all over her tiny, pointed, pixie-like face. 'And whoever did all the dusting this morning, I'd like to know?'

'I have no idea,' I heard Henry reply. He was smiling.

'The same person who emptied the kitchen bin, I expect!' Slipping her arm through Henry's, Mrs Williams drew him inside. I went on my way, and now I was smiling too.

Our house was very quiet. For a moment I thought that everyone was out, but when I went into the kitchen, the twins were sitting peacefully at the table, colouring in pictures with fat wax

crayons. To my surprise, Mrs Brodie was with them.

'Oh – hello,' I said. 'Where's Mum?'

'She asked me to babysit,' Mrs Brodie said cheerfully. 'Said she had to pop out.' She broke off as Davey began trying to wrestle a blue crayon from Debbie.

'I want that one!' Davey yelled, trying to bite Debbie's finger.

'No-o-o!' howled Debbie, lashing out with her other hand.

'Now, now, what's this nonsense?' Mrs Brodie said sternly. 'You know how to ask properly for something, Davey.'

Davey looked shame-faced. 'Please, Debbie, may I borrow the blue crayon?' he said humbly.

'Yes, of course you may,' Debbie replied, and handed the crayon over with a gracious nod of her ponytail.

My eyes almost dropped out of my head.

'That's better,' said Mrs Brodie. She winked at me as she got up and went over to the kettle.

'That's amazing!' I said.

Mrs Brodie smiled. 'I used to be headteacher in a rather tough school in Glasgow,' she replied. 'Now, shall we have some tea? I've brought some shortbread with me.'

I joined the twins at the table and helped them

with their colouring. Mrs Brodie was just serving up tea, juice and shortbread when we heard the front door opening.

'Mum!' the twins roared, and galloped off down the hall.

Mum came into the kitchen a moment later with the twins hanging off her arms. She looked wide-eyed and rosy-cheeked, as if she was excited about something.

'Where've you been?' I asked curiously. She didn't have any shopping bags with her.

'Sunita, I've gone and done something really crazy.' Mum took off her gloves and pressed her hands to her flushed cheeks.

'What?' I asked anxiously.

'I've got a job.'

I thought I'd misheard her.

'I'm sorry? What did you say?'

'A job.' Mum stared at me. She looked petrified.

'Mum!' I ran over to hug her. 'That's great! Where?'

'Only at the burger bar,' Mum explained in a shaky voice. 'I noticed a poster asking for workers when we were in there the other day. So I went back today and – and my first shift's on Saturday morning . . .' She stared anxiously at me. 'Oh, Sunita, do you think I've done the right thing?'

'Of course you have!' I said, my arms still around her. 'I think it's brilliant.'

'Will we get free burgers?' asked Davey eagerly.

'I'll be able to afford to buy them from now on.' Mum laughed.

The four of us stood in a circle with our arms around each other, as Mrs Brodie moved quietly away to put the kettle on again. We were managing, we were coping. No, better than that. We were re-making ourselves into a new family. Re-making our lives without Dad.

I sang to myself as I wandered down the street towards the Williamses' house. I felt good, and there were lots of reasons why. It was Saturday morning. Although it was November, the sun was shining and the sky was a very pale blue. Mrs Brodie was looking after the twins and it was Mum's first day at her new job. I was happy, and happiness was becoming a habit I didn't want to break.

All the same, I did feel a little worried about Mum. I wanted to give her some moral support. So Zara and Henry had offered to come to the burger bar with me. I was meeting Henry first, and then we were going to collect Zara.

As I rounded the corner, I drew in my breath with a little gasp. Jack Browning was strolling

down the street towards me, having just come out of his house, I guessed. His clothes looked cool and expensive – designer jeans and jacket, Nikes, and dark sunglasses perched on his gelled hair.

I tried not to look nervous, or show that my heart was fluttering inside me. Staring straight ahead, I walked on. But out of the corner of one eye, I could see that Jack had noticed me and was scowling heavily.

'Where do you think you're going?' he snarled, stepping in front of me.

I stopped. I had no choice.

'To Henry's house,' I replied. 'Get out of my way.' I could feel my knees trembling, but I refused to drop my gaze.

Jack didn't move. 'You got me into big trouble with Arora last week.' He thrust his face close to mine, so close I could see the pores of his skin. From this distance, he wasn't so gorgeous. He had lots of blackheads. 'I got detention because of you.'

'No, you got yourself into trouble,' I said coldly. 'It was nothing to do with me. Ow!'

With one swift movement, Jack had grabbed my arm and twisted it behind my back. He wasn't really hurting me, but I couldn't move.

'Now we've got to find some way for you to pay me back,' he said in a gloating voice. 'How about you take on all my homework for the next week?'

'Jack! *Jack!* What are you *doing*?'

Jack almost jumped out of his skin at the sound of Mrs Williams's voice. So did I. Immediately Jack dropped my arm, and I backed away from him.

Henry and his mum were standing on the doorstep of their house. Henry was staring at me anxiously, while his mum looked as if she simply could not believe her eyes.

'It's all right, Mrs Williams,' Jack blustered, managing his cocky smile. 'Sunita and me were just messing around.'

'Really,' Henry's mum said in a chilling voice. She marched down to the garden gate, her high heels clicking on the path. 'Well, if I see any more *messing around* like that, I shall be speaking to your father.'

'Shut up, you stupid old bag,' Jack muttered, adding a few swear words under his breath.

Mrs Williams looked outraged as Jack turned and stalked off.

'Are you all right, Sunita?' Henry rushed over to me. It was strange seeing him in weekend clothes, and not his uniform. His jeans looked quite baggy. I had been sure for some time that he'd lost weight, but he hadn't mentioned it, so neither had I.

'*Well!*' Mrs Williams looked as if she needed a sit-down, a cup of tea and a bottle of smelling salts

to revive her. 'Jack Browning behaving like that! Who would have thought it!'

'He's actually not a very nice person, Mum,' said Henry.

'You mean – this isn't the first time he's done something like this?' Mrs Williams seriously looked as if she was about to faint.

Henry shook his head.

'Thank goodness *you're* not like that, darling.' His mum slid her arm round Henry's (smaller) waist and gave him a little squeeze. Henry looked so proud, I almost burst into tears on the spot. 'Now, would you like to come in for a drink, Sunita, or do you have to be going?'

'Thank you, Mrs Williams, but we'd better go,' I said with a smile. 'Zara's waiting for us.'

Henry's mum gave him another hug, went inside and waved us off.

'Somehow I don't think your mum will be thinking that Jack Browning's the best thing since sliced bread any more,' I remarked.

'No,' Henry agreed confidently. 'Funny, I was just trying to get up enough courage to tell her what he was really like when I glanced out of the window and there he was, beating you up.'

'Glad I could help,' I said dryly.

Henry chuckled, hitching up his jeans, which were definitely too big for him.

'Henry?' It seemed a good time to raise the subject. 'Are you losing weight?'

'A bit.' Henry blushed, looking very pleased with himself. 'All my clothes are loose. And now my mum thinks *I'm* the best thing since sliced bread.'

'Because you've lost weight?'

Henry shook his head. 'I don't think she cares about that any more,' he said slowly. 'She just loves all the little things I've been doing for her.'

I smiled. That was the power of the secret good deeds.

'So how do you think your mum's getting on at the burger place?' asked Henry as we walked towards Zara's street.

'I don't know.' I started feeling a little worried again. 'She's never had a job before. She was at college when she married Dad. She didn't even finish her course.'

'I bet she'll be fine,' Henry said comfortingly, stopping outside a purple front gate. 'Is this number twenty-six? That's Zara's.'

Zara's house was like ours, a small Victorian terrace, but that was where all similarities ended. The front door was bright purple, and it had a rainbow painted above it. The window frames were pink and a climbing rose rambled all over the house, the scented flowers a pale, creamy yellow colour. Instead of a doorbell, there was an

159

actual brass bell next to the front door with a rope hanging from it.

'This is great!' Henry said enthusiastically, grabbing the rope and ringing the bell loudly.

Immediately it sounded as if there was an earthquake inside the house. There was a noise of shouts, screams, feet thundering down stairs and dogs barking. Henry and I grinned at each other.

'Get out of the way!' We could hear Zara yelling inside. 'It's for *me*.'

The door was flung open. Two cats, one white and one tabby, came out and started curling themselves around my ankles. I got a confused impression of a small crowd of bright-eyed little children peeping at us from the stairs, while a dog still barked somewhere else in the house. But I was transfixed by Zara.

Henry's eyes were also falling out of his head. 'Zara! *Wow*. You look *great*.'

Zara sighed loudly, pretending to be annoyed. She wore a purple suede Afghan coat with a fluffy white collar, and jeans tucked into knee-high black boots. Her birthmark was almost invisible. She looked beautiful.

'Close your mouths, you two,' Zara said tartly. 'You might swallow a fly.'

'I can't believe it.' I peered closely at her. 'What happened to your birthmark?'

'My mum bought me this special camouflage make-up ages ago,' Zara said casually. 'I haven't bothered to try it out before.'

'You look fantastic,' I said warmly.

'Oh, please,' she said in a prickly tone. 'Was my birthmark really so bad?'

'Of course not,' I replied. 'It's just that you've never worn *any* make-up before. It really suits you.'

'Definitely,' Henry added.

'Well, enough about me,' Zara snapped, trying hard not to look pleased but not succeeding. 'Are we going to Best Burgers?'

She was just stepping outside when Mrs Kennedy popped her head round a door at the end of the hall.

'Zara, aren't you going to bring your friends in to say hello?'

Zara groaned. 'Do I *have* to?' But I got the impression she didn't really mind.

'Yes, you do.' Her mum came forward, a baby on her hip, followed by a big black dog, which galloped straight in our direction. Henry looked a bit nervous, but Zara grabbed the dog's collar before he could launch himself at us, tail wagging. 'Hello. You must be Henry and Sunita.'

We nodded and said hello.

'Doesn't my Zara look absolutely gorgeous?'

Mrs Kennedy said proudly, smoothing down a sticking-up bit of Zara's dark hair.

'*Mum!*' Zara protested loudly, pushing her away. But it was obvious she was pleased.

'She's even prettier when she smiles.' Eyes twinkling, Mrs Kennedy shifted the baby to her other hip. 'But you have to watch for it. She doesn't do it very often.'

'I know,' I agreed. 'I actually think she rather enjoys being grumpy.'

Zara sighed loudly, but her lips were twitching a bit. She pulled open the front door and ushered us out.

''Bye, love.' Mrs Kennedy, the children, the dog and the two cats gathered at the door to see us off. 'Have a good time. We'll go and see Gran and Gramps later when they're back from their holiday. I can't wait to see their faces when they find out we've been decorating their house!'

Henry and I glanced at each other, amused.

'So,' Henry said with enormous glee as the three of us walked off down the street. 'How's life, Zara?'

'Fine,' Zara replied, marching purposefully ahead of us.

'Did you notice a difference in the way Zara and her mum spoke to each other, or am I just imagining it?' I said to Henry in a low voice.

'You're not imagining it,' Henry replied softly.

'Stop whispering, you two!' Zara snapped, spinning round to glare at us. But it was all show really. I could tell.

The High Street wasn't far from Zara's home. As I led the way to Best Burgers, my heart was suddenly thundering in my chest, and I felt quite sick. I didn't want this to go wrong for Mum.

The burger bar was busy, and there were queues at every till. Mum was standing at one of them, taking orders. She wore the green and white uniform, with her hair tucked under a green and white cardboard hat. She looked calm, not at all flustered. I felt relieved.

Zara went to find a table, while Henry and I joined the queue at Mum's till.

'I'm just having a drink,' I said quickly as Henry pulled some money out of his pocket. Mum had only been able to spare a pound for me. 'Nothing to eat.'

'Share with me,' Henry suggested. 'I don't want much.'

'Are you sure?' I asked gratefully.

Henry nodded.

We moved up to the counter. Mum winked at us as she whisked a tray from the pile and placed it in front of us. She wore a name badge with KULJIT on it.

'Good morning, welcome to Best Burgers. How may I help you?' she asked brightly.

'Good morning to you too,' I said with a grin. 'Two small fries, two cheeseburgers and three strawberry milkshakes to eat in, please.'

'Certainly,' Mum replied briskly. She bustled away and began collecting our order.

'I think she's got this well under control already,' remarked Henry.

Mum was back with our food and drink quick-smart. She placed it carefully on the tray, and took our money.

'Are you OK?' I whispered.

'Fine, but my hair stinks of chip fat!' Mum whispered back. She raised her voice. 'Enjoy your meal.'

Zara had managed to get a table quite close to where Mum was serving. Henry and I took the tray over to her.

'Your mum seems to be doing all right, Sunita,' Zara said. She pointed at a copy of the local newspaper which somebody had left behind on the table. 'Here, you two, take a look at this.'

On the front page was a photo, and the caption: *Mayor and family attend opening of new hospital ward.* Henry and I took a closer look. Celina's dad stood in the middle of the picture, wearing his mayoral fur-trimmed robes and gold chain. Celina and her

mum looked rich, glossy and well-dressed, Mrs Patel in a heavily embroidered sari, and Celina in boots and yet another designer coat.

'Sickening, isn't it?' Zara sniffed, tossing the newspaper onto an empty table. 'It's almost enough to put me off my food.' She frowned at the tray. 'Is that all you two are having? I can lend you some money, Sunita—'

'No, it's fine,' I broke in. 'I'm going to share with Henry. He doesn't want much.'

'A-ha!' Zara exclaimed triumphantly, pointing a finger at Henry. 'I *knew* you were losing weight!'

'It's not a crime, is it?' Henry retorted, blushing.

'No, but it's about time,' Zara said bluntly.

'All right, I'll make a deal with you.' Henry divided his cheeseburger neatly, and gave me half. 'I'll carry on losing weight if you wear a bit of make-up to school from now on. Done?'

Zara looked taken aback. 'Everyone'll stare at me,' she snapped. 'They'll think I'm ashamed of my birthmark.'

Henry and I burst out laughing.

'Zara, no one who knows you will think any such thing,' I said with a grin. 'Why not make the best of yourself?'

'Anyway, the only thing everyone will be thinking is how stunning you are,' added Henry.

'Very funny,' Zara muttered. She put up a hand

to smooth her hair down neatly, and Henry and I winked at each other.

As they began chatting about last night's TV, I kept an eye on Mum. She was doing very well, even chatting to the customers every now and again. I relaxed a little.

I noticed the two women who came in a few minutes later, but only because they had six children with them of various ages, who were making a noise. The women pulled them into one of the queues with a good deal of muttering and shoving, and loud questions about what they wanted to eat. They all kept changing their minds.

With a sick feeling in my stomach, I kind of knew what was going to happen a split-second before it did. One of the women, the one in the pink shalwar kameez, glanced at Mum, did a double-take and looked again. She began whispering frantically to the other woman. She stared at Mum, her eyes almost falling out of her head. Then they both began to herd their kids out of the queue they were standing in, and across to Mum's till.

'But this queue's shorter,' one of the boys whined.

'Be quiet, Ajay,' the other woman ordered sharply.

I curled my fingers into my palms until the nails

dug into my skin. Henry and Zara were still chatting, and didn't notice that anything was wrong. I fixed my eyes on Mum, willing her not to notice that the women were staring at her.

She noticed – of course she did. I could see it in her face. Then her head went up, and she stared the two curious women straight between the eyes.

'Can I help you?' she asked in a clear and steady voice.

Looking slightly flustered, the two women gave their order. Mum moved away from the till, her back straight and her head held high. I was filled from top to toe with pride. I knew then that Mum was going to be all right . . .

'You were great,' I told Mum later that evening. The twins were in bed and we were curled up on the sofa, watching TV. 'I wanted to slap those two women, though.'

'I nearly leaned over the counter and banged their heads together!' Mum confessed with a grin. 'But I don't think that would have gone down very well on my first day.'

'You'll be OK now.' It was more of a statement than a question.

Mum nodded. 'Yes, but it's got me thinking. If your dad isn't coming back' – for once, her voice didn't falter – 'then serving burgers and fries all

day isn't exactly going to pay the bills for ever. I mean, what if you and the twins want to go to university?'

'Oh, Mum, that's ages away,' I said with a shrug.

'I know, but I have to think about these things now.' I'd never heard Mum talk like this before, so clear and practical and determined. 'I need to get myself a better job. I was wondering about going back to college myself.'

'I think that's a great idea.'

'Really?' Mum looked doubtful. 'Do you think I could do it?'

'You can do anything you want to!' I declared, throwing my arms around her.

Mum said she still hadn't made up her mind which course she wanted to do, so I decided to give her a secret helping hand. On Monday morning, before I went into class, I hurried over to the careers office in the upper school and found a copy of the local college prospectus. I would slip it into Mum's handbag tonight, when I got home. On the way back to class, I tidied a few bookshelves, watered a few dry-looking plants outside the school office, and picked up a few bits and pieces and took them to the lost-property cupboard. No one saw me.

When I got back to the classroom, the first thing I noticed was the buzz of excited chatter. Celina seemed to be right in the middle of it.

'What's going on?' I asked Henry. 'Are they all amazed by the new, improved Zara?'

'Idiot,' Zara said rudely, touching her made-up cheek gingerly. 'Celina's got some daft idea that the local newspaper has found out about the secret good deeds. Apparently they think it's a great human-interest story.'

'It's true,' Henry chimed in. 'One of the girls in Year Eight, Velma Charlton – her dad's a reporter on the paper. That's how they found out about it.'

I frowned. 'I don't like reporters.' I'd had enough of all that.

Mr Arora bounced – no other word can describe it – into the room. He looked bright-eyed and bushy-tailed. 'Sit down, please,' he called crisply.

'Don't worry about it, Sunita.' Zara shrugged. 'No one knows it was you who started it all. You're quite safe.'

I realized she was right. Something else struck me, and I grinned.

'I wonder what Mrs Bright thinks about it *now*,' I said.

The following morning, Tuesday, Mrs Bright didn't exactly bounce into assembly. But she did look quite excited. Her eyes were gleaming, her skin was glowing and her hair looked even glossier than usual, as if she had a sheen of excitement all over her.

'The theme of our assembly today,' she announced from the stage in ringing tones, 'is good deeds. Good will to all men – and women, I might add – which is highly appropriate with Christmas not far away.'

'She's changed her tune,' I whispered to Zara.

'She's probably dead thrilled about all the publicity the school's going to get in the local paper,' Zara said cynically.

We sang our way through a song or two, and listened to a reading. It was an old story, from Korea, I think, about people in heaven and hell who were both given long, long chopsticks to eat food. The people in hell were miserable and starving because the chopsticks were too long for them to eat with. But the people in heaven got around the problem by feeding each other. It was a good story, and I wanted to think about it a bit, but Mrs Bright didn't seem to want to discuss the reading, as she usually did. She was in a hurry to get to the next item.

'Now, I spoke to you a week or two ago about these secret good deeds which have been happening in our school,' Mrs Bright began, smiling more widely than I'd ever seen before. 'And I said then what a wonderful thing I thought it was.'

You did? I thought, raising my eyebrows.

'And I am not the only person who thinks so.'

Mrs Bright beamed round at us. 'Several local newspapers have been in touch, as well as local TV and radio stations.'

That caused a murmur of excitement around the hall.

'It is very pleasing to me to have the opportunity to stress that kindness and generosity towards each other are the cornerstones of our philosophy here at Coppergate,' Mrs Bright went on, 'and that the idea for these secret good deeds came from one of our pupils.'

Her next words almost gave me a heart attack.

'I am also very pleased to say that I now know the identity of that pupil.'

I thought I was hearing things. I was stunned, shocked, frozen. How could she know it was me? Had Zara or Henry . . . ? But a quick glance at each of them told me that they were as shocked as I was.

'I would like that person to join me on stage now, so that we can give her the credit she deserves.'

She looked down towards me.

Zara nudged me, but I couldn't move. Thoughts rushed through my head. Did I want to be in the limelight again? Did I want to deal with reporters and photographers all over again? Answer awkward questions about Dad?

I was saved from making a decision one way or another. Behind me, Celina Patel rose to her feet and walked to the stage, beaming proudly.

CHAPTER 7

'No!' Zara's furious words were lost amid the gasps and exclamations of everyone else in the hall. 'No, no, *no*!'

For a moment I thought she was going to jump to her feet, but Henry grabbed her arm and held her down.

Myself, I couldn't move. Couldn't speak. Couldn't even hear anything, except for the sickening thumping of my heart in my ears. How had this happened? How had this terrible mistake come about?

Celina was standing on the stage, a fake-modest smile on her lips as Mrs Bright praised her to the skies. *Kind-hearted . . . Generous . . . Great community spirit . . . A wonderful example to the rest of the school . . .* I only heard bits and pieces here and there. I was completely in shock.

'We've got to tell Mrs Bright the truth,' Zara whispered urgently in my ear.

'Just wait a bit, Sunita,' Henry whispered on the

173

other side of me. 'We'll sort this out straight after assembly.'

But was it as simple as that? I stared up at the stage, re-focusing my eyes and ears with a supreme effort.

'And now I'm sure you'd all like to thank Celina for her wonderful idea, which has brought so much pleasure and happiness to our school in recent weeks,' Mrs Bright gushed, looking more animated than I'd ever seen her before. She began to applaud.

The rest of the school joined in. It wasn't thunderous applause by any means. I think most of them were as dazed as I was. Mr Arora, just to my left, looked completely stunned, and barely clapped at all. I didn't join in; I couldn't. Zara folded her arms pointedly and glared at Celina, while Henry stared anxiously at me.

Mrs Bright put her arm round Celina's shoulders and led her off the stage, as the Year 7 classes began to file out into the corridor. We were supposed to leave the hall in silence, but no one was observing that rule today, not even the teachers.

'I can't *believe* it!' Chloe was squealing. 'I never guessed it was Cee! Did you?'

Danielle and Jyoti shook their heads. They all looked tremendously excited.

'How did she keep that quiet for so long?' asked Jyoti.

'She's going to be in the newspapers and on TV now,' Danielle pointed out enviously. 'As if she isn't in the papers enough already! That girl is so-o-o lucky!'

Her face utterly pale with fury, Zara grabbed me and Henry and pulled us out of the line, into the Year 7 cloakroom. 'Right!' she snapped, folding her arms tightly. 'What are we going to do about this?'

'Nothing,' I said miserably. 'There's nothing we *can* do.'

'What do you mean?' Zara practically wrung her hands. 'Of course there's something we can do!'

'We can go and tell Mrs Bright the truth,' suggested Henry.

'Think about it.' I looked from one to the other, my shoulders already slumped in defeat. 'There's no way we can prove it was me and not Celina. All she had to do was go to Mrs Bright and say it was her idea. And that's exactly what she's done.'

'But—' Zara stared at me in horror, lost for words for once, as the truth of what I was saying sank in.

'Anyone in the whole school could have claimed they started the good deeds,' I went on. 'Celina just got in first, that's all.'

'We could still go to Mrs Bright,' Henry said desperately.

I shook my head. 'Don't you see? It would just

look like I'm being spiteful. She knows Celina and I don't like each other.'

'But we can't let Celina get away with this!' cried Zara.

'She already has,' I replied. Turning away, I walked towards the classroom.

Celina was holding court in the middle of the room, surrounded by Chloe, Jack, Jyoti and Danielle. Her face was flushed and glowing, and she looked prettier than ever before. I hated her.

'I can't believe you kept it a secret all this time, Cee!' Chloe was saying in a tone of awe. 'You didn't even tell *us*.'

Celina laughed. 'I wanted to surprise you all.'

'Mrs Bright should give you a medal or something,' said Jyoti admiringly.

'Oh, please.' Celina shrugged. 'I don't want anything like that. My dad's going to be really proud of me, and that's what's most important.'

That hurt more than anything.

'I still can't believe it's her,' I overheard Layla Bishop whisper to Kavita Sharma. 'I mean, *Celina*.'

Looking around at the slightly disappointed faces in the classroom, I got the impression that a lot of other people felt the same way.

As Mr Arora came in, I slid into my seat, ignoring the anxious looks Zara and Henry were both giving me.

'Well, Celina.' Mr Arora gazed across the classroom at her. 'You certainly gave us all a surprise.'

Celina giggled modestly. 'Yes, sir.'

'So how did you get the idea?' Mr Arora asked, looking curious.

'Oh, I saw something on the Internet when I was doing my religious-education homework,' Celina replied. 'Did you know that doing secret good deeds is a Buddhist tradition, sir? I thought it sounded fun, so . . .'

It also sounded horribly convincing.

'No, I didn't know.' Mr Arora regarded her thoughtfully. 'Well done, Celina. What a good idea.'

'Mr Arora doesn't believe her,' Zara said as the bell rang out for lessons to begin. 'You should tell him the truth, Sunita.'

'Yes, go on, Sunita,' Henry urged. 'Zara and I will back you up.'

'I told you, there's no point.' My voice was sharp, but I was too drowned in misery to care. 'Just leave it.'

Somehow I managed to drag myself through the rest of the day. I felt sick and exhausted, as if Celina had somehow managed to drain away all my life and energy and colour and take it for herself, like some evil bloodsucker. I didn't want to talk to Zara and Henry. I didn't want to talk to anyone. My

lips curled into a bitter smile as I remembered how I'd been saving up my story to tell Mum on her birthday. I wouldn't be telling her anything now.

It was a relief when I got home that afternoon to find Mrs Brodie babysitting the twins. Mum would be home from work quite soon, but it gave me a little time to try and pull myself together a bit. I couldn't dump all this on her. Not when things had just started getting better.

'Is everything all right, Sunita?' Mrs Brodie asked me bluntly. After sending the twins into the living room to watch TV, she'd turned her calm blue gaze on me. 'You look as if you've had a bad day.'

'I'm fine.' I wasn't fine. I wanted to be five years old again and lie on the carpet kicking my heels in the air and screaming, *It's not fair!*

Mrs Brodie regarded me thoughtfully for several long minutes. 'You know, Sunita,' she said gently, 'there's a saying that what doesn't kill us makes us stronger.'

'I'm tired of being strong,' I blurted out. 'I'm tired of trying to do the right thing all the time.' To my horror, I felt my eyes fill with tears.

The front door opened, banged shut. 'I'm home!' Mum called.

I blinked hard, not looking at Mrs Brodie, and got myself under control before Mum came into

the kitchen. She had the college prospectus in her hand.

'Look what I found in my bag.' She waved the leaflet at me with a grin, and I forced myself to smile back. 'I was reading it in my break. The business management course looks interesting.'

'You should go to the college and speak to the tutors,' I said, making my voice sound normal with a big effort.

But Mum wasn't fooled. 'What's the matter, love?' She dropped the prospectus on the table and stared closely at me.

I shrugged. 'Bad day at school,' I replied, carefully avoiding Mrs Brodie's eyes. It wasn't a lie, was it? It *had* been a bad day at school.

It was followed by a very bad week. Mrs Bright wasted not a moment in getting Celina into the newspapers. There were pictures in both of the local newspapers, as well as articles. I did not read them. I couldn't. But everyone at school was talking about them. Danielle, Chloe and Jyoti, of course, had multiple copies which they flapped under everyone's noses, shrieking with glee as Celina managed to look modest and humble, yet incredibly smug at the same time. One of the headlines was SCHOOL-GIRL TEACHES US ALL A LESSON IN HOW TO BEHAVE. There were pictures of Celina posing with her dad in his mayoral robes. The papers loved that.

She even got a very short, fifteen-second spot at the end of the local news. It was the feel-good slot, the one that is sometimes about animals or children or something uplifting. I was sitting at home, and suddenly there was Celina being interviewed outside the school gates. I couldn't get away from her. Wherever I turned, she was there. Taunting me. Rubbing it in.

The worst thing was, it was affecting me at home. Mum knew something was wrong, but I couldn't tell her. I couldn't be the bad fairy who brought everybody down with depressing news, just when things were slowly getting better. So I just kept saying that I had a lot of homework and the teachers were stressed because Christmas was coming, and left it at that.

But the most terrible day was when Mrs Bright ordered the whole school into the hall during lesson time to hear Celina being interviewed live on local radio. She'd already done a couple of radio interviews at the weekends, which I had carefully avoided, but there was no getting out of this one. If I'd known it was going to happen, I'd have brought some ear plugs to school that day.

I sat between Henry and Zara, trying anything to block Celina out of my head. I hummed. I counted sheep. I did my times tables over and over. Nothing worked. The whole school was

listening in silence, and all I could hear was Celina's smug and saintly voice echoing around the hall and drilling into my head.

I got the idea from the Internet. Doing secret good deeds is an old Buddhist custom . . .

No, I didn't do it because I wanted to get all the credit. I just did it because I wanted to help people . . .

I only told my headteacher, Mrs Bright, it was me, because I thought she ought to know why I was doing it. I never DREAMED anyone else would be interested!

Of course, my dad's really proud of me. He says I'll probably be mayor myself one day!

I was so slumped in misery, I barely noticed Zara get to her feet and go to speak to Mr Arora. A moment later she was back beside me, taking my arm.

'Come on,' she whispered.

I blinked. 'Where?'

'You feel sick,' Zara informed me bluntly, yanking me out of the line.

I glanced at the stage where Mrs Bright was sitting next to the stereo system. She was staring at us, frowning slightly as we left the hall. Celina's sweet and sickly voice floated after us, until Zara let the glass door fall shut.

'Did you tell Mr Arora I was ill?' I asked her, out in the corridor.

'Well, you do feel sick, don't you?' Zara raised

her eyebrows. 'Sick to your stomach at least. I know I do.'

I turned into the nearest cloakroom, sat down on the bench and put my head in my hands.

'But that's it now, isn't it?' I said desperately. 'Everyone's had their story. Things will go back to normal.'

'I suppose.' Zara leaned against the door and regarded me thoughtfully. 'If we can get over the fact that Celina's a big fat liar, and she took something for herself which should have been yours.'

I tried to damp down the burning fire of resentment that leaped up inside me.

'Well, no one else would believe it, would they?' I said. I tried a casual shrug and failed. 'The mayor's daughter is always going to beat the daughter of a thief hands-down.' My voice wobbled.

'Listen, Sunita.' Zara put her hand on my shoulder. 'Forget about Celina. Think about what *you've* done. Look at Henry. He's so much happier. Me too. And that's all down to you. Everything that's happened in this school for the last month or two is down to you.'

I did not reply. I wanted to be proud of what I'd done, but I couldn't. A tiny, revengeful part of me wanted to make Celina pay for what she'd done.

The glass doors of the hall opened, and pupils began flooding out. They were discussing Celina's interview, but no one looked overly impressed. Maybe that was just wishful thinking on my part.

'Have you noticed how lots of the other kids are a bit down?' Zara remarked, reading my mind. 'I don't think they wanted it to be Celina at all.'

'I hope they don't stop doing the good deeds,' I said anxiously. I wanted that to go on, even if Celina did get all the credit.

'People are still doing them, from what I've heard,' replied Zara. 'But who knows? Celina might put them off from now on.'

Henry came out of the hall with the rest of our class.

'Thanks for leaving me behind to listen to that rubbish,' he grumbled. He took one look at my face. 'Sunita, are you all right?' he asked anxiously.

'Fine.' I gave him a shaky smile. 'That's it. It's all over now.'

But it wasn't over.

Things calmed down at school for the rest of the week. Celina was still being praised to the skies by Mrs Bright at every opportunity, but she'd had her fifteen minutes of fame. I hoped that I would get over it and move on.

But somehow I couldn't. At school, Celina's

smug face made me feel sick. At home, I was trying to be normal because I didn't want to tell Mum what had happened. I would, later, when things were less raw, less wounding, and our lives were firmly back on track. At the moment *my* life seemed to have collapsed again. All I could do was wait. Time passes. Things change.

If I hadn't met Celina in Best Burgers that weekend, who knows what might have happened? But I did meet her. Mum had given me permission to go to the pictures on Saturday afternoon with Zara and Henry. Afterwards we went to the burger bar so that I could walk home with Mum after her shift ended. Zara, Henry and I were sitting at a table near the door. I wanted to be as far away from Mum as possible, because every time I glanced up these days, she seemed to be watching me anxiously. I didn't want her to be anxious. I wanted her to be happy.

We were eating fries and discussing the film, when Celina and her dad came in. I stopped eating and pushed the fries away. They suddenly tasted like poison in my mouth.

'Well, well, well,' Zara said, not at all quietly. 'The mayoral family lowering themselves to eat with the common people.'

The burger bar was busy, and people were recognizing both the mayor and Celina. Celina loved

it. She posed just inside the doorway in her fluffy white coat, pretending to read the neon menu above the counter, but in reality lapping up the stares and whispers of the admiring audience. Which, of course, did not include Henry, Zara and me.

'What do you want, sweetheart?' her father asked. 'Have whatever you like.'

Celina frowned prettily and made her selection. Her dad went off to the counter. He didn't go to Mum's till, which I was glad about.

Celina, meanwhile, looked around the room for an empty table. Then she saw us.

'Oh, hello,' she said, staring down her perfect pointy nose in our direction. 'Fancy meeting you here.'

'Yes, fancy,' Zara retorted. 'Goodbye.'

Celina's lip curled into a slight sneer. 'I don't actually *want* to talk to you, you know. I was just being polite.'

'Doing your good deed for the day?' Henry asked, an innocent look on his face.

'Yes, why not?' Celina raised her arched eyebrows. 'Something you lot would know very little about.'

'We know a good deal more than you,' Zara snapped. 'Secret good deeds is something we know a *lot* about.'

Celina did not flinch. But a very, very slight flush of pink tinged the tips of her ears.

'I don't know what you mean,' she said with a shrug. 'But maybe you'll be interested to know that Mrs Bright has told me I'm going to be presented with the Coppergate Cup.'

'The Coppergate Cup?' Zara and Henry repeated simultaneously. 'What's that?'

'It's a silver trophy that's awarded to a pupil for outstanding achievement,' Celina replied loftily. 'There's going to be a special assembly next week, and my mum and dad are invited. And the local newspapers.'

I felt my stomach tying itself in knots.

'Oh, yeah?' Zara looked extremely scornful. 'Who's won this cup before then, and what for?'

Celina looked lost for words for a moment. 'Oh, who cares?' she said impatiently. '*I'm* going to win it, and that's all that matters.'

'Sounds to me like Mrs Bright has just dreamed up this so-called Coppergate Cup to get some more publicity for the school,' Zara guessed. 'That's what I reckon.'

'I'm afraid you're confusing me with someone who gives a damn what you think.' Celina yawned delicately behind her hand. 'Excuse me.'

She joined her father, who was carrying a loaded tray to a table not far off.

'The Coppergate Cup!' Zara said with deep disgust. 'What a load of old nonsense.'

'It should be Sunita who gets it, if anybody does,' Henry added.

I was watching Celina and her father. Little things hit me like darts of deep, stinging pain. The way he put his arm round her shoulders. The way he put salt on her fries, ketchup on her burger. The way he listened to what she was saying. The pride in his eyes.

I missed my dad.

A great wave of emotion shuddered through me. Not misery. This time it was rage. I was angry, furious. Celina had everything. I had almost nothing, and she'd come along and stolen a huge piece of what I did have.

I had tried to do the right thing, tried to be good. I had been so determined that I would show everyone I was a decent person, despite what Dad had done. And where had it got me? Nowhere, that's where.

One way or another, I decided, Celina would have to pay.

CHAPTER 8

The Year 7 corridor was deserted. Everyone was in lessons except me. I had managed to get out of our English literature class by pretending I desperately needed the toilet. I didn't. I had something else in mind.

I walked towards the lockers. I knew which one was Celina's. It had stickers of a boy band she liked on the metal door.

I stopped, looked around, made sure I was alone. Then I reached out and turned the handle.

It was locked. I frowned, knowing that a few weeks ago, when I'd returned her bracelet, Celina's locker had been broken. Maybe Mrs Bright had had it fixed for her golden girl. But that wouldn't stop me.

I took an envelope out of my pocket. I knew the letter inside by heart.

CELINA,
THERE ARE PEOPLE IN THIS SCHOOL WHO

KNOW THAT THE IDEA FOR THE SECRET GOOD DEEDS WASN'T YOURS. SO WHY DON'T YOU JUST OWN UP?

It had taken me a long time to write. My first attempts had been full of bitterness and resentment. But I'd forced myself to be calmer and cooler. If everything came out into the open, I didn't want to weaken my case by being spiteful. I'd written the letter in capitals so that Celina would not recognize my handwriting.

I slid the letter through the gap between the hinges, where the door met the edge of the locker. The envelope was just about slim enough to fit, although one white corner still poked through the gap. I left it there and hurried away as I heard footsteps.

My English class was working on a comprehension exercise in silence, while Mrs Holland sat at the front, marking books. I slipped quietly into the room and into my seat. Zara and Henry immediately looked up. Ten seconds later, each of them passed me a note. They both read: *Are you OK?*

I shrugged and bent my head over my work. The two of them had been watching me closely all morning, never taking their eyes off me when Celina was around. I hadn't told them about the letter. But maybe, now, things would start to happen . . .

'You sure you're all right, Sunita?' Henry asked me anxiously as we went to the lockers to dump our books after morning lessons.

'Stop asking me that!' I snapped. 'I'm sick of it. Read my lips. *Yes, I'm all right*. Why shouldn't I be?'

'Why *should* you be?' Zara retorted. 'Answer me that.'

'You don't look right, Sunita,' said Henry slowly. 'You look – kind of like you're burning up inside.'

'What, like a volcano?' I asked sarcastically. I was staring over Henry's shoulder at Celina. She was standing near her locker, chatting to Danielle. She hadn't opened it yet. 'Do you think I'm going to explode and boil over?'

'Yes, sort of,' Henry replied solemnly, brow furrowed.

'It was Saturday, wasn't it?' Her head on one side, Zara stared closely at me. 'Seeing Celina with her dad.'

'Oh, *please*.' I sighed, trying not to show that I was shaken by Zara's perception. 'That's just a load of nonsense. Now, can we please change the subject?'

'Mrs Bright says the Coppergate Cup's being delivered today,' Celina announced in ringing, bell-like tones. She was supposedly talking to Danielle, but everyone in the crowded corridor

could hear her as clearly as if she had a megaphone. 'I'm going to her office at lunch time, so I can see it.'

'Ha!' Zara said with deep satisfaction. 'I knew that so-called Coppergate Cup didn't exist until now. It's just Mrs Bright's way of getting a bit more publicity for the school.'

I did not reply and pretended to be busy sorting my books. Celina's locker key was in her hand. Now it was in the lock, and she was turning it.

'The special assembly's on Friday,' Celina went on loudly. 'My mum and dad are really looking forward to it. My dad says he's going to buy me a present, anything I want . . .'

'You've *got* everything you want,' Danielle said jealously.

I couldn't breathe as Celina laughed and began rooting in her locker. She emerged a minute or two later, holding a stack of books. No envelope.

'Let's go and meet Clo and Jyoti,' she said.

I watched as Celina and Danielle walked off, chatting and smiling. It was obvious that Celina hadn't seen my letter, or she wouldn't be acting so normally. What had happened to it?

Zara and Henry were still unpacking their bags, so I wandered casually down the corridor. I wondered if the envelope had fallen out before Celina noticed it, and slipped underneath the lockers.

'What are you doing?' Zara enquired.

'Nothing.'

'Kneeling down and staring underneath the lockers is nothing?' Zara raised her eyebrows. 'What's going on?'

'I told you,' I snapped, 'nothing.' I got to my feet and dusted off my ribbed tights. Maybe the letter had fallen inside the locker, and been covered by books. Yes, that was a more likely explanation.

At least I thought so, until I happened to glance at the bin next to the lockers. There wasn't much in it so the tiny pieces of paper were quite noticeable. Even though they were small, I could still make out that a note written in capital letters had been torn up.

With trembling fingers, I picked up a few shreds and pieced them together. It was my note. And there was the envelope underneath, still intact.

I clutched the bits of paper tightly, crumpling them up in my fist. What had I thought would happen? Had I expected Celina to faint dead away in the corridor like a Victorian lady with the vapours? Did I think she would run screaming and crying to Mrs Bright to confess all?

No, she'd done exactly what I ought to have guessed she would do. Ripped up the note and carried on swanning around the school, boasting

about the Coppergate Cup. I felt sick. How could I have been so stupid? I dropped the pieces of paper and watched them float down, back into the bin.

The letter hadn't worked. So now I had to bring out the big guns.

And suddenly, out of the blue, something Zara had said weeks before swam into my mind.

I don't think I've mentioned Mrs Shulman yet. Mrs Shulman is my history teacher, and she is possibly the scariest teacher in the school, although she's shorter than I am. She has black hair, combed back and clipped off her face. Not one hair ever dares to break free. She has piercing brown eyes and a tongue as sharp as a knife.

If there's one thing Mrs Shulman hates, it's people not handing in their homework on time. A few weeks ago, Layla Bishop left an essay at home, and she practically had to be carried out of the classroom and given mouth-to-mouth resuscitation by the time Mrs Shulman had finished with her.

We had work on the Crusades to hand in this afternoon. I knew what I wanted to do, but I didn't know how I was going to do it. However, it all became delightfully simple when, after lunch, Celina left her bag with Chloe while she went to see Mrs Bright and the Coppergate Cup. Chloe was

distracted by one of the Year 9 boys, a very good-looking one, and when she went across the playground to flirt with him, leaving the bags behind, I seized my chance.

'Secret bad deeds,' I murmured to myself as I opened Celina's bag and neatly extracted her history essay. 'They're not as much fun as secret good deeds, but who cares?' And this would be the first of many . . .

I slipped Celina's essay into my bag. I had my back to the rest of the playground so nobody could see me. Then I wandered innocently away. No one challenged me. Chloe was flirting too hard to notice. All I had to do now was sit back in history, the first lesson after lunch, and watch Celina get destroyed by Mrs Shulman.

'Where have you been hiding?' Zara asked, looking disgruntled. She and Henry had just appeared, after I'd given them the slip fifteen minutes earlier.

'You're being very secretive, Sunita,' Henry added gently.

'Am I?' I asked.

'You know you are,' Zara retorted.

'Oh, well, you know me,' I said flippantly. 'I'm good at doing secret things. Oops, no, I forgot. That's Celina, isn't it?'

Zara and Henry were looking at me strangely,

but I didn't care. Celina might be the golden girl now, but her image would be well and truly tarnished by the time I'd finished with her.

No one dared be late for Mrs Shulman's lesson. In the bad old days, when Mr Arora shambled in to take the afternoon register a minute or two before the bell, we'd all be lurking by the door, hopping anxiously from foot to foot, terrified that we'd be delayed.

Today was no different. We were lined up in a neat, orderly and silent line outside the classroom door before we heard Mrs Shulman's stiletto heels clicking down the corridor towards us.

'Inside, please,' she ordered us, sweeping into the room first. She barely reached Jack Browning's shoulder, but he was just as scared of her as the rest of us.

We marched in like a well-drilled troop of soldiers.

'Kavita, collect up the homework essays, please,' Mrs Shulman ordered briskly, cleaning the whiteboard with one flick of her wrist.

Smiling to myself, I took out my own essay and placed it neatly on the table in front of me. I watched Celina open her bag. *Now wait for the fireworks*.

Can you imagine my amazement, my utter horror, as Celina took out her essay and handed

it to Kavita? My eyes almost fell out of my head. *How???*

Mrs Shulman was telling us which page of our textbook to look at. I wasn't listening. I was slowly, painfully, working it out.

I turned to confront Zara and Henry. They were both staring defiantly at me.

'It was you!' I hissed. 'You took Celina's essay out of my bag and put it back!'

'Of course,' Zara retorted. 'You don't think we're going to let you get into trouble just because of Celina, do you?'

'We were watching you from the other side of the playground,' Henry added. 'We saw what you did.'

'It wasn't *me* who would have got into trouble!' I whispered furiously. 'It would have been Celina, if you two hadn't interfered!'

'And were you going to stop there?' Henry enquired.

I was forced to drop my gaze. 'It's none of your business,' I muttered.

'Yes, it is,' Zara said crisply. 'Henry and I are your friends, and we're not going to stand by and watch you get into serious trouble. Let it go, Sunita.'

I opened my mouth to voice an angry reply, until I saw Mrs Shulman bearing down on us, her eyes flashing a warning.

'*If* you don't mind,' she said silkily, 'we would *very* much like to begin the lesson.'

'Sorry,' I mumbled. I bent over my book, ignoring Zara and Henry. I was going to pay Celina back, whatever they said. They couldn't stop me.

But they did stop me. By mutual consent, Zara and Henry had ganged up to keep me under surveillance like a pair of detectives. I couldn't move without one of them being right behind me. That was how it was for the rest of the afternoon.

'You can't keep doing this,' I said sulkily as we sat on the bus after school. They'd made me so mad, it was the first time I'd spoken to them since the history lesson. 'You can't stop me from getting to Celina eventually.'

'You underestimate us,' Zara said with a grin. 'Give it up, Sunita. You can't win.'

'You'd feel happier if you just tried to forget about Celina,' Henry said wistfully. 'Wouldn't you?'

I ignored them and flounced off the bus. Now I'd fallen out with my friends. No one understood. No one cared how I felt, I told myself self-pityingly.

The twins were watching TV and Mum was in the kitchen when I got home. She was arranging some pink lilies in a vase.

'Aren't they lovely?' she said happily. 'Mr Chan gave them to me.'

'That's nice.' I slumped into a chair and dropped my bag on the floor.

'I've been asked to do a few extra shifts over the next few weeks.' Mum turned back to the lilies and began to tweak them into place. 'Mrs Brodie said she'll mind the twins. It means I'll have some extra money for Christmas presents. Is there something you'd like?'

My dad.

'I don't know,' I said. 'I haven't really thought about it.' *And for Celina to get what's coming to her.*

'And I've made an appointment to visit the college,' Mum went on. She sounded so joyful, my heart ached. I wanted to put my head on her shoulder and howl like I did when I was four. But I didn't. 'It's the same day as the twins' Nativity play at school. It's a shame you can't come, Sunita. Debbie's an angel and Davey's a sheep. He's not very happy about it because he wanted to be one of the Wise Men.' She stood the vase of lilies in the middle of the table. 'When are you going to tell me what's wrong?'

'Why do you think there's something wrong?' I asked, playing for time.

'Your face.' Mum came up behind me and slid her arms around me. I leaned back against her. 'You were happy a few weeks ago, and now you're

not. You're sad all the time.' She rested her chin on my hair. 'Is it your dad?'

I hesitated. Celina was the immediate problem, but really everything came back down to Dad, didn't it? If he hadn't stolen the money, we wouldn't have had to move and I wouldn't be at Coppergate and I'd never have met Celina.

'Well,' I mumbled, 'it *is* coming up to Christmas . . .'

'Oh, I know.' Mum's arms tightened around me. 'I'm thinking about it too. Christmas won't be the same without him.'

'He ought to come back.' I felt a tear steal down my cheek, and was glad Mum couldn't see from where she was standing. 'Even if he goes to prison, he ought to come back.'

'I know.'

We were silent then. What more could we say?

It was Thursday, the day before the special assembly. Zara and Henry were still stalking me, so I'd had no chance to do any more secret bad deeds to Celina. I was frustrated, angry and miserable. I knew I could not sit through an assembly dedicated to telling everyone how wonderful Celina was, but I didn't seem to have any choice.

That was until Mr Arora called me to the front

of the class at afternoon registration, and asked me to take a note to Mrs Bright.

'You should just have time before the bell, if you go now,' he said briskly, handing me a sealed envelope. As I leaned over to take it, he spoke to me again, but in a lower voice. 'Are you all right, Sunita? You look a little stressed.'

'I'm fine, sir.' I forced a smile and put a false spring in my step as I left the room. I knew Zara and Henry were watching me, but I ignored them. Now, if Celina's locker was open . . .

It wasn't. I pulled a face, and walked on through the Year 11 corridor and towards Mrs Bright's office. Zara and Henry might think they had me all stitched up, but sometime, somewhere the opportunity would come for me to get my own back on Celina. And whenever that was, I'd be ready . . .

I knew better than to tap on Mrs Bright's door, which was closed. Instead I went into the school office, which was right next door. Mrs Capstick, the secretary, was on the phone, and she gestured at me to wait until she'd finished.

The connecting door into Mrs Bright's office stood ajar, and I couldn't help peeking in. Mrs Bright, her back to me, was working at her computer. A large silver trophy stood on the table next to her.

The Coppergate Cup.

'Thank you, Sunita.' Mrs Capstick finished her call and took the note. 'I'll see that Mrs Bright gets it. Now, you'd better hurry, or you'll be late for lessons.'

I slipped out into the corridor. The bell was ringing for the start of afternoon class, but all I could hear was the sound of my heart roaring in my ears.

I knew, now, how I could pay Celina back for what she had done.

I thought it would be easy to hide out in the school after all the other kids had gone home, but it wasn't. I'd got rid of Zara and Henry by pretending that Mum and the twins were coming to meet me, so that was the reason I wasn't getting the bus today. I knew from something Mr Arora had said that there was a meeting after school, so all the teachers and Mrs Bright were safely tucked away in the staff room. I'd seen Mrs Capstick drive off in her little car, so the school office was empty. But I kept having to dodge the caretakers and the cleaners, who were mopping and polishing their way around the classrooms.

At last, I decided it was safe to make my way to Mrs Bright's office. My plan? I was going to take the Coppergate Cup. Not steal. *Borrow*. If there was

no cup, there could be no assembly, right? That would shut Celina up. I'd hide the cup somewhere in the school, where no one could find it.

I was so scared, though: I could hardly draw breath. If I was caught, everyone would think I was a thief, just like my dad. No one would believe that I was simply going to hide the cup for a while. Therefore I had to make sure I didn't get caught.

Mrs Bright's door was closed as I tiptoed down the corridor towards her office. My palms were sweaty, my heart was racing, my knees were shaking. I reached for the door handle. One minute, and it would all be over—

'So that's what you're up to!'

I jumped so high in the air, I almost left my heart behind me. I whirled round to see Zara and Henry coming towards me from the other end of the corridor.

'What – what are you two doing here?' I gasped, clinging to the door handle because my legs felt too weak to support me.

'We knew you were up to something,' Zara said triumphantly. 'You were a bit too keen to get rid of us.'

'And you've been funny all day,' added Henry. 'You weren't *really* going to take the cup, were you, Sunita?'

'Why not?' I muttered sulkily. 'It would have annoyed Celina no end.'

'And if you'd been caught?' Zara enquired tartly.

I shrugged. 'I'm the daughter of a thief anyway, so what does it matter?'

Zara frowned fiercely. 'That's just rubbish, and you know it—' she began. But stopped when we heard voices.

'Mrs Bright and Mr Arora!' Henry gasped, looking as if he was about to pass out with sheer fright.

'Quick, in here!' Zara flung open the door of the classroom next to the school office and pushed me inside. Henry scuttled in after us, just as Mrs Bright and Mr Arora turned into the corridor. We didn't have time to close the door, so we just hid behind it, hoping they wouldn't see us.

'I'm still not happy about it,' Mr Arora was saying.

'I see that, but I don't quite understand your concerns,' Mrs Bright replied, quite curtly. 'Surely you're pleased that Celina – who's in your class, may I remind you – is being honoured for her remarkable behaviour?'

There was a pause.

'I'd be pleased if I genuinely believed that she was behind the idea of the good deeds, yes,' said Mr Arora.

Zara and Henry turned wide eyes towards me. I pressed my hand against my mouth.

'Oh!' Mrs Bright sounded quite outraged. 'I suppose those pupils in your class have been spreading rumours again.'

Mr Arora pounced. 'Which pupils?'

Mrs Bright sighed irritably. 'Two children in your class came to see me, the day after Celina owned up. Zara Kennedy and Henry Williams. They both told me that Sunita Anand was responsible, not Celina.'

I stared at Zara and Henry. Both had blushed bright red.

'And you didn't believe them?' This time it was Mr Arora who sounded outraged.

'Well – no,' Mrs Bright said, a little awkwardly. 'After all, I only had their word for it.'

'You only had *Celina's* word for it,' Mr Arora replied.

We heard the office door open.

'She *is* the mayor's daughter!' Mrs Bright snapped. They went into the office, still talking, and the door banged shut behind them.

By mutual consent, Zara, Henry and I did not speak until we had tiptoed silently out of the class-room, down the corridor and into the playground. Then I turned to them, trembling all over.

'You *both* went to see Mrs Bright?'

'Well, I did, yes.' Zara looked down at her feet, embarrassed. 'I didn't know Henry had gone too, though.'

'I didn't know *you* had,' Henry muttered. 'Not that it did much good.'

'I can't believe you both did that.' My eyes were full of tears. 'Thank you.'

'Don't cry!' Zara said in alarm, slapping me on the back. 'But honestly, Sunita, Celina's just not worth it. Please, please, *please* just let it go now.'

I suddenly felt enormously exhausted. I knew Mrs Bright *wanted* it to be Celina because she was the acceptable face of the school. I was just the daughter of a thief. But I was so much more than that. I thought I had nothing, but I was wrong. I had Mum and the twins, I had two loyal friends in Zara and Henry, and Mr Arora believed in me. Celina couldn't take all *that* away.

'I will,' I said. 'I promise.'

'And Celina will get what's coming to her one day,' Henry said solemnly. 'You just wait and see.'

None of us knew, then, just how right Henry was. But the very next morning, the day of the special assembly, Zara, Henry and I walked into school straight into an excited buzz of gossip.

'What's going on?' Zara asked Layla Bishop and Kavita Sharma.

'Haven't you heard?' Layla squealed. 'Celina's mum was arrested by the police last night!'

'What!' I almost fainted with shock. 'Why?'

'For drink-driving!' Kavita could hardly speak, she was so excited. 'She was driving home with Celina's dad and the police stopped her and she was over the limit!'

'Well, well, well,' said Zara slowly, shaking her head. 'Maybe that'll stop Celina acting so superior from now on.'

'Oh, you haven't heard the rest of it yet,' Kavita went on, her eyes like saucers. 'Celina was so upset, she disappeared. She's run away from home, and no one knows where she is!'

CHAPTER 9

It was a kind of justice. How could I not think that? And it seemed so typical of Celina that when the chips were down, she would turn and run instead of facing up to things.

Celina's friends had all the inside information, and they were dishing it out to anybody and everybody. I don't think they knew what the word *loyalty* meant. They were practically holding a press conference in one corner of the playground.

'Mr and Mrs Patel had been to dinner at their friends' house,' Danielle was explaining loudly, 'and Celina's mum was driving home, when she got stopped by the police. They breathalysed her, and said they were going to charge her with drink-driving.'

'And when they arrived home and told Cee, she got hysterical and said it would be all over the local newspaper today that the mayor's wife had been arrested, and what about the Coppergate Cup

and the special assembly?' Chloe announced, all in one breath. 'Then she disappeared!'

'And Mrs Bright will have to cancel the assembly,' Jyoti added, determined not to be left out. 'My dad said he thinks the mayor might have to resign.'

'Where *can* Celina be?' Danielle wrung her hands melodramatically. 'Maybe she's living on the streets. Imagine that, on the streets at Christmas.'

'Aren't they enjoying themselves?' Zara remarked as she, Henry and I moved away from the crowd, who were listening, open-mouthed. 'With friends like those, who needs enemies?'

'After all those things Celina said about Sunita and her dad . . .' Henry shook his head. 'It really does serve her right.'

'I know,' I agreed. 'But—'

Zara rounded on me. 'No!' She pointed a finger accusingly at me. 'If you tell me you feel the *slightest* bit sorry for Celina, I really will not be responsible for my actions.'

I took a moment to think about how I did feel. 'Look, you know I don't like Celina and I'm glad the assembly's cancelled and she's not going to get the cup—'

'Good,' Zara interrupted.

'But I *do* know how she's feeling right now.'

'So *are* you sorry for her?' demanded Zara.

'Not very,' I admitted. 'Does that make me a horrible person?'

'Not at all,' Henry said stoutly. We began to move towards the lower-school entrance as the bell rang. 'I wonder where she's gone?'

'As far away as possible, I hope,' Zara retorted. 'But knowing Celina, she's probably found some cushy little place to hole up for a while. I wonder if the Patels have an attic?'

'Excuse me!'

We all turned to see a red-faced Chloe behind us. Jyoti and Danielle stood behind her with folded arms.

'What?' Zara raised an eyebrow.

'That's not even funny!' Chloe snapped resentfully. 'Cee's our friend and she's missing and all you can do is make stupid jokes about it! So why don't you just shut up?'

'I'll do you a deal,' Zara said coolly. 'I'll keep quiet, if you three will.'

'No chance of that,' said Henry.

'Well, really! Some people have no feelings at all!' And Chloe pushed past us and flounced into school, followed by Danielle and Jyoti.

'Poor Chloe,' Zara said with a shrug. 'I haven't seen her this upset since she lost her Peach Passion lipstick.'

The whole school was alive with rumour and

gossip. The teachers didn't say anything about it to us, but it was obvious that they were discussing it just as avidly. When we met up for assembly, Mrs Bright, who looked very subdued and worried, did mention it briefly at the end.

'I am sure that most of you are aware of – er' – she cleared her throat awkwardly – 'the events of yesterday evening. The mayor and his wife have requested me to ask if anyone here has seen Celina Patel since last night, or knows where she is.'

Behind me, Chloe began to fidget and stuck her knee sharply in my back. I winced.

Mrs Bright stared around the hall. No one spoke.

'Thank you,' she said in her clipped voice. 'If any of you do come across any information you think may be helpful, please come to me straight away. That is all.'

'Celina'll be home by lunch time,' Zara predicted confidently. 'You just wait and see.'

But she was wrong. Our source was Chloe, who spent all day texting her mum to find out if Celina had returned or not, and relaying the news to the rest of the school. There was more excitement later that morning, when some Year 11s, who'd gone into town to buy chips for lunch, returned with copies of the local newspaper. Mrs Patel's arrest was all over the front page.

By the end of the day it was official, according

to Chloe's mum, anyway. Celina was still nowhere to be found.

'OK, so I got it wrong,' Zara said grudgingly as we climbed onto the bus that afternoon. 'But I still don't think she's that far away. She's probably hiding out in a really obvious place.'

'Like where?' I asked.

Zara shrugged. 'Oh, I don't know. But we're talking about Celina here. She can't come to school without full make-up on. She's never going to rough it.'

I was thinking about what Zara said as I walked home from the bus stop. It was a chilly autumn evening, and the sky was a dark and threatening slate-grey above me, so instead of taking the long route with Henry, I was cutting through the estate of posh houses. I couldn't wait to get home. It was so cold, there might even be a frost tonight. I shivered. I wouldn't want anybody to spend a night like this out on the streets, not even Celina.

I slowed down as I passed the Patels' house. The lights were on inside. I snuggled deeper into my thick coat, knowing exactly how the mayor and his wife would be feeling. After all, someone I loved had disappeared without a trace too . . .

As I walked by, I glanced across at Chloe's place. The Maynards' house and the extension next to it were in darkness. Then I blinked, re-focused my eyes.

There it was again. Between a tiny gap in the drawn curtains of the annexe, a small, glowing, flickering flame. Like a firefly. Or a candle.

I frowned. I didn't remember ever seeing a light in the Maynards' granny flat before, on my way home. And why would someone be using candles? The other houses in the street didn't seem to have had a power cut. Quickly, without stopping to think too much, I crossed the road and hurried up the Maynards' drive. I turned left towards the annexe and stopped outside the front door. I might be about to make a huge fool of myself . . .

I rang the doorbell.

No one came.

I rang again, this time keeping my finger pressed down on the buzzer. I could hear the bell ringing inside. But still no one came.

I bent down and lifted the letter box. 'Celina!' I called. 'You'd better open this door right now. If you don't, I'm going straight across the road to fetch your mum and dad.'

For a few seconds there was still no reply. Then I heard the sound of bolts being drawn and a key being turned. The door opened a tiny crack, and a hand reached out and dragged me inside.

'What the hell are you doing here?' Celina scowled. We were standing in a small but comfortable living room, which was lit only by two or

three candles. But although it was dim, I could see that Celina looked much less self-assured than I'd ever seen her before. 'I suppose you've come to gloat.' There were tear stains on her cheeks.

'Of course,' I replied briskly. 'What on earth are you playing at, Celina? Your parents are worried sick.'

Celina ignored my questions. 'How did you know I was here?' she demanded. 'I suppose Chloe gave the game away somehow, the idiot.'

'She was behaving a bit strangely at school today,' I admitted. 'But as I was walking past, I saw the candle flame through a gap in the curtains.'

Celina immediately rushed off and began re-arranging all the curtains around the living room, pulling them together more tightly. I watched her in silence.

'What are you going to do now?' Celina asked sullenly, yanking viciously at the last set of curtains. 'I suppose you can't wait to rush across the road and tell my parents where I am.'

'No, I think *you* should be the one to do that,' I snapped. 'After all, you can't stay here for ever.'

'Chloe's gran lives here, and she's gone to Spain for the winter.' Celina stared defiantly at me. 'She won't be back for months.'

'Don't be so selfish,' I said. 'What about your mum and dad? I *will* go and tell them if you don't.'

'I'll run off again if you do.' Celina glared at me. 'My mum's *ruined* my life!'

I wanted to slap her. 'Oh, don't be so melodramatic.'

'She *has*.' Celina's bottom lip trembled. 'It's probably been in the local newspaper today. Everyone at school knows. I'm totally shamed.'

I stared at her without speaking. I had, very suddenly, realized what a big mistake I'd been making ever since I started at Coppergate. I'd seen Celina as someone who had it all. Not only that, but as an evil demon, a parasite, a bloodsucker. Someone who had great power over me. She was none of those things. She was, quite simply, just a spoiled and selfish girl. She was weak and feeble, and now she was frightened. She didn't have any kind of backbone.

Not like me.

'Look, it's just a five-minute wonder,' I said, not bothering to hide the scorn in my voice. 'By next week people'll be talking about something else. Your mum made a mistake. So what? People do. And you're not so perfect yourself.'

Celina looked as outraged as if I *had* slapped her. 'What do you mean?'

'The secret good deeds,' I said. 'Remember those?'

Celina stared me brazenly straight in the eye. 'What about them?'

'It wasn't you who started them.'

'I don't know what you're talking about.' Celina looked slightly shame-faced, but not much. 'Now, if you've said all you have to say, get out.'

She gave me a shove towards the door.

'Not unless you come with me.' I grabbed her arm. 'Or I'm going to tell your parents where you are.'

Celina tried to pull herself free, but I hung on for dear life.

'I'm not going home!' she hissed furiously, doing her best to fight me off. 'I told you, my mum's ruined my life!'

'Oh, stop being such an idiot!' I snapped. 'If you do run off again, where will you go? The streets? You wouldn't last five minutes!'

Glaring ferociously at me, Celina tried to shove me hard with her free hand. I sidestepped and she lunged forward awkwardly. She let out a cry of pain.

'My ankle!' she groaned, sinking to her knees and clutching her foot. 'I've twisted my ankle because of you, you stupid fool!'

'It wasn't my fault—' I began.

What was that smell?

Smoke.

I turned my head towards the other end of the room. One of the candles sat on a table underneath a window. A long orange flame was licking greedily at the hem of the curtains.

CHAPTER 10

'What's that smell?' Celina looked round a second or two later. Her eyes widened and she let out a loud scream. 'Oh, my God! Fire!'

'We have to get out of here!' I reached out to help Celina up. 'Quick, before it gets any worse.'

Celina slapped away my outstretched hand and climbed cautiously to her feet. 'Don't be daft!' she snapped. 'It's not that bad. I can put it out with a bit of water.'

I glanced across the room. Flames were creeping up the curtains, and smoke was beginning to billow towards us.

'We don't have time for that,' I said urgently. 'We have to get out *now*!'

'Nonsense!' Celina began to hobble briskly across the room. 'I'm not going anywhere—'

'Don't you know anything about smoke inhalation?' I grabbed her sweatshirt and hauled her back. 'If you breathe in those toxic gases, it can kill you. Come on, I'll help you outside if your ankle's painful.'

'It's not that bad!' Celina snapped. 'I can walk by myself, thank you!' She tried to pull away from me, but I held onto her. 'Will you let go, you idiot!'

She began lashing out, trying to hit me. I dodged from side to side, but I still wouldn't let go. I began dragging and heaving her towards the door.

'I am *not* going outside!' Celina screamed furiously. 'I don't want my parents to know where I am!'

'So what are you going to do?' I panted, ducking her flailing arms. 'Stay here and get burned to a crisp? Or die of smoke inhalation? It affects your lung tissues, you know.'

'What are you, some kind of part-time fire-fighter?' Celina shrieked.

'We did a project on fire safety at my old school,' I shouted back. 'So I know what I'm talking about.'

Celina didn't look at all impressed. She grabbed a chunk of my hair and pulled it hard, and I yelled out in pain.

'If you'd just let go of me, I could put it out in two seconds!'

'IT'S TOO DANGEROUS!' I roared. Managing to free my hair, I leaned away from Celina and wrenched the front door open. 'You're coming outside with me, whether you like it or not!'

Celina didn't like it. We fought and wrestled our way out of the door, Celina resisting every

inch of the way. As I was manhandling her out onto the porch, the blazing headlights of a car turning onto the drive made us both look round. I took advantage of the distraction to slam the door shut behind us.

'Oh-h-hh!' With an utterly dramatic change of mood, Celina slumped on the doorstep and burst into noisy tears. 'My ankle! My ankle! I can't walk – I think it's broken!'

'What?' I stared at her in stupefaction. 'You said it wasn't that bad!'

The car had stopped, and people were jumping out. It was Chloe and her parents.

'Celina!' gasped Mrs Maynard, who was the double of Chloe, right down to her skinny frame and make-up overkill. 'What's going on?' She stared at me. 'Who are you?'

I ignored her and turned to Mr Maynard. 'Your granny flat's on fire,' I gasped. 'You need to call the fire brigade.'

Chloe's dad stared at me for a minute in open-mouthed amazement. Then he ran over to peer in through the window by the front door. He groaned in disbelief, and then pulled out his mobile phone.

'Celina!' Mrs Maynard was frowning from her to Chloe as the cogs in her brain finally began to turn. 'Have you been hiding out in our annexe?'

Chloe stared sheepishly down at her feet, biting her lip. Celina ignored her.

'Oh!' she wept, clutching her ankle. 'I'm in agony! Someone get me a doctor!'

'Celina!'

We all looked round. The mayor and his wife were racing across the road from the house opposite, calling their daughter's name. Their faces were alive with relief and concern. As they reached Celina and both flung their arms around her, lifting her to her feet, I drew back into the shadows.

'Where have you been, you naughty girl?' Mrs Patel sobbed. She looked very unglamorous in a green towelling tracksuit which had seen better days. 'Don't you know we've been sick with worry?'

'What's happened, John?' The mayor looked round at Chloe's dad, who had just clicked his mobile phone shut.

'Celina was hiding out in our granny flat,' Mr Maynard said with a frown, 'and it looks like she's somehow set the place on fire.'

'Oh, don't be cross with me!' Celina blubbed, collapsing to the ground again. 'I hurt my leg, and it's really painful! I think it could be broken!'

So *that* was her little game, was it? At last I had realized. Pretend to be more seriously hurt than she actually was, and so get out of any responsibility

for almost burning down the Maynards' granny flat. *And* running away and putting her parents through hell. I had to hand it to Celina. I'd never met anyone so thoroughly aware of how to turn every situation to her own advantage.

'You're a very lucky girl, Celina,' Chloe's dad went on. Unexpectedly, he grabbed my arm and pulled me into the glare of the security light above the garage. 'If it hadn't been for this young lady here, you could have died.'

'Yes, she's a heroine!' Mrs Maynard proclaimed loudly. 'We saw the way she got Celina out of the house. She practically had to carry her because Celina couldn't walk.'

'Well done, Sunita,' said Chloe, and she actually gave me an awkward kind of hug. 'You saved Celina's life!'

I stared around at them. 'But I didn't—' I began.

Celina had stopped crying pretty quickly. 'No, she didn't,' she said sharply. But her words were lost in Mrs Patel's hail of sobs as she dashed forward and caught me in a huge embrace.

'Oh, thank you!' she wept. 'You saved my precious baby!'

'You're a very brave girl, Sunita,' the mayor said in a voice choked with emotion. 'My wife and I thank you from the bottom of our hearts. John, whatever damage Celina has caused, we'll pay for it all.'

'Just a minute!' Celina protested in a furious, high-pitched voice. 'Sunita didn't save me!'

'No, I didn't, really I didn't,' I agreed, but my voice was lost amid the loud protests of Chloe and her parents, and the wail of the fire engine heading our way.

'Of course she did!' declared Mrs Maynard. 'We saw everything!'

'I know you and Sunita don't like each other, Cee,' Chloe added earnestly, 'but you ought to say thank-you.'

The look on Celina's face was priceless. She really was trapped. If she told the truth, her parents would find out that she'd been fighting with me because she wanted to stay hidden. And she'd have to let on that her ankle wasn't as bad as she was making out. She wouldn't want her parents to know any of that. But if she didn't tell the truth, then I would get all the credit.

I could see various emotions flit across Celina's face before she made a decision. Looking as if she was sucking a lemon, she stared down at the ground.

'Thank you,' she muttered through her teeth.

'But—' I began again.

Everyone ignored me as the fire engine screeched to a halt at the kerb. As the firemen jumped down and began unfurling the long rubber hose, I could

stand it no longer. Silently I backed away down the drive. No one noticed. I longed with all my heart to be safe at home, and to forget that any of this had ever happened.

'That was the local newspaper on the phone, Sunita.'

Mum came into the living room, where I was snuggled on the sofa under a duvet. There was nothing wrong with me, but Mum seemed to think I needed pampering. 'They wanted to know all about how you rescued Celina. It's going to be front-page news tomorrow.'

I groaned. I wanted to bury myself under the duvet and never come out again.

'It's all right.' Mum sat down on the sofa beside me. 'I told them I didn't want you to be interviewed so I gave them all the information they needed. And I'm afraid they did ask about your dad, but I just said the situation was the same.' She stroked my hair as I dropped my head into my hands. 'It wasn't too bad, Sunita, honestly.'

'That isn't what's bothering me,' I muttered. My face was bright red. Somehow, out of nowhere, I had become a heroine. When I'd got home I hadn't mentioned what had happened to Mum. I wasn't planning to either. However, a phone call from the mayor to see if I was all right after my 'ordeal'

put an end to all that. The Patels and the Maynards had already talked to a reporter from the local newspaper by then, so it was impossible for me to tell them what really happened.

The twins had got very over-excited and raced around the house screaming that I was a heroine, and Mum wanted to know why I hadn't told her, and Mrs Brodie, who was here having a cup of tea, said all sorts of lovely things about me. It was *terrible*. I felt a total fraud. Now Mrs Brodie had gone home and the twins were in bed, and Mum and I were alone for the first time since it all happened. I knew what I had to do.

'Mum,' I said haltingly, 'if I tell you something, will you just listen? Don't say anything till I've finished.'

Mum looked surprised. 'If that's what you want,' she agreed.

I started at the beginning, on my first day at Coppergate, when Mum and the twins had walked me to the bus stop and I'd seen Celina for the first time. I told her about my feud with Celina, and how I'd started the secret good deeds, and the way everybody at school had joined in. About Celina standing up in assembly and taking all the credit and how it had made me feel, how I'd wanted to get my revenge. Then I stared down at the duvet, unable to look Mum in the eye, as I explained how

I'd found Celina by chance and I hadn't saved her life at all, that we'd actually been fighting with each other, and everyone had just got the wrong idea . . .

When I'd stopped speaking, there was silence for a moment. I took a breath and dared to look at Mum for the first time. My tummy twisted and churned as I saw that she had her head in her hands. Was she really disappointed in me?

'Mum?'

Mum took her hands away. She was smiling, even though there were tears in her eyes.

'Sunita Anand!' She reached out and gave me a big hug that almost knocked the breath out of me. 'I just *can't* believe what a truly amazing person you are!'

'I don't feel very amazing,' I muttered, hiding my face in her shoulder. 'Everyone thinks I'm a heroine, and I'm not really.'

'Oh, yes you are.' Mum hugged me tight. 'You got Celina out of danger, even if you had to do it by force.' I felt her body shake as she began to laugh. 'You could have left her behind, after all!'

I couldn't help laughing myself then. 'I did think about it.'

'And after everything else that's happened . . .' Mum shook her head. 'I wish you'd told me all this before, Sunita. But there's one thing I do know,

and that is, you are *definitely* a heroine in every sense of the word.'

I felt a warm glow steal over me.

'And it looks like Celina has got what she deserves,' Mum went on. 'I don't think she'll be bothering you again after this. Do you?'

'No, I don't think so.' I lay back against the sofa cushions, realizing what this meant. I had a chance to start over again at Coppergate, and be accepted for who and what I was. I wouldn't be dragging what Dad had done around with me, like a heavy burden on my back. I would be free to be myself.

'Make way!' Zara called importantly, brushing a couple of Year 7 kids aside without ceremony. 'Clear the decks! Can't you see there's a heroine on her way into school here?'

I thumped her shoulder. 'Stop it, will you? It's bad enough with everyone staring, as it is.'

'Well, they've never seen a heroine before,' Henry chuckled, pretending to dust the door handle before waving me through into the Year 7 corridor. 'Do come in, Your Highness.'

'Please stop,' I wailed. It was like my first day at Coppergate all over again. Everyone's eyes were on me as I walked into the playground on Monday morning. They had all seen Saturday's local

newspaper with its front-page headline: MAYOR'S DAUGHTER RESCUED FROM BLAZE BY SCHOOLGIRL!

'No chance,' Zara declared, her eyes gleaming. 'I've never been friends with a heroine before, and I'm going to milk it for everything I can get.'

I grinned. 'Look, enough of the heroine stuff. You both know what *really* happened . . .'

The newspaper article had brought Zara and Henry scurrying round to see me on Saturday afternoon, hardly able to believe their eyes and ears. Of course, I had told them the real story.

'That just makes you even more of a heroine in my book,' Zara said firmly. 'The temptation to leave Celina behind must have been *enormous*.'

'Sunita!'

I turned to see Chloe Maynard waving and smiling and nodding at me as if she'd been my best friend for ever. Danielle, Jyoti and Jack Browning were with her. They looked slightly sheepish.

'Are you OK?' Chloe chattered brightly, putting her hand on my arm. 'I just wanted to tell you that Cee's *fine*. Her ankle wasn't broken, just a bit of a sprain, but her mum and dad are taking her away on holiday today. She won't be back till the beginning of next term.'

'Too ashamed to show her face,' Zara muttered in my ear.

'You were pretty brave, Sunita,' Danielle said grudgingly.

'Yeah.' Jack cleared his throat. 'Well done.'

'So how are you, Sunita?' Jyoti chimed in. 'You didn't get hurt too, did you?'

'I'm all right, thanks.' I wanted to be cold and stand-offish, but I couldn't. I didn't *care* enough to act that way any more.

Chloe smiled brightly at me. 'We were wondering if you wanted to hang out with us for a bit?' she offered.

I smiled. 'That's really nice of you,' I said with sincerity, 'but I have my friends.' I nodded at Henry and Zara. 'See you around, though.'

'Well!' Zara exhaled loudly as the three of us walked off towards the classroom. 'Did you or did you not just turn down the chance to join the biggest bunch of drama queens in the whole school?'

I shrugged. 'I'm already a heroine,' I said jokingly. 'I don't need any extra drama in my life.'

As Zara, Henry and I walked into class, there was a burst of applause. I blushed, especially when I saw that Mr Arora was already at his desk and was joining in enthusiastically.

'Well done, Sunita,' he said, his dark eyes twinkling. 'It's very uplifting to know that I have a heroine in my class.'

'Thank you, sir,' I mumbled, 'but I wouldn't mind if nobody mentioned the word "heroine" again today.'

'Get used to it,' Mr Arora said with a smile, and sat down to take the register. Later, when everyone else had lined up to go to assembly, he called me over to him.

'The rest of you go on ahead,' he said as I stood by his desk. He waited until the classroom was empty, then turned to me. 'I just wanted to congratulate you on how well you've settled into the school, Sunita,' he began gently. 'I know it hasn't been easy for you. And now you deserve every bit of praise and credit that you get.'

'Sir,' I blurted out, desperate to stop him, 'I think there's something you should know.' I hadn't planned on telling him the real story of Celina and the fire, but it just seemed the right thing to do.

Mr Arora listened in silence. 'Sunita, I agree wholeheartedly with your mum,' he said firmly, when I'd finished. 'You got Celina away from danger. Whether she came willingly or not is irrelevant!'

'Do you think so, sir?' I said, knowing that Celina didn't see things in quite the same way.

'And anyway, isn't there something else you should be proud of too?' Mr Arora raised his

eyebrows at me. 'I'm talking about the secret good deeds, of course.'

I couldn't stop a giveaway smile from lighting up my face. 'How did you know it was me?'

'Well, perhaps I was the only person who noticed that they didn't begin until you arrived at Coppergate!' Mr Arora pointed out. 'And then there was this.'

He opened a drawer in his desk and took out a book. It was *Stop the Screaming and Start Sleeping!*

I stared at him. 'You guessed I left it on your desk?'

'My niece Amber happened to mention that she'd met you outside the classroom door that day,' Mr Arora replied. 'And when I saw the book there, I put two and two together and came up with the answer.' His smile widened. 'Simi is sleeping right through the night now. Thank you, and my wife says the same.'

'You're welcome,' I murmured, blushing again.

'Now, shall we go to assembly?'

Mr Arora led me out of the classroom. The school was dead quiet, and I realized that everyone was already in the hall. I thought assembly must have started, but I was wrong. They were waiting for someone.

Me.

As Mr Arora pushed open the glass door and

beckoned me through, a thunderous round of applause almost knocked me off my feet. I stopped still, catching my breath.

The first thing I saw was Zara and Henry beaming at me from the rows of Year 7 pupils. Next, I was amazed to see my mum and the twins and Mrs Brodie seated on chairs near the stage. They were nodding and laughing and clapping along with everyone else. Mrs Bright was looking down on me from the platform, a welcoming smile on her face. The Coppergate Cup stood on the table next to her, winking silver in the bright lights.

And then I saw her. *Celina*. She was sitting on the stage with the mayor and her mum. She wasn't wearing school uniform, but jeans and a T-shirt. A pair of crutches lay on the floor beside her chair. She looked red with humiliation, and her eyes could not meet mine.

'That's my sister!' Davey yelled as the applause died down into silence.

'She's my sister as well!' Debbie added, poking him fiercely in the ribs.

There was a burst of laughter. Under cover of the noise, I turned to Mr Arora.

'Sir,' I said urgently, 'I don't think I really deserve this—'

Mr Arora put his hand on my shoulder. 'Sunita, if anyone deserves this, it's you. There's a chair

for you next to your mum.' He gave me a gentle push. 'Go and sit down.'

I stumbled down the hall towards Mum and sank into the empty chair. My legs were trembling so much, my knees knocked together like cymbals.

'You didn't know we were coming, did you, Sunita?' Davey beamed at me.

'No, I didn't,' I agreed weakly.

'We only got the phone call this morning,' Mum whispered in my ear. 'But we wouldn't have missed it for anything.'

'Ssh!' Debbie said loudly, putting her finger to her lips. 'Mrs Fright wants to say something.'

'It's Mrs *Bright*, Debbie,' Mum muttered, turning bright red as the whole school sniggered.

Mrs Bright had stepped to the front of the stage. 'I'd like to welcome everyone to a very special assembly,' she said. 'The theme of our assembly today is courage, and I'd like to begin by highlighting the bravery of one of our pupils.'

I bowed my head, heart racing.

'As you all know, Sunita Anand in Year Seven rescued her classmate, Celina Patel, from a house fire last Friday.'

I knew Mrs Bright must be staring at me, so I forced myself to look up.

'After a difficult start, Sunita has settled into our school very well, and we are proud to have her as

a pupil here,' Mrs Bright went on. 'I have discussed this with the mayor and his family' – here I glanced at Celina, who seemed to be sinking lower and lower into her chair – 'and we are all agreed that we would like to present Sunita with the Coppergate Cup in recognition of her bravery.' She smiled down at me. 'Sunita? Would you join us on the stage please, so that the mayor can present the cup to you?'

I felt choked as I stood up, applause ringing out on all sides. Mum was already crying before I even reached the steps up to the platform.

'Very well done, Sunita,' Mrs Bright said warmly, patting me on the shoulder.

Mr Patel stepped forward and shook my hand, giving it a little squeeze.

'I am extremely pleased to be here today,' he said, beaming around at everyone. 'After the fire, my wife and I decided to take Celina away on holiday for a few weeks to help her to recover from her ordeal. But we felt we simply could not leave without attending this very important ceremony.'

Mrs Patel, who seemed to be trembling on the verge of tears, nodded, while Celina tried not to look as if she'd rather be a million miles away.

'It makes me very proud to present the Coppergate Cup to an extremely brave young lady,' the mayor went on, in a voice quite choked

with emotion. I couldn't help glancing again at Celina, who, head bent, was fiddling with her silver bracelet. 'Well done, Sunita.' He handed me the cup, which was surprisingly heavy. 'You're a credit to Coppergate School, my dear.'

I turned as crimson as Celina – for different reasons, obviously. I felt like I should bow or make a speech or something, but I couldn't speak. Everyone was still applauding as I took the cup back to my seat, and I knew then that at last I *belonged* at Coppergate.

The rest of assembly, the readings and the songs, gave me time to calm down and pull myself together. As the rest of the school began to file out of the hall on their way back to class, Mr and Mrs Patel came over to Mum. Celina, who was making a great show of using her crutches, hobbled sulkily along behind them.

'You must be very proud of your daughter, Mrs Anand,' said the mayor heartily, shaking Mum's hand. 'I can't tell you how grateful we are for what she did.'

'I *am* very proud of Sunita,' Mum replied, smiling. She slid her arm round my shoulders. 'For lots of reasons.'

Mrs Patel clutched my arm. 'I still can't bear to think about what might have happened—' She broke off sharply, and gulped several times.

'Mum, I told you,' Celina muttered, still unable to meet my eyes, 'I'm fine.'

'Have a lovely holiday, Celina,' I said, with innocence. 'And I'll see you when you get back.'

Celina gave me one poisonous glare as the Patels said their goodbyes. *You've got no power over me now*, I told her silently. *You're not the one who's going to decide if I'm happy or sad, if I go under or if I survive. That's down to me, and me only.*

At that moment Mrs Bright came over to us. 'Sunita, we have a reporter and a photographer here from the local newspaper,' she said quietly. 'They would like a picture of you with the cup, but I have told them you may not want to be interviewed.' She put a hand on my shoulder. 'It really is up to you, my dear.'

Mum stared anxiously at me. 'Don't do it if you don't want to, Sunita,' she whispered. 'If you're worried that they might ask about your dad . . .'

'They'll have to get past me first,' Mrs Bright said fiercely.

I looked across the empty hall. A man with a camera and a young woman with short blonde hair, notebook in hand, were coming towards us.

'No, it's fine,' I said, and my voice was strong and clear. 'I'd like to talk to them.'

'Sunita?' The woman held out her hand to shake

mine. 'I'm Lisa Carmichael from the *News*. Would you mind if I asked you a few questions?'

I shook my head. 'But there's something I want to say first.' I took a deep breath. 'I want to send a message to my dad.'

Someone, somewhere, would see this message in the newspaper. I was sure of it. And somehow, in some way, Dad would find out about it and hear what I was saying.

'I want to say' – my voice trembled a little, and I took another long breath – 'Dad, we love you. Will you please come home?'

ABOUT THE AUTHOR

Narinder Dhami is one of three sisters – just like Amber, Geena and Jazz! Narinder originally worked as a primary school teacher but always loved writing. After winning a few writing competitions, she was encouraged to take the leap to work on a book full-time. Her first book was accepted by a publisher and she's now been a full-time author for several years. *Bhangra Babes* is Narinder's fifth book for Corgi and is a sequel to the hugely popular books *Bindi Babes* and *Bollywood Babes*.

To relax, Narinder loves reading murder mysteries, watching football and she is learning Italian. Narinder lives in Cambridge with her husband and four cats. For loads more information, an exclusive web-story and lots of fun stuff, visit www.narinderdhami.com.

Also by Narinder Dhami:

BINDI BABES
BOLLYWOOD BABES
BHANGRA BABES

SUNITA'S SECRET

I thought for a minute. 'Imagine doing a secret good deed for one of your friends. Henry here, for instance.'

Zara raised her eyebrows. 'What, if he loses his bracelet, you mean?'

Henry chuckled.

'No, of course not.' I punched Zara lightly on the arm. 'Something else. Say you knew Henry was worrying about his science project, and you wanted to help him out. You could slip some notes secretly into his locker.'

'Or I could just give them to him,' Zara pointed out tartly.

'Sure you could.' I shrugged. 'But this is much more fun. Imagine how pleased Henry would be. And that would make *you* happy too.'

www.narinderdhami.com

The book begins by exploring fundamental mental skills, then it moves to applying them in specific competitive situations. It focuses first on individual skills and then shows how they are used in team interactions. It is written by some of the most experienced rugby sport psychologists and qualified rugby coaches in the world. It will assist in identifying your strengths and weaknesses to allow you to individualize your training. Numerous examples of mental skill applications in training and competition are presented to help you improve your mental preparation and give you a game-winning edge.

Will it make you a champion? That is for you to decide. All rugby players have to train hard, eat well and play smart to succeed. In my experience, mentally prepared athletes are more likely to play well and perform at the elite level; subsequently, their teams usually succeed. Regular mental training is the simple difference between good athletes and great players. The information here can help every rugby player reach for greatness. Good luck!

Wayne Smith, head coach
New Zealand All Blacks, 2000-2001

acknowledgments

We would like to thank Ted Miller, our acquisitions editor, for his immense patience, never-ending perseverance and technical expertise that enabled us to complete this project. We would like to acknowledge the efforts of all our contributors, who stayed on task over the haul and made requested changes without a fuss.

introduction

Psyching Up for Rugby

Bruce D. Hale
University of Maine

David J. Collins
University of Edinburgh

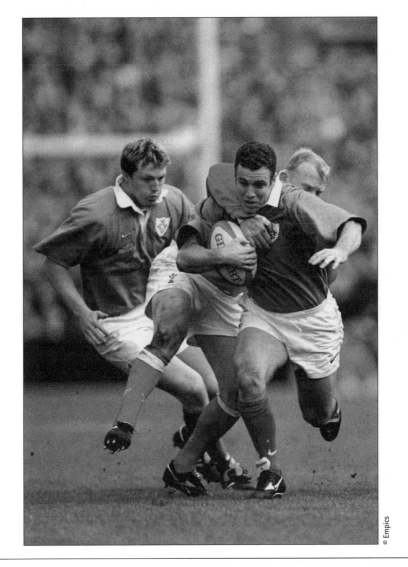

© Empics

What percentage of successful rugby performance is determined by mental preparation for each match? Fifty percent? Twenty percent? Or even one percent? Often your ability to be psyched up, relaxed, positive or focused determines the degree of individual success you experience in any given training session or contest.

Yet many players and coaches still believe there's little they can do to improve the ups and downs of playing performance. Simply put, they're wrong. Every player from youth rugby to national side selection can learn simple psychological skills to improve consistency on the pitch.

In fact, recent research among elite Olympic and professional athletes has revealed that the use of certain mental skills and states have repeatedly been associated with superior performance for the athletes who possess them. These psychological skills and states include goal setting, higher self-confidence, anxiety management, heightened concentration and use of visualization and imagery. These athletes also report having well-developed coping skills for dealing with unforeseen events, regular competitive routines and plans, mental preparation and high levels of motivation and commitment. The best athletes in the world simply can't be wrong. If you want to be the best, you have to train for all aspects of competition.

The State of the Union in Mental Training

Rugby requires expertise in a variety of playing skills. Unlike American football, where players tend to specialize in one or two oft-repeated skills, skillful rugby demands players who can run, pass, tackle and think at every position. It is a free-flowing game where teams of 7, 13 or 15 players have to be able to effectively execute differing techniques at high speed and adjust their play to the event that occurred five seconds earlier! It has now become a thinking player's game that can't always be scripted before a match or practiced exactly as expected. To be successful in rugby, players must be both physically and mentally fit.

In the past, few players were taught mental preparation skills for training and competition. Today, though, professionals practice mental techniques that involve the intricacies of how to make a particular pass or kick. They study and learn the mechanics of a particular break off a scrum; they know more about nutrition for high performance; and they develop warm-up routines and fitness exercises that enable them to excel. It's no longer a case of learn a skill and repeat it. Now it's a case of developing the mental abilities to grow as an athlete. Some elite players have even developed their own brand of useful mental strategies, personally designed for their own psyches. Yet despite this progressive movement towards mental preparation, the majority of today's players have not had systematic training and opportunities to use mental skills to maximize their performance.

Athletes cannot even find this needed knowledge in athletic literature. Most how-to rugby texts deal only with the physical side of the game. They neglect the mental skills that are necessary for success in training and matches. What they fail to communicate, as with many athletic books in general, is that good players must *mentally* prepare for matches, just as they physically and tactically prepare. This book, however, presents both individual and team mental skills that can enable you and your team to achieve maximum playing potential—regardless of the level of ability.

This type of psychological training in rugby is a relatively new area of scientific study for most coaches and athletes. At the elite level, a select few national teams now employ sport psychologists. They work regularly with coaches and athletes to establish year-round mental training programs that seek to enhance the performance of individual players and the team.

But not everyone needs a PhD to be proficient in sport psychology skills. Players and coaches alike can easily adopt these recent training interventions at the grassroots level and incorporate them into daily training and competition strategies. All you need to be is interested enough to read about them, then regularly practice them. As with any other rugby skill, perfect practice leads to perfect performance!

The Nature of Peak Performance in Rugby

All rugby players aspire to play to their potential. But what exactly does that mean? Your potential can be thought of as the following: You execute every game skill to the best of your ability;

you have the fitness and stamina to play energetically and aggressively for 80 minutes; you are mentally skilled to make wise tactical decisions during a match; and you cope with various physical and mental challenges that occur while playing.

After identifying what it means to play to your potential, the next question to ask is, how exactly do you assess your current playing ability? One way to logically assess your physical and mental skills is to use performance profiling, which identifies your strengths and weaknesses as compared with the best players at your position (see chapter 1). After such a diagnosis, you can design training programs that enable you to improve your skills and compete more closely to your actual playing potential.

The best players in the world strive to achieve such a peak performance in international matches. They desire to attain a performance zone in which they are totally absorbed in the match, operating as if they are on automatic pilot and performing flawlessly because they have prepared for every conceivable event during the match. This peak performance zone involves focusing for 80 minutes on rugby tactics, losing self-consciousness to merge into an important cog of the team and having a real sense of control over the outcome of the match. It is an effortless movement where players anticipate opponent's moves and automatically select and execute the proper countermove.

Mental Skills and Qualities Necessary for Elite Rugby Performance

To play at their best, successful rugby players must be physically, technically, tactically, nutritionally and (most important) mentally prepared. You, too, must possess certain mental qualities to get into this zone. These qualities include the ability to achieve optimal arousal levels, a high motivation to excel, an appropriate attentional focus, a high confidence level and an overall positive feeling about performance. In addition, you need to rehearse competitive (and precompetitive) plans to develop positive team interactions. The best players in the world reach their potential by incorporating psychological training into their daily workouts and prematch preparation.

World-class players and coaches have developed repertoires and routines of mental skills that they use daily to reach their rugby goals. Backline players, such as Stephen Larkham of Australia, may verbalize positive self-statements to themselves before making a strong tackle or an offensive break to enhance their self-confidence (see chapter 2). Elite kickers, such as Neil Jenkins of Wales, visualize every successful penalty kick they take at goal to rehearse critical components (see chapter 3). Superior league players, such as Ellery Hanley of England, learned to read defensive cues for tackling coverage by using concentration cues to speed up their decision making and movements (see chapter 4). Scrumhalves, such as Kevin Dalzell of the United States, or hookers, such as Keith Wood of Ireland, may often take a deep breath before putting the ball into the scrum or throwing it into a lineout—all to ensure that their muscles are relaxed and their actions fluid (see chapter 5). Committed coaches, such as Ian McGeechan of Scotland and John Mitchell of the New Zealand All Blacks, and great players such as Michael Lynagh of Australia and Saracens, set out long-term and short-term goals during the preseason to maximize daily effort and maintain motivation over the long season (see chapters 2 and 6).

This text will help you add these powerful routines and team strategies to your playing skills so that you, too, can move your game to a higher level of achievement (see chapters 7 through 9). This book discusses these fundamental mental skills that are necessary to make you a complete player and a better team.

Seven Steps of Success for Skill Learning in Motor and Mental Skills

Mental skills are similar to rugby skills in that they must be logically learned, systematically applied in training that closely approximates match conditions and gradually attempted in competition to be honed to perfection. Few coaches and players have this knowledge base of psychological skills for rugby, and even fewer have the experience of applying them to practice and matches. Without such training, even the elite athletes can make mistakes that limit their play.

Certain elite players have learned by trial and error how to consistently practice and play with mental skills. At any level of competition, it is often the mental game rather than physical abilities that decides the winner. Even beginning players can benefit from effective mental training in practice and competition because they can speed up the learning of new rugby skills or enhance previously learned skills.

One word of caution before you begin to read the skill chapters: None of these skills are magical; they are all skills that must be practiced regularly. This practice routine should be done as a part of your regular training session for at least 15 to 20 minutes a day. These skills won't make you an international overnight, but they do help your game if you commit to practicing them. You must patiently and diligently practice these skills if you want to experience the game benefits.

For example, remember the first time you practiced a pass or a drop kick? Remember how inefficient and unskilled you were? Just like learning to execute a proper dive pass, the process is the same for learning mental skills, such as to set goals, relax or image effectively. Having knowledge about the skills is simply not enough. Effective learning involves (a) *knowledge*, acquiring a conceptual understanding of the components of the skill, (b) *modeling and acquisition*, watching others who demonstrate the skill and working on strategies and techniques for learning the skill and (c) *practice*, creating an opportunity to use the skill in training and competition. With mental skills you can practice anywhere—during weekly physical practices, before competition or at home in the evening. Daily correct practice is the key to changing your undesirable psych-up habits.

The process of skill learning involves seven steps that should be followed sequentially for learning and improvement to occur. The SUCCESS acronym describes each step in the process (see figure 1).

Selection of Components

The selection of components refers to defining the skill in behavioral terms. This first step involves breaking the skill into smaller components. For example, a rugby union skill such as ball retention in the ruck could be broken into body position, the power step into the opposition, continuing the drive onward, turning

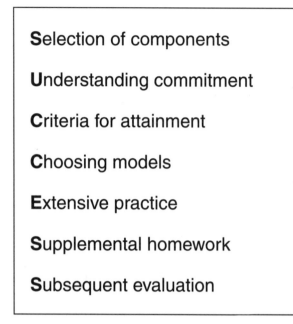

Figure 1   The seven steps to successful physical and mental skills training.

back to your support and placing the ball. A psychological skill such as relaxation training could involve breaking progressive relaxation training into relaxed body position, deep breathing, muscle tension cycle and muscle release cycle.

Once the task is separated into components, you can begin practicing one part at a time. Knowing that you must practice each component in sequence also allows you to continually evaluate your progress on each part for regular motivation and information about your performance.

Understanding Commitment

Understanding commitment means presenting an understandable rationale for learning the skill. Once you know what you need to practice, you need to make sure you understand why it's important to master the skill.

Today's union game is characterized by across-the-field defensive walls that require quick recycling of the ball and quick movement outside. As a player, you know that if you lose the ball in contact, your performance suffers and your team is likely to lose.

From a mental skill standpoint, you are aware that if you have difficulty with prematch anxiety and don't practice a relaxation technique adequately, your overall performance may decline. Once you clearly understand the critical importance of these skills, however, you are more likely to commit yourself to the strenuous practice of the necessary skill.

Criteria for Attainment

Criteria for attainment means to specify a skill level that you wish to attain. Before you begin practice, you need to know your current level of skill execution and what level of correct performance you wish to attain. In other words, you need to specify target behaviors that you wish to achieve. You need to ask yourself the following: What behavior(s)? When? How often and under what conditions? Knowing exactly what you wish to attain beforehand helps to motivate and guide future practice of the skill.

For example, if you retain the ball only 40 percent of the time in your rucks, you may wish to attain a success level of 80 percent in your stated goal (see chapter 7 for team goals). If your heart rate is typically 150 beats per minute before kickoff and you feel uptight, you may wish to learn to relax and drop your heart rate to 120 before kickoff.

Choosing Models

For your body to internalize the proper execution of a skill, you have to develop an idea of what good execution and bad execution look and feel like. Therefore, when you choose your models, select ones that demonstrate both effective and ineffective use of the skill. Afterwards, you can develop a standard of achievement that provides consistent feedback so that you know whether you have achieved optimal performance or not.

Once you know the difference between good and bad performance and once you develop a standard, you can focus your effort on reaching your actual performance goal. For example, with a rucking retention skill, you would need to watch other players perform the skill; you would need to get a visual and verbal lesson from the coach; or you would need to watch videotapes that depict rucking skills. For a relaxation skill, you may need to have a sport psychologist or coach take you through a relaxation procedure to feel the difference between being anxious and being relaxed before you play. You may even be able to watch other players use prematch strategies to get themselves to an optimal level of arousal.

Extensive Practice

Extensive practice requires opportunities to practice many matchlike situations. Practice the various components of your physical or mental skill to improve your execution. Use what is called the *part–whole method of practice*, where you practice each component separately and then put them together to practice the skill in the proper sequence and timing. Coaches and other players can give you feedback concerning your execution of the components and total skill. For mental skills, the coach or sport psychologist can give you feedback about thoughts or technique.

Once you have a basic grasp of the skill, try it before or during basic drills or scrimmages. For rucking retention, this might involve trying the skill first at half speed during a learning drill, then gradually performing it at full speed with more aggressive opposition. For a relaxation skill, first learn the long version of the skill by listening to a tape or working with a sport psychologist daily outside of practice. Gradually reduce the time it takes to relax until you can reduce tension in minutes with several tension-release cycles or just deep breathing and positive suggestions.

Supplemental Homework

For supplemental homework (transfer of training), generalize the skill to a variety of game situations and critical moments in competition by practicing it in simulated game situations of increasing difficulty. Gradually incorporate the skill into low-key competitions until you feel comfortable with your ability to execute it properly in important matches. Try it before or during a variety of game situations so that you can perform it in any difficult match situation. In other words, practice the way you expect to play. When you structure practices to mirror actual competitive situations, you feel as if you have been there before.

You need to rehearse physical and mental skills exactly as you expect to perform them in competition. Visualize it in your mind before executing it with your body. Because your goal is peak performance, you want to be able to make automatic physical adjustments or mental decisions in different competitive environments without much conscious effort. For example, for rucking retention, you can practice maintaining possession when no support is nearby, when you need to produce a quick ball on a diving tackle or when rolling back over to place a ball when you're facing the opposing team.

For a relaxation skill, this practice might involve doing a relaxation session the night or morning before a contest or a short deep-breathing session on the bus or during warm-ups. Incorporating deep breathing and relaxing thoughts for instantaneous relaxation before a lineout throw, scrum in rugby league, penalty play or penalty kick would be typical uses of relaxation skill in the height of competition. Many mental skills can be practiced in other important life events and become life skills. For example, once you learn to relax before matches, you can use that skill to relax before giving a speech or going for an interview.

Subsequent Evaluation

Finally, subsequent evaluation means devising drills or testing opportunities to make sure you have achieved the attainment level you set. Have someone collect statistical data or rate you on form or technique execution in practice and matches. Make sure they rate all the components of the skill you have identified. You can keep these training records as part of your performance profile (see chapter 1).

Constant evaluation of your strengths and weaknesses and your feedback showing improvement keeps you motivated towards attaining elite status in the execution of critical rugby skills. Many coaches today keep accurate statistics on individual and team tactical skills such as ball retention that are based on detailed match analysis of game videotapes. Some athletes have devised behavioral ratings and self-report inventories that evaluate how well they were mentally prepared during a match. For a problem such as anxiety management, there are validated scales available in many sport psychology self-help books or from sport psychologists that can help you to keep track of your progress towards being optimally aroused during a match.

Applying Skills to Your Training Needs and Position Requirements

This book is designed to allow you to personalize your mental training program to meet your individual, positional or team needs. Chapter 1 begins with an opportunity for you to assess the mental and physical strengths and weaknesses that are critical to elite players in your rugby position. Once you identify which mental skills need improvement, you can begin planning your goals (chapter 2) and setting up a regular training session in and out of practice to perfect your psychological skills.

Choose the mental skills that you have pinpointed as being weakest, then follow the training exercises to practice those skills in training for competition. Remember, just reading about a skill does not improve your skill level and mental preparation. You must be committed to regular practice of your mental game if you want your physical game to improve.

Once you have perfected the fundamental mental skills presented in part I and incorporated them into your game plan, you can move on to the team skills covered in part II. Coaches should be able to formulate comprehensive, year-round mental training plans for their teams. Examples of team skills and game situations are included in each chapter to allow you regular practice of these critical skills. Part II pulls together basic mental skills into a team format that can help coaches and athletes plan training sessions to enhance team skills such as decision making, creating team goals, formulating attacking and defensive strategies and designing team mental preparation and competitive routines. Opportunities for homework are provided in each chapter to allow your team to practice under competitive conditions. Our goal is to make your team more mentally tough.

Mental Skills As Life Skills

For most of us, rugby is only a small part of our lives, and some day in the future, active participation ceases for all of us. Rugby, though, can teach many participants skills that can help them be more effective in other life situations during and after their playing days. Basic psychological skills can be used across situations to become basic life skills, which any individual needs to survive. They are usually categorized as either *interpersonal skills,* skills used to communicate with a variety of individuals in different situations, or *intrapersonal skills,* commonly called psychological skills, which include both mental and physical skills.

In rugby, you can learn both kinds of skills and effectively transfer their use to nonsport situations. For example, if a rugby player has learned to effectively relax before and during matches, he could use the same skill to help him relax during other stressful life events, such as job interviews, social situations or examinations. Another primary goal in life could be developing personal competence: the ability to do life planning, to be self-reliant and to seek the resources of others. Personal competence can easily be taught through the use of rugby, then transferred over to daily life. These skills, however, must be carefully and systematically practiced in nonsport situations if they are to enhance performance in life.

For instance, when certain factors are present, these life skills can be generalized from rugby settings to nonsport settings. First the individual has to believe that the skills are important in other situations. Second he must be aware of which life skills he has mastered. Third he has to know how the life skills were learned. Next he must believe that he can effectively apply the life skills in other situations, then he must be open to trying these skills in other nonsport situations. This step usually requires the individual to seek out other people to help in these new situations. Finally, he must develop the ability to adjust to initial failures using the skills in nonsport settings and be willing to keep applying them. Athletes can be guided through this transfer process by coaches or sport psychologists without undue effort.

In sport, most sport psychologists emphasize the teaching and implementation of a small group of performance-enhancing life skills. These typically are arousal management, attention control, decision making, goal setting, positive self-talk, stress management, time management and others. These very skills, all described in this book, can be used in a number of life areas such as work planning, self-exploration and self-appraisal.

Other life skills learned in sport are often neglected by athletes (see figure 2). These skills can be taught for transfer from rugby using the same skill-learning steps described earlier. Coaches and sport psychologists can provide knowledge, experience, feedback and support to players to help ensure that these skills transfer quickly and efficiently.

Performance under pressure

Organization

Meeting challenges

Handling both success and failure

Acceptance of others' values and beliefs

Flexibility and success

Patience

Risk taking

Commitment and perseverance

Knowing how to win and how to lose

Working with people you don't necessarily like

Respect for others

Self-control

Pushing yourself to the limit

Recognizing limitations

Competing without hatred

Accepting responsibility for behavior

Dedication

Accepting feedback and criticism as part of learning

Self-evaluation

Wise decision making

Setting and attaining goals

Communication with others

Ability to learn

Working within the system

Self-motivation

Figure 2 Life skills learned through rugby and other sports.

In the following chapters, you will have the opportunity to learn new life skills that will bring you improved performance in rugby if you make them a regular part of your training program. You can enhance your individual physical and mental skills and increase your team skills, all to improve overall team performance and lead to success on the pitch. If you use the skills systematically, your game will improve and you might become an international that we will watch and read about some day. At the very least, you will improve your game skills and enhance the quality of your life in other areas. Enjoy the journey!

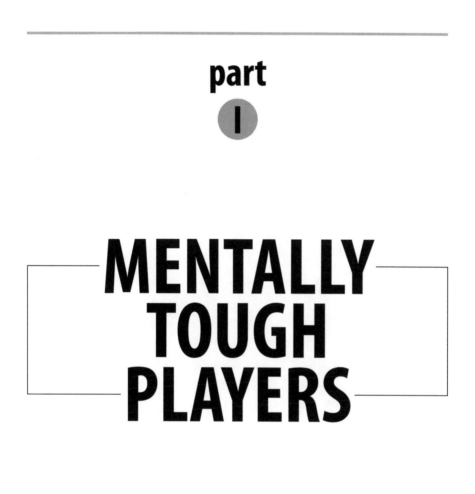

part

I

MENTALLY TOUGH PLAYERS

chapter

1

The Mental Profile

Angela Abbott
University of Edinburgh

Bob Easson
Scottish Institute of Sport

© Tony Demin/International Stock

From sports to art, practitioners and sport psychologists are interested in finding effective means of identifying talented individuals. Optimal methods of identifying and developing excellence facilitate the appropriate distribution of limited resources. Conversely, inappropriate methods develop players who are unable to excel, or those with potential might be overlooked.

Talent Identification

The most common method of identifying talented players in rugby has been through the observation of performances on the field. Such methods are intuitively appealing because the ultimate aim for players must be to outperform their opponents. Consider talented Fraser, a hard-running and physically mature youngster whom no one can stop from scoring once he has the ball. Because of his 'obvious talent', much time is invested into his development; however, as Fraser gets older and his opposition become more physically equal, his runs become increasingly contained. Whereas strength and size were initially the key factors influencing his performance, other skills such as passing and decision making are now critical. Because he did not originally need these skills to succeed, Fraser may not have developed them.

Procedures that base identification on performance alone fail to consider a person's potential to develop necessary skills, which may lead to the demotivation of many late-maturing athletes. Current selection of talent in rugby is based on individual performance levels with little emphasis placed on psychological factors of excellence. Our aim in this chapter is to offer a better way, based on the identification and promotion of those factors—namely, mental skills—that best discriminate between the elites and the almost-but-not-quites.

Recently, coaches and managers have given more consideration to identifying the characteristics that typify successful rugby players. A substantial amount of scientific research has shown that certain physical measurements correlate highly with success in top champions. For example, gymnasts tend to be short to medium in height, whereas rowers tend to be tall and have long limbs.

These distinctive profiles have led to the development of talent identification programs that compare a youngster's physical profile with the gold medal profile. For example, Australia's Talent Search program profiles youngsters on body dimensions, such as arm span and height, to consider their physical suitability for different sports. Scotland has recently piloted an adapted version of Talent Search that also considers physique—for example, weight is positively correlated with rugby but negatively correlated with gymnastics.

Although less systematic, player position in school and club rugby is also often based on physique. For instance, because tall players have an advantage when playing in the second row, the club coach or schoolteacher often places the tallest youngster into this position. Although height is an advantage to a second-row player, a person may not remain tall into adulthood, which reveals a basic flaw in this system.

As an example, big Owen, who at the age of 13 stands 5 feet 11 inches, appears to be the perfect lock forward. Consequently, a lot of time is invested into his development because of his 'obvious potential'. Six years later, however, Owen is of average height relative to his peers and is therefore too small to be an elite, second-row player.

Even if it were possible to accurately predict adult physical values such as height, we still could not effectively identify rugby talent because other skills and variables, such as mental skills, influence performance. Rugby is a complex and rapidly changing environment generated by current strategy and capabilities. It is a sport too intricate for any baseline formula that attempts to predict success.

Psychological Skill Identification

Although it is clearly beneficial for a centre to be strong and powerful, performance is also mediated by contextual factors, such as the ability to make the right decision when under pressure in a game. The ability to optimally perform under pressure is partly influenced by the psychological strategies the athlete uses.

Scientific research also illustrates that consistent performance at the world-class level depends on the psychological strategies an athlete employs. A highly consistent international player, such as Lawrence Dallaglio (England and Lions back row), will have a psychological approach to training and competition that is overtly different than the one used by the local club player. These psychological factors must be recognized within any talent identification program.

The major aim of any talent identification model must be to identify the young players that are able to develop the level of skills required to be successful senior rugby players. Research has shown that players who successfully compete at the senior level are mainly distinguishable through their psychological approach to training. These findings emphasize the importance of determination, initiative and concentration in the learning of skills.

Any talent identification program must consider not only determinants of performance but also the psychological characteristics that support skill learning and development. Psychological skills, such as decision making, concentration, confidence and coping with anxiety, must be assessed in all players early in their playing careers so that programming can be developed to enhance their weaker mental skills. The following profiling strategy helps coaches and players better assess players' rugby qualities and identify the areas that are most critical to improvement.

Individual Profiling of Rugby Skills

To develop into top-class rugby players, younger players (and coaches) must learn how to evaluate their *own* strengths and weaknesses to provide the information and motivation necessary to create effective training plans to enhance rugby skills. They need to be able to identify the qualities that are necessary for excellence in performance in their rugby position. These qualities may include physical skills, technical knowledge, attitudes or psychological skills that are crucial in achieving elite performance.

Once players can accurately assess their own qualities in comparison with the best international players in their positions, the coaches and athletes can plan individual and team training sessions that increase the skills of the developing players. In addition, this regular self-assessment generates motivation in players, and they will therefore work harder on their own or in a team setting to achieve their playing potential.

The following section covers a self-assessment technique called *performance profiling* (Butler 1996) that enables coaches or players to identify playing strengths and weaknesses, which forms the basis of talent identification. This easy, step-by-step procedure is an efficient means of self-assessment that leads directly into individual and team goal-setting strategies (see chapter 2).

Step 1: Identify the Qualities of Elite Players

This step can be done by a single player, with or without a coach, or with a coach leading a group of players. A simple form can be developed for keeping track of the information. Table 1.1 is a sample profile form using Gavin Hastings, former Scottish captain and fullback, as the hypothetical example.

Think of the ideal player at your position using a 15-player team. What are the ideal characteristics of this elite rugby player? Brainstorm all the physical skills, technical abilities and knowledge, attitudes (emotions and dispositions), psychological skills and other qualities that make this person an ideal player. List as many as you can think of under the appropriate heading.

Look at table 1.1 and notice the list of qualities under each category that we have generated for Gavin Hastings in his fullback position. Think of an ideal player in your position and list all the necessary qualities for elite play in each category. The ideal player at your position may have these qualities or others.

Step 2: Rate the Importance of the Qualities

Not every position in rugby has the same skill requirements. Forwards may need to be better ruckers or maulers than fullbacks, who need to be able to kick and run with passing flair. You need to rate the relative value and importance (I) of each skill listed for your positional example. On a scale of 1 (not important at all) to 10 (of crucial importance), rate how important each of the selected qualities are to the ideal positional player you have selected. Most of your ratings will be the higher numbers with some possible 10s (if they are critical skills for elite performance). For example, as a thinking, offensive-minded fullback, Gavin Hastings might need a 10 in goal kicking, tackling or leadership (as captain), but he may only need a 9 in aggression or communication.

TABLE 1.1   SAMPLE PLAYER PROFILE: GAVIN HASTINGS, FORMER SCOTTISH CAPTAIN AND FULLBACK

Quality	Importance (I)	Self-Assessment (SA)	10 (ideal) −SA	Discrepancy (10 − SA) × I
Physical skills				
Passing	10	7	3	30
Goal kicking	10	5	5	50
Running attack	10	7	3	30
Tackling	10	8	2	20
Catching high ball	10	7	3	30
Rucking	9	6	4	36
Speed	10	7	3	30
Strength	9	5	5	45
Fitness	10	7	3	30
Technical knowledge				
Counterattacking	10	6	4	40
Positional kicking	10	7	3	30
Defending kicks	10	7	3	30
Attitudes				
Leadership	10	7	3	30
Aggression	9	6	4	36
Psychological Skills				
Concentration	10	6	4	40
Confidence	10	5	5	50
Being relaxed	10	7	3	30
Using imagery	10	7	3	30
Self-motivated	10	7	3	30
Risk-taking	10	6	4	40
Other				
Communication	9	5	5	45

Scale: 1 (lowest) to 10 (highest)
Ideal score is 10

Step 3: Assess Personal Qualities

The next step involves self-assessment **(SA)** of your current ability on each of the ideal qualities. In the example, our hypothetical player is an 8 in tackling and a 7 in leadership but only a 5 in goal kicking. Rate yourself on each quality in your list. Use feedback from coaches, videotape assessments and comparisons with your teammates as the basis for your self-assessment. Think about your best and worst performances to judge the range of your abilities.

Step 4: Subtract the Self-Assessment Rating From the Ideal Value

Subtract each self-assessment rating from 10, the ideal score. Do the subtraction for each quality listed. In the example in table 1.1, the goal kicking difference score is 5 and the tackling score is 2.

Step 5: Identify the Highest Discrepancy Scores

This step also involves some simple calculations. Take the difference score (10 – SA) and multiply it by the importance rating **(I)**. In the example, the discrepancy for goal kicking is 50 (5 × 10). For tackling, it is 20 (2 × 10).

Circle the four highest discrepancy ratings on the list. These are the four qualities or skills that you need to improve immediately to become a better player. In the example in table 1.1, the four highest are goal kicking (50), confidence (50), strength (45) and communication (45). The athlete's weakest qualities influence the athlete's four prominent individual goals (see chapter 2) to be adopted for preseason. With this information, the coach and athlete can plan individual and team drills to help the athlete increase skill in these qualities. Additional practice time could be set aside to enhance these abilities. If you have more than four weak qualities because of tied scores, pick the four you want to improve immediately. The additional areas can be included once you improve the primary choices.

Coaches are also an important part of the assessment process. Once the ideal qualities for the position have been listed, coaches can also assess individual players on each quality. After doing the computations and obtaining the highest discrepancy ratings in skill, coaches and players can compare the coach's assessment with the individual player's assessment. This comparison offers coaches and players a great opportunity to discuss perceived strengths and weaknesses in the player's skills. They can come to agreement on the skills that need additional, immediate training, and players can add these skills to their goal-setting forms.

An individual rugby profiling form can also function as a continual feedback and motivational tool for both players and coaches. Players can undertake new self-assessment ratings on each quality once a month and evaluate their potential improvement on each quality, especially in critical playing skills. Evidence of improved ratings can lead to enhanced playing confidence and subsequent improved performance. This regular evaluation process can also allow the coach and player to rationally discuss the player's growth and pinpoint areas that need additional training to meet the player's playing potential.

Profiling Mental Skills for Rugby

To improve overall rugby performance, a player or coach might use the profiling technique just to enhance psychological preparedness for matches. Instead of listing all the different ideal qualities that go into overall performance, you may want to assess only psychological qualities to track skill before, during and after play.

This process is identical to identifying other qualities that make up the ideal positional player who is your role model. Looking at the example in table 1.1, you can see that eight mental qualities have been listed under attitudes and psychological skills—leadership, aggression, concentration, confidence, being relaxed, using imagery, self-motivated, and risk taking. Think of other attitudes and psychological qualities that might also be included.

In our example, it is clear that this player has a major problem with self-confidence. In fact, this player approaches each match with trepidation, thinking negative thoughts that lead to a dismal performance before the match even starts. Our hypothetical player should plan individual goal-setting steps, focusing on positive self-talk and confidence-building mental skills in practice as possible interventions.

It is also clear that this player's concentration wanders during the match and correlates with poor performance. A coach would notice that after making a mistake in the game, this player gets angry and loses focus for several minutes, where repeated mistakes occur. Strategies for improving concentration (see chapter 4) would be useful in learning how to incorporate refocusing mental skills into the game.

Let's presume this player is also the team's goal kicker. Visualization, therefore, is a required skill for good play (see chapter 3). This player tends to be a streak goal kicker who is inconsistent in his mental approach and mechanics. Incorporating imagery scripts into training and game routines would help him become a dependable kicker.

Finally, his risk-taking score suggests that he plays a conservative, defensive-minded fullback position with little attacking movements. In fact, he is afraid to come into the line on the burst for fear of dropping the ball and having it kicked through for an easy try. He also is afraid to try running counterattacks; he just kicks every time he receives the ball deep in a defensive position. Strategies to develop attacking moves in training and build confidence that his teammates are supporting his runs would help make this player more aggressive.

Profiling can be used on a match-by-match basis for each position by listing every playing behavior that is critical to top performance. Each player can be rated repeatedly on each of the listed behaviors after each match to map progress during the season and identify behaviors that require additional training. Individual goal-setting plans should emphasize further practice in identified behaviors. Coaching feedback, reinforcement and selection can be based on prior performance, assessed by a weekly behavior profile for all team members.

Profiling can also be used to identify team strengths and weaknesses and to help create effective training sessions to improve team performance (see chapter 6). Team profiles can help in the creation of overall team goals in the preseason, aid in the development of team strategies for various opponents, help coaches regularly assess match performance post hoc and build overall team confidence as improvement occurs.

Talent identification is an initial step that coaches can take to identify potential qualities of excellence. The regular use of this profiling technique can help both coach and athlete develop the potential that has been identified. Training to improve weaknesses is the key to success.

Characteristics of Excellence in Training

Selection procedures must identify and encourage those psychological characteristics that allow for excellence (see figure 1.1). These characteristics can be observed and evaluated through behavior in training and competition. Although the characteristics of excellence are relevant to all sports, certain behaviors are specific to rugby.

Commitment

Quality practice

Goal setting

Imagery

Planning at all levels

Distraction control strategies

Perceptions of pressure

Performance evaluation

Figure 1.1   Eight characteristics of excellence.

For example, imagery has been highlighted as important to successful development and performance in many sports, but a high jumper and a rugby player use imagery in different ways. When watching an elite high jumper, we likely will see that athlete mentally rehearsing a successful clearance before each attempt. In rugby, however, it is less common to see players carrying out similar mental rehearsals. Nevertheless, top players do report using imagery during skill preparation. Neil Jenkins, now the scoring leader in rugby, employs a consistent mental rehearsal process before taking a penalty:

> I have always been meticulous in the time between placing the ball and taking the kick. Going for goal is probably the loneliest task on a rugby field and you have to get your preparation right. Any interruption to your routine clouds concentration and you start to

be filled with doubts. Noise has never been a problem for me—I just imagine I am back on Cae Fardre [the field near his house where he spent hours practicing]—and I have been fortunate in that I have not had many wretched days when nothing goes right. (Jenkins and Rees 1998, 137)

Similar preparation procedures are possible before performing any set move in rugby, such as the scrum or throw-in. Additionally, as part of their pregame strategy, successful players also prepare themselves for open play by mentally rehearsing different scenarios they may confront. For example, Scotland's standoff Duncan Hodge says, "On the morning of a game I will read game situations in my head before they happen."

Within Training

The young player who is most likely to have the potential to acquire skills and progress within rugby must be committed to producing quality practice. High-quality practice is based on personal goals that have been established as a result of evaluating performance after competition and training. According to Chris Patterson, Scotland's fullback, "I have secret goals that I want to achieve, and if I get close to achieving them, then I set them higher."

The committed player works on these personal goals within both individual and team training sessions. For example, it is common to see goal kickers perfecting their skill outside of the group session. Chris Patterson used to stay on the pitch practicing his goal kicking until he made a perfect 10 out of 10, even if it meant being late for class! It is less common, though, to see a player individually perfecting skills such as tackling, body position and ball handling. Consider the developing player who rarely, if ever, practices his evasive running outside of normal training time.

This commitment to practicing outside of team sessions should be expected from a player who has the potential to develop into a world-class player. To successfully transfer skills to the game situation, players must practice these skills under pressure. Facilitating this environment is the coach's responsibility.

The quality of training is also enhanced if the player establishes images of ideal plays within the game. For example, Michael Jones, the great All Black flanker, used to visualize different game situations and the lines of defensive coverage he would run. He would change his tactics according to the opposition's various strategies.

Within Competition

The successful player learns to effectively transfer the skills developed during training into the game situation. This transfer requires careful planning and preparation—including both simple tasks such as kit preparation and more complex physical and mental preparation—in the days and hours leading up to a match. Carrying out a personalized prematch preparation routine minimizes the possibility of being distracted before and during the game and may include psychological strategies such as positive self-talk and imagery.

A good example comes from a New Zealand provincial player who set goals for himself before every game. These goals were based on match statistics, such as tackle counts, forced turnovers, ball retention and effective backrow moves, and were recorded in his training logbook. He felt more confident, motivated and psyched up before each game, without being over-psyched.

Establishing clear, effective, competitive process goals is another characteristic of successful and potentially successful players. A commitment to these personal goals ensures that focus and concentration are maintained throughout the match. For example, in the Scottish victory over France in the 1995 Five Nations Tournament, France went ahead with just five minutes to go. In this situation, not only did Gavin Hastings remain committed to winning the match, but he also encouraged the same level of commitment from all the team: "We have come too far to give up. At least let us give ourselves a chance of scoring." Hastings went on to score the winning try under the posts just seconds before the final whistle.

Successful game players also establish their roles within the actual game. For example, the open side wing forward knows her role during a preplanned move from a set scrum. Additionally, the player has considered every possible scenario—the move going successfully, the move being adapted from the alignment of the defense or the move breaking down.

To ensure continued progress, players should regularly evaluate their match performances as a follow-up to initial performance profiling. Effective evaluation allows a player to identify areas that need to be improved, which leads to appropriate mental rehearsal and physical practice between matches. For example, the scrumhalf who suddenly identifies accuracy and speed of passing from the base of a ruck as new weaknesses should undertake extra work with the stand-off before or after a team session.

Additionally, the scrumhalf may use elements of team training to achieve this personal goal. This practice could occur during rucking drills with the forwards or during a team run. An effective postmatch evaluation allows personal goals to be targeted within both individual and team training, and it maximizes the opportunity for continued development.

Facilitating Player Development of Characteristics of Excellence

Some psychological characteristics can influence both the development and performance of a player. Once coaches are aware of these characteristics and how they can be used to facilitate training and performance, they can then promote their development. Three key processes can be used to assist the development of these characteristics of excellence.

Plan and Publish Training Sessions in Advance

For the U21 Scottish Rugby Union team, session plans are published on a white board before the start of a training session. Plans include details about the elements to be practiced and the reasons for the practice. An important part of this process is the clarification of individual roles in different phases of play (see the example presented in figure 1.2). This process helps players focus because they are aware of what is required before beginning the training session and will therefore optimize the use of practice time.

Additionally, this process enables players to identify how they can work towards their own personal goals within a team training session. For example, a player who has identified the need to improve accuracy of passing in a game situation may want to practice passing when fatigued and under time pressure as part of attack and phase play during defense drills.

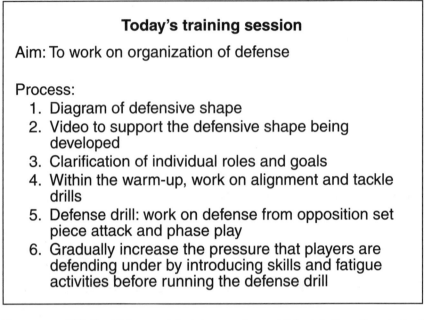

Today's training session

Aim: To work on organization of defense

Process:
1. Diagram of defensive shape
2. Video to support the defensive shape being developed
3. Clarification of individual roles and goals
4. Within the warm-up, work on alignment and tackle drills
5. Defense drill: work on defense from opposition set piece attack and phase play
6. Gradually increase the pressure that players are defending under by introducing skills and fatigue activities before running the defense drill

Figure 1.2   U21 Scottish squad training session published before the start of training.

Evaluate Training and Competition

In the U21 Scottish Rugby Union team, the structure, content and overall effectiveness of training sessions and competitive performances are analyzed in relation to individual and team goals. Players are encouraged to establish clear goals that follow the principles outlined in chapter 2. Goals should be specific, measurable, achievable, realistic, time-framed, enjoyable and rewarded. A range of methods is employed to optimize the evaluation process.

For example, individual video footage is produced for each player and is evaluated by the coach and player in one-to-one sessions. The video may be used to reinforce what was meant by verbal feedback, such as "That was a good leg drive", maximizing the possibility of the player's consistently reproducing this performance. Additionally, slowed video sequences may identify reasons for a skill breaking down, which were not apparent in real time. As a result of these evaluation sessions, players are able to continually monitor progress towards goals and adjust and identify new goals where appropriate.

At all times, the importance of evaluating training and competitive performances independent of outcome is stressed. Consider a player who delivers most of his passes within a game situation, but when under pressure, his passing accuracy decreases so that the receiving player has to check his forward run. If this player is unable to distinguish between outcome and process, he will not identify passing under pressure as an area that needs improvement.

Once individual goals and roles are clarified, athletes are encouraged to work on these both in team sessions and independently. A hooker who identifies as a goal the increased accuracy of lineout throw could practice throwing the ball against the post or with one of the lineout jumpers away from team training. To maximize progress towards achieving goals, the hooker should also practice lineout throws within the team-training situation.

© Empics/Kenny Rogers

Training under gamelike conditions prepares players for aggressive, high-pressure game situations.

Once a skill has been mastered, it is essential that the player be given the opportunity to test the skill in a gamelike situation when fatigued or when under time or space pressure. It is common to see players practice goal kicking and lineout throwing, but it is less common to see players carry out the same skills when fatigued, as they would be required to do towards the end of a match. Because goals should be established as a result of performance evaluation, they often focus on skills that have broken down under pressure situations. If training situations do not adequately re-create this pressure, players may continue to display the same problems during matches.

Provide Quality Feedback When Appropriate

To help athletes evaluate their competitive and training performances optimally, the coach regularly provides feedback to the U21 Scottish Rugby Union squad. Feedback is constructive when it is based on the process that the athlete needs to change or consolidate ("Good tackle. Your leg drive drove them backwards.") as opposed to being outcome-oriented ("Well done!"). The use of process feedback provides players with the opportunity to develop clear strategies for improvement.

For example, a player who is deselected because of poor tackling is able to develop strategies for improving his tackle technique if process feedback is provided, such as, "You need to get lower in the tackle; you need to bend your knees more." To facilitate the feedback process, individual performances can be videotaped and evaluated by the coach and player in one-to-one sessions that emphasize process goals.

Training systems that include performance evaluation, goal setting, commitment, planning and performing under pressure facilitate the development of psychological characteristics of excellence that optimize player potential. It is important to recognize, however, that all the psychological characteristics of excellence are interrelated. For example, if individual performance evaluation is inaccurate, a player may set inappropriate goals, which can result in a training focus that is not optimal for development. Consequently, training systems should be developed that recognize and encourage the development of the full range of psychological characteristics of excellence.

Summary

The process of skill learning and performance is largely influenced by psychological factors. An inadequate focus on the psychological characteristics of excellence currently exists within talent identification and development programs. Profiling strategies and proper training programs can facilitate both skill development and performance in rugby. Coaches and players need to distinguish between performance levels and true potential. A major role of the coach is to create skill training systems that promote the development of psychological characteristics of excellence through team mental skills for competition.

chapter

Motivation and Confidence

Ken Hodge
University of Otago
New Zealand

Alex McKenzie
Highlanders Super 12 Rugby Team
New Zealand

© Empics

Our job in this chapter is not to motivate you or give you confidence. The only person who can do that is you. To be effective and meaningful, motivation and confidence must come from within yourself. Motivation provided by someone else—your coach, captain or the opposition—is unlikely to be as meaningful or have a lasting effect.

It would be hard to imagine that All Black Andrew Mehrtens' motivation to play a test match comes solely from the All Black captain or All Black coach John Mitchell. Likewise, Wallaby George Gregan did not need team captain John Eales or head coach Rod McQueen to motivate him to train for, or to play in, the World Cup. Too often captains and coaches portray themselves as being able to motivate others, but in reality it just isn't possible to motivate someone unless that person wants to achieve the dreams and goals the motivator is providing.

These motivators only provide an inspirational sparkplug. Although inspiration is useful, it is little more than a spark that can start a fire only when the right fuel is available. That fuel must come from within—the dreams and goals that matter to you. Motivation is your own internal combustion engine.

We often refer to the motivational-inspirational approach to motivation as gas station psychology: Someone fills your fuel tank and blows up your tires, but the benefit is short lived because the fuel tank will soon be empty and the tires will eventually go flat. In the long run, you must be able to supply your *own* fuel for effective motivation. In other words, you are responsible for your own motivation. Therefore, you should take time to identify not only a long-term dream goal but also a set of short-term goals that provide you with a sense of purpose—ones that excite you and ones that satisfy you once you have achieved them.

Motivation is important for success in rugby. You need motivation for the season, fitness training, skill training and practice, and for pregame psych-up. The reality of motivation is that it is both *wanting to* and *having to* do something. For rugby, you obviously must identify rugby goals that you want to achieve, but you also need to be realistic enough to realize that you will need to motivate yourself during those times when you feel you *have* to do something—your training motivation, that is. In other words, when you reach the stage of *having to* do something rather then *wanting to* do it, you will need strong self-discipline to tough it out.

Motivation is a skill that you need to have truly mastered before you can expect to gain consistently high levels of confidence and performance. Goal setting is the starting point for such motivation and confidence for peak performance. If your goals are clear in your mind, then peak performance becomes more achievable on a regular basis, and your motivation remains high. When you begin to see regular improvement in your performance as a result of achieving your goals, your confidence also becomes high.

You can benefit from setting goals in several areas, such as the following:

- Physical goals: Improve endurance, power, strength, flexibility, weight, diet, sleep patterns.
- Technical goals: Keep shoulders relaxed when sprinting; pass accurately with left and right hands; follow through when goal kicking.
- Tactical goals: Improve ability to read opposition backline defensive patterns and quickly identify the best point of attack; improve ability to read the right lines to run in support.
- Psychological goals: Practice mental preparation techniques; practice imagery of performance in pressure situations; cope with criticism from coach.

Steady progression through short-term goals allows you to reach long-term goals. First choose the areas in your peak performance profile (see chapter 1) that need improvement, then set long-term goals for each area. Next set short-term subgoals for each long-term goal. Each key area should have its own staircase of subgoals (see figures 2.1 and 2.2).

Before you go any further, ask yourself some key questions about your rugby performance: Where am I now? Where do I want to be in a week, next month, in six months, two years? What are my strengths and weaknesses? Your mental profile can help you answer these questions (see chapter 1). You may also want to talk to your coach about the results of your mental profile, and on the basis of that discussion, set long-term and short-term goals for each area.

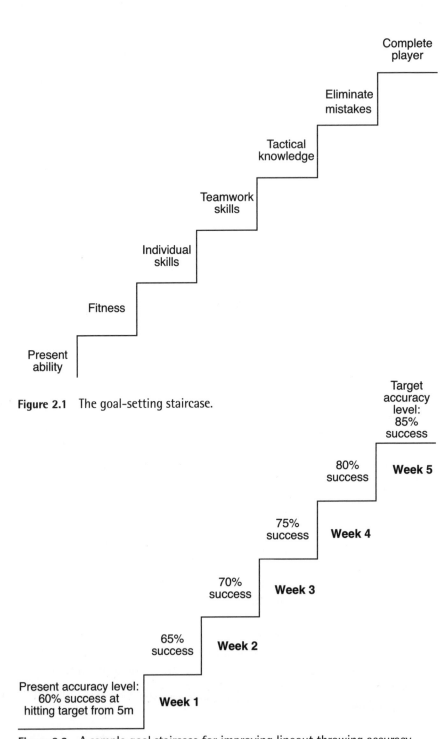

Figure 2.1 The goal-setting staircase.

Figure 2.2 A sample goal staircase for improving lineout throwing accuracy.

Self-Motivation Through Goal Setting

Goal setting definitely works. I've found that if you write down your goals and what you've done, see what you've achieved, you feel your goals are more attainable.

—Zinzan Brooke, All Black 1987–1997

A goal is an aim, objective, target or dream. More specifically, it is a particular standard of performance that you wish to attain within a specified time limit. When deciding on which areas to set goals, you need to select the skills that you believe to be the most important or those most in need of improvement.

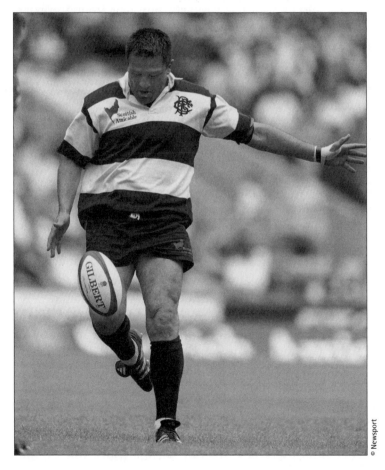

Elite players like Zinzan Brooke set goals to increase their motivation to improve.

Achieving your goals shows that you are making improvements in both your training and playing performances. As a result, it helps in maintaining your motivation as well as optimal levels of confidence and activation. The process of goal setting also helps you identify your strengths and weaknesses, which is the ideal starting point for designing your training plan. Goals help you to determine what is important in your training by providing direction and forcing you to prioritize your needs. Goal setting is like a road map: The long-term goal is the destination while the short-term goals are pit stops along the way; the goal achievement strategies (the training methods) are the choice of route.

A long-term goal is a dream goal. It is the ultimate objective and provides direction for your training plan. Achieving short-term goals allows you to regularly monitor your improvement. It enables you to reward yourself for the effort and hard work you have put in while reaching the goal, and it can increase your intensity in training and competition.

We took this season just step-by-step, establishing short-term goals as we went along.

—*Todd Blackadder, All Black 1996–1998, 2000 and Canterbury captain 1996–2001, talking about the 1997 Canterbury team that won the NPC 1st Division in New Zealand*

Set positive rather than negative goals. For example, instead of saying to yourself, "I will not lose my temper every time a refereeing decision goes against me", say, "Whenever a refereeing decision goes against me, I will stay calm and focused on my game". That is, instead of focusing on "I won't fail", focus on "I will succeed". Focus on what you want to do, not what you don't want to do!

Performance Goals Versus Outcome Goals

In top-level rugby, there is enormous pressure from many sources (especially the media) to set outcome goals, such as winning against a particular opponent. Outcome goals are similar to long-term goals in that they provide motivation for ultimate objectives in the future. The dream of becoming a champion or winning an event can keep you going during tedious training sessions. Outcome goals can be set initally as your "wannabe" goals. However, outcome goals are not within your control, and they can become a major source of anxiety, which in turn can lead to poor performance. Therefore, rather than only setting outcome goals, you should also set performance goals that are based on the peak performance skills identified in your profile.

Performance goals (some sport psychologists also call them *process goals*) differ from outcome goals in that they focus on mastering specific tasks or skills, such as passing, kicking, tackling, scrums, lineouts and second phase ball retention. Playing well and being successful depends on correct execution of these basic tasks and skills. If you perform these tasks well, then you are more likely to achieve the outcome you are seeking. As a consequence, performance goals encourage you to focus on how to win rather than winning itself.

All I want to do is play well and enjoy it. The only thing I can do is to play as well as I can. The rest of it is out of my control.

—*Todd Blackadder, All Black Captain 2000*

With performance goals, the criteria for success is being better than you were last time at a specified task—such as lineout throws with a higher percentage of accuracy, correctly executed back-row moves, passes or kicks for touch. Rather than determine success by comparing yourself with your opponent, you compare yourself with your own previous performance. You have more control over these goals, and they are an honest and demanding way to measure success.

For example, an outcome goal might not provide a complete evaluation if you win easily against a poor opponent, but a performance goal gives a better picture of how well you did that day. Conversely, if you lose against a good opponent, performance goals still provide you with information about improvements and the effectiveness of your training. Outcome goals are just too crude and imprecise to be used as a helpful measure of success.

Goal Setting With SMARTS

Good goals share certain characteristics that you can remember with the acronym SMARTS. Good goals are **s**pecific, **m**easurable, **a**djustable, **r**ealistic, **t**ime-referenced and include **s**trategies to achieve the goals.

First set goals that are *specific* to the skill you are trying to improve. These need to be difficult to reach yet still realistic. They should be performance goals, stated positively, and they should involve a detailed description of the goal so that it can be measured. For example, a specific goal might be "The team will cross the advantage line for 90 percent of backrow moves attempted during the game against Pirates on May 18."

Set goals that can be *measured* in numerical terms. If you state your goals in readily measured, numerical terms, it then makes it simple to determine whether you have achieved the specific behavior that you are focusing on. For example, you could set goals in terms of the following:

- Percentage of tackles made
- Number of rucks hit in good body position
- Number of successful backrow moves executed
- Percentage of times that specific moves made the advantage line or tackle line
- Exact times for specific sprint or endurance distances
- Amount of weight lifted for specific weight room exercises

Specific, measurable goals make it easy to determine whether you have achieved them. Writing a detailed description of each goal enables you to see whether you've attained it or not.

An example of a poor goal is "I want to improve my upper-body strength to help me burst through tackles in midfield when coming into the backline from fullback." This goal can be improved to this simple, measurable one: "Before the start of the season, I will be able to perform 3 × 8 reps of 100 kilograms (220 pounds) in bench press and 3 × 8 reps of 70 kilograms (154 pounds) in shoulder press." Another example of a poor goal is "I want to be more accurate in my throwing in to the lineout." To make this goal specific and measurable, change it to "I will be able to hit a 30-centimetre-square (11.7-inch), 4-metre-high (13-foot) target 9 times out of 10 at distances of 5 metres, 7 metres and 10 metres (16, 22 and 32 feet)."

Goals and goal schedules may need to be *adjusted* as you work through them. You may find that the goals you initially select are too hard or too easy or that sickness or injury has interfered with progress towards your goal. You must be prepared to modify your goals, strategies and target dates as required. For example, if one of your training goals was to be able to bench-press 120 kilograms (264 pounds) eight times by a certain date, and you suffered a shoulder injury that prevented you from weight training for four weeks, then it may be necessary to adjust your goal from 120 kilograms to 90 or 100 kilograms (198 or 220 pounds) by that date.

To set *realistic* goals, know your own limitations, but aim to stretch your capabilities by challenging yourself. Remember, goals must be out of reach but not out of sight! Make sure they are achievable if you put the work in. For example, a goal of successfully making 100 percent of attempted kicks during a game is an unrealistic goal. It would be better if this player were to get an indication of his actual successful kicking percentage and then set a goal to increase this percentage by a realistic amount. Using a more realistic percentage would also mean that he still had the opportunity to reach his goal even if he missed a kick during a game.

There's no point in having an unachievable vision, but it has to be big enough to be a little frightening, big enough so that there is a fear it won't be achieved.

—*David Kirk, All Black 1983–1987*

If you set goals that are too difficult to achieve, then you are virtually guaranteeing failure rather than increasing your chances of success. Let's return to our example of demanding a 100 percent success rate. If you set a goal of making 100 percent of your tackles in your next game, and you miss a tackle in the first five minutes, you have already failed. However, if your goal were to make 70 percent of your attempted tackles (based on last week's tackling rate of 60 percent), then you still have a chance of achieving your goal when you miss a tackle. Your performance can even improve overall. So instead of feeling like a failure in the first five minutes of a game because you missed out on achieving your unrealistic goal, you are likely to be more motivated to make the next tackle attempt a successful one because you still have a chance.

To make goals *time-referenced,* set target dates for achieving them. When you fail to set a target date, you can always use the excuse that you're still working towards achieving the goal. But when you have a target date, the closer to that date you find yourself, the more effort you are likely to put into making sure you achieve the goal. For example, a player who sets the goal of attaining a certain level of fitness by next season should specify exactly when that might be, as the season extends over a period of months. If the athlete specifies that she will achieve her fitness goal by April 1, then by February and March she is more likely to put in the extra work to achieve her goal within the time frame.

After you have set your goals, you must outline a specific *strategy* to achieve them. For example, a goal strategy for improving passing accuracy for a scrumhalf might be "I will practice an extra 30 passes from the ground (as if from a scrum or ruck) and 30 passes from the air (as if from a lineout or maul) after training on Tuesdays and Thursdays. I will also ask for an hour of one-on-one coaching each week from an expert passing coach."

Tracking and Evaluation

To help you think through the key questions in setting goals, fill out the goal achievement worksheet (figure 2.3). This tool will help you think through your goals in depth as you strive to express yourself in writing. Make sure the goals you set follow the SMARTS guidelines and that you include a specific strategy to achieve each goal. Record these in your training logbook.

Through Otago University rugby I became more convinced of the need . . . to set high standards and be ruthless and proud in executing them.

—*Josh Kronfeld, All Black 1995–2000; Leicester RFC, 2001-present*

You must be committed to pursuing your goal strategies. Writing a contract with yourself can be helpful (see figure 2.3). Support from significant people in your life—teammates, parents, partner, friends, boss—is also vital. Make sure you inform these people about your goals and goal strategies; they can't support you if they don't know what you are trying to achieve and why it matters to you. After following these guidelines, you should

Goal Achievement Worksheet

Name _____ Playing position _____ Date / /

Specific statement of *performance* goal:

_____
_____
_____
_____

Target date for goal achievement / /

What is the payoff from achieving my goal? _____

_____
_____
_____

What are the consequences of *not* achieving my goal? _____

_____
_____
_____

What is my *strategy* to achieve my goal? _____

_____
_____

Possible obstacles in the way of achieving my goal: _____

_____
_____

Strategies for *overcoming* these obstacles: _____

_____
_____

What *excuses* do I usually make? _____

_____
_____
_____

Is is worth the time, effort, and commitment to reach my goal? Yes _____ No _____
Why? _____

_____
_____
_____

Goal-Setting Contract

I _____ hereby do solemnly swear that I am committed
to achieving the goal that I have set out above. I will achieve this goal by following
the goal achievement strategy that I have developed and outlined above. I am fully
committed to this goal and my achievement strategy.

Signed _____ Date _____

Witness _____ Date _____

Figure 2.3 A goal achievement worksheet and contract.

insert your performance goals and goal strategies into a training plan.

To ensure your commitment to your goals and your training plan, you should do the following:

- Write out your long-term and short-term goals.
- Write down at least one achievement strategy for each short-term goal.
- Write down target dates. Deadlines provide an added incentive and help plan the time frame of your goal achievement.
- Record goal evaluation procedures to use with your training log.

Do remind yourself of your goals by maintaining a training log. Other options include making a wall poster as a visual reminder of your goals, target dates and overall training plan. You may want to write your goals on index cards and display them on your mirror or the fridge door. Ask yourself, "What did I do today to become a better player?" Remember, monitoring is *your* job, and self-monitoring and self-evaluation lead to self-motivation. Be organized, responsible, committed and assertive. Have the attitude that if it's to be, it's up to me!

Monitor your progress regularly. Not only should you monitor your progress, but you should check your target dates as well. They may need to be adjusted according to how well you are progressing towards your goals. Your training methods and strategies should also be reviewed periodically for their effectiveness. Remember, setting goals does not in itself improve performance. The hard work and training detailed in the strategy are what enable you to achieve your goals and subsequently improve performance. When you achieve your short-term goals, make sure you reward yourself with a special treat or compliment yourself with positive self-talk (see p. 54). Success breeds more success and more confidence!

If all you care about is winning, if you aren't enjoying the play, if the relief of not losing is the biggest emotional gain, then the best of it is lost.

—David Kirk, All Black 1983–1987

Self-Confidence

One of the key ingredients of successful performance in rugby is belief in your own ability. Players who are self-confident think and act differently than players who lack confidence. If we think of some great performances by union players such as Christian Cullen of New Zealand, Stephen Larkham or George Gregan of Australia, Waisake Serevi of Fiji, Olivier Magné of France or league players such as Gary Connolly of Ireland, Martin Offiah of England or Lee Briers of Wales, we can probably come up with some common characteristics of their play that would cause us to label them as confident players. Each is willing to take risks, and they seldom hesitate or make unforced errors (if they do, they are still willing to try a particular move again, even if it didn't work the first time). Bottom line, they are all confident players.

So what is self-confidence? In relation to rugby performance, it can be defined as a player's belief in his ability to execute the various skills required for playing the game. Essentially, it is whether or not you expect to be successful when you attempt a particular skill. If you expect to succeed, then you are confident.

The saying "If you think you can, or if you think you can't, you're probably right" tells us that belief in one's own ability is often a self-fulfilling prophecy. If we expect something to happen, then that expectation helps to cause it to happen, provided we have the necessary skills and the willingness to do it. For example, if you have high confidence in your ability to tackle an opposing player who is running straight at you, then you are more likely to be successful than you would be if your confidence is low. In fact, the positive relationship between self-confidence and success is one of the most consistent findings in research relating to peak performance in sport.

So what are some of the other benefits of having a high degree of self-confidence? To begin with, self-confident players are more likely to remain calm in pressure situations because they believe in their ability to succeed. This is one of the reasons good team captains are always self-confident players; they must remain calm when there is three minutes to go, their team is two points behind, stuck deep in their own 22, and they have to decide how to get them down to the other end of the field and score.

In these situations, the ability to remain focused on the task is crucial, and confident players are able to do this. They will also be less likely to give up, and in fact they will increase their efforts to overcome the pressure situation because they believe that they can do it. So not only does confidence affect emotions such as anxiety, it can also have an effect on concentration, motivation and decision making.

In addition, players and teams that play with confidence are more likely to adopt positive tactics that involve calculated risk taking. Teams that lack confidence often play "not to lose", which is reflected in their conservative and sometimes tentative approach to the game. Players who lack confidence are afraid to make mistakes. They don't take risks, and they generally wait for things to happen rather than taking control over their own performance. They wait for the opposition to do something rather than making something happen themselves. The goals that the players set for themselves are likely to be less challenging than if their confidence were high, and as a consequence, they are less likely to develop to their full potential. Confident players, on the other hand, set challenging goals and are likely to exert a great deal of effort in attaining these goals. Their confidence helps them to realize their potential.

Increased confidence can cause you to attempt more skills, and it can have a positive effect on emotions, concentration levels, amount of effort, the types of game plans that you adopt and the types of goals that you set. Being confident, though, doesn't mean that you won't have any negative thoughts or self-doubts. It is normal to be nervous or apprehensive about an upcoming game; however, confident players still believe in their ability to perform well. Despite any self-doubts that they may have, they have learned to counter those negative thoughts.

While high self-confidence is vital to the success of a rugby player, this characteristic alone will not guarantee success. You need to have a realistic level of confidence that matches your ability level. When your confidence exceeds your ability, you are likely to fail and will continue to fail until your confidence is eventually brought down to a more realistic level. The danger here is that while you are overconfident, not only does your own performance suffer, but your team's performance suffers as well. Despite your ability to perform well, if you lack confidence, you are also likely to fail because your lack of confidence results in self-doubts, excessive nervousness, tentative performances, a lack of concentration and conservative decision making that restricts you from performing to your potential.

Sources of Information

How can you attain self-confidence? Is it something that can be developed and improved? The best way to answer these questions is to look at the various sources of information that players use to assess their confidence levels and the various strategies that coaches use to boost a player's confidence. There are four major sources of information that influence your level of self-confidence:

1. Whether or not you have performed successfully in the past—performance accomplishments

2. Watching other players perform the skill—vicarious experiences

3. Having other people tell you that you can perform a skill successfully—verbal persuasion

4. How you interpret your physical and emotional feelings about an upcoming performance—activation level

Performance Accomplishments

Not surprisingly, the most powerful source of information about whether you believe you are capable of performing a particular skill is whether you have successfully performed that skill in the past. For example, if you are a hooker who can accurately throw to the back of the lineout most of the time, you are likely to feel confident that you can do it again in subsequent lineouts. On the other hand, if you have been consistently called for not throwing straight, then your confidence for performing this skill is not likely to be very high.

Coaches should create situations that allow players to experience success. The best place to do this is not during a game but in practice, and the philosophy is simple: Success increases confidence and leads to further success. Good practice structure is essential to this process. Drills and techniques can be organized, taught, demonstrated and practiced to ensure that players experience success. These experiences can be reinforced through encouragement from coaches and other players. Players are more likely to feel confident about performing a certain move or a certain skill during a game if they can successfully perform it in practice.

One of the most effective ways of building self-confidence using performance accomplishments is to set and successfully attain specific, measurable, achievable and realistic goals within a specific period of time. If your stated goals follow the guidelines for effective goal setting (see pp. 41-44) and you are committed to doing the work to achieve them, then improved confidence and performance is an inevitable consequence, whether it is for practices, games, or individual or team training sessions.

Vicarious Experiences (Modelling)

The second source of information from which you can gain confidence is watching someone else successfully perform a particular skill during a game or a practice. In doing so, you can then gain some measure of confidence that you can do it as well. Of course, this method of gaining confidence is nowhere near as powerful as knowing that you've successfully performed the skill in the past, but it does work, especially if the player who demonstrated the skill is similar to you.

For example, let's assume that you are a #8 who is 1.85 metres tall, weighs 90 kilograms and plays club rugby. You are more likely to believe that you can break the advantage line from the base of the scrum if you watch someone of a similar stature to you do it in a club game than if you watch a video replay of Ron Cribb—1.93 metres tall, 108 kilograms—doing it for the All Blacks against South Africa in a test match. The message here is that the most powerful effect on the observer's self-confidence occurs when the model is similar to them in terms of playing position, age, height, weight, gender and ability level.

Verbal Persuasion

Coaches can be a great source of confidence if the player trusts the coach's credibility. If a trusted coach tells a player that he is capable of breaking the advantage line from the base of the scrum, then he will gain some measure of confidence from the coach's words. In this case, the coach has used verbal persuasion to instill some confidence in the player about his ability to perform this particular skill. Again, this kind of strategy is not nearly as powerful as actually performing the skill successfully, but it will have an influence if the player believes that the coach knows what he is talking about.

Activation Levels

A player's perception of her level of physical and emotional activation can directly influence her confidence levels. Most players would admit to feeling apprehensive or nervous before a game, and this is a normal reaction. In fact, many players consider nervousness a desirable feeling because it means that they care about the game, want to do well and are probably more focused on their performance. However, these feelings are sometimes accompanied by tension in the muscles, a churning feeling in the stomach, sweaty palms or wanting to urinate more than usual during the buildup to a game. If a player perceives these physical feelings as an indication of fear, it can negatively affect her confidence levels, but a player who perceives these feelings as an indication that she is excited or psyched up for the game can increase her self-confidence. She sees it as a sign that she is ready to perform and eager to get out there.

So how can you change perception of these feelings from fear to excitement and an eagerness to perform? One way would be to learn how to use relaxation, imagery or stress management techniques to reduce activation levels—that is, when they are too high and you perceive them as fear and anxiety. Another method would be to train yourself to believe that the feelings are positive (called *relabelling*). This can be accomplished through the use of several strategies including imagery and various self-talk techniques. On the other hand, if you feel that you are too relaxed going into a game, you can increase your activation levels by using techniques such as imagery and self-talk or by increasing your activity levels through running, exercises, or warm-up drills.

Traditional Methods to Improve Confidence

Imagery is simply an extension of the notion of modelling. Instead of observing another person performing a particular skill, you can imagine yourself performing the skill. By imagining yourself successfully executing skills or successfully shutting down opposition moves, you can approach an upcoming game with more confidence. But imagery should not only be restricted to situations or skills during games. You can imagine yourself successfully performing practice drills or making it through an especially hard training run or fitness session. Chapter 3 outlines imagery in more detail and provides some useful imagery exercises for players and coaches.

Acting and thinking confidently can raise confidence . . . even if you don't *feel* particularly confident. The more confident you act, the more likely you are to feel and perform confidently. In addition, if you portray an image of confidence to others (head up, chest out, erect body position), then your opponents may begin to feel uneasy and perhaps even lose some of their own confidence. They will feel as if they are playing against someone who seems totally calm and in control. By the same token, when you show that you have lost confidence—either by negative self-talk or body language (chin down, slouched over, lacking energy)—you will actually boost your opponent's confidence because they will believe that they've got the better of you in the game. Portraying confidence, again, even if you are not *feeling* confident, can also lift your own teammates' spirits if they themselves have begun to lose confidence. It may not help you to win the game, but it might help prevent the team from giving up and conceding defeat.

Similarly, coaches should maintain an air of confidence because it rubs off on the players. Confidence, like enthusiasm, is contagious. Coaches should remain calm and focused, and when they communicate with the players at halftime, they should maintain that air of confidence. This aura can be accomplished by briefly emphasizing the positive aspects of their team's performance, making them aware of some of the things that they can improve on and encouraging them to do some specific things in the upcoming half. Coaches who yell at their players at halftime and appear to panic risk destroying the confidence of their players.

You should also try to maintain a positive attitude during practices and games. Negative thoughts can quickly undermine confidence. You should actively encourage yourself and your teammates through the use of positive self-talk and affirmations. When a mistake is made, it's no use getting down on yourself for making it. If you find yourself in that position, you should quickly replace the negative thought with a positive one.

For instance, if you're a flyhalf and miss a touch from behind your 22-metre line or knock on the ball during an attacking backline move, rather than say to yourself, "You idiot!" you should immediately refocus and say something like "Okay, hang in there, things will get better. What do I have to do now?" Self-talk should either be motivational ("You can do it") or instructional. For example, when kicking goals, Grant Fox, All Black goal kicker from 1984 to 1993, used to say to himself, "Head down, follow through".

The bottom line is that thoughts translate to action. Players who are more positive in their thoughts and self-talk are likely to be more confident and positive in their play. In fact, self-talk is such an integral component of self-confidence that the following section further discusses the identification and development of positive self-talk strategies (see p. 54).

Being as well prepared as possible for games or practice sessions gives you the confidence that you have done everything you can to maximize your chances of being successful. When you go into a game with a well-prepared and well-practiced game plan, well-rehearsed moves and techniques (scrummaging, back-row moves, backline defensive screens, continuity techniques, tap penalty moves) and with well-learned and practiced individual skills, it can only increase your confidence about an upcoming performance.

An integral part of preparation is individual off-season fitness training. If you know that you are as fit, fast, strong and powerful as you could possibly be when the season starts, you will be confident in your ability to play at maximum intensity for 80 minutes, to handle the physical aspects of the game and to focus on your own performance without worrying about your lack of fitness, strength, pace or power. In addition, a well-rehearsed pregame routine (see chapter 9) is another important aspect of good preparation. If you know the exact routine that you will follow in the build-up to a match, in terms of what you will do and when you will do it, you will be more confident that you are as prepared as possible.

Self-Talk

I've always used my mind-talk when I'm training or playing. It might be as simple as saying to myself, 'Come on, come on', or grunting. And I've got no time for negative thoughts. It's something I've cultured over years and it signals a certain response in me.

—Zinzan Brooke, All Black 1987-1997

Thoughts have a direct influence on the way we behave or perform. If you think that you are capable of playing well against an opponent, then your chances of doing so are infinitely greater than if you think you will play poorly.

Self-talk may be described as intentional thinking or as an inner conversation with oneself. It is clearly linked to self-confidence, motivation and concentration. A player who thinks positively is more likely to perform positively. On the other hand, a player with low self-confidence thinks negatively and performs accordingly. The trick is to learn to control self-talk so that it remains positive or to replace negative thoughts with positive ones.

Intentional thinking is the basis of controlled self-talk, but it does not mean having a long conversation with yourself during the game. The words or phrases that you use need to be brief and precise so that the message is received and understood quickly and so that your response is equally as quick. Self-talk is like having your own cassette player in your head—you make your own tapes and then play them when you need them. Your self-talk should enable you to create and maintain your ideal performance state (IPS).

Uses of Self-Talk

Self-instructional talk or cue words are useful for learning and practicing physical skills. For example, a goal kicker might use the phrase "head down, follow through" before attempting a shot at goal, or a hooker might say "hit the dartboard" before throwing into a lineout. Similarly, a lock about to hit a ruck or a maul might repeat the phrase "slot, sink, smack" to remind himself to pick a target to drive into (slot), adopt a low body position and keep his head up (sink) and drive through and beyond the ruck once contact is made (smack). Perhaps the best example of the use of cue words to remind players what to do in certain situations is when referees say "crouch", "hold" and "engage" when calling the front rows together for a scrum.

Cue words should be brief but precise, and they should indicate something that you should do at that particular moment. The words themselves might mean nothing to anybody else, but as their name suggests, they should cue you to do something specific. In addition, you should use your self-talk to guide you towards automatic execution of the skill.

I command myself [before I kick], 'Head down. Follow through'.

—*Grant Fox, All Black goal kicker 1985-1993*

Many players use a specific set of self-talk cues to keep their attention focused on the task at hand (see chapter 4). For example, they might say to themselves "here and now!" when they find themselves dwelling on a past mistake. After they verbalize it, they then realize that focusing on that mistake is not going to help them with what they have to do at that particular moment. Another example: If you are a halfback who has just kicked a box kick out on the full and conceded a lineout to the opposition, you should immediately try to put the mistake out of your mind and concentrate on your role in that lineout. You may have time to think about what you have done wrong and work out what you should have done instead, but then you must immediately refocus and concentrate on your next job. It is okay to get mad at yourself for making an error, but you must quickly learn to refocus. This is where self-talk can be quite useful.

Words or phrases with a clear, specific emotional message are also useful for cueing performance. For example, words such as "go" or "explode" could be used to express how a winger might want to sprint after a box kick from a lineout. Similarly, words such as "smooth", "easy", "oily" or "rhythm" could be used to indicate how a flyhalf wants to execute the leg-swing for a shot at goal. A loosehead prop could silently repeat the word "rock" to symbolize being as solid as the Rock of Gibraltar in each scrum. You can also use simple phrases to maintain energy, effort and persistence when the going gets tough during a match. For example, phrases such as "go for it", "push it", "pick it up", "keep going" or a whole host of others could be used that are meaningful to nobody else but you.

Use cue words or phrases to assist you with your pregame mental preparation. When you are going through your physical and mental warm-up routines, you can incorporate cue words, phrases or affirmation statements to help you reach your ideal performance state before kick-off. In addition, self-talk can be used in conjunction with other mental skills such as imagery during pregame preparation (see chapters 3 and 9).

Affirmations for Building Confidence

Affirmations are self-statements that reflect positive attitudes or thoughts about yourself. Remember, you are only able to do what you think you can do, so affirmations can help you believe in yourself and develop self-confidence. For example, Muhammed Ali used to publicly state, "I am the greatest!" which is an example of a positive affirmation. While this may be extreme, and probably not accurate for most rugby players, phrases such as "I play well under pressure," "I can do this" or "Nerves are a sign of readiness" would be examples of types of affirmation statements. You might use such statements before or during a game if you felt the need to regain, maintain or attain your ideal performance state.

Techniques for Controlling Self-Talk

Once your awareness of negative thoughts and feelings is heightened, you need to develop techniques to deal with the negative thoughts and to focus on positive thoughts. Develop a list of key words and phrases that have specific purposes (self-instruction, creating mood, holding attention, affirmation/confidence statements). See the sample self-talk list in table 2.1.

Thought stopping is a relatively simple technique that is useful for eliminating negative thoughts and replacing them with positive thoughts. It involves the use of silent, or sometimes overt, cues or triggers. For example, you might silently say, "Stop!" or "Bin it" when you recognize that you are having negative thoughts. You could then use imagery to mentally write the negative thought on a piece of paper, then throw it in the rubbish bin or set fire to it. You might even imagine that the negative thought is written on a television screen, then change the channel to one that has a positive replacement thought written on it.

TABLE 2.1 **SELF-TALK CHART**		
Statements I will use	**When**	**Purpose**
Focus words/phrases: "smooth leg action" "pass in front, chest height" "concentrate, focus" "hit the bull's eye"		
Mood words/phrases: "calm and relaxed" "strong and aggressive" "power" "feelin' fine"		
Positive self-statements: "I have trained hard, I deserve to play well" "I'm ready"		

The key is to use the trigger to eliminate the negative thought. You want to have an positive alternative thought with which to replace it. This ability requires some planning by you to identify your most common negative thoughts. After you have done so, you can then develop a positive replacement thought to insert once the negative thought has been eliminated.

Here is one method of changing negative thoughts to positive thoughts. Make a list of typical negative and self-defeating thoughts, then design a positive substitute thought for each negative one. Consider the following as examples:

Negative thought: "I don't want to screw up. I don't want to take this shot at goal."

Positive thought: "Relax. All you can do is give your best effort. Enjoy the challenge!"

Negative thought: "I hate the rain! I never play well in the rain."

Positive thought: "Relax. No one likes playing in the rain. It's the same for them as well as us, but you can handle it better."

Develop a list of personal affirmation statements. On this success list, note your strengths, skills and qualities, and state these in positive, action-oriented self-statements. Examples might include, "I have trained hard; I deserve to succeed", "I play well under pressure" or "I always make my first-time tackles." You can print these on index cards and carry them in your gear bag or stick them to your mirror as consistent visual reminders of your affirmations. You might also want to create an audiotape on which you have recorded your affirmation statements, cue words and refocusing or coping statements with your favorite music in the background. Repeated listening to these positive self-talk tapes helps program your mind for positive thoughts during training and performance.

Summary

Once you have identified your performance goals, you can begin to design your training plan. You must choose the appropriate training methods to develop the performance qualities identified in your mental profile. Goal setting is the first step in prioritizing your needs for your training plan. To achieve your goals, you must then identify the specific training methods you will need to put into action.

Self-confidence is crucial for peak performance in rugby. You need to develop a realistic level of confidence in your ability to perform the variety of skills that you need during a game. This awareness can be achieved in a number of ways, most of which involve using the four main sources of information regarding your level of confidence. Techniques such as goal setting, imagery, self-talk, relaxation and pregame routines can all be used to maintain or improve your confidence when used with good practice, training habits and sheer hard work during the off-season to develop the basic physical skills required for your playing position. You should always try to have a strong sense of confidence without being overconfident or underconfident. A realistic sense of confidence helps you consistently perform to your potential and more easily overcome occasional performance fluctuations because of your belief in your capability to perform.

Self-talk is linked to concentration, self-confidence and stress levels. Self-talk is not an in-depth conversation with yourself or a long list of self-instructions. Effective self-talk is short and precise, and it requires a minimal amount of thought to correctly complete a skill or affirm your confidence in yourself. Practice your positive thoughts in training so that they automatically occur in matches. Remember, confident players think they can, and they do!

chapter

3

Visualizing the Perfect Match

Bruce D. Hale
University of Maine

Bruce Howe
University of Victoria

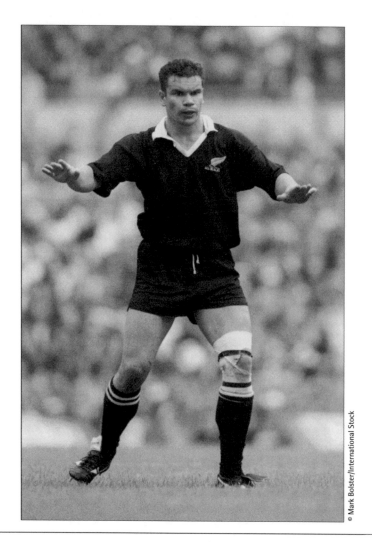

© Mark Bolster/International Stock

Here's a recent match-deciding situation that actually occurred in an international match. This scenario suggests how a top-notch goal kicker and captain may have used mental imagery to prepare for his kick.

A penalty is awarded to Australia and team captain John Eales thinks through his options. The match is four minutes into injury time in the Blediscoe Cup against New Zealand. The ball is about 20 metres from goal and about 10 metres from the left touch line. The Kiwis lead the match 22 to 20, and this may be the last play of the match.

"Can I make the kick? It's a tough angle but with no time left on the clock, we will take the lead and the championship is ours." Captain John Eales signals to go for goal and the win with a penalty kick. The responsibility rests solely on his shoulders.

The captain takes the ball from the referee and the team moves away into position. Eales signals for the tee and begins his mental preparation as the tee is relayed to him. He checks the wind, decides the direction for the kick and feels the action of striking the ball. The tee arrives. As he positions it and begins to line up the ball, he breathes deeply and shifts his focus from the game in general to the specific task in hand. Internally, he begins to review the process. "Five steps back and two left", he says to himself, and he imagines his even-paced steps back with eyes on the ball.

As he looks to line up the ball, he imagines it sailing clearly, starting towards the right upright and moving slightly with the wind before ending between the uprights of the post. He places his left foot to the side of the ball and sees it in that precise position at the end of his run-up. The right foot goes at the rear of the ball, and this time he imagines the feel and sound of the instep of the boot hitting the invisible sweet spot on the ball.

Eales steps back and only thinks of the point of contact on the ball. Nothing interferes with his concentration on the task. He reaches the end of the run-up, pauses, looks up to view the posts and once more establishes a picture in his mind of the ball taking an unerring path to the target. The crowd is roaring, but he barely notices the noise. One last time, he runs through the image of the entire action, takes three breaths and gives himself the cue reminders of "head down" and "follow through". He moves forward and strikes the ball firmly, feeling relaxed and confident in the performance of the entire skill. The ball leaves his foot. Even before he looks up to watch it fly between the posts, he knows that it will be successful. The cheering crowd certifies the result, and as he bends to pick up the tee, the referee blows his whistle for full time. Eales jumps three feet in the air and is swarmed by his delirious Australian teammates. Australia has won the Blediscoe Cup on Eales' foot in injury time, 23 to 22.

Defining Imagery and Mental Practice

The most successful kickers in the modern game have used this imagery process with only a few variations. Unfortunately, most other rugby players do not use the technique to aid them in the more continuative game skills, nor do coaches encourage its use during practice and games to aid their teams' performances.

At one time or another, every rugby player has dreamed of huge success on the pitch—scoring the winning try, kicking a match-winning drop-goal, making a big hit on the other team's

© Sporting Pictures, Ltd. (UK)

Successful kickers such as John Eales use imagery to prepare for the kick.

star player or making a perfect long pass out to the winger. Some may even imagine disastrous failures, such as missing a big tackle or missing a kick at goal. The mind constantly creates pictures, experiences various emotions and produces lifelike bodily sensations that seem like an actual game.

There has been some confusion about what is included in the practice of imagery. Historically, *mental practice* was used to describe the process, but it was directed only towards the technique of rehearsing a skill mentally before completion of the physical task. This definition is now seen to be limiting. The term *imagery,* on the other hand, is considered a broader term in which structured mental activity is utilized to assist performance in several ways. Players may also call this process *visualization,* which is a type of mental rehearsal that emphasizes using the visual senses to imagine rugby situations.

Imagery is best described as a process of using all the senses to re-create or create an experience in the mind. Imagery is more than just creating pictures in the mind's eye; imagery can be so real and intense that some people actually believe they are in a real-life rugby match. With practice and regular use, it can become an enormous tool to enhance rugby play.

Uses of Imagery

Imagery is used primarily as a means of improving performance, which is usually accomplished through mental rehearsal of the skill before the physical action. As described in the goal-kicking example, it means that the kicker would go through perfect execution in his mind before the physical action. It may occur immediately before or some time before the actual performance.

It may be necessary to remember movement feelings—for example, how it feels to make a dummy pass and step inside the defender. Movement feelings may also help players practice correcting physical errors, such as coming into a tackle situation with the centre of gravity too high or the upper body too straight. Imagery can also be used to review a performance on completion, especially during practice sessions. For instance, between trials during tackling practice in rugby league, players can mentally review their body position in tackling technique, the level of success they achieved and what adjustments might need to be made.

In addition, mental imagery helps a player rehearse strategies to retain focus during the match, make split-second decisions and solve problems before and during a match. Furthermore, imagery can improve focus on the task and eliminate distractions. For example, during a game, the defensive back-row players can review the likely options for the attacking team before packing down for a scrum. They also can imagine their own successful counterresponses, which enables them to stay prepared for the action.

Finally, and less directly, imagery provides an excellent way to improve a player's mental skill arsenal. It can enhance confidence by providing coping responses to new situations, such as an unfriendly crowd in an unknown stadium. It can also improve confidence through imagining successful performances in the past. The memory of strong performances in an earlier match can be recalled to help a player believe that he can succeed again in an important game.

It may also help players retain motivation by reliving and restating rugby goals in their minds and imagining reaching those goals. For many teams, practicing focus and motivational cues called by the captain on the pitch can help to maintain concentration when the match is at a critical point. Imagery is also a critical part of many stress management techniques (see chapter 5) in which athletes learn to reduce their anxiety levels to a controllable level or even increase arousal level when an extra push is important to win a scrum down near the goal line. Coping images can help players overcome opening-minute jitters and the first experience of playing in front of a large crowd. Bottom line: Imagining successful use of certain mental skills can lead to enhanced performance in actual matches and is well worth the investment of both the coaches' and players' time.

When to Use Imagery

Many players use imagery before, during and after training to improve rugby skills and performance (see table 3.1). Learning a new pass more quickly, a new attacking play in the backs and a defensive scheme from the scrum are all good examples of rehearsing skills in practice to enhance game-day performance.

TABLE 3.1	**CRITICAL MOMENTS TO USE IMAGERY**	
When	**Critical moment**	**Purpose**
Before, during and after practice	Performance rehearsal	To rehearse skill learning and performance
Before matches	Quick preview	To focus on relaxing images, repetition of simple and advanced skills, competitive strategies, past successes, goal programming
During matches	Match preview	To review actual skill execution, strategies and plays; to rehearse action movement and events before they occur
	Instant rehearsal	To rehearse the feeling of a movement or play after successful execution (to commit to memory); to identify or correct an error
After matches	Match review	To evaluate good and bad aspects of performance after a match; to help plan training and to reward good play

Many players also use imagery during their prematch routines to make sure they are ready to play at a high level and to give themselves a sense of control over their environment and opponents. During warm-ups, players who imagine a series of positive images of basic and advanced skills will raise their minds and bodies to a peak of competitive spirit and confidence. Some players and teams in rugby league and union have even begun to script the first few plays of a match to provide a clear sense of direction and to make decisions more easily in the first few minutes. Players can rehearse these plays until they don't have to consciously think about them while playing.

Rehearsing competitive strategies such as kicking high balls to the opposition's fullback or turning the scrum past 90 degrees could be a regular part of pregame preparation. Imagining old successful plays and performances can add to confidence, and imagining the performance steps that will lead to victory that have been voiced by the coach and team can be a critical part of pregame mental preparation.

Although it is more difficult to use imagery in-depth during a match (and most preparation should be done before the match, anyway), there are instances in which imagery during competition can be beneficial. During natural breaks in the game tempo—such as injuries, infractions, penalties and lineouts—players can learn to use brief imagery cues that help them rehearse successful skill execution and plan competitive strategies.

A common example is the great Welsh kicker Neil Jenkins and his elaborate pre-kick routine: He actually goes through some of the kicking motions and visualizes the ball going through the posts. During a break in the action, the captain might call a play or yell a verbal cue so that players can imagine their parts in the movement. Hookers often spend several seconds visualizing the exact spot where they want to throw the ball on a lineout. During breaks in the game, a player could also review his prior play and try to correct a simple error, such as being too high going into a ruck. He could also review his kinesthetic memory: how his back felt on the last scrum when he was able to keep it straight with his hips down, all while driving forward.

Finally, even though more and more clubs videotape games to review individual and team play, players can always go to the movies in their minds, anytime, for no cost after the match is finished. Identifying good and bad play can help make future training more efficient and give players a sense of being in charge of their own improvement. By taking a few minutes to review their own play and by emphasizing their positive plays, players can build confidence for the next match and get enthused to come to practice. It's easy to correct mistakes in the mind and to rehearse the perfect execution of a skill over and over again.

Mental imagery can be used almost anywhere—in the changing room, before going to bed, after waking up—in a short amount of time (in seconds!) or for long periods with minimal fatigue (although short sessions may be better). The key to effective mental imagery practice is to learn how to rehearse mentally to optimize potential. As with any other physical skill, use it daily as part of the training routine.

Why Imagery Works

There are many explanations of why imagery works. Each reflects the principle that the mind controls every activity of our body. This idea can be demonstrated by the fact that when a player is thinking about throwing a pass, the muscles show a small amount of activity in the same manner as if the pass were actually undertaken. Some evidence suggests that mind-muscle connections may be solidified by this kind of imagery practice. Skills become more automatic over time because the neural circuits are reinforced over and over.

A different, more straightforward model suggests that mental rehearsal increases the amount of time available to practice. Research has shown that imagery is most effective when combined with physical practice; that is, you can't substitute it for live, physical practice. Imagery's advantage is that it can be achieved away from the site and without specialized equipment. Furthermore, it can be continued when a player is unable to practice because of injury. Another explanation for imagery's success may be that the image raises the central focus on the key factors of the task to be accomplished; thus, it reduces the intensity of distractions before and during performance. These distractions could be external, such as weather or noisy spectators, or internal, such as anxiety or fear.

In conclusion, imagery has the indirect advantage of building confidence in the player's ability to succeed through the imagining of previous and future successful performances. Seeing is believing because the body performs better when the mind is positive and under control.

Types of Imagery

There are two types of imagery. The first is *external imagery,* which is more visual in approach and can be described as viewing action from outside the body. It is almost equivalent to viewing a videotape of a performance, such as if a player were to imagine watching herself take a kick at goal for a conversion. Frequently, this process is called *visualization*.

External imagery has particular value in early stages of learning skills involving simple tasks, such as passing to a teammate properly off the far foot. It also has the important purpose of enabling the performer to reinforce correct performance and to isolate and correct errors. For example, in learning a reverse pass, the player can think about and see how she executed a pass. She can recall that when she passed the ball, it was delivered too hard for the receiver to catch. This review would allow the player to make the adjustment without reference to the coach. As you can see, one of the advantages of external imagery is that people learn most sport skills by watching others demonstrate the skill. In this case, the athletes are visualizing themselves. They learn by visualizing what that skill looks like when they do the performing. Coaches should encourage their players to use external imagery often when they try to get the picture of what a new skill is and when they try to correct mistakes in execution.

The second type of imagery is *internal imagery*. Internal imagery is more multisensory; it is performed from a within-body perspective. For example, a player imagines a pass coming to her through her own eyes, and she sees a defender converge on her. She then feels herself planting her left foot hard and sidestepping the defender on the right.

Internal images are so powerful for the athlete because they are strikingly vivid. The player not only sees the world as it usually looks, but she also can feel her body moving during the imagined movement (kinesthetic feelings). She can smell the grass, hear the grunt of a hard tackle and feel the pebbly surface of the all-weather cover of a rugby ball. Internal images usually require well-learned physical skills and real-life rugby movement experience so that the athlete has a better idea of the feel of the task.

Internal imagery should be more beneficial for match performance because it can use all the senses; therefore, skills practiced in a more realistic image should be readily transferred to real-game situations. Players can take advantage of internal imagery in quite a few contexts: They can rehearse attacking and defensive strategies; they can practice reading offensive movement as cues; they can correct kinesthetic movement problems such as poor body position or timing; they can learn to cope with debilitating anxiety by practicing feeling more relaxed; and to speed up injury rehabilitation, they can feel injured body parts moving as if they were healed.

Internal imagery rehearsal also has application in the employment of tactical activities. For example, back-row attacks can be visualized: Players recognize internally where and when the play is initiated before they attempt execution. Players imagine their play and their timing in the task according to their individual roles. In practice, coaches can cue these activities and require the players to review their roles before the physical effort.

To summarize, evidence suggests that internal imagery has a significant effect in aiding performance. It is agreed that elite performers have gained advantages from both types of imagery, external and internal, and are able to switch from one to the other with ease depending on the nature of the task.

Imagery Exercises
to Develop Rugby Skills

In *Imagery Training: A Guide for Sportspeople*, Hale (1998) suggests that successful imagery has four principles, which he termed the four Rs: relaxation, realism, regularity and reinforcement. For each principle, practical examples and exercises are included to help improve imagery training and rugby skills.

Relaxation

For imagery to be effective the player must have a relaxed mind and body. To concentrate fully on rugby images and become totally involved in imaginary movements, the player should find a quiet place where he can rehearse his images without distraction and anxiety. Relaxation can assist in calming and controlling the mind before actual imagery rehearsal is undertaken.

When players have imagery sessions, they need to ensure that their bodies and their minds are relaxed so that they can feel their bodies moving, see their images clearly and experience any emotions they generate. Some players may need to learn a simple relaxation technique such as deep breathing before they imagine so that they can clear their minds and put their bodies in touch with the images. This routine is more likely to be of use during practice and before a game rather than during competition. Nevertheless, when time is available during the game—as in goal kicking, lineout throwing and restarts—use of simple relaxation exercises help to clear the mind and can be used with imagery rehearsal.

Breathing Exercise

If you have already learned a relaxation technique, such as progressive relaxation, yoga or deep breathing, simply find an isolated spot and practice relaxing for 10 to 15 minutes before imagery training. If you are new to these techniques, simply close your eyes, let your mind go blank and concentrate on breathing deeply for several minutes. Focus on the sound of the air going in your nose on the inhale, and try to push your abdomen out while breathing in as much air as possible. Exhale fully by pulling in your abdomen and by paying attention to the air as it rushes out of your nose. If your mind wanders, just come back to the sound of your deep breathing. Continue deep breathing for about 5 to 10 minutes until your muscles feel limp and your mind is clear of distracting thoughts. Begin your imagery routine.

Gradually try this breathing exercise in practice during the stretching routine. As you start stretching, keep your eyes open and begin breathing deeply with your abdominal muscles, totally filling your lungs with air and then slowly exhaling all of it out. As deep breathing continues, imagine a simple rugby skill such as passing the ball to a teammate. Try an external image; try to visualize how you look passing the ball. Switch to an internal perspective. Imagine the scene as if you are looking through your eyes: You see the ball passed to your teammate, noticing the weight on your far foot and your wrist and fingers snapping the ball on its way. Imagine the passing skill several times from both perspectives; try to feel how your body feels during the internal image of passing the ball.

Make this relaxation habit a regular part of your imagery sessions. With practice, you will soon be able to relax quickly and become fully immersed in your imagery practice within seconds, both on and off the pitch.

Realism

Realism refers to making images as realistic as possible so that imagery practice transfers maximally to live, physical practice and matches. Players should use as many senses as possible, and they should imagine them so vividly that it feels that they are actually playing a match. This exercise involves creating a precise, detailed image of the action. Players should try to structure their images to mirror the actual competitive situations they expect—the roar of the crowd, the smell of new cut grass, the feel of the clean ball in their hands, how their bodies feels when they move. They should see the competitive scene clearly and in living color.

Being able to reproduce the image with clarity increases the likelihood of more effectiveness in improving performance and focus. New players find it difficult to imagine with such clarity because the visual images are not set in their minds. With proper practice, clarity and control can readily be enhanced. Vividness means incorporating as many senses into the image content as possible so the scene is as realistic as an actual match. Players should pay close attention to body movements and sensations when training, such as feeling body position when entering a tackle or a wrist snap when passing the ball. Images should include emotional feelings. When there is concern about the field or crowd, it is helpful to provide videotape of the location and a preliminary visit so that players can practice coping with the surroundings in images.

Clarity Exercise

In an isolated and relaxed atmosphere, find a fairly new rugby ball and closely examine it, carefully noticing all its details such as the colors, designs, insignias and company logos. Now with your eyes closed, imagine the ball with all its intricate details—colors, designs, insignias, logos. Open your eyes and rate the clarity of your image on a scale of 1 to 10, with 1 being "can't see anything" and 10 being "perfectly clear". Repeat this exercise several times, each time observing the ball closely and trying to re-create its image in your mind. Remember to self-assess your ability.

Vividness Exercise

Now pick up the ball again, but this time focus on the texture and smell of the ball. Close your eyes as you handle the ball. Notice the all-weather dimples, and smell the leather and grass on it. Put down the ball. Try to imagine how it felt and smelled. Try this several times, alternating actually feeling and smelling the ball, then try to re-create these sensual images in your mind. Rate the clarity of these sensual images using the 10-point scale.

Sometimes by blocking out your dominant visual sense, you can enhance other senses in your imagery rehearsal. By closing your eyes during slow, constrained rugby movements, you can pay close attention to the kinesthetic feelings of movement and then remember how they felt in images that include movement sensations.

Clarity-Vividness Exercise 1

Choose a relatively simple skill to practice kinesthetic imagery, such as taking the ball into contact on the tackle. Execute the movement several times against an opponent with a rucking bag. Practice power-stepping into the opponent by dropping your centre of gravity and by putting the ball in a protected position. Lead forcefully into the bag with your other forearm and shoulder as you extend your hips and shoulders up and under the tackler, all while keeping your legs driving.

Close your eyes and imagine the same movement in your mind. Visualize the defender from an internal perspective as you feel yourself lower your centre of gravity and square up for contact. Focus on the kinesthetic feelings in your shoulders, hips and centre of gravity as you feel yourself driving up and through the defender. Repeat this several times to solidify the neuromuscular connections. If you need to reinforce the feelings, intersperse the visualization with actual physical practice. Remember to rate your kinesthetic imagery ability. Focusing on critical body parts during physical skill execution can help to make kinesthetic images more vivid.

Clarity-Vividness Exercise 2

Watch the best player on your team or a skilled coach execute a simple skill several times, such as a pop kick or a spin pass. Focus on two specific components per action: for the pop kick, the ball position and the pointed toes with instep driving up through the ball on the run; for the spin pass, cranking the ball down with the wrists and fingers and snapping the ball laterally away with the upper hand sliding up and over the top of the ball.

Close your eyes and imagine what this skill component clearly looks like in reality. Try to imagine it several times, then physically practice the movement without the ball. Focus first on the visual action, then close your eyes and try to feel the movement sensations as you move your hands or kick through the imaginary ball. Once you can feel the kinesthetic sensations of the movement, close your eyes and try to imagine seeing the movement through your eyes and feeling the sensations of the action. Imagine this several times to enhance the vividness of your visual and kinesthetic imagery. Evaluate the effectiveness of your imagery every time you attempt it.

Controlling the content of images is another subcomponent in the production of effective realistic images. For example, the first jumper in a lineout can imagine a ball that he jumps forward to receive and then change the image to adjust his action if the ball is overthrown. Similarly, it is important to imagine a positive outcome in the situation. If a player feels able to do it in his mind, then he is more likely to succeed in the real match. On the contrary, if he sees himself failing, he probably will.

Control Exercise

It's important that the image content mirrors reality as close as possible. One way to enhance the ability to control what is seen and felt in an image is to break a skill into parts. First imagine each part successfully, then put the parts together into the whole skill.

Select a skill that you can break down into components, such as a drop-goal attempt. Observe the best kicker on the team practicing the drop-goal, or watch an expert demonstrate it on a videotape of an international match. Next, try to imagine the whole sequence of movement by closing your eyes and duplicating what you saw. It may be difficult at first to clearly visualize the whole movement, so break the action down into components. For example, the drop-goal could be broken into the ball positioning and drop, the point of contact and the follow-through. Now practice the first component physically several times—practice receiving a pass, turning the ball to a vertical position and bending over to drop it closely to the ground on the point. Focus on what you see, then close your eyes and focus on the movement sensation of catching and dropping the ball with your hands and wrists.

Once you can feel the kinesthetic sensation of the ball drop, close your eyes again and imagine seeing the movement through your own eyes and feeling the movement in your hands. Do this several times. Afterwards, try this physical/mental practice sequence for the next component, the contact on the kicking instep with toe down and support foot alongside. Practice the follow-through phase next with the observation of demonstration, physical practice and mental rehearsal sequence. After you feel that you have confidently mastered imaging the separate components of the action, observe a demonstration of the whole drop-goal action and try to visualize the entire sequence of movements several times. If you have difficulty with the whole skill, repeat the imagination of each skill component, and, if necessary, watch the demonstration of the whole action again.

Once you can visualize the whole skill, physically rehearse the various components sequentially first with your eyes open, then with them closed. Physically rehearse the whole skill together until you can successfully perform it. Finish by imagining the whole skill through your own eyes and feeling the body movements that accompany it. Do this several times until you can clearly see and feel every component of the skill. When this skill is mastered, try others, such as tackling actions—body position, contact and wrap, drive, release and ball gathering—or jumping in the lineout—step and drive, lift, catch, descent, clean and drive/pass.

Controlling Speed and Duration Exercise

To maximize the transfer from practice to competition, learn to imagine rugby skills and situations at real-life speed. Select a skill that has a fairly clear beginning and end, such as a passing/running move in the backs or an attacking move in the forwards. Using a stopwatch and teammate or coach, time how long it takes to execute the whole skill from start to finish. For example, in a switch move, start the watch when the initial lateral run starts, and stop it once the outside runner accelerates back inside past the passer. Time it several times and take the average time.

Now from an internal perspective, imagine the switch move as you have just performed it, seeing through your own eyes and feeling your body move. Close your eyes, start the stopwatch as you begin imaging and stop the watch after you have imagined sprinting past the passer. Compare the time it took in real life with the time it took in your imagination.

If the imaged task was too fast, try it again and add more skill components to the image or slow down the speed of the image. If the image was too slow, speed up the image by processing it faster and leaving out some of the imagined components. With several repetitions of this process, you should be able to closely approximate the imagery time to the actual execution time. Evaluate the effectiveness of the imagery vividness when you do it. Try it with other closed rugby skills that are easy to break into a concrete start and finish.

Positive Outcome/Emotions Exercise

What you think is what you get! If you want your play to be a successful, positive experience, make sure you imagine positive outcomes in your images. Experience the positive emotions that accompany success in a match, and include as many senses as possible to make the image as realistic as you can.

For example, select a simple skill, one you can readily imagine as a successful execution and positive outcome. A simple two-on-one attacking move for a try might be a good example. If you have a videotape of yourself on a successful two-on-one move, watch it after practice. An alternative is after you have executed a successful two-on-one in a drill or scrimmage, immediately stop the action and rehearse the skill mentally.

Imagine being inside your body; imagine seeing and feeling yourself effectively complete the move. Visualize yourself running at and drawing the defender, slowing and turning at the last second to make a perfect pass off your inside foot to your teammate just outside of you. If you physically executed this move recently, try to remember the exhilaration and excitement of assisting on a scoring move by beating the last defender. Rehearse this positive outcome several times until you can feel the thrill of throwing a scoring pass every time you imagine the skill.

Coping Imagery Exercise

Unfortunately, we sometimes make mistakes in a match and don't perform up to our own expectations. Good players learn to overcome mistakes without dwelling on past mistakes and turn the game around to a positive outcome. Coping images can help you successfully deal with negative emotions and refocus your efforts on positive cues and outcomes.

Imagine feeling anxious at the beginning of a match, starting poorly or even making an early mistake—such as dropping a pass, missing a tackle or losing a ball in a tackle. Imagine the negative emotions of frustration, anger and failure interfering with your performance. Take a deep breath, clear your mind and imagine yourself coping successfully with the situation.

For example, a rugby defender who missed a tackle, might say something positive such as "I'll get the next one." He then might imagine concentrating closely on the runner's midsection, quickly reading the defender's direction and feeling himself move quickly with low, squared body position, driving into leg or midsection with a shoulder while wrapping up the defender's legs to drive him backwards onto the turf before getting up and grabbing the loose ball. A receiver who just dropped a pass might also say something positive, then imagine giving the passer a good target, focusing on the ball entering his hands and watching it cradled safely into his fingertips for a successful pass and run.

Use action verbs and feeling adverbs if you write a script (see pp. 83-86), or use kinesthetic imagery to feel yourself responding with a successful execution. Always finish imagery sessions with a perfect, successful execution of whatever skill you are practicing to end on a positive note.

Regularity

Like rugby skills, mental skills such as imagery have to be practiced regularly to transfer the training effects into matches. This skill is not hard to achieve, and it can aid learning and confidence by increasing the practice time for skills and tactics away from the site. Spending time on a daily basis (about 10 to 15 minutes) to image the critical skills and tactics of the game strengthens the likelihood for success in the game and practice.

Alternate periods of actual physical practice with imagery practice to optimize imagery use during training. When rugby players engage in this activity during breaks in physical practice (during water or training breaks), it aids focus and reduces the requirement for long and boring rehearsal of basic skills. Mental imagery can also be a regular part of a prematch warm-up routine, where players imagine themselves performing skills flawlessly, reviewing strategies and plays and seeing themselves scoring the winning try.

Evidence suggests that for optimal effect players should spend several minutes of uninterrupted concentration on each imagery scene. Too little time results in a poorly developed memory trace and inconsistent execution of skills. Too much time on the same image leads to boredom and fatigue, which decreases concentration and subsequent performance. If a player needs to concentrate on an image for a long period, intersperse the imagery sessions with short rest periods.

Imagery Practice Schedule Exercise

Write down your imagery practice schedule for the next week (see table 3.2). Begin thinking of possible times before, during and after practice when you can take 5 to 10 minutes to rehearse images—for example, before falling asleep, after studying, after watching

TABLE 3.2	IMAGERY REHEARSAL SCHEDULE	
Day	**Time**	**Content**
Monday		1. 2. 3. 4.
Tuesday		1. 2. 3. 4.
Wednesday		1. 2. 3. 4.
Thursday		1. 2. 3. 4.
Friday		1. 2. 3. 4.

Prematch routine   Content
1.
2.
3.
4.

Match images   Content
1.
2.
3.
4.

Postmatch images   Content
1.
2.
3.
4.

a rugby video, during stretching exercises, at water breaks, while waiting in line for a turn during a drill, in the locker room and so on. Write down times during the day, and write down the content of the images to be rehearsed, such as passing the ball, concentrating on the ball and kinesthetically feeling yourself properly bound in for a scrum. Post the imagery rehearsal schedule inside your training book, on your desk or in your locker.

Pick one of two different images each day to practice that help you improve the most in a physical or mental skill area. Practice each image during and after practice for a week. See if the quality of your images begins to improve, then see if your quality of play improves. Find a regular practice routine and write it down, one that includes mental rehearsal during practice and at night. Practice it regularly throughout the season.

Decision-Making Exercise

Here's a good example of a practice-based image to use to improve rugby skills and strategy. Select a typical situation on attack in which there is an overload of players against the defense, such as a two-on-one or three-on-two running situation. Use an internal imagery perspective. Be inside your body and see the situation through your own eyes—your position with the ball, your teammates' positions and the defenders' positions. Make the imagery as real and vivid as in a match, at the same quick pace.

Your decision is to select the right pass or move to make to a teammate. Are you going to draw the defender in, turn and make a perfect pass to your teammate who is accelerating beside you? Do you notice that the defender is sliding into the gap between you and trying to play both of you so you dummy the pass and step inside the defender? Mentally rehearse both scenarios in your mind several times; feel your body making the right decision as you visually read the defender's movement cues. You may need to rehearse how to react to different defensive cues, such as the distance of the defender, the distance between you and your teammate, how closely the defender is marking you, how fast your teammate is moving and how much space you have around you and your teammate. Rehearse all these possible variations until you can feel and see yourself making the proper decision that opens up the running attack.

Try to imagine the same decision-making situation with a three-on-two break in which both defenders are moving up quickly and tightly, leaving a wide skip pass open to your outside teammate. Rehearse the proper decision in real time; see the ball spinning outside to your breaking teammate for a huge gain. Practice this image several times. When the situation happens in a match, your brain will be hard-wired to automatically make the right decision and execute the correct move. Regular visualization results in regular improvement.

Practice and Match Routines

Do the same for pregame and competition routines. Start with equipment preparation (uniform, boots, taping, ball), then physical preparation (stretching, running, passing, kicking), and include important mental images in the process. For example, during stretching, imagine making solid tackles, passing accurately on a two-on-one break, catching lineout throws, kicking for goal or scoring the winning try. Write down the content of images in the imagery rehearsal schedule.

When you want to use imagery during breaks in the match, such as lineouts or penalties, you need to do a little preparation. In the imagery rehearsal schedule, write down the images to be rehearsed, then use them during breaks in practices and scrimmages. Gradually incorporate these critical images into match breaks to help maintain focus during the match, keep motivation high and keep working towards match goals. Make imagery a regular part of practice and match routines.

Reinforcement

Reinforcement means using visual and kinesthetic aids to improve the quality and control of images. Imaging is not helpful if the image is unclear, so use videotape or good models to aid in developing clear images for your memory. For example, to clearly imprint proper passing technique in their minds, scrumhalves could watch videotape segments that show sound body position, leg push and hand and wrist follow-through on effective scrum-half passes. Videotape of games can also help pinpoint errors for correction and strengthen the vividness of external images to correct those mistakes. Other visual aids might include competent demonstrations by coaches or veterans, visual cues, hand-held minicameras, videotape analysis systems and biomechanical analysis. All of these aids improve clarity and control of imagery and should be taken advantage of.

Another option for effective reinforcement that powerfully enhances imagery clarity is focusing on the kinesthetic feel of the body during movement. For example, for front-row players, paying attention to the feel of a tight bind enhances the imagery of effective scrummaging. Alternating videotape, imagery and actual practice effectively speeds up skill learning and significantly improves performance.

To improve both internal imagery and feel for movement, try videotaping drills from a normal visual perspective (a helmet cam perspective) and learn to look for important decision-making cues to enhance the vividness of images. Try using a weighted rugby ball, performance feedback instruments on scrum and rucking sleds, biofeedback systems and soon (perhaps) virtual reality imaging system, which could help develop kinesthetic awareness of correct rugby moves and how these movements feel during execution.

Using Visual Aids

Ask someone to videotape your next rugby practice so that you can watch yourself practice a specific skill, such as passing, kicking, tackling or rucking. Study the videotape, then close your eyes and imagine yourself executing the same skill from this external perspective. Try alternating the film and imagery several times to enhance imagery for clarity and control. Imagine seeing yourself execute the skill correctly to finish this rehearsal session.

To develop a more powerful ability to use internal imagery, videotape from an internal perspective with a hand-held camera. Pick a skill that you can videotape easily, such as kicking a penalty kick or passing effectively on a two-on-one offensive break. Focus on the same cues that you look for during actual play, such as the sweet spot in kicking or the position and speed of the incoming defender on a passing play. Close your eyes and visualize the same cues you see on the tape. Imagine the kinesthetic feelings in your body that accompany a passing or kicking movement. Try to improve these movement feelings by alternating watching the internal videotape and imagining the same perspective immediately afterwards with all the senses. If you can program your brain before matches about what to look for to make good decisions and to retain your focus, your performance during matches becomes more automatic and highly skilled because the neural connections are well trained.

Writing Imagery Scripts

To maximize the effects of imagery on learning and performing rugby skills, plan the content carefully. Writing an imagery script to use in training helps develop more vivid images, more controllable images and images that use more of the senses. Follow this three-step process.

Step 1: Tell the Story

Select a skill or event in a game. Tell the basic story of the scene by outlining the components or behaviors that make up the action in its normal sequence of occurrence. For example, let's return to the penalty kick example from the beginning of the chapter (pp. 62-63). John Eales might break his actual kicking routine into the following components:

1. Check the conditions.
2. Position the ball and angle.
3. Review positive thoughts and technique.
4. See a good result.
5. Hit the sweet spot.
6. Repeat reminder cue(s).
7. See a successful result.

After this example, write down the components of the skill in sequential order.

Step 2: Add the Details

This step involves adding appropriate adjectives and descriptors to each component. To enhance the details, use as many sensory details as possible from practice and competitive environments: colors, directions, weights of objects, qualities of noise, smells, feelings. Add details about the actions and emotions to make the script read as if the skill were actually being performed or the event were being experienced. The more vivid and powerful the actions and emotions are portrayed, the more powerful the subsequent image. Use strong kinesthetic verbs and adverbs to describe the action.

Go back to the second step in the penalty kick example. "Position the ball and angle" might read "Position the blue, decorated Gilbert ball leaning back towards me at 45 degrees in the blue kicking tee. Place the ball so that it faces squarely at the right post, positioning my black, left supporting boot alongside the ball with my instep level with the tee, and my right boot instep lined up behind the ball."

Step 3: Refine the Script

This step involves combining the descriptions and components into a clear, easily readable paragraph that stimulates the imagination. Use a point of view in the first person to describe in detail the thoughts, movements and feelings that would be experienced. Once it's written, make sure it evokes a vivid image that contains plenty of sensory action and emotional details. Reading it should make you feel as if you are actually performing the skill or experiencing the event.

Make and listen to an audiotape of the script with other images or read it over and over until the content of the image is memorized. Try it in practice and see how effective it is. If it is not as powerful as desired, add expressive kinesthetic and emotional verbs and adverbs to make it more vivid. Practice the script repeatedly until the image can be imagined in competition, then simply let the body do its thing.

Here's an example of a script that John Eales might have written for himself for his goal kicking imagery (see table 3.3):

TABLE 3.3 SAMPLE IMAGERY SCRIPT USING JOHN EALES GOAL KICKING EXAMPLE

Step 1: Tell the story	Step 2: Add the details	Step 3: Refine the script
1. Check the conditions.	Pick up loose grass, toss it up.	I pick up some loose grass in my right hand and toss it up and watch for any wind currents.
2. Position the ball and angle.	Carefully position ball, kneel behind, walk up to ball, position left foot, curl my right boot, line up my hips.	I walk up to the ball and position my left black boot next to the ball . . .
3. Review positive thoughts and technique.	Five steps back and two left. Just keep your head down and follow through.	I think to myself "five steps back and two left" and slowly pace back to my . . .
4. See a good result.	See the ball curve right through the posts.	I stare at the posts and imagine seeing the ball curving right through . . .
5. Hit the sweet spot.	Fixate on the sweet spot. Feel my instep thumping. Feel the ball explode.	I fixate on the sweet spot on the ball and feel my right instep thumping the . . .
6. Repeat reminder cue(s).	Take three breaths. "Nice and smooth."	I take three deep breaths, and my final thought is "nice and smooth".
7. See a successful result.	Confidently approach the ball. Drive it effortlessly through the posts.	I confidently approach the ball and drive it effortlessly through the posts.

The referee blows his whistle and awards us a penalty kick. I pick up some loose grass in my right hand and toss it up and watch for any wind currents. He hands me the ball, and when the tee arrives, I carefully position it on the penalty spot. I kneel behind the tee and meticulously position the ball at a 45-degree backwards angle facing directly at the right goal post. I walk up to the ball and position my left black boot next to the ball with my instep even with it. I curl my right boot behind the ball and line my hips up with the goal posts. I think to myself "five steps back and two left" and slowly pace back to my starting position. Then I say to myself, "Just keep your head down and follow through and you'll make it!" I stare at the posts and imagine seeing the ball curving right through the posts as it ascends end over end toward the howling crowd. I fixate on the sweet spot on the ball and feel my right instep thumping the ball on this highlighted spot. I feel the ball explode off my foot toward the posts. I take three deep breaths, and my final thought is "nice and smooth!" I confidently approach the ball and drive it effortlessly through the posts as the crowd raises the roof.

Summary

After reading this chapter carefully, you should have a good understanding of how to use imagery techniques to enhance rugby skill: what imagery is, how to use it in practice and matches and where and when to use it. The best ruggers in the world use it to take their game to a higher level, but it works just as well for novice players. It takes regular practice, proper instruction and good effort to bring positive improvements to performance.

Imagery is another life skill that can enhance your ability to perform in a variety of life situations and enable you to cope with stressors with confidence. It has many varied uses that can improve your quality of life at home, school, work and on the athletic pitch. It allows you to be more in charge of your life. Anything you can imagine, you can do.

chapter

Focusing On the Game

Jeff Summers
*University of
Tasmania*

Steven Christensen
*University of
Southern Queensland*

Paul Sheath
*St. Peter's
Lutheran College*

© Empics

Being able to concentrate during a performance is a vital ingredient in performing well. Though it is most obvious in individual sports, such as shooting, tennis and gymnastics, concentration is equally important in team sports. In rugby the levels of concentration can vary from the intense and focused, required of the placekicker, to a ball-starved winger, just keeping his mind on the game. It is not surprising that coaches constantly remind players to stay focused and concentrate on their roles in the game.

The manner in which we conceded a try early in the second half was due to a lack of concentration in the scrum. You cannot afford that against a side such as England.

—*Donal Lenihan, Irish rugby manager (Moran 1996, 101)*

Although lapses in concentration usually occur during breaks in play and pass without incident, sometimes they coincide with a critical event and result in a costly error. One of the most famous lapses in concentration occurred to Greg Martin in the 1989 Australia vs. British Lions Test. The incident occurred towards the end of a tightly contested match, with the Wallabies just three points ahead. David Campese, the brilliant but unpredictable Australian winger, caught a misjudged kick by the Lions in the in-goal area, but instead of touching the ball down for the expected 25 yard drop-out, he decided to run the ball from behind his own line. As he was being tackled before reaching the field of play, he threw a poorly directed pass to a totally surprised Greg Martin who knocked the ball on and watched in horror as Lions winger Ieuan Evans dove on the ball to claim a try! To make matters worse, the Lions won the game by a solitary point.

What does this example tell us about concentration? Although most athletes have their own conception of what concentration is and how they feel when they are not concentrating, a universally accepted definition is hard to come by; thus, this question is a complex one to answer. For our purposes, we will define concentration as simply focusing mental effort on only one source of information. As the previous scenario illustrates, a vital part of successful concentration is that the mental effort must be directed to the appropriate information. Greg Martin may have been concentrating on getting into position for the anticipated ensuing 25-yard drop-out, rather than focusing on what Campese was doing.

Dimensions of Attention

The ability to control attentional focus is a fundamental prerequisite for optimal performance in any sporting activity. Attention is a multidimensional construct and is generally believed to involve at least three psychological processes:

1. selectivity of perception,
2. regulation of concurrent actions (divided attention), and
3. maintenance of alertness.

So far, our examples of the importance of attention in the game of rugby have illustrated its selectivity. Selective (or focused) attention appears to have evolved to protect humans from being

Crowd noise is an external distraction that needs to be overcome.

overwhelmed by the vast amount of environmental information constantly bombarding them. When a player is waiting to field a towering garryowen as opposing tacklers charge towards her, she needs to maintain attentional focus on the ball while blocking out distracting or irrelevant sources of information, such as crowd noise, movements of players and negative thoughts ("This is going to hurt!").

Concentration can be likened to a spotlight that comes with an adjustable lens. The spotlight illuminates different parts of the external environment (selective attention). The beam can be narrowed to allow detailed processing of a small area of the world (focused attention), or it can be broadened to allow less detailed processing over a wider area (broad attention). Portions of the world outside the attentional beam receive little or no processing.

There is some evidence to suggest that optimal, attentional beam width may differ across sports, across ability levels within a sport and in team sports such as rugby. It may also differ according to the athlete's role in the game. For example, broad attention may be optimal for a fullback, whereas focused attention may be necessary for a front row forward. The beam can be directed inward, resulting in distraction by the player's own thoughts and anxieties, as well as being directed outwards, leading to distraction by factors in the external environment.

There are times when mental resources need to be spread across a number of activities concurrently, such as running, monitoring the position of opposition players and kicking the ball precisely to land in no-man's-land behind the opposition's backline. The ability to divide attention across several concurrent actions is quite difficult and develops only after extensive practice. Although most experienced rugby players are able to accurately kick the ball on the run with ease, watching under 11-year-olds play rugby shows how difficult this skill is to perform.

Attention can be thought of as the allocation of a limited supply of mental resources (fuel) or energy to different tasks in a way that reflects expectations and priorities. Performance of any task depends on the amount of attentional resources assigned to the activity. Likewise, multiple tasks, such as running and kicking the ball while monitoring the position of teammates and opponents, can be performed simultaneously only if the combined demands do not exceed the common pool of resources.

As a result of extensive practice, skilled players are able to run and kick the ball almost automatically, using little mental energy, thereby allowing their remaining resources to be devoted to monitoring the positions of the opponents and deciding on strategy or tactics. Novice players, in contrast, have to use nearly all of their available resources to execute the action of kicking the ball on the run. Through automation of lower-level skills, skilled players can devote their attention to higher aspects of the game.

Interestingly, there is some evidence to suggest that once a skill has become automatic, a player can disrupt performance of the skill by applying conscious attention to the execution of the activity. For example, an expert placekicker who misses a couple of easy shots may start to consciously attend to his kicking action on the next attempt. In the worse-case scenario, such an internal attentional focus may lead to what is known as paralysis by analysis.

Another dimension of attention involves the state of alertness and readiness for action, or the maintenance of optimal sensitivity to environmental information. Fluctuations in the level of alertness are related to changes in physiological arousal level. Although there are momentary increases in alertness during a rugby game, such as when making a tackle or when receiving a pass, the ability to maintain alertness through a game is crucial. One lapse of concentration at the wrong moment can result in a missed tackle or dropped ball and a game-winning score for the opposition. Because maintaining a high level of concentration for long periods of time can be mentally tiring, players need to develop strategies to exert mental effort at the right moments during a game. As the Welsh legend Jonathan Davies remarked:

> For a back, there are long periods of inactivity in which it is easy for your mind to wander and for you to lose your focus. I used to cope by switching off completely while waiting for a scrum or lineout to be set up and then refocus when the action was about to start. The ability to turn it on or off like a tap worked for me, but there are others who have to maintain their concentration at all times otherwise they cannot get it back. (*Independent on Sunday*, 25 October 1998, p.12, Supplement)

Players use a variety of cues to signal when to increase concentration, when to relax and where to direct their attentional focus. These cues can be auditory, such as the referee's whistle, particular calls for various moves and self-talk to increase concentration or reduce arousal. Visual cues, such as looking at the goal posts for the placekicker or the picking-up of the ball by the hooker for the lineout jumper, can also be used to intensify concentration. Finally, many players use habitual actions, such as the half-back twirling the ball in his hands before putting it into the scrum or the centre slapping his thigh as the ball is thrown into the lineout, to trigger concentration.

The ability to maintain concentration is particularly important towards the end of a game when fatigue begins to set in. A player who is not in top physical condition is in danger of becoming internally focused on how tired he feels and may miss important external cues. The professionalism and rule changes in rugby union have demanded that players be tougher, more athletic and more resilient than ever before. They need to be able to turn on intense concentration to produce an extremely high standard of play week after week. In competitions like the Southern Hemisphere Super 12 involving teams from Australia, New Zealand and South Africa, each game is like a test match.

Equally important to be mastered is the ability to refocus attention after being distracted. Distractions can come from external sources, such as crowd noise, public address systems or the taunts of an opponent, and from internal sources in the form of task-irrelevant thoughts. Paradoxically, sudden decreases in noise can also prove distracting and stressful. In rugby the great sportsmanship of the crowd in maintaining an eerie silence when a player prepares to kick a penalty may be just as distracting as the thunderous noise that greets the teams as they run onto the field at grounds such as the old Cardiff Arms Park. Whatever the distraction, it is imperative that correct attentional focus is restored quickly.

Attentional Flexibility and Style

In addition to being able to direct sufficient mental energy to task-related information and sustain concentration over time, the ability to effectively switch attention is a vital ingredient of skilled performance. Attentional flexibility is the ability to alter the width and direction of attention; that is, respectively, the number of cues focused on at once (from broad to narrow) and where the focus of one's attention is (external or internal). For example, a flanker drives into the ruck, but the opposition clears the ball. The player must be able to switch quickly from the narrow focus of attention demanded by the ruck situation to scanning the surrounding environment (broad focus) in order to pick up the opposition player with the ball.

To account for individual differences in concentration skills, Nideffer (1976) proposed that people have a preferred attentional style or propensity to adopt a particular attentional focus in different sport situations. Combining the dimensions of width and direction yields four attentional styles: broad-external, narrow-external, broad-internal and narrow-internal (see figure 4.1).

A broad-external focus is required when a player scans the field of play to rapidly assess the game situation before deciding what to do, such as pass the ball, kick or go for the interception. Not surprisingly, research has shown that positions requiring swift, tactical decision making, such as halfback and first five-eighth, are usually occupied by players who have a strong broad external focus. Conversely, a narrow-external focus is required when a player is about to make an action, such as the placekicker focusing on the ball before kicking or the lineout jumper focusing on the hooker's call before the ball is thrown in. A broad-internal focus is needed when discussing the match plan and tactics with the coach. Finally, a narrow-internal focus is used by a player to tune into his body, as when the prop forward concentrates on producing maximum effort in the scrum.

Although a player may have a preferred attentional style, a key to performing well in rugby is to be able to switch rapidly between attentional styles, as demanded by different skills and situations. The halfback, for example, who is about to put the ball in the scrum needs to quickly scan the field to assess the situation (broad-external focus), then decide on a strategy (pass or run the blindside) using a broad-internal focus. He may then go through the move in his mind (narrow-internal focus) before adopting a narrow-external focus to execute the required

External

Broad-external

- Peripheal awareness
- Ability to read the game, anticipate, and react to game changes
- Good for scanning the run of the play
- Enables choice of tactic or play
- Team playmakers spend more time in this quadrant

— Players with this dominant style are subject to distraction by unimportant information, such as crowd noise

Narrow-external

- Required at the moment an action is made (kick or pass the ball, tackle)
- Focused on a limited number of external sources of information
- Ability to block out distractions
- Forwards spend more time in this quadrant (scrums and rucks)

— Players with this dominant style may not adjust to or notice changing game situations

Broad —————————————————————— Narrow

Broad-internal

- Analysis based upon information gathered in broad-external mode
- Creative thinking and problem solving
- Coaches spend more time in this sector
- Enables choice of tactics or play
- Those in this quadrant are good at using breaks in play to discuss what they see occuring in the game and how to fix it

— Players with this dominant style can overanalyze the game (dwell on mistakes) and lose focus

Narrow-internal

- Focused on thoughts or ideas
- Quadrant for kinesthetic (body) awareness and use of mental imagery
- Often players who are most aware of their own tiredness and pain are found in this quadrant

— Players with this dominant style can be distracted by internal thoughts that are not action-oriented, are negative, or provoke anxiety

Internal

Figure 4.1 Nideffer's (1976) attentional style model adapted to rugby.
From Nideffer, 1976, "The inner athlete," New York: Crowell.

sequence of actions. While it may seem overwhelming and complex, the process becomes more natural with practice, to the point where it becomes completely automatic.

Detriments in performance may occur when the player is dominated by a particular attentional style and is unable to adopt the attentional focus more appropriate to the situation. For example, the prop forward maintaining a narrow-internal focus when running with the ball in open play (when a broad-external focus is required) may not be aware of a teammate screaming for the ball on the right or the huge opposition second rower looming to the left. The notion of attentional style, therefore, provides a useful, if somewhat oversimplified, framework to identify the various types of attentional focus required in rugby.

Practical Skills for Improving Attention

Attention is a limited resource and forms a major component of the overall performance of any athlete. It requires energy to drive it and can be affected adversely by a large range of factors, particularly in a contact sport such as rugby. However, concentration is a skill, and as such, it can be improved with training. As a resource, the amount of concentration available can be improved, as well as the way the resource is used. The following techniques help players monitor and improve their attentional skills. Three case studies are presented to illustrate a systematic approach to dealing with concentration issues at both the individual and team level.

Rugby is a complex game, and naturally, there is no way to cover all eventualities that may affect a player's attention. The first step is to understand the attentional demands of the sport and the particular attentional skills required for each playing position. The four attentional styles outlined in figure 4.1 can be useful in this exercise as well as talking with and observing elite players.

Once players have a feel for the ideal attentional profile they should adopt for various roles in the game, an evaluation of their own attentional strengths and weaknesses is needed. This exercise can be quite difficult for most athletes. Although there are a number of self-evaluation instruments available, there is little evidence to suggest that athletes are capable of accurately evaluating their own concentration skills. If possible, players should watch themselves play on a video and attempt to relive the concentration mode they adopted during various game situations. Often the coach can provide valuable insights into concentration abilities.

Although the exerise is difficult and can be an investment of time, it is well worth doing because concentration problems are the most common performance issues athletes and coaches present to sport psychologists. This phenomenon is largely due to the fact that concentration of some sort is required in nearly every sport performance. Players and coaches must be careful, however, not to infer that a concentration problem exists if the team loses or the player performs poorly and makes frequent skill errors.

For instance, consider the performance of Australian rugby union fullback Matt Burke in two test matches played on consecutive weekends in 1998. In the first game, Burke was the hero, landing five out of seven kicks to help the Wallabies end a four-year losing streak to the All Blacks. The following week against South Africa, Burke landed one out of five goal-kicks as the Wallabies went down 14 to 13. Both matches were played in Australia—a hostile crowd cannot be blamed, and the difficulty of the kicks appeared comparable in the two games. While it is tempting to attribute this dramatic reversal of form to a concentration problem, other factors such as the wind conditions, a slight change in technique or more complex issues may be the culprit.

The challenge facing the coach, athlete and sport psychologist is to understand whether the distractions and lapses in concentration (which are relatively easy to identify) are the *cause* of the athlete's performance problems or are a *symptom* of the problems that the athlete is facing. Athletes, coaches, parents and teachers are encouraged to look beyond the quality of performance. They should consider issues that influence performance, and they should examine the reasons for playing well or playing poorly and winning or losing. On many occasions, coaches and players are able to competently address the problems.

The hypothetical cases discussed later in the chapter are intended to encourage coaches and players to undertake a systematic approach. However, on those occasions when things are less clear-cut, coaches, teachers and parents may need to discuss matters with an accredited sport psychologist.

Dealing With Concentration Problems

Traditionally coaches and rugby captains have solved concentration problems in much the same way that Francois Pienaar adopted with the 1995 Springboks:

> We were leading 19 to 15 with three minutes left to play when Joel (Stransky) failed to kick a restart 10 metres, and the French were given a scrum on halfway. It was an uncharacteristic error and placed us under pressure. France won the ball and fly-half Christophe Deylaud launched an up-and-under. I was running back, and I saw James Small steady himself under the ball. Perfect, I thought. James will claim the mark. But he didn't. He knocked on. Two unforced errors had awarded France with an attacking scrum, and I could hardly contain my anger. Gathering the entire team around me, the air turned blue as I urged the guys to concentrate. 'We've come so . . . far,' I shouted, drenched with sweat, rain, and mud. 'Let's not . . . give it away. Please . . . concentrate.' (Pienaar 1998, 169-170)

From schoolboy level to the World Cup level, the approach is to implore players to just concentrate or pay attention. This approach has both benefits and shortcomings. History shows that Pienaar's Springboks limped to a narrow victory over the French in the 1995 World Cup semifinal following a try-saving tackle by James Small and Hennie Le Roux in the final minutes of the match. Pienaar's appeal to concentrate was a success. James Small and teammates listened, heard the message and refocused their attention after a lapse in concentration.

This immediate and often animated strategy can successfully address temporary lapses in concentration, such as those that may occur because of fatigue and other external events that distract players from the game. But it may not work in all situations. The strategy has the best chance of success when concentration problems lead to a decrease in performance from a shortcoming in maintaining alertness, caused by players failing to refocus attention away from these distractions.

Team leaders such as Francois Pienaar often have to passionately urge their team-mates to concentrate.

Contemporary approaches to concentration training are more systematic than repeated appeals to concentrate and are characterized by three steps. First, understand the nature of the concentration problem. Specifically, is it a cause or consequence of a performance problem? Is it explained by skill deficits in selective attention, divided attention or alertness and refocusing of attention?

Second, consider alternative approaches for solving this problem and establish a treatment plan. Experienced coaches often get another perspective of the problem and consider alternative solutions by discussing it with assistant coaches, teachers, sport psychologists and other professional staff. Coaches should cautiously view the various strategies, though, as they may not be appropriate with players of different ages and abilities or in every situation.

The final step is to put the plan into action and evaluate its success or failure. Many sport psychology books describe generic concentration activities such as grid exercises, the unbendable arm, the stork stand and soft-eyes–hard-eyes. These general activities are useful for demonstration purposes in university classes and professional development workshops only. They offer little to train concentration skills that are needed in rugby training and competition, and there is little empirical or practical evidence to conclude that general exercises have much effect on concentration skills for competitive performance.

As an alternative to these general concentration exercises, the following case studies provide examples of distractions in training and competition and offer some strategies for improving concentration. The three case studies have been selected to illustrate a systematic approach to understanding and acting on recognizable concentration problems. The cases are fictional and used for illustration purposes only.

In each case, a plan to remedy the situation is suggested. This plan is structured to recognize whether the concentration problem is due to a deficit in the functioning of a particular attentional dimension. Additionally, in each case the intervention approach is described in some detail to convey how the activity would be conducted with the player or team. The various concentration activities used in the case studies illustrate the five different approaches to addressing concentration problems:

1. Focus training
2. Organize the concentration focus
3. Cope with distractions
4. Use plans and routines
5. Sensory expertise and trust refinement

Case Study 1: Anxious and Unfocused

James is a 16-year-old student at Lichfield Grammar School, which is the leading school in a large provincial city. Lichfield is modelled on an English public school and boasts fine rugby and cricketing traditions. James is a member of the Lichfield's Second XV rugby team. The 200- and 400-metre athletics champion at his school, James has the speed and agility to make him an asset as a rugby winger. He views rugby as his second sport, however. His primary sport is athletics, and he hopes to one day represent his country at the Olympic Games.

James has recently been promoted to the First XV team because of season-ending injuries to the team's two wingers. He was apprehensive about playing the last four games of the season at this level of competition. Although he has sound ball skills, his tackling skills are only just adequate for Second XV competition. It is widely recognized that James' ectomorphic body-shape and modest tackling skills are problematic for a winger playing at First XV level. Some wingers at this level of competition are more similar in speed and size to New Zealand International Jonah Lomu.

Following a poor tackling performance in his debut match, James appeared to be anxious and more apprehensive. At a meeting with the school counselor, who is a qualified sport psychologist, James disclosed that he was worried about being hurt in a tackle and being humiliated in the school community by his poor performances in the First XV team. Furthermore, he believes that opposing teams will focus their attack through his wing because of his tackling weaknesses. James adopted this view because of some taunting that he received from opposing players during the first match. He said that there were several periods during the match when he was more concerned with what was being said about him and how anxious he was feeling than the actual rugby play. Because of these distractions James was standing too upright in the tackles, perhaps focusing on the face and shoulders of opposing players.

James' concentration problems have a psychological origin; he is having problems maintaining an appropriate focus during matches. His selective attention skills are inadequate to focus on task-relevant information for the duration of a First XV level match. Three intervention activities were designed to help the situation:

1. Using plans and routines
2. Coping with distractions
3. Organizing the concentration task

Activity 1: Using Plans and Routines

James' first concentration activity focused on correcting his selective attention problem through organized plans and routines, which are excellent concentration guides. They serve to organize relevant and irrelevant cues for the player, and they provide a blueprint for intentional focus and action.

For the activity, the rugby coach obtained videotapes of the 1995 World Cup Semi-Final and Final. At the conclusion of the next practice, the coach called a special backs-only team meeting to discuss the tackling situation confronting James. The coach introduced the issue sensitively and asked the players to help find a solution to the problem. He then showed video excerpts from the 1995 Rugby World Cup, initially showing New Zealand powerhouse Jonah Lomu running through English tackles during the second semi-final. This was followed by excerpts of Springbok James Small looking after Lomu in the World Cup Final.

The players hatched a game plan during the meeting drawn from the discussions prompted by the video footage. Like Small, James was to stay on the outside of his opposing winger and force him inside where he would be tackled by other players. This maneuvre was practiced repeatedly at practice with James and his outside centre developing a more effective partnership.

James was asked to maintain a wide position when his team is in attacking and in defensive situations. Specifically, he was to stay on the outside of his opposing winger when his opponents had possession of the ball. When his opposing wing gained possession, he was to approach him at an angle forcing him to move in-field where he would be tackled by the outside centre.

The coach could have imposed his solution on the players, but he believed the solution would be more widely accepted and adhered to if it emerged from within the backs themselves. Of course, the plan was the coach's preferred solution all along, hence the choice of video footage; however, the player-generated approach provided an opportunity for James to save face in front of his peers. It also prompted his teammates to show empathy and concern for the difficult situation that he was experiencing.

Activity 2: Coping With Distractions

James' second concentration activity focused on helping James let go of negative thoughts and replace them with positive ones. Many psychologists believe that negative thoughts precede negative emotions, behaviors and motivations. Thought-stopping activities aim at stopping negative reactions by breaking the chain of negative responses and reactions. They provide an effective method of eliminating negative thoughts before they have sufficient time to start a negative cycle of feelings, motivations and behaviors. This activity was aimed at reducing feelings of anxiety and uncertainty by preventing negative thoughts from stimulating these emotions.

For James' thought-stopping activity, he obtained one thick rubber band. He placed the rubber band over one wrist. The rubber band did not interfere with the circulation to his hand but was sufficiently tight so as to not fall off during rugby activities. James was instructed to monitor his thoughts during rugby practices, matches and nonrugby events. When he detected a negative thought about becoming injured, being humiliated or tackling inadequately, James was to stretch the rubber band and release it, giving himself a painful snap to the wrist. At the same time, he was to loudly say, "Stop!" then immediately think of his cue phrase "hips and back".

After repeated use, the trigger word "stop" may be replaced with a word selected by the athlete. Alternatively, other physical actions, such as snapping the fingers, clapping hands or slapping one hand against the thigh, may be used as physical actions to replace the rubber band.

Activity 3: Organizing the Concentration Task

The third concentration activity used double-team tackling to simplify the concentration focus. Concentration problems can arise when players become overloaded with relevant and irrelevant information. An effective strategy is to simplify the concentration task by determining a single objective and one or two action statements that enable this objective to be fulfilled.

The rugby coach aimed to simplify James' attacking and defending roles in the First XV team with the assistance of Louis, the team's outside centre. The coach held three meetings to address James' problems. Each of the meetings aimed to limit and clarify the responsibilities that James fulfilled in the team and to simplify the concentration focus that was required to satisfy these tasks.

The first meeting was with James himself. The coach reinforced the competition plans hatched at the backs-only players meeting. A discussion followed of the attacking and defending roles that James was to play and how he was going to work together more effectively with Louis, the outside centre.

In the second meeting, the coach spoke with Louis about James' difficulty focusing his attention when opposing players were taunting him. The thought-stopping activity was explained, and Louis was asked to engage James in the play as soon as possible after a taunting incident. In attack, Louis was to throw a pass to James as soon as possible after a taunting incident. James was instructed to go directly up the field with the ball, take the first tackle, and position the ball for a second-phase play. If the team was in defense, then Louis was to remind James that he was part of a dynamic tackling team and to be ready to show teamwork.

In the third meeting, the coach spoke with James and Louis together. He singled out their defensive functions as an area that needed improvement and suggested that they adopt a double-team tackling approach. In double-team tackling, James was to tackle an opponent at the hips to slow his momentum with Louis joining the tackle as soon as possible. Louis was to complement James' initial tackling movement by putting the opponent on his back. Together the three devised the cue phrase "hips and back" to signal James and Louis' partnership in tackling an opponent.

Case Study 2: Old Ways and New Ways

Lyndon is a 23-year-old professional rugby league player. He has played first class rugby with the same premier division rugby club for seven years since joining the club as a youth player. Lyndon has represented his country at under-19 and under-21 levels and has received a senior A cap as a replacement. Lyndon has held the primary goal-kicking duties for his team during his club and representative career.

During round six of the domestic competition, Lyndon injured his left anterior cruciate ligaments resulting in a 10-month layoff for surgery and rehabilitation. Lyndon was highly motivated to return to first-class rugby within the time frame agreed upon with the orthopedic surgeon. The club reassured Lyndon that his playing contract was secure, and they subsequently provided him with unlimited access to physiotherapy and psychology services throughout the injury rehabilitation. The psychologist introduced him to long- and short-term goal setting, self-talk, imagery and simulation training, all of which Lyndon used to assist his rehabilitation.

The injury was rehabilitated, and he made a successful return to first-class rugby the following season. However, midway through the season, Lyndon asked to visit the psychologist once again. Although he had regained full confidence in his ability and felt that the injury no longer interfered with his performance in field-play situations, he felt uneasy about his goal kicking. Lyndon explained that although his goal kicking statistics were only slightly below his average, his goal kicking felt unnatural, conscious and effortful. Asked to explain how things felt before the injury, Lyndon was only able to offer that it felt like nothing much at all. "I would just do it! I'd place the ball, take a few steps back, look at the goals and run in to kick the ball between the posts."

The psychologist suggested that Lyndon had become more attentive to information and more analytical in his decision making as a consequence of his injury rehabilitation program. The thought-based sport psychology activities—goal setting, self-talk and simulation training—had taught Lyndon to adopt a more logical and analytical thinking style. Similarly, the body-scanning skills that helped him manage the painful injury trauma, surgery and demanding rehabilitation regime had also contributed to the problem.

The psychologist explained that during general play the intensity of the game kept the analytical-type processing balanced with automatic processing. However, during stoppages, Lyndon's body-scanning skills, goal setting and self-talk shifted the balance in favor of controlled information processing. This temporary imbalance was corrected as play restarted, allowing Lyndon to play his natural game. However, during the stoppage in play before a penalty kick, Lyndon had learned to be more analytical and consciously attentive, despite his preference to be more intuitive and automatic in his goal kicking.

Lyndon's concentration problems are learned behaviors, balancing both controlled and automatic processing of information during matches. His divided attention skills are currently inadequate to spontaneously switch to automatic processing when kicking for goal. The psychologist suggested two intervention activities:

1. Sensory expertise and trust refinement
2. Focus training

Activity 1: Sensory Expertise and Trust Refinement

Sensory expertise refers to activities that encourage players to use auditory and proprioceptive cues to control their skilled movements. (Coaches in Western cultures often emphasize using visual cues to monitor physical skills and ignore using other sensory resources.) Lyndon has sound imagery skills and positive attitudes about using imagery to improve his rugby. For the activity, he is asked to obtain videotapes of rugby matches. While watching the videotapes, he is encouraged to take up the role of an imaginary goal kicker whenever a penalty is awarded in the game. He is to use one or two calming breaths to settle his mind and body, and he is to begin visualizing that he is taking the goal kick. Because the aim of this intervention is to encourage goal kicking with limited conscious thought and control, Lyndon is only provided a brief imagery script that simply initiates the imagery. He is encouraged to complete the visualization on his own:

When watching the rugby game, consider taking up the role of an imaginary goal kicker whenever a penalty is awarded by the referee. Use one or two breaths to calm yourself, clear your mind, and steady yourself for the kick. Begin visualizing by seeing your hands pick up the ball. Feel the ball in your hands. Take steps to dry or wipe mud from the ball. Feel your hands securely place the ball in position for the goal kick. Step backwards, marking out your kicking approach and determining your starting position. Look at the target and anticipate the ball's trajectory. Steady yourself before approaching the ball, then do it. Feel yourself kick the ball. See only the last part of the ball's path as it travels over the goal posts. Imagine that the ball has left a rainbow-like trail to mark its trajectory, starting from where you initially kicked it and finishing over the posts.

Encouraging greater kinesthetic activity can enhance the sensory components of this activity. Lyndon can partially undertake this goal kick in his living room by symbolically placing an imaginary ball in position, retreating to his starting position and moving forward to kick the imaginary ball. Closing his eyes while making the kick can also help enhance his kinesthetic awareness.

Activity 2: Focus Training

This approach aims to manage the myriad of mental, physical and external information that is available to a player by training a simple "if X situation, then Y action" contingency plan. This activity trains Lyndon to pay attention to the right things, at the right time and for the right duration. Lyndon understands the appropriate focus for goal kicking and is able to perform this concentration focus. However, he needs to improve his control over this concentration skill so that he can improve his goal kicking under a range of different and challenging conditions.

For this exercise, Lyndon needs ready access to three rugby balls. His task is to complete 15 goal kicks during each rugby practice, completed as five sets of three goal-kicking repetitions distributed throughout the training session. Lyndon is encouraged to discuss this activity with his coach and undertake each goal kicking set during a naturally occurring break in the session.

Additionally, Lyndon is encouraged to select challenging moments during training to complete each set, times when he may have an inappropriate focus of attention for accurate goal kicking. In choosing these moments, he will be required to shift his attention to automatic processing or control of the goal-kicking movement. During each practice, Lyndon should aim to vary the difficulty and distance of his goal kicks.

Supplementing the five sets of goal kicks with one or two additional goal-kicking sets as requested by the coach can enhance the uncertainty and application of this task. In addition to the coach selecting the difficulty and distance of his goal kicks, the coach can implement positive or negative consequences for Lyndon or other members of the team, based on Lyndon's performance. These variations are aimed to strengthen the stressful conditions and uncertainty upon which Lyndon may be required to kick for goal but also challenge him to kick without conscious thought and control over the skilled movement.

Case Study 3: One Moment in Time

Harlequins Rugby Club celebrated the 100th anniversary of the founding of the club by staging a centenary celebrations weekend during the middle of the 2001 rugby season. The celebrations had been well planned with activities on Friday evening and throughout the weekend. The program included invitations to all former club members, including the 1953 Triple Championship Team. The legendary 1953 Harlequin Invincibles completed an undefeated season by winning the President's Cup, the League Cup and the Challenge Cup, which is played on a knockout basis between first, second, third and fourth division teams.

The centenary celebrations program included presentation dinners, luncheons, president's breakfasts and other functions attended by association officeholders, local politicians and officials, sponsorship representatives and current and former club members. For current club captain Alex Delgardo, the honor of leading the A-side XV team during the centenary year was a bittersweet experience. Delgardo appreciated his place in the history of the club as the 100th club captain, but this responsibility weighed heavily, as the Harlequins had qualified for the President's Cup Final for the first time in several years.

The President's Cup was held between the first- and second-place teams after the first round of matches. Harlequins had just qualified for the President's Cup after narrowly winning their last game. While the President's Cup Final made for a fitting finale for the centenary celebrations, Delgardo and his first-grade players approached this match feeling the pressure of some 100 years of expectations. The President's Cup Final was scheduled on the Sunday afternoon of the centenary celebrations weekend, and many hoped that a Harlequins victory would conclude a truly memorable celebration for the club.

Anticipating the distractions and pressures of the centenary celebrations, Delgardo chose to read Francois Pienaar's autobiography *The Rainbow Warrior* to get a sense of how Pienaar and his South African Springboks coped with the distractions and pressures of the 1995 World Cup. The Springbok campaign itself had a rocky pathway but culminated in a finale that unified 43 million South Africans.

Delgardo recognized similarities between his team and Pienaar's Springboks. Concerned about the impact of the centenary celebrations on his team's performance, Delgardo borrowed several ideas from Pienaar's book and wove them into a focusing and refocusing plan for the President's Cup Final. Before the weekend of celebrations, Delgardo approached the club coach, club president and legendary 1953 club captain Alex D'Silva, asking for their support. Under Delgardo's leadership, the four men choreographed a plan to help the team's concentration.

The Harlequins' anticipated concentration problems have a psychological origin. The nature of the anniversary celebrations are likely to test the best selective attention, divided attention and alertness and refocusing attention skills of the players. Alex Delgardo suggested five steps:

1. Organization of the concentration focus
2. Coping with distractions
3. Focus training
4. Sensory expertise and trust refinement
5. Plans and routines

Step 1 aimed to organize the task. Delgardo arranged for a pre-match team meeting to be held at the president's home. There the president spoke briefly, followed by the club coach and Delgardo. The president followed a script similar to Springbok coach Morne du Plessis. He calmly congratulated the team on their achievement of making the President's Cup Final and thanked them for their contribution to the centenary celebrations. The club coach drew inspiration from Springbok manager Kitch Christie's message, encouraging players to play their hearts out but also conveying how proud he was of each player. Delgardo spoke third and followed Pienaar's script closely. He acknowledged that mistakes will occur in the final, and he encouraged players to keep their heads up—not to worry about mistakes—and simply to get on with the game. Each person spoke calmly and encouraged players to keep the game simple and straightforward.

Step 2 aimed to cope with potential distractions. Delgardo arranged for players and officials to travel from the president's home to the grounds by bus. Anticipating the quietness and tenseness of this journey, Delgardo again followed Pienaar's example and played Roger Whitaker's song, *If*. He, too, felt that many players would be concerned about what would happen if they knocked on or if they dropped a pass. Like Pienaar, Delgardo wanted to get the message across that they should forget about the ifs and just play their natural game without being fearful of failure, inhibition or humiliation.

Step 3 aimed to train an appropriate focus for the game. The 1995 Springboks were inspired by Nelson Mandela's presence and the personal message he delivered in the changing rooms before the World Cup Final. Delgardo believed a similar effect could be created by inspirational former club captain Alex D'Silva. As the players moved into the changing rooms of the local rugby stadium, D'Silva was waiting for them. Highly regarded by all current Harlequin players, D'Silva moved from one player to another, as Mandela did, shaking their hands and wishing each player good luck. Before leaving the changing rooms, D'Silva asked Delgardo for permission to address the team. As previously arranged, Delgardo agreed. D'Silva spoke in a calm and considered voice emphasizing that the day was for playing rugby in the manner for which the club had become known and respected. His words encouraged players to focus on the present, disregard the past and ignore the future.

Step 4 aimed to reinforce trust and expertise among the players; it occurred in the warm-up area a few minutes before the team was to take the field for the match. Delgardo called the players together and with arms linked asked them to join him in singing the club's anthem. But rather than sing this song with the loud and celebratory tone as was the team's tradition after a victory, Delgardo asked the players to sing softly, emotionally and in harmony. The team obliged. Delgardo recalled the unifying impact that the South African national anthem had on the 1995 Springboks and aimed to repeat this influence in a modest way with his team. Shortly after this the team took the field and commenced the President's Cup Final.

Step 5 was held in reserve and aimed only to reinforce an appropriate focus if, during the latter stages of the game, fatigue were to affect the team's concentration and commitment. Influenced by Pienaar's orders in the second semi-final against France, Delgardo prearranged for Sampedro—a tireless, hardworking and personally inspirational Lock—to make the emphatic and colorful appeal for players to concentrate if it was required.

Summary and Conclusions

Rugby requires the use of attention in its various contexts of selectivity, resource allocation and alertness. Furthermore, while the sport shares many aspects with other team sports, it also has some unique features that have implications for attention control. Although many team sports, such as soccer and hockey, divide players into forwards and backs, the difference in the roles and activities performed by these two groups of players is arguably greater in rugby (especially rugby union) than in most other team games. The different roles also require general attentional styles (broad-external versus narrow-external, for example). However, unlike some other team sports where players only function within a clearly defined role, such as American football where some players never actually touch the ball, rugby players can and often do perform outside their normal role, such as when forwards run, pass, and kick as backs do, and backs ruck as forwards do. It is the ultimate team sport, and a vital ingredient of a successful rugby player is attentional flexibility.

In recent years, there has been a proliferation of self-help books on sport psychology. All these books contain a chapter on concentration and provide a fairly standard set of tools and activities for improving attention control in any athletic endeavor. Rather than continue this trend, in this chapter we tried to illustrate the use of sport psychology to help with concentration problems through three hypothetical case studies, each dealing with different aspects of attention. The case studies are designed to show that pure concentration problems rarely exist. The first step is to understand the context in which the problem occurs, then tailor the intervention to the particular situation, individual or group. With an organized concentration plan, players can learn to focus effectively at any level of participation.

chapter

5

Using Stress for a Competitive Advantage

Kirsten Barnes
England Women's Rugby

Austin Swain
Loughborough University

© Empics

When faced with an opponent of equal ability at the elite levels of rugby, one factor separating the winning team from the losing team is often the ability to cope with pressure, as shown by the players individually and the team collectively. France's thorough demolishing of the favored All Blacks during the semi-finals of the 2000 World Cup and the inability of the All Blacks to respond to a series of quick tries during the match speaks to the difficulty of handling pressure in important matches.

Some players naturally thrive under the pressure of competition, more so than they do in training. For many players, though, the ability to use pressure to enhance their rugby is a difficult prospect and more of a challenge. Handling pressure before, during and after a game often can be an overwhelming obstacle. The challenge for any rugby player operating at this level is to be able to interpret a potentially negative or threatening situation in a positive and challenging way.

Many rugby players never achieve their potential because they allow the occasion to get the better of them. Pressure environments, where expectations and rewards are high and where the fear of failure can invade even the most resilient mind, can affect players negatively by preventing them from playing to the best of their ability. This negative impact impedes the players' thoughts and actions, and suddenly they are unable to transform what they do successfully in training to the game situation.

This chapter provides ideas and tools to help players cope more effectively in stressful situations. Up to this point, we have deliberately used the generic and somewhat ambiguous word *pressure* because it is a word more people can identify with without necessarily being able to accurately define. Sport psychology literature, however, talks conceptually about the term *stress,* which is the term we shall focus on because the two can be used synonymously.

Stress Is Good

There is nothing mystical about stress. All rugby players experience it to varying degrees. Stress can be defined as any situation in which the environmental demands are perceived as threatening and outweigh an individual's ability to cope, which then results in an individual effort to resolve the problem. In these terms, stress can be negative yet potentially positive. Players can galvanize their personal resources and raise their effort to meet a challenging situation. The stress and coping model process shown in figure 5.1 identifies the different levels at which various coping tools can come into play (Jones, G., in press).

This model is covered in more detail later in the chapter. Briefly, level 3 focuses on ways to minimize the potential of stress to emerge at all and includes the most basic forms of stress and their solutions. Level 2 explores ways of turning threatening perceptions into more positive impressions if the strategies at level

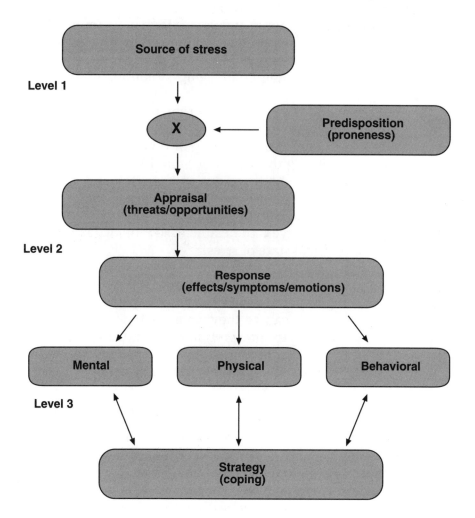

Figure 5.1   The stress and coping model.

3 did not work. Level 1 focuses on ways to manage symptoms in dealing with stress when the reappraisal activity at level 2 has not succeeded.

The consequences of stress on a player's actions and team's performance are enormous but conquerable. Stress affects all players differently, and different situations can have various effects on the same player. Some players are more naturally prone to negative stress. For example, they might experience high levels of cognitive and somatic anxiety in response to relatively nonthreatening situations, such as a cloudy day that may or may not bring rain. These types of players are known as high trait-anxious players and generally have a tendency to interpret most situations as threatening rather than challenging. For those who are less trait-anxious, their stress levels are activated by an upcoming challenging situation, such as the game.

Some players find they get very nervous before competition, which helps them play well. Other players who don't get very nervous feel that helps them achieve. For others, the nerves prevent them from playing the way they would like to. Those who don't get nervous sometimes go out on the pitch and find they are not fired up for the game. The different ways in which stressful situations affect each rugby player are numerous, and it is important for rugby players to be able to identify when they are in a mental or physical state of stress.

The key is for players to be able to identify within themselves the way they want to feel before and during the game to get the most out of a rugby performance. Some elite players will be as nervous for their final cap as they were for their first. The difference is their ability to interpret stressful situations as challenges and use the skills or tools they have learned to control their levels of stress to enhance their performance.

Sources of Stress: Level 1 Interventions

Many factors affect a rugby player's or team's performance (table 5.1). These factors may be experienced during training, in the lead up to a game, moments before kick-off or during an actual game.

There are many ways to deal with stress. Often by becoming aware of the source, a player can relieve the stress temporarily

TABLE 5.1   SOURCES OF STRESS

Internal factors	External factors
Importance of competition	Weather conditions
Perceived ability of opposition	Distractions during the match, such as family, friends, the crowd, media
Performance in previous game (self-belief)	Travel and disruption to routine
Previous injuries	Referee decisions
First time back after injury	Competing out of season
Motivation during training and season	Other people's expectations (pre-match)

by putting some perspective on it and maybe even preventing its reappearing in the future. These problem-focused strategies nullify the potentially stressful situation before it grabs hold. A useful strategy may be to control those things that are controllable when planning competitive routines. Uncertainty can contribute to stress, so a proactive way of dealing with this concern is knowledge of the opposition and how the team is going to respond.

Dealing with the what-ifs is another effective planning exercise in preparation for a game or tournament. The team can split into small groups and identify key themes that relate to each game, such as the hotel, transportation, grounds and venue and weather. Under each of these headings, players can try to identify every possible problem that could occur and come up with feasible solutions. The small groups can then share their issues and solutions with the rest of the team, and the team can discuss and decide the best way to deal effectively with these issues.

Another effective way to deal with potential stress is the use of precompetition and preperformance routines to provide a sense of familiarity and calmness during pressure situations (see table 5.2). The precompetition routine is a flexible but planned, step-by-step process the player and team go through to prepare for a game.

Most players have sound instincts about the things they need to do before playing, which is a good start, but can they remember the details from game to game, month after month? After a

TABLE 5.2 **SAMPLE ROUTINES**		
Competition routine	**Positional, skill-specific routine (throw-in at lineout)**	**Unit-specific routines for key skills (scrummaging, lineout, kicking)**
Get changed, go out onto pitch, warm up physically and mentally, skill-based warm-up, return to changing room for taping, team huddle and captain's words	Foot placement, position of hips and shoulders, correct hand position on the ball, arms raised above the head, deep breath and a split second image of where to throw the ball before making the call	Quick front row formation, four heads, sink-hit

successful performance, it is advantageous for players to remember exactly what they did to prepare and note the details that possibly made the difference. Taking the time to commit the routine to paper helps the players cover all the bases in their preparation. (This habit works for teams as well.) Each time the players step on the pitch, they will feel the confidence that comes from doing everything possible to be ready to play.

Player or unit skill-specific routines focus on the steps taken before executing a skill, such as a lineout throw-in, scrum or placekick. Effective routines allow players time to prepare for what they are about to do rather than rushing into the skill and leaving the outcome to chance. Using table 5.2 as an example, write down your own precompetitive routines. Practice using them in training, scrimmages and low-key competitions until you are comfortable with them. Afterwards, you can more confidently use them before the high-pressure matches.

Familiarization is another way for a team to prepare and be confident in the surrounding venue in which they are playing. When possible, the team should arrive early, preferably a day or two before (or at least a few hours before), to check out the facilities and become familiar with the grounds. Find out some specifics of the area that may become part of preparation on game day, such as the typical wind direction, the softness of the pitch or the direction of the sun. Ask a veteran player or coach who has played there previously to describe the grounds so that the description can be used in imagery (the use of imagery is discussed in more detail in chapter 3). Familiarity with surroundings is clearly an important variable, but effective imagery skills can minimize uncertainty as a negative influence, even without a prior visit.

Have regular meetings with coaches and players to reinforce communication in terms of preparation, as well as a debriefing after the game. In preparation for any game, especially during tournaments, stress levels can be greatly reduced if regular, effective communication takes place. Players, coaches and staff benefit from being informed, and each party needs to take responsibility in the communication process, which is another good example of proactively exerting influence over what can be controlled (problem-focused coping). Robust team communication processes that do not break down when a team is under pressure provide a further buffer against the effects of stress. South Africa's great defensive stand against England in the 1995 World Cup stands out as an example of continual, defensive team communication on the pitch, which led to final success. Team rules that identify agreed codes of conduct and social support mechanisms are further examples of this planning.

Another source that may heighten stress is when players don't have clear goals or objectives either for themselves, their unit group or their team prior to the match. Therefore, make time before a game to discuss and commit to paper the main goals of the game and what each unit group wants to achieve, such as the disruption of the opposition scrum ball in both 22s. Because these goals are discussed openly, the whole team knows exactly what they are working towards, and no player or unit is left running onto the pitch confused about their objectives. Role ambiguity is a stress-inducing variable in any environment, and a lack of clarity over expectations or the game plan can contribute further to pregame anxiety.

A factor off the field that can contribute to stress is the fact that today's elite rugby player is a professional, which brings with it a dramatic lifestyle change. Being a professional athlete carries many responsibilities but none more important than those to the athletes themselves. The process of being able to self-reflect is crucial as the pressure to perform to potential and produce good results increases. Staying focused on rugby as well as maintaining a balanced lifestyle is a new challenge many players face.

For any level player, a training diary to plan and record what is being done daily is a useful tool to monitor training. Following a game, players may want to conduct their own type of debriefing of the game—review how things went and record three things that went well and three things that could have been better. This retrospection provides a log of playing experiences and something the player can reflect back on as the season moves on.

It is critical to set regular goals to improve rugby skills and plan the next step forward (see chapter 2). In the past, the time devoted to training was team focused, and individual players had to squeeze in personal skill development wherever possible. Now that individual players have higher expectations, they must take more personal responsibility for their own personal development, training, and time management in their sport.

Threat or Opportunity: Level 2 Appraisal

Players interpret the information they receive differently. Some players see situations as challenging while others may feel more threatened by the same situation. No matter how hard players prepare for a match or tournament, their ability to deal with every eventuality that may occur is limited. There will always be circumstances that create stress, simply because they are unexpected or are out of the player's control. So what can be done to cope?

Level 2 provides ways to react to these situations effectively. This process is called *appraisal/reappraisal,* a way of thinking positively when under pressure, rather than thinking negatively. If the strategies at level 1 have worked, then usually there is no need to go to level 2—no bad stress materialized because the player anticipated and prepared. However, for unexpected moments for which the players cannot always prepare, or when they have to react successfully during a critical moment, their ability to view the situation as a challenge rather than a threat is critical.

Appraisal is the way people interpret the information they are receiving. Can the thoughts and feelings of threat and negative anxiety be converted into a more positive mindset? In other words, can the stressful situation be used to create an invigorating performance state as a result of the way the player thinks about the situation, or do the stressful thoughts overwhelm focus and confidence? *When the going gets tough, the tough get going* is a common catch phrase that illustrates this idea. Appraisal is an ongoing process used at every stage of a performance. For players to use stress as an advantage and make the most of every competitive situation, each player's appraisal has to be an effective, positive step in the stress-coping process.

For many players, the initial, primary appraisal of a situation is threatening, not constructive, and one that can potentially damage performance. In these circumstances, the ability to reappraise the situation or reinterpret it in a way that creates a positive mindset is an invaluable skill. What is believed to be threatening to one player may be viewed as a challenge by another. For example, if the captain leaves the pitch because of injury, some players may panic and believe that they won't be able to play without the captain. Others positively cope with the new player who comes on as replacement, saying, "Come on, we can do this—we have all trained together and know what to do".

Appraising information differently can be a consequence of any number of reasons: past experiences—one of the players heard some distressing news moments before going to the grounds; mood—someone didn't sleep well the night before; beliefs—a player did not play well on this pitch last time; or unexpected circumstances—the team receives huge amounts of attention from a large crowd as they arrive at the grounds, or the bus is late to the grounds. Furthermore, if players feel that the demand is beyond their capability and that the result will have serious consequences, then they will feel more open to a threatening appraisal. Therefore, it is important for coaches to recognize that in the stress-coping process, each player appraises information differently at different times and at different stages in development. This knowledge in itself may seem a threat (or opportunity) to some coaches who have to learn to work with every individual on the team.

The consequence of typical negative appraisal is that it may lead to irrational thinking. Players lose sight of the task at hand and find themselves doing one or more of the following:

Catastrophizing—make a mountain out of a molehill. "Every time I miss an early tackle I have a terrible game."

Overgeneralizing—use extreme statements. "We always play badly against this type of team."

Discounting the positive—focus on the negative. "We never win any drop-outs or kick-off restart balls."

Mind reading—anticipate comments from others. "I know the coach is going to say I was useless today."

Predicting the future—assume the worst will happen. "The way we have been playing recently we are bound to lose."

Black-and-white thinking—no grey area. "The only way we are going to beat this team is to move it wide."

Taking things personally—see comments as a personal attack. "Just because I missed the tackle, the coach thinks I'm a terrible player."

Why does one player see the positive side to a stressful situation (the opportunity), while another player reacts negatively and sees the same situation as a threat? Often the initial appraisal in a stressful situation, especially an unexpected situation, is one of threat—for example, "I am not going to play well in this wet weather". This type of response promotes worry and doubt about playing the game, which leads to thinking that often generates a self-fulfilling prophecy of failure.

At this point the player needs to develop the skill of adopting a secondary appraisal (a reappraisal) of the situation, learning to turn the threat into an opportunity. Reappraisal is a skill that can be learned. A player who can cope at level 2 does not have to resort to emotion-focused strategies at level 3. These players are capable of appraising and reappraising a situation by using skills such as positive self-talk, negative-thought stopping and imagery to help them identify a more effective frame of mind that allows them to play to their full potential. Generally, elite players have developed the ability to interpret stress in a facilitative way, minimizing the destructive effect of negative thoughts and feelings.

The essence of reappraisal is being able to challenge irrational thinking. In an attempt to reappraise a difficult situation, positive thinking can have a powerful impact. Positive thinking refers to different ways in which players develop and maintain confidence in their ability and keep rugby situations in perspective. The art of positive thinking can be achieved through positive affirmations and self-talk for general and specific rugby situations. Table 5.3 lists some examples in which England players initially had irrational thoughts but were able to reconstruct them, making them rational, positive and challenging.

TABLE 5.3   **TURNING NEGATIVE THOUGHTS INTO POSITIVE THOUGHTS**

Irrational thought	Rational thought
I never play well three times in a row.	I am on a roll, coming off the back of two great performances. I am going to go forward to everything.
I never play well against France. They wind me up.	I am going to concentrate on my own game. I am ready for any niggle. This is a sign I am playing well.
This is going to be a crooked throw.	Stick to my routine, focus on the steps, breathe, centre, preview.

Positive self-talk refers to the ability to identify words, phrases and images that bring feelings of confidence and control. This process is not always an easy one, as we tend to pick on our faults more often than our strengths, which sometimes contributes to our own downfall. When they are repeated, however, positive words, phrases or images can act as a buffer to recurring negative thoughts. This repetition of positive thought helps maintain focus, keeping the players positive about themselves, their ability and their performance before an event, and either on the pitch or on the bench. It is important for players to stay focused on the process of how to succeed rather than on the final success itself. Positive thinking about the task at hand helps keep the mind focused on the present.

Here's a training example. A player has a timed, 2,000-metre run to do in training, and his goal is eight and a half minutes. He might be thinking that he will never be able to accomplish this feat and therefore appraise the situation as threatening. As an alternative, he could use positive affirmations. He can remind himself that he has done the training for the event and has the endurance and strength to successfully complete the task. He could repeat "Go for it!" to himself during the buildup to the run and use it if he starts to feel the negative thoughts entering his mind. Positive thinking provides the tools to counterattack negative thoughts when they enter the mind, arming the player to fight back mentally. He is in control to maximize his capabilities.

When players appraise situations and see the opportunities available—that is, they reappraise the situation positively—they will be excited, happy and calm, and they will feel in control when contemplating every opportunity. Strategies at the appraisal level are designed to reinforce confidence. A positive self-image and perception of ability leads to confidence and good performance.

When Reappraisal Isn't Enough: Level 3 Coping

A player moves to level 3 coping strategies if the appraisal/reappraisal process is not effective or is not appropriate—for example, if the player still perceives the stress as negative and needs a way to deal with the impact of the stress. In the midst of competition, feelings of worry, concern or doubt most likely lead to thoughts such as "What are we going to do?" or "That's it, the game is over now," which then lead to negative actions such as knocking on the ball while being tackled to the ground. Level 3 interventions offer a host of physical, mental and behavioral strategies to overcome a negative reaction to stress.

At level 3, players becomes aware of the signs and also experience the symptoms of stress. They may need a way to cope during a match, as well as before and after. Level 3 teaches strategies to deal with the mental, physical and behavioral consequences of stress.

Stress affects us mentally, resulting in worry, self-doubt, team doubt, lack of concentration or changes in perception. For example, before a match a player may wonder if her family or friends are in attendance and worry whether she is going to have a good game. During the match, she might doubt her ability to kick, focus on a mistake she has made or be distracted by the crowd during a lineout. After the match, she may dwell on the bad parts of her performance.

Stress is also experienced physically, such as butterflies or a retching sensation in the stomach, sweaty palms or limp legs. These symptoms are often conditioned, prematch responses that need to be controlled if they become too invasive. Excessive muscle tension is not conducive to flowing movements.

Stress can also affect behavior. For example, the night before a match a player may not sleep well or may eat more than normal, thinking more energy is needed. During the match, he may become more talkative or forget to communicate regularly with teammates. After the match, he might forget to review his performance and just walk away from the game.

For optimal and effective coping, a player needs to develop mental, physical and behavioral strategies to deal with stress. Because the type of stress experienced (mental, physical or behavioral), the frequency and duration may be different for each case. It is advisable to match the coping strategy to the stress symptoms, and the players should pick their coping strategies based on their own stress experience.

Coping Mentally

Cognitive anxiety is the worry or negative thoughts a player may experience. A player may also experience negative expectations, lack of concentration, negative images of failure, a decrease in confidence, and an increase in self-doubt and team doubt about performance. The following strategies are designed to tackle some of these problems.

Concentration Cue Words and Activation Words

A player who gets nervous or feels stressed in a situation often loses the ability to stay focused and concentrate, which can have a debilitating effect on performance. When concentration is lost, the players' focus of attention shifts, and they often begin to identify irrelevant information, such as noticing people in the crowd during a lineout. One way to enhance concentration skills when under pressure is to develop concentration cue words or activation words (see chapter 4). These words may vary from motivational cues to technical or tactical calls. Players may say them to themselves to refocus or call them out loud to teammates, but their main purpose is to keep the player on task.

To identify these words, phrases and images, players should begin by recalling positive aspects of their rugby playing ability and skills as well as previous performances, including preparation and warm-up, or instances in which they reacted well to overcome odds. Players should write down and rehearse these positive affirmations in training (see table 5.4). By recalling such information, the player is sending conscious positive reminders that develop into positive self-talk and become particularly helpful in stressful situations when concentration begins to falter.

A key component to all of these statements is belief! The player must believe in the words, phrases or images they choose in order to be effective in focusing attention on what is relevant to the game at that point in time.

TABLE 5.4 POSITIVE AFFIRMATIONS	
General positive affirmations	**Specific, personal rugby achievements**
I am strong.	I had a great match against this team.
I feel ready for this game.	I play great in the rain.
My speed is great.	

Imagery

Using imagery is another effective way to cope with nerves and prepare for competition (see chapter 3). With imagery, the players clearly see themselves playing rugby, feeling themselves playing, feeling the ball in their hands and seeing themselves running on the pitch. In preparation for playing, imagery is a useful technique for players to use to familiarize themselves with the venue (especially if it is their first time there) and to calm themselves by rehearsing their warm-up routines and possible game situations.

When imagery is useful and realistic, players may actually feel nervous about the game by just imagining it. This emotional reaction suggests that the players have effectively created the moment in their minds and when the real moment arrives, they will feel in control, confident and prepared because they have already practiced dealing with the anxiety.

Imagery can also be used to build confidence. Don't imagine losing; imagine winning! Players should decide beforehand what the goal is and make sure they see themselves achieving that movement or action. Imagery is great for building self-confidence, rehearsing game preparation and focusing attention. Don't leave imagery to the last minute and expect it to work; try it out during training periods and in preparation for each game.

Coping Physically

All of our bodies react differently to nervousness and stress. Some people experience butterflies in their stomachs, jelly legs, sweaty palms, shaky hands, an increase in heart rate, or they breathe faster. These are all physical responses to stress. Fortunately, strategies for physical relaxation exist and have been well researched to help calm players and control physical nervousness. Different forms of relaxation can benefit a player the night before a game, pregame, at the ground and during the game.

There are many benefits to learning ways to physically control breathing and relax. The model in figure 5.2 demonstrates the range of situations in which relaxation techniques could be useful, such as inducing a deeper sense of relaxation the night before a match or calming a player down moments before executing a crucial dead-ball skill.

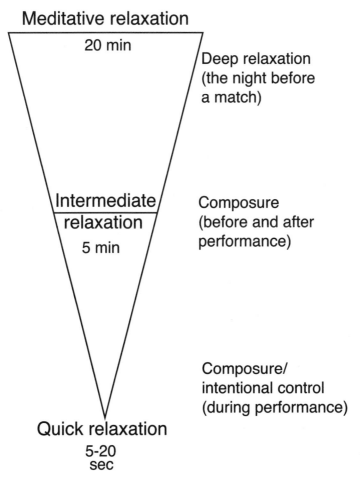

Figure 5.2 Level 3 stress intervention model.

The techniques used depend on personal preference and the timing of the exercise in relation to the start of the game. In general, breathing and relaxation techniques help control nervous energy. This ability yields significant dividends: It leads to better sleep before a big game; it prepares the player for imagery training; it improves concentration; and it can help improve overall body awareness.

There are different techniques for controlling breathing and physical relaxation with two being the most common. The first breathing technique, with its variations, is called focused breathing, and the second is a physical technique known as progressive muscle relaxation (PMR). Both techniques help achieve meditative, intermediate and quick relaxation by reducing nervous tension by lowering the heart rate and generating a feeling of control of the body.

Focused Breathing

Find a comfortable place to sit or lie down with feet uncrossed and hands on your abdomen. Make sure you are comfortable and generally feeling overall body relaxation. Begin breathing in through your nose and out through your mouth. Each breath should be deep, using your abdominal muscles. With your hands resting on your abdomen you should be able to feel your belly rising and falling with each breath.

Try to focus all your attention on the centre core of your body. Feel your abdominal muscles expand as you breathe in and relax as you exhale. To slow your breathing down even more, introduce counting to your breathing. As you take deep breaths, count to yourself as you inhale *(in, two, three, four)* and exhale *(out, two, three, four)*. Repeat this counting pattern to slow your heart rate down.

You may also find that a particular word—such as *relax* or *calm*—helps you relax. Introduce this word into your thoughts once you have established a steady, slow, rhythmical deep-breathing pattern. Every time you exhale say the calming word in your mind. You should feel an overall body sense of relaxation. This technique is particularly useful to help you fall asleep at night if you are feeling anxious about the game. It could also be used several hours before competition to relax away any useless, debilitating muscle tension.

Centering Technique

This technique is a shorter version of focused breathing that can be used moments before going on the pitch or during breaks in the action. By taking a moment to take in more oxygen and slow your breathing down, you are putting yourself in a better playing state. Centering involves taking a few deep breaths while sitting or standing, allowing the body to feel in control and relaxed, yet not in a deep state of focused breathing relaxation.

Focus your attention on your abdomen and feel slow deep breaths coming from your diaphragm as your abdomen pushes out as you breathe in through your nose. As you exhale, feel the tension leave all your muscles. (You might focus on a particular muscle group for every breath to make sure those muscles feel loose and relaxed.) When you are ready, stand up and shake yourself into an energized state and out of feeling overly relaxed.

One-Breath Relaxation

This technique is useful for on-pitch situations when you need to slow or calm down before executing a particular skill, such as a throw-in for a lineout or taking a penalty or conversion kick.

Take a long, slow inhalation followed by long, slow exhalation, letting your shoulders rise and fall at the same time to release any tension that may exist in the upper body. This is also a good time to use a cue word, phrase or imagery to refocus your thoughts directly on the task at hand, such as focusing on the goal posts or the spot where you are throwing in.

Progressive Muscle Relaxation (PMR)

Progressive muscle relaxation helps distinguish a tense muscle from a relaxed muscle. Use PMR after focused breathing technique when the body is relaxed and you want to feel even more relaxed. This exercise is good to do before falling asleep, especially if you have trouble sleeping the night before a game.

While sitting or lying comfortably, take some deep breaths and feel an all-over body relaxation. Focus your attention on your feet and tighten up all the muscles in your feet. Hold the tension for four counts (mentally count *one, two, three, four*) and then relax. For about 10 seconds concentrate on the feelings of heaviness and relaxation as they occur in your foot muscles (use the cue word *relax)*. Repeat two more times. Move to your calf muscles. Tighten your calf muscles. Hold the tension for four counts, then relax and repeat. Move up to your quads, glutes and abdomen, then to your hands, forearms, upper arms, shoulders, neck and face. Do three sets of hold-and-relax focus for each muscle group. Try to isolate each muscle group; it helps to increase your awareness of the major muscle groups in your body and the tension that can sometimes exist during pressure situations.

You can speed up your progress on the exercise as you become more skilled at it by combining the muscle groups. You can tense and relax all the muscles in your legs at once, then progress through the middle part of your body, upper body, then your face. At even later stage, you can tense all the lower body muscles and relax them several times, then you can tense and relax all the upper body muscle groups together. With additional practice, you can just tense your whole body and relax it several times to reach a state of total body relaxation.

Use PMR the night before a game. As you lie comfortably in bed, do some deep breathing to relax. Try some imagery of situations in the next day's game. Following the imagery, you may feel nervous about the game. Now is a wise time to do muscle progressions in PMR along with some more deep breathing to lower your heart rate. See if you can create a feeling of overall body relaxation and a clear mind. You may feel a sensation of heaviness and sinking into your bed, and sleep will quickly follow.

Movement

Another way to remove tension from muscles is by physically moving them around. The physical warm-up is a great opportunity to relieve nervous tension. If you have been travelling to the venue, waiting around before the game or rushed off the bench to play, you will want to reactivate yourself physically and mentally. A light jog, some short running bursts or a little stretching to simply elevate the heart rate and breathing can create an energized feeling to switch your mind and body into its playing mode and help dispel excess nervous energy. While activating yourself, you may find that listening to music also helps to get you switched on and takes your mind off the game, allowing you to feel relaxed but energized.

Coping Behaviorally

When some players become nervous, they decide to change the way they normally do things. It is not uncommon for them to feel they need some extra help, time or something out of the norm to help them perform better. Actually, this deviation from routine is probably the worst thing they could do to themselves. Even during times when they have done all they can do to prepare for a game, players should stick to what they know works and use their regular routines. We often notice changes in behavior in other players before we realize how we have changed our own routines. To think and act as normally as possible, develop and use performance routines.

Players on a team need to be aware of other players' responses to pressure, and they need to support them. For example, some players might show a short fuse or display needless attention-seeking behavior while others may become very quiet. Other behavioral changes to game stress might include not eating anything the night before or morning of a game. Be conscious of any change in behavior that might have an adverse impact on a teammate's play.

While we discussed performance routines in the context of level 1 interventions, they are also relevant at this behavioral level when a player starts to experience debilitative levels of anxiety. Focusing on a routine can act as a positive distraction to negative thoughts and feelings that a player may experience (see chapter 9). It is a safety net to fall into during times of stress and anxiety.

Personal Time

Members of a team often find themselves constantly surrounded by team members and feel like they never have any time alone. It is crucial for players to create time to be alone during a tournament (especially when on tour) as well as when preparing to play if isolated preparation time is needed.

Before you leave home (or the country), think about the things you like to do on your own and take the necessary items. For example, you may be able to take your mountain bike with you and have it to get away when appropriate. Or it may mean a collection of books, magazines, music, games or a cell phone to talk to friends outside of rugby. Use anything that allows you to create time for yourself, especially when you are nervous or when others may be winding you up. Use your precompetition routines to help map out the time you will spend preparing on your own and when you will be with the team.

Body Language

Nervousness has a certain look; it gives confidence to the opponent. Players need to find ways to look confident on the outside as they cope with nervousness on the inside. A key strategy is to be aware of body language. If you see someone walking around with her head down, shoulders drooping, pacing up and down the hotel lobby, or kicking the ground or slowly getting into position after a mistake during the game, your first thought may be "That person looks nervous." This message is not a confident one to send to the people you are playing with or playing against.

The New Zealand All Blacks perform their infamous Haka dance to try to psych out their opponents.

Be aware of your own presentation. You may be feeling nervous inside, but you certainly don't have to show it. Walk with conviction—head up, shoulders back. Be quick to refocus after a mistake and get back into position. It is not arrogance but attitude. A great example of team body language and confidence is the classic, in-your-face performance of the Haka by the All Blacks before an international to try to psych out the opponent.

Finally, control the controllables. There are many things in rugby that can't be controlled, and worrying about them wastes valuable energy. There is no point in worrying about those things that you cannot control, such as the weather. Equally, there is no need to worry about the things you do have in your control. If you have already taken the time to prepare for them in your routine, then you have a great chance at succeeding.

The next time you are nervous, look at the situation as an opportunity, not a threat. Being nervous is good. Use that extra energy to play better than ever, use these skills to help keep your focus on your play, and believe in your ability and the team's potential to achieve.

part

II

MENTALLY TOUGH TEAMS

chapter

6

Cohesion and Teamwork

Krista Munroe
University of Windsor

Peter Terry
*University of
Southern Queensland*

Albert Carron
*University of
Western Ontario*

© Empics

Rugby has a fantastic bonding effect . . . It brings friendships to the fore . . . You get strong guys up front, quick guys in the back, you get poets, you get freemasons, everybody playing in the same team, and it's a fantastic culture.

—*Francois Pienaar, Captain, South Africa, World Cup Winners 1995*

Team cohesion describes the tendency of a group to stick together and remain united as it pursues its goals. As the Pienaar quote illustrates, team cohesion (or team unity) can generate strong emotions among team members. But, as anyone who has been a captain, manager, player or observer of rugby can testify, achieving team unity and getting a team to work together to achieve a common goal can be difficult. Individual team members sometimes have personal goals and aspirations that bring them into conflict with the team's goals and objectives. As a consequence, those individuals may try to pull the team in different directions. Teammates may dislike one another, which may lead to poor or nonexistent communication on and off the pitch. On the other hand, teammates may like one another so much that to maintain harmony, they do not risk honest appraisal, accurate feedback and open communication.

So what steps can team leaders and coaches take to ensure that the team is actively working to become unified and cohesive? This chapter seeks to answer that question by focusing on four strategies that have been used successfully in sport teams: team performance profiling, team goal setting, a game-plan exercise to develop role clarity and role acceptance, and an exercise to promote mutual respect.

Team Performance Profiling

Team performance profiling is a method that teams use to identify the ideal characteristics necessary for success and the degree to which those characteristics are currently present. Performance profiling provides a foundation for decision making and goal setting because it helps athletes understand

- their own team's areas of perceived weaknesses,
- their own team's areas of perceived strengths,

The authors wish to acknowledge Mark Pink and Cameron Henderson of Brunel University for their assistance in researching material for this chapter.

- the concept of an ideal team,
- areas in which their team might resist improvement,
- where there is a discrepancy within the team about strengths and weaknesses,
- where there is a discrepancy among athletes in what is considered important,
- where there is discrepancy between athletes and coaches in what is considered important, and
- strategies for monitoring performance.

Essentially, team performance profiling allows coaches and athletes an open and communicative environment to facilitate goal setting.

Several positive psychological consequences can result from the process of engaging collectively in team performance profiling. First, and most important, the team's task and social cohesion will be improved. Teams high in task cohesion work together to attain the group goal, and teams high in social cohesion work together to maintain social relationships in the group. With greater task and social cohesion, there is greater satisfaction with the team's goals. Finally, when teams act together to participate collectively, other psychological perceptions that reflect a sense of unity are enhanced. Team interactions that occur during team performance profiling can lead to the development of common perceptions and beliefs about the group—such as the team's goals, its unity and the level of current satisfaction.

Team performance profiling has received considerable attention over the past several years, and one reason has to be the simplicity of the process. There are eight steps to follow, and to facilitate the completion of these steps, each athlete is given a copy of both the Athlete Performance Profile sheet (see table 6.1) and the Team Performance Profile sheet (see table 6.2, p. 141).

1. Each athlete, working independently, identifies up to 10 elements of team play that are viewed as most critical to rugby team success and records these in the first column of the Athlete Performance Profile sheet. These 10 elements should represent all aspects of team play—offensive play, defensive play, lineouts, scrums and tackles. In the example in table 6.3 (p. 142), notice that the rugby forward has listed both offensive and defensive elements of team play.

TABLE 6.1 **ATHLETE PERFORMANCE PROFILE SHEET**			
Performance element (individual)	Performance element (group)	Importance score (1 to 10)	Current level (1 to 10)
1.			
2.			
3.			
4.			
5.			
6.			
7.			
8.			
9.			
10.			

2. The athletes divide into two subgroups—backs and forwards. The leader chosen for each subgroup lists on a blackboard or flip chart all the elements identified by individual athletes. The subgroup then discusses the elements listed.

3. After a thorough discussion, the subgroup comes to a consensus on the 10 elements considered most significant for team success. The leader of the subgroup then copies these elements on the Team Performance Profile sheet. In the example in table 6.4 (p. 142), notice that for brevity only four elements have been listed—lineouts, rucks, mauls, tackles.

4. Each athlete then copies the 10 elements from the group consensus into the second column of the Athlete's Performance Profile sheet. In the example in table 6.3 (p. 142), notice that the group consensus items are slightly different than the individual player's elements. Using a scale varying from 1 to 10 (where 1 means "not very important" and 10 means "most important"), the athletes decide on an importance score for each element. To provide a frame of reference for developing an importance score, encourage the athletes to think of a highly successful team and

TABLE 6.2	**TEAM PERFORMANCE PROFILE SHEET**		
Performance element	Mean importance score (1 to 10)	Mean current score (1 to 10)	Discrepancy (importance – current)
1.			
2.			
3.			
4.			
5.			
6.			
7.			
8.			
9.			
10.			

Element in need
of immediate attention:

1. _____

Elements that need work over
the season:

1. _____

2. _____

3. _____

4. _____

how that team would rate on these elements. Generally, when players engage in the process of performance profiling, the elements listed are either rated at or very close to 10.

5. Next, the leader of each subgroup calculates the average importance score for each element (all the individual scores are added and then divided by the number of individuals in the group). The answer is then entered in the second column of the Team Performance Profile sheet.

6. The athletes independently assess their subgroup's current level for each of the elements; that is, the athletes use their own perception to rate the subgroup at that time in the season. The following question can be used as a prompt: "Where would you rate our unit at the present time on each of the 10 elements?"

TABLE 6.3 SAMPLE ATHLETE PERFORMANCE PROFILE SHEET

Performance element (individual)	Performance element (group)	Importance score (1 to 10)	Current level (1 to 10)
1. Lineouts	*Lineouts*	10	7
2. Rucks	*Rucks*	10	5
3. Mauls	*Mauls*	10	8
4. Tackles	*Tackles*	10	8
5. Passing	*Passing*	10	6
6. Ball retention	*Ball retention*	10	6
7. Defense in rucks	*Scrummaging*	10	5
8. Attack from scrum	*Receive kicks*	10	5
9. Defense in scrums	*Penalty defense*	10	6
10. Lineout defense	*Penalty plays*	10	7

TABLE 6.4 SAMPLE TEAM PERFORMANCE PROFILE SHEET

Performance element	Mean importance score (1 to 10)	Mean current score (1 to 10)	Discrepancy (importance – current)
Lineouts	10	6	4
Rucks	10	4	6
Mauls	10	7	3
Tackles	10	7	3

Element in need of immediate attention:

1. Rucks

2. Lineouts

Elements that need work during the season:

1. Mauls

2. Tackles

Again, a scale ranging from 1 to 10 is used (1 means "could not be any worse" and 10 means "could not be any better"). The athletes record their evaluations in the fourth column of the Athlete's Performance Profile sheet.

7. The leader calculates the mean score for the subgroup's current level for each of these elements. The mean current level is then entered in the third column on the Team Performance Profile sheet.

8. The leader subtracts the mean current level of the subgroup from the mean importance level. This calculation provides a discrepancy score for each of the 10 elements (fourth column), which helps the athletes clearly see their unit's perceived strengths and weaknesses. The higher the discrepancy score, the more work that is needed on the element. Notice that in the example in table 6.4, lineouts and rucks are calculated to be the two areas needing immediate attention.

These eight steps can be used for the game of rugby as a whole or can be repeated for four separate areas of rugby: performance, technical, tactical and mental aspects. After identifying the elements that need the most work in each of the four areas, the team can then set goals related to various elements. The team must decide which elements in each of the four areas need improvement immediately. These would be targeted as the short-term goals for the group, and the remainder of the elements could be designated as long-term goals. Experience has shown that only one or two elements should be chosen from each of the four areas as short-term goals. Any more than that may be too many.

Team Goal Setting

In any group situation, athletes naturally have individual goals and aspirations for themselves: to score more points than the previous year, make more tackles or have a greater involvement in the team offense. Individual goals are not only inevitable, they are also essential for individual progress. What are essential for team progress, however, are team goals. Research has shown that in collective endeavors, group goals are far more effective for group success than individual goals. It is important to note that group goals are not the sum of the group members' personal goals.

Group goal setting has been found to foster respect, cohesiveness and a means to provide the team with focus and direction. Group goals should focus on performance processes, such as *Secure the ball from at least 80 percent of our line-outs*, rather than outcomes, such as *Win the championship*. Performance processes are the foundation for team outcomes because they are simply more under direct, personal control.

To engage in group goal setting, coaches and players should develop an open environment that encourages honest dialogue. The process of group goal setting can increase the cohesion of a group by fostering common beliefs about the team's goal, its unity and the level of satisfaction present. When individual members help to establish goals for the team, cohesion is enhanced, goal acceptance is increased, and team members are more com-

Setting group goals encourages the development of mutual respect among team-mates, creates cohesion and provides direction for the team.

mitted to the achievement of the goals. Furthermore, the leadership behavior of the coach in the goal-setting process also influences group cohesion. When coaches emphasize the importance of goal setting and allow members to participate in team goal-setting processes, what results is a stronger sense of task and social cohesion.

For the team to engage in team goal setting, two sets of information are essential. The first is knowledge of the area (or areas) in which team goals are to be set. Team performance profiling is the process you should use to identify such elements targeted for goal setting. The second set of information required is current (or baseline) statistics for the targeted elements. For example, if securing lineout possession was identified as a problem area through team performance profiling, the team's current standard must be known before a goal can be established. Knowing that the team is successful in securing the ball only 45 percent of the time provides a frame of reference for setting a future goal.

Players can follow five simple steps to participate in team goal setting. The information gathered can be recorded on a sheet, such as the one shown in table 6.5.

TABLE 6.5 **TEAM GOAL-SETTING SHEET**

Performance element	Baseline	Personal estimate	Group's estimate	Team's estimate

1. Each athlete identifies the short-term goal (the performance element having the largest discrepancy score) from the team profiling exercise (see table 6.4 for a sample). These goals are recorded in the first column.

2. The baseline data (current performance level) for each element is entered in the second column. The coach can gain access to this information by referring to previous play statistics or video footage.

3. Working independently, the athletes record a personal estimation or target for the team goal in the third column.

4. In their subgroups (backs and forwards), athletes come to a consensus on the group's estimate for the team goal. This target is recorded in the fourth column.

5. Finally, the entire team comes together to discuss the team's goals. One leader for the team records the total team's estimate for the team goal in the fifth column.

Establishing a period of time in which to achieve the team's goals is extremely important in the goal-setting process. The team must decide when to reassess the goals and examine the progress that has been made. Because the elements identified are short-term goals, reevaluating the goals is recommended after two or three matches. At that point, the coach should provide feedback with regards to the goals that were set. The team may discover that the targets were either too high or too low, and they need adjustment. A new target date is then set. These same five steps can be carried out for long-term goals as well. Reassessment of long-term goals should be done every four to six weeks.

Understanding and Accepting Individual Roles

The synergy effect is paramount. But, for the whole to truly become greater than the sum of its parts, everything has to come together in a common understanding of what it takes to win the game. Each player has to understand how his cog fits into the whole machine, each player working to achieve his individual objectives in the knowledge that his teammates will do the same, each player knowing his role in the context of the collective role.

—*Kevin Bowring, Welsh Rugby Union National Coach, 1996-1998*

Successful rugby teams generate order out of apparent chaos. For 15 individuals to function effectively in a fast-moving, ever-changing environment, the planning and practice of group processes is required. This task can be aided by the game-plan exercise. The purpose of this exercise is to develop a common understanding of the specific task ahead, clarify individual and group roles, generate role acceptance and identify key words and concepts to be used on the field of play. Role clarity is the degree to which a player understands what behaviors are expected while role acceptance is the degree to which the individual is satisfied with his or her role responsibilities.

The game-plan exercise represents the forum for discussing and agreeing on strategy before it is implemented, and it is carried out in four stages. In stage 1, the strengths and weaknesses of the opposing team are summarized in as much detail as is available. In stage 2, the team comes to an agreement on how these strengths and weaknesses will be countered or exploited. In stage 3, the team members identify key words or phrases that reflect the game plan. Finally, contingency plans are prepared by considering various what-if scenarios.

One strength of the game-plan exercise is that it provides a mechanism for public acceptance of team strategy, and it crystallizes lists of issues into a few key words or phrases. The example in figure 6.1 shows more specific details of the four stages of the game-plan exercise. Bear in mind that this exercise is designed to build on the existing strengths of the team, to emphasize to each player the critical elements of a successful team performance and to identify key words that summarize the qualities of the team at its best.

First, at a team meeting, team members identify verbally what they perceive to be the strengths and weaknesses of the opposition. A facilitator collates this information on a blackboard or flip chart. The coach should have significant input in this process but should not dominate the proceedings. To encourage a sense of ownership of the process, the coach should prompt each team member to make a contribution. Once the list is completed, team members identify how the perceived strengths can be countered and the perceived weaknesses exploited. Once the team has discussed and agreed on a strategy, the facilitator lists the strategy

Stage 1: Opposition assessment

Strengths:

1. Rucking speed

2. Back breaks

3. Kicking high ball

Weaknesses:

1. Scrums

2. Lineouts

3. Ball retention

Stage 2: Counters

Strengths:

1. Get quickly to breakdown

2. Up hard on defense

3. Wings drop and help

Weaknesses:

1. Drive backwards, wheel

2. Catch and drive

3. Hard tackle and drive

Stage 3: Cue words

1. "Tackle and drive"

2. "Up hard"

3. "Drop and cover"

4. "Be aggressive"

Stage 4: What-ifs

1. If they score early, tackle hard, drive over the ball, retain our possession.

2. If they kick to fullback, flyhalf and scrumhalf help with coverage.

3. If their backs break gain line, drop flanker into the backline.

Figure 6.1 Game-plan exercise example.

on a separate sheet and crosses out the specific opposition quality that has been addressed.

(Note: An emphatic swoosh of the pen across a substantial opposition strength can do much to engender team confidence. Obviously, the opposition is not encountered on a flip chart, nor does crossing out a team's strength nullify their threat in reality; however, there is a link between the pregame mindset of a team and their performance on the field of play. It is this mindset that the game-plan exercise seeks to influence.)

It is important during this process to achieve acceptance of the potential consequences of a particular strategy for some team members. For example, let's presume that it is agreed that the outside half should kick a higher percentage of first phase possessions than normal, perhaps because the opposition's fullback is perceived to be weak under the high ball. This decision inevitably means less ball-in-hand for the three quarters. Because backs prefer to run with the ball (versus chasing kicks), any concerns they might have about the agreed-on team strategy should be voiced at this point, rather than during the game.

As the agreed plan evolves, the facilitator should start to request key qualities that the team intends to display, such as "discipline", "aggression" or "patience". Team members should be encouraged to suggest how these qualities will be shown during the game. For example, will aggression be better reflected by knocking the opposition backwards in the tackle, by pumping the knees when rucking and by driving low with the ball into contact situations?

Finally, a few key words or phrases should be highlighted to the players as take-away messages from the agreed game plan. Teammates should be encouraged to remind one another of these during the game, especially if things are not quite going according to plan. For example, during a British Student Championships final at Twickenham in 1995 between Brunel and Swansea Universities, the lead changed hands three times in the final two minutes of a desperately hard-fought game. A towering drop-goal put Swansea into a 30-28 lead with only a few seconds remaining; most people believed Swansea had secured victory. However, the key words "patience" and "discipline"—

agreed on by the Brunel players before the game—strengthened their resolve. Swansea saw them storm back from the kickoff, win a penalty almost immediately and kick the goal for a famous 31-30 win. The beneficial impact of the agreed key words in this nail-biting situation were identified by several Brunel players after the game.

To test the effectiveness of the game plan, coaches should offer a few what-if scenarios for players' consideration: What if the opposition scores immediately from the kickoff? What if the referee makes a series of bad decisions against us? What if we are failing to win our own ball from the lineout? What if we are 10 points down with five minutes to play? Team members should discuss what elements of the game plan might need to be changed in such situations (if any). They should determine whether the key qualities agreed by the team are the right ones to cope with all possible scenarios, and they should know whether a distinct, alternative game plan is required or just variations on the agreed plan.

The wisdom of a process that focuses on how to respond positively to potentially negative events might be questioned by some people, but rugby is not a game of perfection. Knowing how to get the most from a team on a bad day is a key skill. Ignore such preparation at your own peril.

Promoting Mutual Respect

The main reason the Lions beat the Springboks in 1997 was because we became a team in the true sense of the word, we understood each other, we had respect for each other, we had a deep sense of a common purpose.

—*Richard Hill, British Lions flanker*

Rugby is a highly interdependent sport. Teammates are mutually reliant for both team performance and physical well-being. Consequently, the development of mutual respect among teammates underlies the task cohesion and team spirit that form the bedrock of a successful team. The following mutual respect exercise is a simple strategy to help develop such mutual respect and enhance the self-confidence of each individual. This exercise is a way of letting players know the reasons why their peers value and respect them, a process that fulfills an important psychological need. The mutual respect exercise requires all team members to identify why they want their fellow players on the team. This strategy has been used to good effect with the national teams of England and Wales.

The principle underlying this exercise is that the natural bond among teammates has great potential to strengthen the self-belief of each individual and, hence, of the team. Teammates often have great respect for each other's personal and playing qualities, yet they may not feel inclined to express that respect openly, perhaps for fear of creating the appearance of a mutual admiration society. The net result of such reluctance is a missed opportunity to boost team cohesion. The mutual respect exercise allows the expression of respect without the burden of speech making. All players like to know that their teammates appreciate them. While they may know this intuitively, it does no harm to be told explicitly, especially before a big game.

For the mutual respect exercise, each player is given a form containing the names of all their teammates. At the top of this sheet is the phrase "I want [teammate's name] on my team because . . . " After each player has independently and confidentially written their comments about every other player, the forms are collated by the facilitator or group leader. All the comments about a particular player are transferred onto a single summary form. This is repeated for each player. The summary sheets are distributed in sealed envelopes to each player.

Questions arise of how often to do this, whether to include all squad members or only the 15 starters and when and how to present the feedback. Our advice is for the coach to use this strategy sparingly (saving it until an important occasion), to include every squad member and to provide the summary sheets for players in sealed envelopes. We recommend distributing the envelopes the evening before the game to allow players to sleep in the warm glow of their teammates' positive comments. Figure 6.2 provides examples of the types of comments made by international players about one another. All involved in the process knew that there was no room for empty flattery and that the sentiments had to have a solid basis in reality.

I want Player A on my team because:

He never takes a backwards step.

He has huge heart, spirit and pride.

There is no tougher player in world rugby.

He is as hard as a rottweiler.

He is a born leader.

He is an inspiration.

I want Player B on my team because:

He is the old master.

He has sound stability and control.

He is known for steering the ship up front.

He has a motivational, calming influence.

He is a great reader of the game.

He is a superb player.

Figure 6.2   Sample comments from the mutual respect exercise.

The comments tend to reflect qualities well justified by performances over the years. As a result, they positively affect the self-image of the player receiving them. Player A is clearly seen by his teammates as someone who plays with passion, determination and the sort of physical robustness that inspires those around him. The image of this man as a rottweiler dog may provide the same sense of identity enjoyed by Brian Moore, the ex-England hooker affectionately known as Pit Bull. Player B is seen by his teammates as someone whose effectiveness is based more on his experience and decision-making ability than aggression. He would probably be encouraged by their comments to view his age (mid-30s) as an asset, rather than a potential source of anxiety.

Summary

Will Carling, England and British Lion, once said, "Most of all things, I love being part of this squad. I can't express how much it means to me . . . It's a team, a group, it's a pride of brothers . . . That's it. Whatever happens, we are brothers in pride." As this quote illustrates, players develop strong bonds with their teammates, a genuine sense of team unity. The reasons for this cohesion are obvious to anyone who has experienced the joys and pains of sport—the sacrifices, the training, winning, losing and so on. It is inevitable that some sense of unity develops in every team. The exercises outlined in this chapter are intended to speed up this process, to facilitate the bonding of individuals on a team, for that team to become more unified and for that unified team to become better and more successful.

chapter

The Attacking Mindset

Eddie O'Sullivan
Irish Rugby Football Union

P.J. Smyth
University of Limerick

© Empics

By now you should be well aware of what sport psychology is and how it can be applied to enhance performance. Players can acquire an array of mental skills that control anxiety and arousal and also develop confidence and concentration. Through questionnaires and self-awareness exercises, you should have an awareness of your own psychological profile with its strengths and weaknesses. After doing so, now you simply need to select and develop the mental skills that can benefit you most and mould them into a routine to be used in match situations. Remember, mental skills first need to be learned and practiced in nonpressure situations (such as at home), then built into your skill drills and team practices, then applied in match situations. As with physical skills, they may not always work for you in the initial stages, but with perseverance and practice the benefits become obvious.

In this chapter we consider how psychological principles and skills can be employed to enhance attacking play in rugby. Attacking skills and tactics break down for a variety of reasons. One reason is a lack of physical fitness, such as being too fatigued to sustain a burst of pace or lack of muscular strength to hold up the ball for recycling in a tackle. There could be technical deficiencies, such as a weakness in passing off the left hand or inability to control running pace. Skills and attacking tactics can also break down because of mental factors, such as anxiety, lack of confidence to carry out a particular role or lack of appropriate focus.

For example, consider the case of a player who, when a move is called, becomes anxious and focuses his mind on either a previous mistake or on what might happen if he drops the ball in the upcoming move. In both cases, cognitive anxiety prevents his mind from focusing on the present moment and on what is relevant. In addition to lack of focus, the player may also have somatic anxiety, which creates muscular tension and affects coordination and timing of actions.

Another example of inappropriate focus is a player who at the instant of receiving the ball has his mind focused on the advancing defender instead of the ball. Before receiving the ball, he is so focused on the ball that he fails to notice a change in the opponent's path and fails to adjust his own path. At a lineout, an attacking opportunity could be lost because a thrower, jumper or supporter is not focused on what needs to be done. In a dynamic situation, the appropriate focus is changing all of the time.

Players experiencing cognitive anxiety are in danger of focusing too narrowly (tunnel vision) or of focusing on irrelevant and negative thoughts. This deficiency may cause them to miss crucial relevant information that results in poor decision making and ineffective actions. Somatic anxiety may also cause an excess of muscular tension that can cause coordination problems affecting the actions of catching, passing, kicking and running.

The Ideal Performance State and the Attacking Mindset

Before we devote the rest of the chapter to illustrating how to achieve the attacking mindset, perhaps we should ask an important question: What defines an *attacking mindset?* The characteristics of the attacking mindset and the ideal-performance state include total focus, relaxation and confidence. Players must enjoy

The attacking mindset is focused and confident and is able to make good, quick decisions.

the feeling of automatic and effortless performance without fear of mistakes.

Many players have experienced this mindset at some stage in their careers, but they have also found that it is difficult to achieve on a consistent basis. With appropriate use of mental skills, integrated with technical and physical preparation, you can increase the probability of achieving the ideal attacking mindset more frequently. Although these mental skills help you achieve this mindset, keep in mind that they also help at the other end of the spectrum when you are not in the attacking mindset. When you experience a lack of focus, loss of confidence and an increase in error making, the use of mental skills enables you to cope with these situations and make adjustments to improve your mindset.

Taking Advantage of Opponent Errors

When opponents make errors, such as dropping a ball or missing a tackle, chances are that their mindsets are still on the error at the next set piece rather than focused on the present. It is precisely at this time that they are vulnerable to an attack, such as another high kick or a move where their opposite number gets another run at them. Keep your radar tuned in to these opportunities; they *will* happen. It is up to each player to take advantage of the moment when it spontaneously presents itself.

Before becoming an international, Richard Wallace, former Ireland and Lions winger, sought help with his ability to maintain concentration. The problem was highlighted for him during a provincial game when the opposition launched a high kick in his direction, and he was out of position and missed it. At the following scrum, the opposing out half realized that he was vulnerable and put up another high kick. This time Richard was in position, but he missed it again. When questioned as to what his mind was on for the first kick, he said it was on nothing in particular; he had just drifted out of the game because he had not received the ball for a long time. With respect to the second kick, he said his mind was still on the previous missed catch and the possibility of it happening again.

Richard therefore devised and practiced a mental routine that ensured that this concentration problem did not occur again. He was surprised that more teams did not take advantage of such mental vulnerabilities in opponents. It happened to him; certainly it could happen to other players throughout the course of any match. Coaches then must teach players to develop an awareness to recognize these situations.

For example, players and coaches could discuss the opponent's past mistakes and mental vulnerabilities, as in stage 1 and 2 of the game-plan exercise from chapter 6. They could select several verbal strategy cues that would alert their teammates that they intend to attack the vulnerable player(s) on the next possession. The team also could discuss these strategies quickly during breaks in the action.

Fear of Failure and Mistakes

One of the characteristics of the ideal-performance state for the attacking mindset is absence of fear. Fear causes lack of focus and muscular tension, both of which have a detrimental effect on skillful performance. Effective attacking play involves taking risks and increases the probability of making errors. This combination of risk taking and error making naturally tends to create a fear of failure.

It is not uncommon to see teams who are usually skillful and adept in handling the ball in their opponent's 22-metre area become quite jittery, tense and error-prone when they attempt the same thing within their own 22. Why is this? The skills and actions are the same, and they probably have more space and time. The answer is that the consequences of making a mistake are greater in their own 22, and this fear leads to focusing on possible negative consequences, rather than on relevant cues for the skills and moves.

There are several ways to deal with fear of failure and become comfortable with taking risks. One way is to acquire and use mental skills for focusing: process goals, controlled breathing, self-talk and focusing words, imagery and routines. Another way to become as mentally skilled as possible is to practice under the pressure of simulated match conditions or to carry out moves in high-risk situations in actual matches. Initially, this rehearsal could be done in less important matches, then gradually extended to important matches. With contexts such as real-life game situations, fear is conquered by facing up to it.

An important influence in preventing or conquering fear of failure is coaches' attitudes about risk taking and making mistakes.

Australian coach Bob Dwyer, whose teams were renowned for their brilliant attacking play and risk taking, says, "Rugby is a game that deserves to be played positively, by which I mean that every team should be willing to risk defeat in the pursuit of victory" (Dwyer 1992, 41). When talking about David Campese, Dwyer says, "I have come to the conclusion that his single greatest asset is courage. Campese has always been willing to achieve the best" (1992, 68). Dwyer points out that many players of flair tend to withdraw into their shell after they have been criticized for mistakes.

Interestingly, though, making mistakes can also positively affect skill development. Recent research shows that practice with more errors leads to higher skill levels than practice with fewer errors. Through making mistakes, the players learn about the boundaries of what they can achieve. They develop a feel and appreciation of what is correct and what is incorrect, and they learn how to adapt a skill to what is required for a particular moment. In short, smart coaches encourage players to explore and experience what works and does not work. In fact, at times some coaches even ask their players to experience the incorrect techniques and compare it with the correct technique.

Inevitably, all players make mistakes, and when they do, there is a tendency to dwell on the mistakes, express anger and scold oneself. The mind is in the past and not focused on what is currently relevant, increasing the probability of further error. To combat this temptation, players must have mechanisms or routines to get themselves back into the present after an error. There are several different routines, but their intention is the same—to trigger the players back into the present. Some do controlled breathing, then utter a refocus word such as "next" or perform an action such as slapping the hip. Others give themselves a few seconds to vent their anger with an appropriate action; it clears their mind and they can then refocus. Keith Wood says,

> There was a time when [if] I made an error, I wanted to immediately make up for it by doing something spectacular. Inevitably I would make a further error and compound the situation. Now I have developed a routine whereby I repeat a mantra word to myself. This clears my mind, and I then focus on next doing a simple thing well.

As with all the other mental skills and routines, routines for dealing with errors must be progressively practiced and developed. Imagery can also be used to visualize the error-making situation; the refocusing routine can then be undertaken to replace the negative focus with a positive mindset.

Developing Decision Making

Effective attacking play requires the ability to identify spaces and weaknesses and the ability to exploit those weaknesses through the choice and execution of appropriate tactics and patterns of play. This procedure involves several psychological or mental processes. For example, from the set piece, the out half must know where to focus her attention, and she must interpret (perceive) the situation correctly to identify spaces and weaknesses. She then decides on the most appropriate tactic or pattern of play to employ, which she communicates to the team. The out half narrows her attention to focus on receiving the ball, then delivers it appropriately.

Ireland and Lions outhalf Ronan O'Gara says,

> At each set piece I look up and scan the defense as soon as it begins to form. Based on what I see, I decide on what attacking ploy to use, and I communicate this to the players around me. Once again, before I receive the ball, I scan the defense to see if it has changed in any way that would force me to amend my first decision.

This process of attending, perceiving and decision making should continue in the second and third phases of play. Again O'Gara says,

> As an attack develops I like to think at least one phase ahead of where the play is. This helps me come to quick decisions and allows me to communicate earlier with my teammates.

O'Gara's statements illustrate that he has a highly developed routine for focusing his attention on what is relevant so that he can obtain the necessary information on which to base his attacking decisions.

This scanning routine has been developed and honed with practice over the years, and the mental processes involved in attention and decision making can be developed and practiced as well. These practices involve the coach's manipulating defensive alignments while the attackers are unsighted with their backs turned. As quickly as possible, the attackers have to turn and scan the defense to identify where the spaces to attack are, then they need to choose the appropriate method of attack.

Practicing for Competency and Confidence

One of the most effective ways for individuals and teams to build confidence in their attacking skills and tactics is to achieve the highest possible level of competency. Competency is achieved through practice, and practice affords the opportunity to integrate mental skills and strategies with physical performance. Former Ireland and Lions out half Ollie Campbell says he got his confidence for big matches from the preparation he underwent with his skills and fitness in the months beforehand. He says,

> Usually big match days were very relaxed for me. I was very calm and surprisingly relaxed and would be looking forward to going out knowing I had done the work. I would just let go and let instinct take over.

For attacking play to be successful, each player must be confident of his role. When a new pattern is introduced, sometimes even the best coaches can make the erroneous assumption that because they are dealing with skilled, experienced players, they automatically are able to understand and perform what is required. Such an approach can make players feel uneasy and uncomfortable about what they have to do. It is important to take a player's preferred learning style into account.

As part of his work for a doctoral thesis, Robin McConnell, author of *Inside the All Blacks* (1998) and *The Successful Coach* (2000), observed the All Blacks closely for three years as they prepared under Laurie Mains for the 1995 World Cup. He noted how concerned Mains was that the players fully understand and be comfortable with a new move when it was introduced and how willing he was to listen to their concerns. To this end, he would first walk the players through the pattern before gradually speeding it up. He then would perform it under match conditions with opposition.

As part of his work, McConnell assessed the preferred learning styles of the players and how they would like new moves to be explained to them. The results showed that Mains' method was compatible with player learning styles and confirmed his belief that both the coach and the players should be reciprocally involved in the learning process. When coaches take account of how players learn best, they greatly contribute to them being more knowledgeable and secure about their roles. This investment of time, in turn, greatly improves player confidence, and the end result is more effective play.

An essential aspect in the process of developing player confidence with respect to their roles in moves is that practice should progressively become more similar to match conditions. The presence of opposition is essential. It is ironic that coaches and players sometimes forget that the purpose of practice is to rehearse skills and tactics so that they transfer into the competitive match situation. The greater the similarity between the practice conditions and the match conditions, the greater the probability of this transfer occurring. It is only with the presence of opposition that the players can gain any sense of how effective they are. Knowing that they can beat a realistic tackle line in practice greatly boosts their confidence at beating the tackle line during an actual game.

For example, here's a practice sequence for developing an offensive attack move off the back of the scrum or in the backline:

1. Walk through the move with coaching explanation of roles.
2. Practice the move without opposition, gradually speeding up the execution to game pace.
3. Practice the move against token opposition, then full opposition at game pace.

At a seminar, Eddie O'Sullivan noted:

> It would be ludicrous to attempt to practice defense without the use of attackers. Why then would you even consider practicing attack without using defenders?

Rugby is played in a dynamic environment that is constantly changing, and the dynamics of the match situation ensure that the same skills and patterns are not performed the same way each time. This state of flux affects moment-to-moment decisions and adjustments that individual players have to make regarding the timing of runs and precise execution of these actions. Therefore, simulation training should include variable practice with running the patterns from different starting positions and angles, and players should learn to adjust to their opponent's positions and angles. This type of practice prepares players for the novel situations that occur during matches.

The point about variable practice is well illustrated by an example involving David Campese. In the semi-final of the 1991 World Cup, Campese set up a try for Tim Horan by moving infield and throwing a pass over his shoulder to an apparently unsighted Horan. Afterwards, as they marveled at this piece of brilliance, journalists and pundits used words and phrases such as "genius, what improvisation" and "This cannot be coached or practiced". Campese's reaction was that there was nothing he did in a match that he had not already practiced. He simply completed many variations of similar skills in practice and therefore was ready for the opportunity when it presented itself during a match. He said, "I have performed that skill many times in practice. The movement may not have been exactly the same, but I have performed many similar movements".

Practice also affords the opportunity to simulate the psychological conditions and pressures of the big match situation to rehearse and develop mental skills for keeping in control and well focused. An example of simulating the psychological conditions of the big match atmosphere was created by former coach Geoff Cook when preparing the England team for a match against Wales in Cardiff, as described in former out half Rob Andrew's biography *A Game and a Half* (1994). At the training session on the Wednesday before the match, the Welsh national anthem was played on the speaker as the team ran onto the pitch. Two days before the match when they travelled to Cardiff, the Welsh anthem was played again as they crossed the Severn bridge into Wales. Andrew says:

> By the time we walked through the packed lobby of our hotel an hour and a half before the kickoff and began our solemn march

to the ground through thousands of milling supporters, we were totally immune to the Welsh and Wales. (p. 51)

It is not practical to have simulation practice at every training session, but it is possible for individual players to use imagery to simulate what happens in a game and to practice controlling anxiety and keeping focused on the task at hand. Some years ago Irish and Lions wing three quarter Richard Wallace found that when a move was called in which he had a key role he began to feel anxious and have doubts and negative thoughts. As he stood waiting, he had visions of himself overrunning or dropping the ball. To counter his negative thoughts and feelings, Richard used the skill of imagery that he was already using for other aspects of his play.

First, at home he would create the specific match situation in his mind by imaging the situation on the pitch, the atmosphere with crowd noise, the move being called and him executing his role successfully. In addition, he re-created the accompanying feelings of negative thoughts and feelings. He would then repeat the key words *focus* and *ball* to keep focused as he waited and during his run.

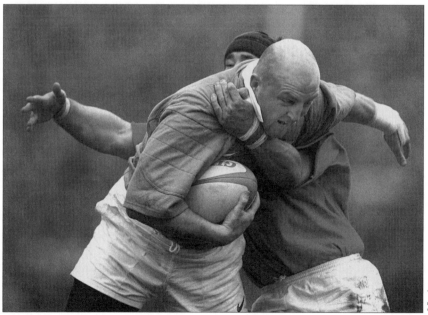

© Empics

Keith Wood visualizes game situations in his mind, works through them, then executes on the field.

As well as practicing this routine at home, Richard would perform this routine in practice and in club matches, then in an international game. He did not wait until the next international game to employ this routine. Rather, he developed it in his mind at home and rehearsed the international situation with imagery. Richard's mental discipline made him ready for an international game, and he is a great example of how to integrate mental practice with physical practice.

Former Ireland and Lions outhalf Tony Ward is another player who made extensive use of visualization in his preparation. He says,

> I was always visualizing myself beating defenders whether I was sitting at home or walking down the street. When out practicing on my own, I would do some evasive running and imagine the defenders being there and me beating them. In the weeks and days leading up to an international match, I would mentally place myself in situations and see myself beating the actual defenders I would be playing against. Then when it came to the actual game, it was as if I had been there before, and I felt totally at home. I found that visualizing situations like this not only improved my skills but gave me great confidence.

Ollie Campbell experienced a similar routine. He explains by saying,

> I was totally immersed in the game. When not physically practicing I was all the time practicing in my head. I would imagine myself in all sorts of situations where I would be kicking, passing, running, sidestepping, swerving and changing pace to beat opponents. When walking down a crowded street where I had to avoid colliding with people, I would imagine I was evading opponents in an upcoming game.

Use of imagery to develop an appropriate attacking mindset need not be confined to backs. Ireland and Lions hooker Keith Wood has scored 13 international tries. The secret, he says, is that he scored many of these tries in his mind beforehand. He spends his time visualizing situations that occur in matches, and he rehearses his possible roles, including opportunities to score tries. The result is that when these situations arise, he has been there before and knows exactly what to do.

Goal Setting for Attacking Play

Goal setting greatly enhances the development of an attacking mindset. The process of goal setting contributes to several important psychological characteristics necessary for optimal performance. They include the development of self-awareness (from the process of identifying strengths and weaknesses), motivation from having a sense of purpose and direction, concentration from having an appropriate focus and confidence from achieving appropriately set goals.

To be an effective attacking entity, a team needs to be capable of crossing the gain line frequently. Teams need to analyze the rate at which they cross the gain line in matches. Once they establish their average rate of success, they then must establish a higher target rate as a goal to achieve. This goal must be challenging yet achievable. The goal should be set both by players and coaches, and once the long-term goal is established, short-term goals must be set.

Next, a strategy for achieving the goals must be put in place. This strategy includes exploiting the strengths of the team—fast breaking by the scrumhalf and back row or wide ball to fast wingers and full back. Appropriate patterns of play are then developed for these players to improve the strike rate for getting across the gain line. The strike rate and strategies should be reviewed each week and, if necessary, appropriate adjustments made.

In addition to having appropriate patterns of play, the strategy should include the development of the attacking skills and physical attributes of individual players. Goals and strategies can be set for improving such skills and physical attributes as passing, sidestepping, decision making, strength, speed and acceleration. As with the attacking goals set for the team, progress on individual goals contributing to the attacking goals should be reviewed and evaluated frequently.

When an attacking move is called in a game, it should be clear to each player that the goal is to cross the gain line at a particular point. Each player has a role in the process of achieving this goal. For example, players could do any of the following: give a correctly weighted skip pass at a particular point; receive a pass; go on a decoy run; or run at a particular angle and timing to receive the ball at a particular point. Having clear process goals keeps players focused on the task, moment by moment, when they are "in the flow".

In addition to having process goals, players can also use trigger, or cue, words to help them keep focused on the process goals. Players can create tailor-made words per situation. For example, for giving a skip pass, they could say, "follow through"; for a controlled decoy run or strike run, "control" or "smooth"; for receiving the ball as it arrives, "ball" or "focus"; and for keeping the hands relaxed as the ball arrives, "soft hands".

Being focused on particular moment-by-moment process goals enables the player to make slight adjustments to keep the move on target. Often the adjustments are subtle, yet their effects are significant to the match. Players must learn to identify not only opportunities for adjustments but what specific adjustments to make. For example, in one situation, a player may need to recognize that she can execute a skip pass that is slightly stronger, softer or delayed. A player can make an earlier or later run, or she could make a slight change in the angle of the run or the position at which the ball is taken. Once players practice under variable conditions while focusing on their process goals, the monitoring and adjustments will occur automatically, and they will identify these opportunities to make these adjustments within a split second of thought.

Increasing Intensity in Crucial Situations

Often 10 minutes before halftime and 10 minutes after halftime are crucial points in the game. When the team trailing at these periods can get some points, it provides a significant psychological boost. For a team in the lead, scoring additional points has a demoralizing effect on opponents, and it is often enough to keep them out of the game for the duration.

The purpose of increasing intensity is to generate new momentum. The hardest scrums are often in the first 10 minutes of a game as teams endeavour to stamp their authority and gain an advantage over each other. As the game progresses, the scrums tend to become more relaxed—looser binds, dropped heads and not pushing as hard. If a team on a signal can make a concerted effort to tighten the bind, lift the heads and generate a combined special shove, it generates a tremendous momentum that surprises the opposition. This element of surprise should be taken advantage of by taking the ball to the opposition with support to score before the opposition can recover.

Each player must tune into the code word for a special effort, perhaps doing a quick mental rehearsal of their role and having their own mood word or self-talk. For example, a prop might repeat "drive" before a pivotal scrum. The designated cleanup player on a lineout catch might say to himself "drive and bind" on a driving maul from a lineout. They need to realize that they must sustain the effort in the follow-up rucking and mauling. Often the advantage of such momentum can be lost by a player knocking on the ball because of this lack of control and focus.

Such an increase in intensity and momentum can be generated in other aspects of play as well, such as a drive at the lineout, a high kick or a crash ball through the centre. The choice of play for this increase in intensity and momentum generation must be one where the probability of gaining an advantage is high. For example, if your team is under pressure in the scrum, then that area of play would not be an appropriate choice.

Teams need to practice how to increase intensity and generate momentum. They need to identify areas of their game in which they can increase the intensity to generate momentum, and they should have a repertoire of tactics to call on. Match situations need to be replicated—such as the 10 minutes before and after halftime, when they are either in the lead or behind. Each player should be asked to visualize and feel the situation as it would be in the match, and they need to rehearse what they are going to do. Players who have a tendency to get too worked up or lose focus in such situations should have their own routines and focus words to enable them to keep focused and in control. It should not be left to chance on the day of the match, nor should it be just discussed in practice by going through the motions.

Coming From Behind

The classic example of a team coming from behind occurred in the Ireland versus Australia 1991 World Cup match. Australia was the overwhelming favorite and led throughout the match, but Ireland fought hard and kept in contention. With five minutes to go, Ireland scored an unexpected try to take the lead; an upset looked certain.

Captain Michael Lynagh stepped up for what coach Bob Dwyer regards as perhaps his finest hour: "Lynagh's composure at this point was critical. It may well have been the finest moment of his career" (Dwyer 1992, 140). Lynagh called his players around him and told them there was time enough to win the match. He told the Australian forwards that he was going to kick off deep and that it was up to them to keep the Irish down at that end to win the possession. At that point, the backs would attempt to score.

And that is exactly what happened. The try came from a standard move that had been practiced endlessly during the week before. The Australians remained focused, purposeful and they retained their self-belief. Lynagh called them together, outlined the plan and helped them focus on what to do.

This scenario illustrates how individuals react differently in such situations. Some lose confidence, give up and are not prepared to fight back, believing the cause is lost. Others fight back but, unlike Lynagh, may do so in an uncontrolled, frenzied effort that can be nonproductive and lead to errors. The appropriate mindset must be developed through simulated practice so that players remain in control and avoid a chaotic performance executed under the guise of fighting back.

First, individuals need to become aware of how they tend to react in such situations; then, with the aid of routines and mental skills, they need to work at developing the appropriate mindset. Players need to be reminded in a few words of what has to be done in their individual roles. The captain, for example, needs to become adept at focusing the team on what needs to be done when there is little time left. Captains must ensure that they have their players' attention and are able to make eye contact. The captain's job is to remind the players of what has already been done in practice.

In the simulated practice, the team should gather behind their goal line as if they had conceded a score to fall behind. The coach asks each player to become fully aware of what has happened. The players should pause, visualize and feel the situation. They should then use their routines and mental skills to get focused for the restart. The captain should remind them of what has to be done and perhaps use a practiced cue word or phrase to motivate them. Next the team will restart and go through their planned attack.

Attacking Through the Lineout

The tactical decision has been made to attack from a catch at #5 in the lineout. The first priority is to gain possession, which comes from an accurate throw-and-catch from a fully focused thrower and catcher. The important factor to keep in mind is that a team could fail to gain possession because of lapses in concentration by the thrower, jumper, supporters or other support players.

For example, distractions for the thrower can lead to anxiety or inappropriate focus, and these can range from external to internal. The crowd noise may prevent the thrower from being able to hear the lineout call, or the referee may tell the player not to delay as they try to hear the call. The thrower's mind may be on a previously missed throw, or it may be fixated on the importance of the current throw (two points behind with five minutes to go). Throwers in these situations need to be calm, collected and know exactly what they have to do. When the lineout is eventually called, the thrower needs to calm down and adjust level of arousal, especially following a robust phase of play. Controlled breathing helps here, both to reduce general arousal and to focus the mind.

The thrower then needs to get the call. Once the call has been obtained, the thrower moves to the throwing position and checks where the catcher is. The thrower may then gain further focus by looking at a point on the ball, taking two or three controlled breaths and using a cue word such as "focus", "calm" or "smooth", which they say to themselves (self-talk). The thrower then corrects foot positioning, putting the ball overhead, sighting the target and mentally rehearsing the throwing action by imaging the force and the flight of the ball going to the target. Finally, the thrower throws to the jumper.

This example of a routine is one that contains process goals, enabling a player to become focused on the throw. Such a routine helps the thrower block every distraction, such as what previously happened, the importance of the throw, what may happen after the throw and so on. A routine that incorporates mental skills must be well rehearsed, developed and refined in practice and in matches. Every throw, whether in practice or in a match, should be preceded by the routine. It is the catalyst that triggers the automatic chain of events in a well-executed skill.

The difficulty of the lineout throw—and the importance of being mentally ready for it—was stated very well by Ireland and Lions hooker Keith Wood in an interview with Vincent Brown of *The Irish Times*. In it, he said,

> Throwing the ball into the line-out is not as simple as it may seem. You go from one situation where you are running, and at my weight of 16 1/2 stone, running into somebody that's 18 stone at full tilt is an incredibly aggressive encounter. The adrenaline is bursting through the system, and then suddenly there's a stop in play. You have to be incredibly calm, composed, put the ball into a moving target 10 yards away, three or four yards up in the air. It is difficult, it's a very difficult skill (Brown 2001).

To prepare himself for the throw, Wood performs a routine as soon as the lineout is called. This routine involves controlled breathing to calm and clear his mind. During this process, he consciously perceives his arousal dropping to a comfortable level. As captain, he then decides where the throw is to go and calls it. Next he focuses on the target and mentally rehearses the throw going to the target along the appropriate flight path. With his focus totally on the target, he executes the throw.

Wood has developed and refined this routine over several seasons. In earlier years, he developed his basic technique by throwing at targets on a wall. Now, most of his physical practice is done with the different jumpers he plays with, and he spends a substantial amount of time mentally practicing his throwing. This mental practice is done immediately before a match as part of his preparation and also at other times.

While the thrower gets ready by going through a mental routine, the jumper should be doing likewise. Jumpers may use controlled breathing along with some appropriate cue words such as "relax", "focus", "leap", "catch". They can also imagine themselves stepping back or forward, then jumping and catching. Similarly, the blockers and the other support players should rehearse moving to their positions and performing their actions. In fact, once the target has been identified, all players must focus on their immediate upcoming roles.

Attacking Wide From the Lineout

Again the thrower, jumper and support players would go through their routines. This time, however, the catcher would deliver a fast ball off the top. The principal support players—open side flanker, #8 and blind side flanker—should also prepare themselves for getting to the breakdown as quickly as possible.

This preparation can include controlled breathing, mentally rehearsing upcoming actions or using appropriate self-talk or focus words. As throwers are preparing to throw, they could say phrases such as "first to the ball" or "sprint to the ball". As with the forwards, the backs involved in the attacking tactic must also be focused on their roles.

Attacking off the Scrum

From a defensive point of view, the most successful method of preventing a team from attacking from a scrum is to disrupt the opposition and diminish the quality of their possession. For that reason, the most important goal for the team feeding the scrum is to supply controlled possession from the selected channel of the scrum.

An effective scrum requires a scrumhalf to coordinate and all eight forwards to participate. All eight players in the scrum must have a mental routine that ensures their foot positions, binds and body positions are correct before engagement. Additionally, every player must know the type of ball presentation required from the scrum—channel and speed—before engagement. Before the scrum engagement, they need to mentally rehearse their roles both in the scrum and after the ball is released from the scrum. Once the scrum has engaged, each player needs to concentrate on keeping the scrum stable—before, during and after the feed—to channel the ball appropriately to launch an attack.

The individual and collective preparation of the players before engagement is the key to effective coordination when the unit skill of scrummaging must occur. Good scrummaging teams tend to scrummage frequently in training. Both individually and as a unit, they learn to prioritize a mental rehearsal routine, which includes a checklist of techniques and cue words that ensures a stable platform from which to attack. For example, players may use cue words such as "head up", "back straight", "feet under hips" or "shoulders higher than hips". To ensure unity as they engage, the unit may say aloud "hit" or "hit and squeeze".

In addition to their role in securing a good ball in the scrum, players must be fully aware of their roles in the ensuing attacking move, especially back-row players. To be fully tuned in, they should mentally rehearse their roles in the attack. It is not uncommon for back-row players to have their minds on their roles in the upcoming back-row attacking ploy after the scrum has engaged. This habit results in less driving from the back row—hence, less support for the front five. This chain reaction allows the opposition to disrupt the scrum after the feed and ultimately cause the cancellation of the back-row attacking ploy.

Regarding the importance of mental rehearsal, Ireland flanker David Wallace says,

> Before the scrum engages, I mentally rehearse my role in the planned attack and my support lines to the ball. If I don't do it then and leave it until the scrum engages, it will interfere with my contribution to the scrum.

So the procedure is to mentally rehearse the upcoming move and then focus on the scrum. These physical and mental routines must be developed with scrummaging practice, otherwise they will not be put into operation in matches. As a result, both the quality of the scrum and the ensuing attack are adversely affected.

Attacking From Starts and Restarts

Normally on a kickoff, the forwards line up on the kicker's left-hand side and the backs on the right. The ball is then kicked to one of four main areas: left high and short to the 10-metre line where the kicking team competes to regain possession; long to the corner of the same side; down the centre towards the goal posts; or the right-hand side. For the latter three situations, the team either concedes possession for territorial advantage, or they may regain possession by pressuring the opposition to kick to touch.

No matter what option is taken, it is crucial that the team is well organized with players knowing their roles. There must be organized follow-up patterns with the first line of players pressuring the receivers and the second line either taking advantage of this pressure or stopping an opponent who has managed to take the ball and break the first line. A third line should be organized to cover clearing kicks from the receivers. As with other aspects of play, kickoffs must be well rehearsed with simulated plays against opponents. Players must see it as a new phase of play with a particular focus, one for which they should mentally rehearse and have practiced cue words.

Starts and restarts also occur after scores have been conceded. Players should have refocusing routines ready for restarts after scores so that they are focused on their roles in regaining the attacking advantage. These refocusing routines should be well rehearsed, and the captain and pack leader must remind players of these roles. They should be particularly aware of players who are vulnerable to losing their focus.

Restarts afford the opportunity to regain the initiative. Very often, the team that has just scored is in a self-congratulatory mode and not fully focused; they are vulnerable to not being mentally ready for receiving a kick with intense follow-up pressure. All members of the kicking team have to be fully refocused and committed to pressuring the opposition. The kicker, of course, must be well practiced in visualizing and delivering an accurate kick.

A quick restart from a 22-metre drop-off affords a team that has been defending an opportunity to regain the attacking initiative. The team must become organized for the drop-off before their opponents. The defending team has the advantage because they have less ground to cover for the kick as compared with their opponents. The process of reorganization must be well rehearsed with simulated practices. Mentally, each member of the team must be able to switch from a defending mode to an attacking mode quickly. Well-rehearsed refocusing words and routines are needed from individual players for themselves and from team leaders for the whole team.

For receiving restarts, teams must cover all areas to receive the ball, knowing their roles and moving to support once they see where the ball is going. Receiving restarts affords opportunities to launch counterattacks. Teams are vulnerable to counterattack when kicks do not go to the intended area or when the defending patterns are not organized to provide sufficient pressure and cover.

For example, when the short high kick goes too far and is not close to the touchline, and the players in midfield have not followed up sufficiently, the receiver can throw a long pass infield and set up the team for a counterattack. Players should practice recognizing the situation and implementing the action. Keep in mind that a danger in this situation is when the receiver focuses on getting the ball to midfield rather than focusing on the ball first.

Attacking Tactical Kicking

Tactical kicking can occur off set piece possession or phase play, and it can be executed to regain possession or gain territory. As with starts and restarts, tactical kicking from set piece play is a matter of organization and communication with each player having a well-defined role.

To kick to where the opposition is vulnerable, kickers aim for one of four main areas: the high kick (Garryowen) towards the full back; the box kick; the diagonal kick towards the open side wing; or the chip over the three quarters. If the kick is to have full effect, it must be accurate, but it also must be chased aggressively by designated players who form the front line, supported by second-line players. (Third-line players cover clearances if the ball is retrieved by the opposition.) Once the tactical decision is made to kick, players must focus on their roles. This tuning-in process can be aided by mental routines and appropriate cue words given by team leaders or kickers.

Kicking may also be used when a plan to run has been cancelled because of a bad pass. Players have to adjust their roles quickly without time to rehearse. Players can learn to anticipate and react early to these situations by learning to read early cues for what is about to follow. Kicks in phase attacks usually occur when the attack with ball-in-hand stalls out. With practice, players can learn what type of kick is appropriate and how to anticipate and support it.

If teams are to develop the appropriate attacking mindset for attacking tactical kicking, the coach must set up appropriate simulated practices in which players practice and develop the physical and mental aspects. With respect to changes in tactics, where a running tactic has to be cancelled and a kicking one substituted, players can be taught to read the cues of the situation, such as the body language of players, to adjust quickly to the new situation.

Research indicates that players can be directly taught to read these cues by instruction or by implicitly being exposed to the relevant areas over a period of time. As with running tactics, kicking tactics need to be first practiced in low-pressure situations with minimal opposition. Gradually, the pressure should be increased until match situations are being fully simulated.

Summary

Psychological principles and skills can be used to develop an attacking mindset. Characteristics of the ideal mindset for attacking rugby are being totally focused yet relaxed, being confident, having no fear and feeling that performance is automatic and effortless.

From time to time, you experience this mindset or aspects of it. To get in the attacking mindset on a more frequent and consistent basis, players need to acquire and develop mental skills and routines. It is not enough to acquire mental skills, such as imagery, controlled breathing, muscle relaxation and goal setting on your own. Rather, you must develop these skills with practice of the physical skills of rugby integrated and rehearsed in simulated match conditions. Take these examples of various attacking situations and put them to use to develop your own mentally tough, attacking mindset.

chapter

8

Tough Defense

Hugh Richards
University of Edinburgh

Dean Richards
Leicester Tigers, Leicester, England

© Sport the Library/Robb Cox

From the perspective of a spectator, it may seem artificial to try to distinguish attack from defense and forward play from back play in the modern era of fast, integrated rugby currently played by top international teams. This chapter concerns the psychology of defense, but keep in mind that when players play well, they execute a variety of skills in all aspects of play. Rapidly turning defense into attack can be a most potent strike weapon; and the offensive tackle, ruthlessly introduced to the world stage by Western Samoan sides in the 1980s, clearly demonstrates how a defensive skill can be employed for motivational and offensive purposes.

This chapter reviews the important psychological considerations associated with defense in rugby. It is organized around four broad areas that make up the defensive wall (see figure 8.1), which includes quality training as the essential foundation of every good performance. What follows is the performance of individual players and coaches, then the overall performance of the team.

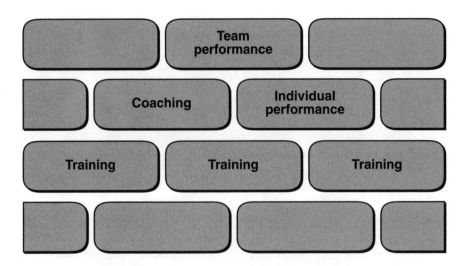

Figure 8.1 Components of defense. Training is the foundation of performance for every other element.

Importance of Defense

Defense has never been more important in rugby union. Professionalism has produced more physically skilled athletes playing in teams that are better organized. Every facet of the game, including defense, has to be executed at a high degree of competence to be successful. Teams need to follow the rules of simple economics, finding the ideal combinations of maximum benefit (scoring as many points through attack) and minimum cost (conceding as few points through effective defense). Opponents, the weather and other variables affect the achievement of even the most successful cost-benefit ratio in each match.

Changes to the laws of rugby, including increasing the value of the try from four to five points, have also increased the emphasis that successful teams must give to defense. Conceding a try is now more costly relative to other sorts of scores. A team on defense must prevent their try-line from being crossed at all costs. One consequence of this is an increase in the number of penalty tries that are awarded. The importance of defense is also reflected in the fact that international teams employ specialist coaches to concentrate on the effectiveness of a team's defense.

The view that good defense is necessary for success was emphasized by media reports during the 1999 Rugby World Cup (RWC). The winning Australian team conceded only a single try in the entire tournament. This fact suggests that defense is critical, especially when the results from past RWC competitions are examined thoroughly.

We reviewed the results of every match in Rugby World Cup competitions in 1991, 1995 and 1999. We focused on the eight teams that made the quarterfinals and ranked them in order of the place they achieved. The top four were ranked on the results of the final and playoff matches, and the other quarterfinalists were ranked on their point difference throughout the competition. The rank order for each competition can be seen in table 8.1.

We wanted to see the extent to which good defense was associated with better ranking. As a measure of defense, we took the average number of points scored against each team, the logic being that a good defense concedes fewer points. The results, shown in figure 8.2, show that in each of the Rugby World Cups, the eventual champion was the team that had the best defense.

TABLE 8.1	RUGBY WORLD CUP TEAM RESULTS: 1991, 1995, 1999		
Rank	1991	1995	1999
1	Australia	South Africa	Australia
2	England	New Zealand	France
3	New Zealand	France	South Africa
4	Scotland	England	New Zealand
5	Ireland	Scotland	England
6	France	Australia	Scotland
7	Samoa	Samoa	Wales
8	Canada	Ireland	Argentina

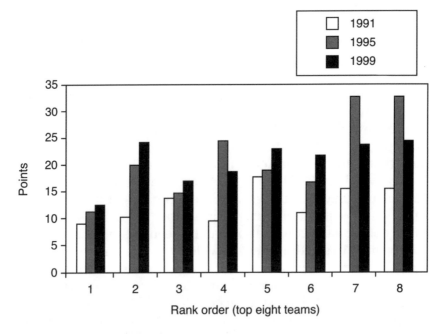

Figure 8.2 Average points conceded per game in the World Cup in 1991, 1995 and 1999.

The data in figure 8.2 show a clear trend that the better-ranked teams consistently concede fewer points. What is so striking is that this overall pattern is true in all three competitions, with different teams, different players, different opposition in the earlier pool games and even different laws! Despite these variations, this pattern suggests that the relationship between tournament success and defense is very strong.

In contrast, when we looked at the attacking ability of teams, assessed by average number of points scored, there was no clear pattern associated with final ranking in the tournament (see figure 8.3). In fact, in the RWC in 1995, South Africa still won the competition despite scoring, on average, fewer points than any other team in the top eight. These results show that there is not a strong relationship between the attacking capacity of a team and overall success in these competitions. (Those who remember the 1995 World Cup will remember the 145 points that New Zealand, eventually ranked second, put past Japan in the pool match. This anomaly goes a long way towards explaining the unusually high average for the team ranked second in 1995.)

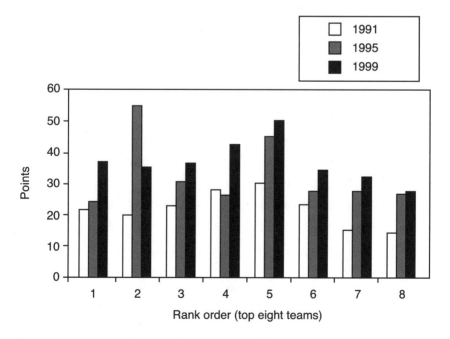

Figure 8.3   Average points scored per game in the World Cup in 1991, 1995 and 1999.

The evidence suggests that although attacking ability is important, it is an effective defense that differentiates those teams that perform best on the world stage. From the Rugby World Cup statistics, it seems reasonable to suggest that defense represents the essential bedrock of long-term success. Paul Zimmerman, discussing American football, described the relationship between the two facets of play: "Offense wins games; defense wins championships".

Individual Performance

Every individual in the team needs to be able to effectively perform skills ranging from general to specific. Everyone needs to know how to tackle; the forwards must be able to clean out the opposition at rucks; and specialist lineout jumpers need to be able to compete for opposition ball. In each case, doing it right is not just a matter of physical coordination and technical proficiency—the players need to make the correct decisions at the right time.

Practical Applications: Individual Performance

- Develop and practice use of task-relevant thoughts for certain key skills.
- Plan and use individualized preparation routines to achieve optimal controlled arousal.
- Make instructions clear, specific and game-relevant.
- Train anticipation through identification of relevant cues.
- Simplify tactical decision making to reduce errors.
- Use mental rehearsal to practice decision making.

The ability to make good decisions can improve considerably when players develop their ability to anticipate. Players who are able to read the game and anticipate the likely moves of the opposition are able to react quickly using the best option available. Basic psychological factors and an individual's mental set influence the way a player thinks and what he feels during a match.

The Mental Set

The four aspects of the mental set that are particularly relevant in rugby are confidence, attention, arousal control and aggression. It is quite clear from casual observation and scientific research that performance is better when confidence is high. To defend well, players need to feel confident in their own abilities and the team's ability to tackle, cover and regain possession of the ball. The greatest source of confidence comes from recent successful performances, and it is important that coaches regularly give accurate information about defensive play to promote confidence. Keep in mind, though, that confidence is fragile. A couple of errors in a game can quickly undermine even the confidence of a player who has numerous good games under his belt.

It is also clear from research that anxiety erodes confidence. With this picture, it is easy to see how a rapid slump in performance can occur. A fullback who fumbles a high ball becomes more anxious to catch the next one cleanly. If the next one is also missed, then the two failures and the increasing anxiety will have a potentially disastrous influence on confidence.

At the individual level, concentration of attention can be used to alleviate this downward cycle. Players can learn to focus their attention through the use of task-relevant thoughts, which can be developed in training for tasks that they are required to perform. For these tasks, one to four words representing essential physical and technical features are used to self-coach their performance.

For example, successfully catching a high ball in defense means running to arrive just at the right time, jumping for the ball, twisting sideways, having arms and hands in the right position and watching the ball. These actions could be converted into cue words such as "pace, jump, twist, arms and eyes" (the terms should be chosen by the player). If players develop and use these phrases in training, this refocusing cue could help to put the execution of a well-learned skill back on track. It can also be used after an unsuccessful attempt at the skill and in the period immediately preceding when the skill is needed again.

In general, task-relevant thoughts help in two ways. First, the words provide a reminder of the basics and may even help the player realize what is going wrong—for example, arriving too early, then jumping from standing. Second, by having something to do to remedy the situation, you reduce the available thinking space that you might have otherwise used for anxious worrying. It is important that your task-relevant thoughts are kept short, simple and deal with the broadest elements of the skill. The cue words need to be easily remembered, used quickly in the game and should be able to gently jog you back into performing the skill. Too much detailed instruction actually has a negative effect by intruding on your smooth movement patterns that are the hallmark of well-learned skills.

When you begin to lose self-confidence, general encouragement ("Come on you can do it") is relatively ineffective in improving the situation. If verbal statements are to have any effect, then they should remind the player of recent occasions when the skill was completed well. For example, a coach might shout, "Hit low and drive through like you did in the first half" to reestablish good tackling habits. Seeing an example of similarly skilled teammates performing the same skill well is even more effective than encouragement.

The capacity to maintain focused attention is further challenged in rugby by the intensity of physical contact. The arousal level must be higher than normal so that the physical energy systems are working at high intensity. In addition, a player's perception of being hit is dampened. The same blow to the head would feel more uncomfortable and disorientating if received while walking around a supermarket rather than during a rugby match!

Clearly, the level of arousal needs to increase, but if arousal levels become too high then attention suffers. At the extreme, very high arousal causes a player to become hyperattentive, which means that his narrow focus of attention shifts rapidly from one feature to another. Unfortunately, this type of shifting results in focusing on irrelevant cues during the game. Imagine trying to play with a pair of cardboard tubes strapped to your eyes with your head turning uncontrollably from side to side. Once the game is in progress, arousal levels tend to find equilibrium. Problems in arousal commonly occur at the start of or just before a game when a deliberate psych-up session has been too intense.

One problem with psych-up sessions is that they ignore the fact that each player has different initial arousal levels and different ideal arousal levels for play. Consequently, every individual needs a different approach to arousal control, and it is up to each player to identify what is needed, how it can be achieved easily and when it should be used as the time for competition approaches. Players should develop their own patterns of preparation based on what has been most effective previously. An established routine is simply one of the easiest ways of achieving controlled change in arousal to optimal playing level. A standard preparation routine can include the following elements: practical—changing, getting taped, going to the toilet; physical—warming up, doing simple handling drills; and mental—mentally rehearsing making the first tackle, checking calls with teammate, recalling team strategy for first 10 minutes.

Although a team talk would be common to all members of a team, preparation routines before a match need to be different for each individual. For example, some emotional players might thump lockers to get themselves ready while ex-England wing Rory Underwood reportedly got ready by doing the *Times* crossword puzzle or reading the *Financial Times.*

The last component of mental set for individual defense is the use of aggression. One of the problems with aggression is that the term is really not specific enough to describe a single type of behavior. Legitimate head-on, high-speed tackles, vigorously rucking a player who has not rolled away from the ball in a ruck and unprovoked punching would all potentially fall under the category of aggression, but actually they represent different types of behavior.

The head-on tackle is a legitimate part of rugby and is sometimes called assertive behavior. Vigorously rucking a player who has not rolled away can be described more accurately as instrumental aggression. With instrumental aggression, the potential hurt is intended to have some functional purpose and falls within legitimate behavior in the game. Making life uncomfortable for players lying on the wrong side of a ruck is instrumental in that it makes the player think twice about getting in that position again. Finally, punching someone simply to inflict pain or injury is hostile aggression and is illegal in rugby.

These various sorts of behavior are distinguished not by what a player does but by what they intend to achieve. A player who punches an opponent who joins a maul illegally from the side may claim that it was for the good of the team to stop this opponent from infringing (instrumental aggression). But if the same player frequently commits aggressive acts, it could be that the real intention is hostile aggression (he just wants to hurt somebody) and is using the explanation of team benefit as cover. While the real motives behind aggressive acts are notoriously difficult to uncover, most competitive teams take a dim view on any behavior that might leave them a man down, temporarily or permanently. Any repeated hostile behavior should be avoided and addressed by coaches and referees.

There are always exceptions to every rule. The infamous "99 call" used by the 1974 British and Irish Lions tour of South Africa—in which the entire team retaliated simultaneously—was illegitimate instrumental aggression designed to address the problem of being physically intimidated. The chance of them all being sent off was remote, as they proved. This was an example of illegal instrumental aggression, designed to minimize any risk of being sent off. As Gordon Brown, who played lock that day recalled, "It was really just to save our souls because the refs were letting them [the South Africans] get away with everything".

There is often a fine distinction between aggressive acts that are instrumental but legitimate and those, such as the 99 call, that are instrumental yet illegal under the laws. For example, a flyhalf who has been the recipient of a heavy, illegally high tackle may not be quite as prepared to run the ball next time. As a consequence, this aggressive act is instrumental because it is advantageous for the defending team; however, it is illegal within the laws of the game. A slightly lower tackle, equally hard, would have a similar effect and be legal. The emphasis on legitimate instrumental aggression is worded neatly in a quotation taken from Robin McConnell's book *Inside the All Blacks* (1998). While outlining how the opposition players (the Irish in 1992) who infringe at rucks will be treated, the coach said, "I tell you, we're going to deal with some of these guys with legal ferocity" (30).

The term *aggression* does not refer to a clearly defined set of behaviors, and it may be misunderstood by certain players. So that players avoid being sent off or having to spend 10 minutes in the sin bin, instructions should be specific, and they should focus the minds of players on game-relevant components. Instructions to "knock the opposition back in the tackle, rip the ball, clear the opposition off ruck ball and put the man down" are specific behaviors that can be focused on and are preferable to the nonspecific "be more aggressive".

One example of legitimate instrumental aggression that may have influenced the self-confidence of teammates was the tackle Mickey Skinner (England) put on one of the back row of France in the Five Nations encounter in Paris in the 1980s. Skinner tackled his opponent head on as he charged towards the English try-line, lifted him up and drove him backwards. The England pack secured the ball, and the pressure was lifted from the English try-line. Most people would label the tackle aggressive, yet it was legitimate and instrumental. The single tackle was also symbolic of England's defense and marked a change in the psychological momentum of that period of the game.

Anticipation

In the modern game, no first-class player takes the field without some information about his opponent, including general information about the team's style of play—their moves, preferences and strengths of opposite numbers. This information increases the ability of the player to anticipate the game more accurately. Despite the immense value of video homework, players still need to be able to anticipate the game as it unfolds.

Research has confirmed that elite athletes have the ability to spot relevant cues that provide information about what is likely to happen. For many players, this ability develops naturally through experience and interaction with other good players, but it can also be deliberately targeted for more rapid development in younger players.

One way to facilitate this development is to get players to watch other matches with a coach or more experienced player. Throughout the match, the players take turns predicting out loud what is going to happen, and the predictions need to be accompanied by the cues that were used to reach them. As well as looking carefully at alignment and where there is space that might be attacked, players should be encouraged to watch relevant cues, such as where the opposition is looking, which players they are signalling to and where players are out of position or injured. It also is possible to gain valuable cues from the position and behavior of the player about to receive the ball.

For example, a flyhalf standing deep and not facing straight would be more likely to kick towards the touchline than a flyhalf standing flat and facing square to the defense. Equally the player who is going to receive a crash ball is likely to be scanning the defense much more thoroughly and be more attentive to catching the ball than a dummy runner.

Progressive anticipation training and cue identification need to be regularly practiced to become a part of competition behavior. Coaches and other players can assist players by reminding them to try to read the game as they are playing, by giving them verbal reinforcement when they anticipate well and through postmatch debriefings. Players can also learn to communicate their read to other players on the pitch.

In addition to anticipating the opposition, each player needs to be able to predict what his teammates are likely to do so that he can then provide effective cover or support. A well-coordinated defense relies on this kind of mutual understanding, or, in other words, coherence.

Tactical Decision Making

Tactical decision making refers to the rapid decisions that each player has to make at any given moment during the game. In defense, players need to decide what their primary aim is in any situation, such as putting the man down versus smother tackle, or showing the outside as opposed to forcing the player to cut back in. Having too many decisions can create difficulties in performance resulting in none being executed effectively, as the player would be caught in two minds.

As the number of choices increases, so does the time taken to select one and do it. One way to combat this overload is to consider the overall team strategy, then exclude some of the options. Players need to play to their strengths and avoid their weaknesses. For example, a small winger would be unwise to attempt high smother tackles on much larger opponents because there is much greater chance of an ineffective tackle.

Players should be encouraged to mentally rehearse the likely situations they will encounter in the days before the match and decide on effective responses in advance. For example, a fullback may rehearse the scenario of the opposition outside centre— already identified as a key threat—breaking through the defense between the 10-metre and 22-metre lines. The fullback should think about the lines of defensive running to close down the player for a tackle. This rehearsal makes it more likely that an effective response will be chosen quickly at the appropriate time. Players need to move from daydreams to rehearsal by structur-

Each defender must know his primary aim in any situation.

ing the mental practice scenario to assist the player in anticipation and decision making (see chapter 3).

When decision making is difficult for a player, reduce the number of alternatives to an either-or decision to overcome the problem. A front-row forward who picks up the ball in his own 22 may be told to either pass it to players in space, if there is time, or run in front of his own support, take the contact, stay on his feet, and drive. In this case, there is one cue—is there time and opportunity to pass to supported players? If not, the player should take the default option and go for contact and drive. This is a straightforward method of reducing the complexity of decision making.

Tactical decision making can also be evaluated and trained retrospectively using video footage. Players should be asked to explain why they chose the option they did and also to identify any alternatives that might have been available to them. If the same situation occurred elsewhere in the game with a more effective outcome, it can be used as a vivid demonstration of better decision making. To focus on regaining possession may cause the player to concentrate on the ball and result in a missed tackle, whereas to focus on stopping the progress of the attacker, smothering a pass or knocking the opponent down may be more likely to produce an effective tackle.

During training, decision making can also be assessed by suddenly halting play so that players can be asked to look at their positioning, why they are doing specific things and what they think is going to happen. This process can also increase team understanding because teammates become more aware of what their colleagues are thinking at specific points in the game.

Coaching Strategies and Plans

A survey of past and present All Blacks identified a number of dimensions for an elite coach (McConnell 1998): complete knowledge of the game and tactics, ability to plan and implement a game plan (including training) and communication.

One of the primary roles of a coach is to develop defensive strategies that reflect the strengths and weaknesses of the team and provide the focus for training. In terms of defense, it is logical to consider general strategies, such as how to work a drift defense, and strategies specific to a situation or a particular opponent. One advantage of overall strategies is that they provide a general picture of what should be going on in any given situation.

Practical Applications: Coaching

- Ensure defensive strategies are well explained and check players' understanding.
- Identify and practice specific game plans to block opponents' attacking strengths and preferences.
- Give players clear, specific roles for critical defensive phases of the game.
- Check that feedback is provided to all team members and is specific to components of performance.
- Use techniques to increase feedback provision (summary feedback/player feedback).
- Highlight examples of good play to act as models.
- Reinforce any good play you want to see repeated.

Players need to not only recognize when something is wrong but when to do something about it. For example, a winger may realize that an injury to the centre has left an overlap in a man-on-man defense. The winger should call across additional cover or attempt to tackle the opponent with the ball fast enough to prevent him from releasing it. At a more advanced level, this player may call for a change in defensive strategy, perhaps to a drift defense.

Time spent explaining the overall picture of defense is important if the team is to be able to play coherently and adapt to changes in the attacking play of opponents. Video footage can be valuable in the initial stages of explaining overall strategy by showing the overall shape of defensive strategy.

One of the most effective models to use is footage of the team itself. When players see their own personal best performance in relation to a particular defensive skill, they are likely to develop the confidence to emulate it. This process uses a team's performance as the model that most closely approximates the target style, and it can be refined as the team becomes better.

Coaches also need to develop game-specific strategies for particular opponents. Each team has its own strengths and weaknesses in relation to attack and defense, and coaches need to identify these for their teams and opponents. For opponents with a small pack whose forwards go to ground quickly and try to ruck, a coach might instruct his forwards to only go into contact in threes or fours, allowing the remainder to fan out in defense. On the other hand, a larger pack might tend to use rolling mauls, meaning that defensive players should be instructed to drive against the maul and tie it up.

Key opposing players may also warrant particular attention. One obvious defensive strategy is slowing down the release of the ball to a scrumhalf well known for his sniping runs off the base of rucks and mauls. Coaches planning defensive strategies also need to make players aware of what must be avoided. An accurate, long-range goal kicker should be a danger that every player knows could cost the team points if they unnecessarily infringe within their own half.

Few players have attracted more specific attention than the impressive, large Jonah Lomu of New Zealand in the Rugby World Cup in South Africa in 1995. His combination of size, speed and power proved a potent attacking force in the pool games. None of the competition seemed to develop any specific strategy to negate his influence, including England, who went down in the semi-final after some critical early scores from the winger.

In the final, it was immediately apparent that South Africa had developed a defensive strategy to stop Lomu by using at least two defenders tackling together, with the first one trying to pull him off balance before the second attacker took his legs. Previous matches had shown that the first tacklers attempting to stop his legs had simply bounced off. After their victory in the final, Kitch Christie, the South African coach, admitted that aspect of the game plan: "Our defense won the game. It was unbelievable from forwards and backs." Asked about Lomu, he said, "He got the ball eight times and we took him out eight times."

Roles and Responsibilities

Each player needs to know exactly what his defensive role is in major phases of play. Assigning roles helps players focus their attention on key components of defense. For example, a blind side flanker (defense) may have the specific role of ensuring that the opposing #8 does not carry the ball over the gain line. Other attackers are ignored because the player knows that they are the responsibility of other defensive team players. Having a clear role can benefit self-confidence because it removes unnecessary complexity from defensive plays where attackers are deliberately trying to create as many alternatives and as much uncertainty as possible.

Players need to clearly understand what they are being asked to do. In unusual situations or where mistakes occur frequently, it is a sensible first step for a coach to check the players' understanding of their roles. A coach who focuses purely on getting players to do the right thing without worrying about whether they understand what they are trying to do will produce a team with limited capacity for adaptation.

Players also need to accept responsibility for their given roles. Players may be asked to provide cover when another player moves to attack. Players who insist on doing their own thing or who are new to the team may severely reduce the effectiveness of an overall defensive strategy.

Finally, players need to be able to actually perform their roles. Assigning a player to mark an extremely powerful or fast opponent in a man-to-man defensive lineup may falter simply because the defender lacks the size or speed to keep up. If any of these three components—understanding, acceptance and ability—is absent, then both individual performance and overall defensive strategy is compromised.

Skill Development and Feedback

Players at all levels can benefit when they fine-tune positioning and timing of their defensive play. Soon after performance, it is critical for players to have accurate feedback, dominated by positive explicit instruction ("Start running earlier; watch your man") as opposed to negative instruction ("Don't watch the ball; don't get bound in"). The use of reinforcement is also important, but with mature and committed performers, this aspect need not be as frequent as when coaching children.

An important factor to note is that feedback should be linked clearly to specific behaviors. With inexperienced performers learning a basic skill, providing summary feedback every five attempts produces a better balance of learning than feedback after every attempt or summaries over 10-plus trials. This approximate number of five trials per summary may increase if the performers are more experienced, but it may decrease if the skill is more complicated, such as a drift defense.

Training sessions can also give coaches the opportunity to teach players to develop their own ability to give feedback to each other and to analyze their own performance. Skills sessions in which groups of players take turns providing feedback is one way to promote this ability. Asking players to rate their own performance on specific skill components helps increase their learning of exactly what they did when they performed well. Players who cannot distinguish good from bad performances struggle to develop their full potential. For coaches, player feedback, buddy coach observation or even simply listening or watching a tape of one of their own training sessions can all be used to maintain and improve their coaching skills.

Motivation

It is easy to ignore the contribution of defensive work when try scores and penalty kicks take the limelight. Awards for the Player of the Match or Most Valuable Player (MVP) tend to go to individuals who score. But on the contrary, the analysis of Rugby World

Cup tournaments confirms that the difference between tournament winners and the rest was their defensive ability, not their attacking. A coach must find ways to highlight and reward players specifically for defensive prowess. Coaches need to identify examples of good defensive play, and the subsequent reinforcement should be equal to the attention given to attacking play.

While many players would feel pleased if a coach quietly acknowledged their hard work, the effect would be limited to that player. Openly praising a player, perhaps for covering back, highlights the specific behavior as a model to other players. We are all more likely to do something that we know meets with social approval. Coaches who use video review sessions have the ideal situation in which to show examples of what they want. Praise and reinforcement are much more effective when they are linked to a specific, observable event or behavior. General praise ("You covered well today") has much less effect.

Finally, reinforcing good play openly with the team is likely to promote players to participate in this behavior among themselves. Developing the team into a self-reinforcing and constructively self-critical unit is a much more efficient process than relying exclusively on the coach to critique and reinforce. Players often have a better view of what might have happened than those on the touchline. Coaches may want to adopt a questioning style ("Okay, so who was the key player in halting that attack? Why?") in video debriefings to develop the ability to critically analyze and reinforce each other's performances.

At Leicester RFC, an award known as Tigers Tackle of the Match goes one step further than simply involving the team in the reinforcement process. In this case, the crowd is also involved, and the importance of the defensive skills have much more overt emphasis. The crowd actively looks for and vocally supports important tackles in the match. Neil Back, Leicester's and England's outstanding flanker, has often been singled out for this public award given to defense, in accordance with its critical game importance.

Training

Players and coaches cannot expect to do things in competition that they have not trained for, which applies as much to mental components, such as tactical decision making and specific strategies, as it does to physical skills. The importance of defense in the game warrants that defensive work should represent a significant proportion of the total time spent training on and off the pitch. Training should be planned and organized correctly, structured to maximize learning and include simulation to increase the ability of players to transfer skills learned in training to the intense environment of competition.

Practical Applications: Training

- Plan training thoroughly; include alternatives so that training can be flexible.
- Inform players of training aims in advance.
- Determine optimal time for training; it increases the likelihood of quality training.
- Random and variable practice structures maximize long-term learning.
- Aim for quality performance; know when it is achieved (through evaluation).
- Improve the transfer of skills from training to competition (through simulation).

Organization

Input from players can greatly maximize quality practice. Research in other sports has shown that elite athletes prefer training when they know in advance the training schedule (though not detailed drills) and the focus for specific sessions. They also indicated the importance of being kept busy and being challenged.

While players should train and get used to producing maximal effort at the time of day that they need to compete, the need to simulate the time of competition does not need to apply to all training. Training should be scheduled to maximize the effort, intensity and quality produced. Players should be encouraged to personally train on their own when they feel most energetic. The organization of team training, particularly for teams that are training and playing away from home, should be carefully planned because disruptions to usual training patterns can negatively affect training quality.

For example, a U19 team going on tour may have morning and afternoon training scheduled for most nonplaying days. If this training frequency is significantly greater than what the players have been used to before tour, then there is a danger that within a week players will begin to feel chronically fatigued. Radical departure from what they are used to will have a potentially negative impact on training quality.

A mature coach who regularly gets up at 7 A.M. each day may perceive an early morning training session at 9:30 A.M. as a sensible time. Most 19-year-olds, however, not only sleep in but are in the habit of staying up late. The consequence is that the players will have their sleep cut short so that they can get up to eat before training. In this example, players would incur one or two hours of sleep deficit each night. Some players may sleep through breakfast but then attempt to train without breakfast, and, of course, the quality of training will be impaired. Clearly, to plan training effectively, coaches must have a realistic appreciation of how players will work around a particular schedule.

The organization of training should also include the work that needs to be completed away from the training field, such as video review of matches to train tactical decision making, develop anticipation, explain broad strategies and analyze opposition strengths and weaknesses. Furthermore, some training-related activities, can be walked through in any suitable area before being practiced on the pitch, such as planning how best to defend against specific moves from a five-metre (16-foot) scrum. Training organization should give players genuine free time during which they can completely take their minds off rugby. Clearly stated expectations of when work is required and when it is not help to maintain effort and attention.

Practice Structure

Traditional rugby training sessions that use repeated skills on the same drill before moving to another are not the best for maximizing long-term player learning. They simply do not hone players' ability to retain and perform the skill when required. Once players get into the groove of performing the skill well, they stay in that focus and repeat the skill. What they need to learn is how to get into that groove time and time again.

An example of a varied practice structure might require players to switch randomly from catching a high ball to making a man-on-man, head-on tackle to setting up a maul and secure possession. This approach is much more effective for learning than a block of catching drills, a block of tackling and a block of mauling. Research on learning suggests that practice that requires players to be more actively engaged in the process increases the learning effect.

Long-term learning refers to how well the skill can be remembered and recalled after a period of no practice. In general, a coach wants forwards to develop excellent long-term learning for rucking. But if the aim changes to achieving rapid skill acquisition, then traditional blocks of repetitive drills are most effective. For example, if a winger is drafted at fullback because of injury but is unsteady under the high ball, then practice structure should be designed so that he performs a high volume of catches. Even in this situation, practicing different variations of catches in a random order—running back to catch overhead, running forward to take catch, timing run to jump and catch—enhances the learning of the skill so that it is more adaptable to the varying conditions in competition.

But if a coach wants to arrange practice to teach this new fullback other long-term playing skills, he might arrange drills that change from high ball catching, to kicking for touch from lineouts and scrums, to counterattacking off low-balls, then to kicking high balls in return or kicking for the corners. Randomly changing the practice pattern of different skills enhances long-term retention and performance.

In conclusion, practice should be goal-directed and flexible. Elite performers in any sport aim for quality practice, not quantity. If the goals for one element are rapidly achieved, then it makes sense to practice another skill. A forwards training session may have as its goal to practice defensive lineout throws aimed at securing possession and driving forward to move the opposition backwards. If the forwards perform this well with all different combinations of jumpers and numbers in the line, then practice should move to another skill, such as attacking moves.

Simulation

Movement patterns produced under stressful conditions are not the same as when the task is completed without any pressure. Performance under stress is actually a different skill than without stress. As a consequence, it is important that the right training environment and conditions are used to make training as similar as possible to performing under competitive conditions. Players should heed this ideal: Practice as you play!

It is important to ensure that players are completely familiar with the competitive situation through realistic practice conditions. Any number of factors can be manipulated to increase the degree of simulation and improve the transfer of skills from training. Players should wear similar kit to that in which they will play in, particularly with regards to boots and protective equipment. Neoprene supportive clothing may be marginally restricting, for example, when reaching for a lineout ball, so players may need to practice lineout work under the same conditions as in a match.

The training environment should closely match the one that is going to be played in. For example, if the team is going to play a night game, then a few training sessions should be completed under floodlights to familiarize players with the conditions, particularly skills such as catching high balls while facing the lights. Training should also simulate competition with regards to fatigue because skilled performance tends to degrade with fatigue. Consequently, skills should be practiced at different stages of fatigue. To allow for practice during a fatigued state, players should switch some of their solo sessions to the time immediately after squad training.

During the 1990s, the Welsh team conducted practice sessions before the Five Nations tournament in the national stadium at Cardiff. These sessions were completed against a background of recorded crowd noise played through the stadium speakers. The intention was to simulate the difficulties of playing with loud crowd noise, which may have an impact on aspects such as calling moves.

Coaches also move performance towards competition level by changes in the speed or distances used in drills. Both of these restrict the time available to think and react, but they also create a situation that is more realistic of competition. The increase in substitutions in recent years, along with the introduction of blood and sin bins, means that teams need to practice reorganizing quickly and changing strategy to suit situations in which they are a man down or playing with individuals out of position. This ability is particularly critical if the player removed is a key decision maker or has a primary role in organizing defense. Roles need to be explicitly stated among teammates to allow them to compensate for any absences.

Finally, all skills must be practiced at match intensity and in the order in which they are likely to occur. Skills should not continually be practiced in blocks because the game does not normally follow this pattern. Skill training must include continuous practice involving all sequences of skills. Defensive practice must be structured so that players learn how to transform defense into attack. Defense is simply one of the situations that affords good offensive opportunities, and a team practicing defense should be encouraged to launch attacks once possession has been regained.

Team Performance

On match day, there may seem to be little input from the coaching staff, other than in a supportive role and making substitutions. But the coaches' presence, reassuring instruction and ability to engineer space for players to focus can be instrumental in providing the optimal conditions for preparation. Every coach should recognize that the time for learning new skills or planning new strategies has passed and the focus must be on playing with what has been practiced. Coaches must recognize that they can be a source of stress if they try to remind players of too many things or introduce new ideas on match day. Sound preparation is critical to performance, whether defense or attack, and it should not be left to chance.

Practical Applications: Team Performance

- Plan preparation backwards from kickoff.
- Stick to timing so that players can complete preparation around the schedule.
- Practice competition-style communication.
- Devise and practice calls and signals for quick, clear communication.
- Maintain quality communication to allow defenses to adapt to attacks.

While most players communicate reasonably well in training, in competition the quantity and quality of communication typically decreases, especially when a team comes under pressure and grows tired. Communication changes from training to competition: In the former, players exchange ideas and develop skillful play; in the latter, the only emphasis is on maximizing performance. In match-play simulation, though, players should communicate as they would in competition, and they should reserve additional feedback until later.

Communication is also essential for organizing the defense, particularly against novel attacking moves of the opposition. Changing from one strategy to another should be clear and quick, accomplished by a single call. Clear calls should be devised and used all the time in practice. For example, "hit the maul" or "weak side break" might be practiced calls. New team members should be assigned a veteran player who teaches them all the calls required for their positions to accelerate their full integration to the team. At the simplest level, communication can help teammates identify who is marking each opponent. Calling this out may increase the pressure on opposition players, as they hear that they are in somebody's sights!

Finally, communication is critical to maintain the capacity to adapt as the game progresses. If players realize that particular attacks are penetrating their defense, then they need to communicate to organize alternative solutions to stop their opponents. For example, the pack leader could tell the weak-side flanker, "Make sure you tackle the #8 on the pickup." The ability to adapt in the heat of competition is the ultimate test of the level of communication.

Communication can break down when too many players begin to communicate at once and confuse the issues. Teams need to have explicit channels of communication and adhere to these in match-play training sessions. Coaches should designate players to make the calls in key aspects of play.

One interesting example of a situation in which the defense needed to adapt to counter attacking strategy was the game England lost to South Africa in the 1999 Rugby World Cup quarterfinal. South Africa played a clear game plan that recognized England's strong defense. Instead of expending huge effort in crossing for tries, South Africa was content to play into drop-goal range and take these much easier points. South Africa scored five drop-goals, but the defensive alignment of England did not appear to adapt to this threat. Even after the game plan should have been apparent, slow forwards were still trying to close down the South African flyhalf.

Mental skill training is a critical part of defensive preparation and execution in rugby league and union. In today's fast-paced game, the team that has mentally prepared the best defense will likely succeed. Remember, defense wins championships!

chapter

9

Mental Sharpness for Every Match

David J. Collins
University of Edinburgh

Patrick Mortimer
University of Edinburgh

Bruce D. Hale
University of Maine

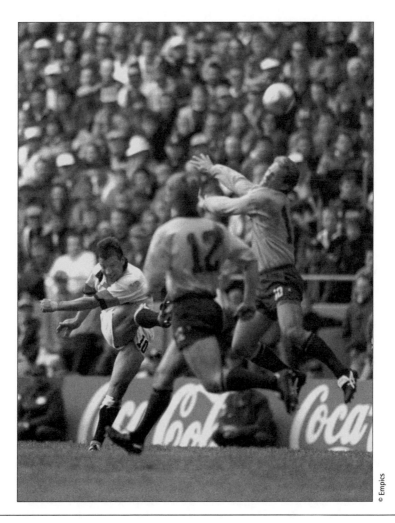

© Empics

Rugby is played in an unpredictable environment—after all, the ball doesn't even bounce the same each time! Consequently, victory doesn't just hinge on sound planning and preparation. To win consistently, both the team and individual players must be prepared to identify and think through challenges set by the opposition and the playing environment, and they must be ready to solve problems on the hoof in a way that best suits the team's collective skills. In short, being mentally sharp for a game revolves around preparation that enables players to spot problems and empowers them to come up with acceptable and effective solutions.

Mental preparation needs to take place both in training and just before competition. Each process is interdependent with the other. Players need to first become skilled in general psychological rugby skills during training; then they need to develop more specialized preparation routines and plans for specific matches. In this chapter, we examine the common causes of challenging problems and finish with some practical hints for creating personalized individual and team preparation routines for games.

Mental Preparation in Training

Sport vision is a recent addition to the sport science armory, and more players are receiving help from specialists to improve their visual acuity. Sometimes, though, the issue is an apparently simpler but more common problem—getting players to simply *look*. Frustrated at his players' lack of ability to see spaces and attacking possibilities (does this sound familiar?), Great Britain's field hockey coach Jon Royce developed the Decision Web (DWeb), a structured format for developing players' ability to effectively attend to, or scan, the game environment.

Figure 9.1 shows the DWeb model, a structure for the continual cycle of visual scanning that any rugby player must constantly employ to avoid missing any key information. Because it is a cycle, we can start anywhere. For convenience however, we'll start at the top, with the player moving without the ball.

Prescanning means looking at what is happening in front and behind, which is essential no matter how far away from the ball a player is. Players ideally know what they are going to do with the ball before they get it, and prescanning is a skill that enables

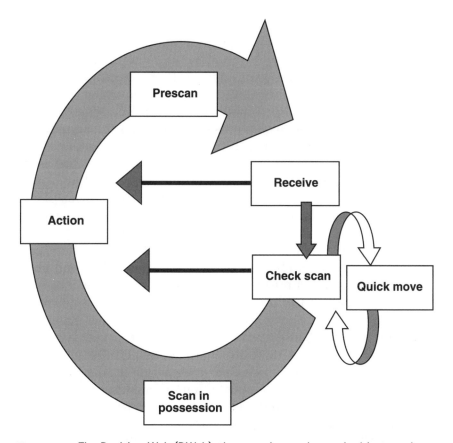

Figure 9.1   The Decision Web (DWeb), the scanning cycle required in team invasion games.
Adapted from *Coaching Focus* (1994) Vol 26, pp. 20-22, with kind permission of *Sports Coach UK* (scUK). All rights reserved. ScUK subscription and membership services provide a range of benefits to coaches including insurance and information services. For further details please ring 0113-274 4802 or visit **www.sportscoachuk.org**.

fluid and fast play—how could a player execute a tap pass unless he knew where his supporting player was before the ball came to him? If players are weak at this facet, they will constantly be the source of a move breaking down or a sudden halt to forward progress. Acute prescanning skills allow barbarian-like play and help players receive and give in one movement, hence the arrow from *receive* to *action*.

Keep in mind that this fluidity isn't always required, or even always sensible for that matter. Players must learn to *check scan*, taking another quick look to make sure before they execute. Weakness here results in many interceptions. Effective check scanning helps the player know when to close up and take the hit. If the check scan shows no danger, then the player can take the preplanned option, hence the arrow to *action*. But if there is a problem, such as a potential intercepting defender or a block further down the pitch, a *quick move* often allows the situation to move forward and the danger to clear. After a second quick check scan, the pass, swerve or kick can be executed safely and effectively. Lack of the ability to momentarily stop everything (often seen to good effect in Sevens play) means that the hapless player seems to run blindly into problems, and the move will therefore falter.

In the final analysis, if there is still nothing on, then the player must move purposefully, *scanning in possession* to spot likely options. After the action—whether a pass, kick or swerve—the player once again starts prescanning to stay in the game. Beware of the prima donna player who, after making the half break and dumping the ball off, looks around for adulation . . . yes, you know who we mean!

So that's the DWeb. Notice that a weakness at any particular facet results in an observable problem. Of course, we all make mistakes, but if match statistics show a consistent type of error by one player, the coach should be reaching for the DWeb to see what can be done. Most players have a weak spot somewhere in the web. Systematic checking and training is a useful step to fully develop players while avoiding crucial errors. Also recognize that the scanning skills within the DWeb are essential for developing decision-making skills, arguably the hottest topic for coaches in the game at present. It's simple—if you aren't aware of it, then you can't make decisions about it. Coaches ignore DWeb development at their own peril.

Great. But what can be done about it? Designing DWeb drills is relatively straightforward once you understand the stages of the web itself. Consider a simple passing game—a group of players pass several balls around a circle. To create a prescan drill, require passes to be made to anyone in the circle within one second of receiving the ball. Without looking before the ball is passed, a player cannot dispose of it safely in the time limit. Now increase the number of balls to just below the number of players, but allow a slightly longer time on the ball. This is a check scan drill, developing the key habit of preplanning (based on prescan) but checking to avoid passing to a player who already has a ball.

More complex drills are easily designed. Just consider what sort of things the player has to look at (the display) and when, then design the drill accordingly. Figure 9.2 shows a scan in possession drill that gives the player a game-realistic display that must be scanned on the move. A defender (square) and an attacker (circle) set off around their respective cone markers at the same time. The coach feeds a ball to the attacker as early as possible, which triggers a second attacker to start a run up the other side of the waiting players. The waiting players act as

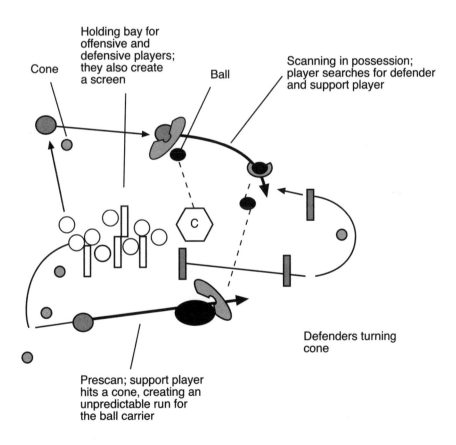

Cone

Holding bay for offensive and defensive players; they also create a screen

Ball

Scanning in possession; player searches for defender and support player

Defenders turning cone

Prescan; support player hits a cone, creating an unpredictable run for the ball carrier

Figure 9.2 A preliminary scanning in possession drill, involving a full team.

a screen to prevent the first attacker from viewing the support player too early, which mimics the kind of traffic seen in a game. An added bonus is that players have the opportunity to watch, encourage and (God forbid!) learn from their teammates.

The attackers' collision distance is determined by how far the defender travels from the starting bay. The coach's objective is to find the correct distance to allow the ball to get away . . . but not too easily. This feat is achieved by simply moving the defender's turning cone up or down the practice channel.

The use of the drill is in itself a test of decision making. The drill provides the coach with situations that provoke errors (yes, we want errors) and therefore enables feedback to be focused on individual weaknesses. Common errors result from miscalculation of distances and times to cover before collision. Common but dysfunctional solutions seen might include the first attacker taking evasive action, such as slowing down or turning across field to link up, actions seen in international players.

As in the basic circle drill, practices can be designed that address different parts of the DWeb; it depends on the timing of the pass by the coach. The Saloon Doors drill is an excellent example, equally suitable for Rugby Union or Rugby League. In this drill, two or more players with tackle shields act as the saloon doors, swinging open or shut as required at times dictated by the coach through both verbal instruction and by the timing of the pass to the practicing players. A prescan variation is shown in figure 9.3.

The drill depends on the coach's feeding, with the feed completed only once the player has scanned the saloon door players' positions. The ball can be fed earlier or later, governed by the time between collision and depending on the player's skill level. In this variation, the two defenders remain together or apart once the ball has been received. The coach can throw the ball onto the ground to encourage the support player's prescan and communication role.

Common errors appear in the form of ball watching. Players' stride patterns become hesitant, and they appear rushed once the ball is received. To add even more pressure, allow the defenders to advance, which reduces the amount of time the attacker has to view the defense.

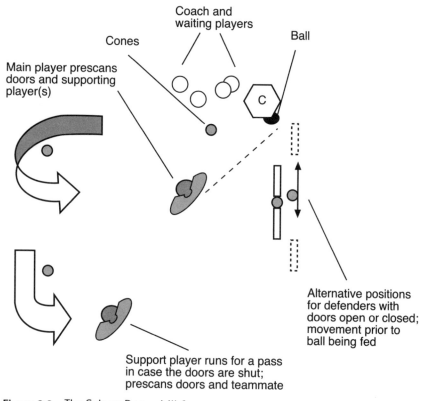

Coach and
waiting players

Cones

Ball

Main player prescans
doors and supporting
player(s)

C

Alternative positions
for defenders with
doors open or closed;
movement prior to
ball being fed

Support player runs for a pass
in case the doors are shut;
prescans doors and teammate

Figure 9.3 The Saloon Doors drill for prescan.

The drill can easily be modified to test the player's check scan skills. Version I, shown in figure 9.4, involves a single runner changing his running line in response to moves made by the defender. This drill relies on the defender altering his position when the ball is 20 to 100 centimetres away from the receiver. The receiver must be running fluently, from when he rounds the cone through receiving the ball to running past the blocking defender.

Version II, shown in figure 9.5 (p. 213), presents the player with a game-realistic display and represents a challenging combination of the two previous drills. Not only do the defenders move before the ball is fed, but they can also alter their position as the ball is in the air. Thus the attacker now has to prescan and check scan, altering his plan accordingly. A second attacker adopts a support role for the distribution pass. This practice depends on both the precision of the feed and the defenders' movements.

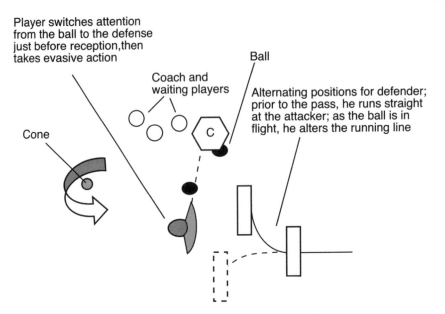

Player switches attention
from the ball to the defense
just before reception,then
takes evasive action

Ball

Coach and
waiting players

Alternating positions for defender;
prior to the pass, he runs straight
at the attacker; as the ball is in
flight, he alters the running line

Cone

C

Figure 9.4   The Saloon Doors drill for check scanning, version I.

The most common error is that the attacker gets a good smack in the chops, commonly known as *man and ball*. Alternatively, the second attacker may not prescan properly and always go up the outside (the right) of the primary attacker. This is not a problem if the doors are open, although this option equals lazy play, but it does cause problems quickly if the defenders close the doors at the last moment. In this case, the primary attacker usually needs a short and easy dump-pass option, which is entirely dependent on the support player's position. Of course, this situation is also avoided if the attacker is able to look away from the ball without discernible change in pace or stride. In this case, he avoids man-and-ball contact and is able to perform an avoidance maneuvre.

Because the DWeb can be used to highlight individual weaknesses, it can also be used as the basis for individual development, with specialized drills designed to address the player's personal needs. To demonstrate this process, we include a sample intervention that was completed on a junior international, as part of an ongoing development program for talented players.

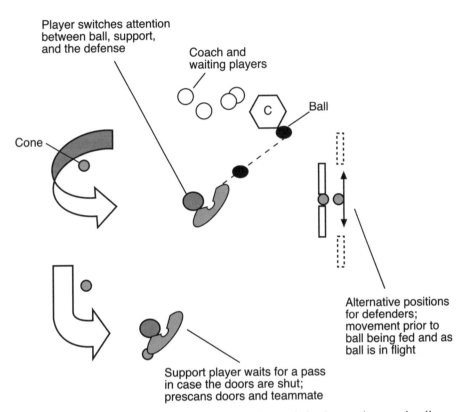

Player switches attention between ball, support, and the defense

Coach and waiting players

Ball

Cone

Alternative positions for defenders; movement prior to ball being fed and as ball is in flight

Support player waits for a pass in case the doors are shut; prescans doors and teammate

Figure 9.5 The Saloon Doors drill for prescanning and check scanning, version II.

Case Study

Player A was a back-row forward with specialist experience at blindside and #8. This player was noted for his ability to make adjustments during passing and ball reception, which prevented him turning the ball over—all the while receiving man and ball at the same time. DWeb assessment of Player A clearly showed that he was able to check scan, which nicely explained his ability to avoid defenders at the last second. On consultation with Player A's coach, the next step was for him to be able to capitalize on his check scan ability (avoidance of players during reception) by developing the ability to release other players around him.

To assist Player A, his coach and sport psychologist identified a particular situation, together with target behaviors and mental actions, that appeared to be a common challenge for him. During videotape review of the errors in his games, we were able to identify that he was indeed check scanning, often taking his eyes off the ball before reception to check what teammates and opponents were doing. On questioning, Player A revealed that as a result of the information he gleaned through these check scans, he adjusted his body position to ride the oncoming tackle but was uncomfortable with taking the alternative option of releasing the ball as it often resulted in a fumbled reception and pressure on the team.

The initial target of behavior change was to build upon his support role during defensive retreat situations. His outstanding ability to recover ball and slip tackles would become "phenomenal" (in his coach's words) if he could learn to release the ball for counterattacks and not always take safety first options, such as making mauls or rucks. It was clear that check scans were desirable and that adding prescans to ball watching before reception would allow Player A to make the outlet passes desired—the distribution of recovered ball obtained during frenzied situations into controlled directions of play.

At this point we educated the player and the coach on the DWeb to assist the player's learning and transition. Once the education had been completed, we then assessed his performance, identifying the lack of a prescan in the retreat phase of his game and the available time for prescanning as issues for attention. This evaluation was achieved first through analysis of video footage of him retreating to recover ball, then through quantifying the amount of time he spent staring at teammates.

Two core-coaching strategies were implemented. First, Player A had to develop the ability to scan away from the ball during retreat phases of his game. This action depended on his capacity to predict the actions of teammates and defenders and also on reducing his dependence on ball security. Second, he had to adjust his body position during the retreat phase to carry out the prescan, which meant opening himself up to a side-on tackle or facing up to the oncoming players. He anticipated a potential loss in pace to the appropriate field position, but the coach felt further effort in his physical training would compensate for this loss. Once all this diagnosis and planning had taken place, the coach, player and sport psychologist set about building prescan drills to target retreat scans.

The coach, player and sport psychologist agreed that all should be present during feedback, and this decision was important to the success of practice for two reasons. The coach would be able to reinforce the player more often than the sport psychologist, and the coach could concentrate on the other players while the retreat scan work was being carried out (figure 9.6).

Feedback was accomplished first through practice video footage, then game footage in front of the player. Video feedback was conducted pitchside during practice. A review followed immediately after each attempt. Following repeated blocks of practice, pressure was increased through the use of random, distributed and combination practices. Game support became a two-part process. First, retreat situations underwent videotape review to reinforce positive behavioral change and subsequent reinforcement by mental practice. Second, the player and coach enlisted

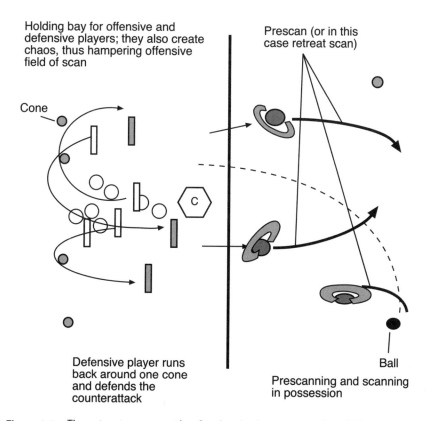

Figure 9.6   The retreat scan practice for developing prescanning skills.

the support of fellow players to provide verbal triggers in practice and open play.

From start to finish, the whole intervention took six playing weeks to initiate and nine weeks before the target behavior was achieved. The rapid success of the intervention was also dependent on the instrumental cooperation of the coach and other players. The use of the DWeb enabled everyone involved to both conceptualize the problem and rapidly design drills and challenging practices to address it. As a result, Player A was mentally sharper and more able to react positively to a crucial part of his playing role.

Team-Specific Problem Solving

Once the players identify the problems set by the opposition, they need to come up with solutions. This facet of play is currently receiving a great deal of attention, with rugger gurus creating decision-making (DM) drills regularly for training. A rather neglected factor in DM—the team dimension—is also important to concentrate on, and this new construct relates to the old idea of playing style.

Some teams just seem to have distinctive styles, which dictate the action they take in any particular setting. For example, England was known as a forward-oriented side (until recently, at any rate). Accordingly, players would tend to take keep-it-tight options, reflecting the style of the team and demonstrating a characteristic psychologists call a shared mental model (SMM).

Players with a common SMM look at a situation in similar ways, focus on the same factors in the display and come up with answers that fit the team consensus. The SMM is crucial; without it players may focus on different aspects of the display and come up with different answers that ultimately confuse their teammates. The consequences are failure to follow the game plan and not making the best use of the team's talents, which explains a lot of what is seen in the elite game. For instance, players may play together really well on one team, only to struggle when selection or transfer places them in a group with a different SMM.

The degree of commonality in SMM, or how similarly the team perceives situations and solves problems, is called coherence. Coherent teams are more effective because their responses are both similar and quicker than less coherent teams.

Figure 9.7 presents coherence in pictorial form. The team on the right has several players with tight SMMs. These players demonstrate a common understanding of opposition challenges, weigh factors in the display in similar ways and quickly follow or even anticipate each other's actions. The player outside the circle is trying to learn this system and until doing so will struggle to match the speed and apparent smoothness of his teammates' DM.

The team on the left is in similar shape, with several players possessing a common SMM. Consider the player between the circles, just touching the outside of the circle on the right. This player, perhaps transferring between the two teams, or even trying to adjust his style from club to country, will demonstrate slower, even confused DM. Players in this position have to rely on a conscious, think-it-through style, rather than the more automatic, gut-feeling style that is increasingly essential in today's fast-paced game.

Ideally, the advantages of coherence are clear. Ongoing research shows that coherence is a clear characteristic of elite teams and that this advantage is independent of how long players have played or practiced together. The implications therefore are simple: Coherence is a characteristic of good sides, but it doesn't happen automatically. This conclusion leads to the inevitable question, So how can this extremely desirable characteristic be developed? Research shows that the way to change the SMM—and therefore increase coherence—revolves around

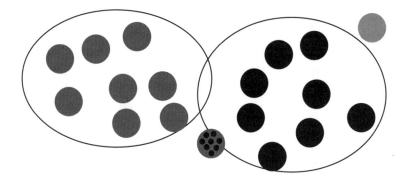

Figure 9.7 A pictorial representation of coherence and the presence (or absence) of shared mental models (SMMs).

long-term discussion and structured practices focused on the reasons underlying the decisions taken.

Consider two examples, one simple and one complex. The best and simplest exemplar of SMMs can be seen in the classic two-versus-one drill shown in figure 9.8. Notice first that to promote prescanning, the attacking players run around cones before receiving the ball, rather than just starting at the end of a grid (as in the drill shown in figure 9.2, p. 209). The main point relates to the defender's position. The two extremes shown are the lower and upper boxes, in which the attacker's decision is simplest. The top position means draw and pass while the lower is a dummy and go.

There is, however, a position of maximum confusion in the middle, in which any sensible defender will stand because it offers the smallest clue (and hardest decision) for the attacker. But where are the positions that automatically cue one or another of the two options? In other words, how far in one direction or

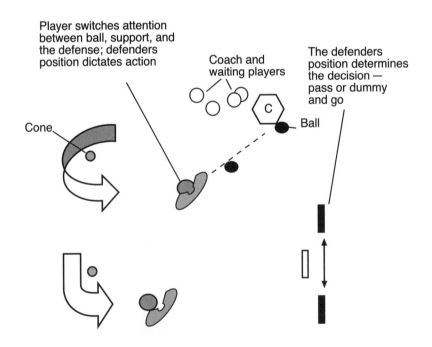

Figure 9.8   The two-versus-one drill (with DWeb variation).

the other must the defender move before the attacking option is clear? No one knows for sure, but there had better be general agreement about it if one of the attackers is not to be caught by the unexpected actions of the other. In situations such as this one, which presents multiple scenarios to consider, an SMM clearly becomes a survival skill when a team wants to win with cohesion.

A more subtle example relates to the defender's body position. Work on this can be quite useful in developing a defensive stance that is maximally confusing to attacking opposition, one that gives little clue to the defender's intentions. In all cases, discussion helps to expose each player's weighting scale as to which factors of the display—the defender's foot position, gaze, on the toes or balls of the feet, and so on—are the most important and what his preferred option is. Greater agreement enables players to anticipate each other's actions and react to them, each taking actions that cover for or support their teammate (back-up behavior).

Team coherence at the other end of the scale is illustrated in figure 9.9. Consider the options that any particular team can take from an attacking scrum at position A. Preferences depend on relative strengths and weaknesses, and they vary from team to team; however, the effective team is coherent and holds a pretty tight SMM as to what the best option may be.

What happens if the scrum is at position B? How does the team plan change, and what must each player do differently to optimally support this plan? Once again, that depends on the team DM. The coherent team has a tight SMM, which means that each player is aware of what options are likely.

Many coaches try to generate tightness by the development of elaborate playbooks. Such choreographic coaching can be effective, but unfortunately, the complexity of the game means that the prearranged moves rarely, if ever, meet the players' needs. Prelaid plans inevitably lack flexibility, but coherence, by contrast, is based on a deeper but broader understanding that relates to principles, rather than procedures. These principles of play can be simple and individual (as shown in figure 9.8, p. 216) or they can be complex, total-team systems. The latter are well developed by meaningful discussions and practices, such as the

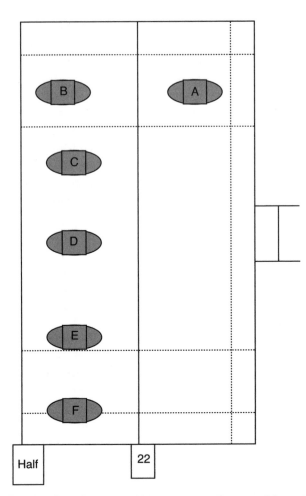

Figure 9.9 Team options from attacking scrums—a clear need for coherence.

changes in tactical plans that occur with scrums at positions B, C, D, E and F.

One more point about coherence. When we introduce this idea, some coaches express concerns that these types of structures can inhibit creativity and make teams predictable and easy to read and counter. Not at all, a prime example being the similarities and differences between top-class flair players (such as the second author) and total donkeys (such as the first!). Both do unexpected things. The key difference is that the flair player's actions fit in with the team's overall aims, and other players' actions rapidly fall in with the plan. The unaware idiot does the unexpected and rarely does this action contribute to the greater good. Thus, the flair player's common SMM with his teammates is paradoxically liberating, enabling creative actions that can be supported by the team.

Developing coherence is a long-term project that is not commonly addressed by many of the elite coaches we have observed. Developing coherence offers so much potential benefit that we endorse it as effort well spent for any coach. In fact, it may even generate greater benefits than the technique emphasis that predominates in junior rugby!

Mental Preparation for Competition

In addition to developing general mental skills such as decision making and team coherence in daily training, each player and every team should organize their mental skills training programs as systematic, year-round plans to be fully prepared for the competitive season (see table 9.1) . Mental skills training can't be a hit-or-miss practice strategy used on the odd occasion. It must be a regularly scheduled component of the comprehensive training program if mental skills are to be optimally implemented in competition. It is not a magic pill that can be taken the night before the big game for dramatic behavior change.

We used Bompa's (1983) and Bacon's (1988) periodic training model to provide you with examples of a year-round mental training plan for both individual players and teams. Because we believe in a scientific, educational learn-by-doing approach to training, basic mental skills are first learned in the preseason phase and then gradually adapted to rugby situations. These skills are regularly practiced in and out of basic training sessions for the one to two months, encompassing general fitness and rugby skills training.

For example, a player or team might first be taught different strategies of imagery use, then they are given opportunities in and out of practice to try it out. In particular, they might learn how to visualize decision-making strategies we previously discussed in two-versus-one passing drills or how to imagine their role in lineout throwing, binding or jumping.

TABLE 9.1 YEAR-ROUND MENTAL TRAINING PLAN

Time of year	Primary purpose	Specific activities
Preseason (Aug. to Sep.)	Learn basic skills	Individual goal setting Team goal setting Anxiety management Imagery and visualization Concentration and attentional focus Self-talk and confidence building
Precompetition (Sep.)	Put skills into practice	Individual and team goal setting Anxiety management Imagery and visualization Concentration and confidence building Team cohesion Offensive simulations Defensive simulations Decision making Individual prematch and match routines Team focusing/refocusing plans
Competition (Oct. to May)	Use skills to enhance performance	Specific team cohesion strategies Specific offensive and defensive simulations Specific decision-making strategies Individual prematch and match routines and assessment Team focusing/refocusing plans and assessment
Off-season (June to Aug.)	Prepare for next season	Year-end program evaluation Performance profiling Individual and team goal setting

The second phase of training (precompetitive) typically lasts one to four weeks. Teams are given opportunities to practice certain mental skills for specific, competitive situations that involve unopposed simulations, team scrimmages and low-level scrimmages against other teams. In addition, individual players should also be trying out their personalized, precompetitive routines and competitive focusing/refocusing plans (see the discussion in the next section and also chapters 7 and 8). With coaching feedback, players can then assess their mental toughness and tweak the techniques to make them more effective.

A good example would be concentration cues. Individual players can use their own special cues to help them remain focused or motivated during breaks in the action during scrimmages. Coaches and team leaders can verbalize rehearsed team or subgroup focus calls during different situations to test their effectiveness in matchlike settings. Players or coaches can fine-tune their individual or team focus cues based on the success or failure of these trials.

Phase 3 (competition) typically lasts for three to eight months and involves using mental skills interventions before, during and after competitions. Specific prematch routines and game strategies can be adapted for each specific opponent within the framework of the regular routines—for example, a player can become highly energized and aggressive in the first 20 minutes against a very hard-hitting side or visualize moves against a specific opponent. The goal of interventions is for the individual player and team to be mentally tough and to perform at a consistently high level in all matches. If mental weaknesses are discovered, the player or team can return to a more intensive retraining of basic mental skills to help regain playing form or adapt basic routines to cope with the new problems.

The final phase (the off-season) lasts one to three months, and it is a time when coaches and players assess their mental strengths and weaknesses of the past season to begin planning for the next season. Through individual evaluation, each player can complete a Rugby Performance Profile (see chapter 1) and with the coach's feedback, can create a step-by-step goal-setting plan (see chapter 2) for enhancing rugby and mental skills the next season. Players and coaches could even do some sport psychology reading during this rest period between Sevens matches!

For practice to become perfect, training must be thoroughly organized and planned. Players who want to effectively train their mental game so that their reactions are automatic and successful must regularly schedule their efforts. There are no miracles for becoming a better player or team.

Individual and Team Prematch Routines

Players and teams that are full of confidence immediately before a match have a better chance of victory than anxious, doubting players. Individuals who have a perceived sense of control over their actions and their impact on the surrounding environment tend to be more confident about their abilities. A sure way to create this feeling of control is to provide players with a sense that extraneous events and the environment are organized, orderly and under their control. On the other hand, if players feel the environment or task is constantly changing and feel doubt and uncertainty about their ability to control their actions, then their self-confidence wanes and their chance for success is severely reduced.

Therefore, it is imperative that each player and team develop various means of removing as much uncertainty as possible from the competitive atmosphere and create ways to build a sense of order and control in the immediate run-up before the match. Individual and team prematch routines are powerful strategies to enhance confidence levels and mental toughness. The key is to include a set of physical and mental acts, events or evaluations that function as a mental checklist for each player. Besides ensuring that all aspects of preparation have been covered, performing this routine before every match reduces anxiety and increases confidence. The routine occupies each player's mind and prevents anxiety. Confidence rises because the players believe they have controlled every possible part of pregame preparation and can cope with any eventuality.

Some team-oriented match preparation and simulation have already been discussed in chapters 7 and 8. In this section, we discuss how to build an individual prematch routine and organize a team prematch routine so that players are mentally sharp for every match.

Preparing an Individual Routine

Rugby is a game of ebb and flow in a changing environment lasting 80 minutes. The player who has prepared for the most options and can quickly cope with changing conditions or strategies ultimately succeeds. Individual routines can be broken down into four components (see table 9.2). Good players practice these routines until they are second nature, and they use them to reach consistently high performances.

Prematch Preparation

The prematch preparation period typically lasts from several days before to the night before the match. Players need to ensure that they have adequate sleep and consume energizing, healthy meals and fluids (seek nutritional advice if necessary). For psychological preparation, players should review videotapes of opponents' tendencies and watch their own prior good performances to build confidence. Mental rehearsal of planned match moves and roles can help sharpen individual and team execution and reinforce the benefits of training. Listening to self-talk audio tapes made by sport psychologists or players themselves can enhance self-belief. From a team perspective, this time period can be used for team discussions of game plans or pep talks, videotapes of prior excellent team performances, videotapes of opposition matches and action movies to motivate team intensity and aggression. Coaches and team leaders should organize the time management schedule for the final days before competition.

Prematch Routine

On the day of the match, routines need to be well learned and organized, and they need to provide a sense of control over events. Prematch routines should include good eating and drinking habits, physical and mental warm-ups and basic rugby drills. The routines should begin early on the day of the match with

TABLE 9.2 SAMPLE INDIVIDUAL MENTAL PREPARATION ROUTINE

	When	Activities or focus
Prematch preparation	Night before	Sleep Diet and nutrition Mental rehearsal Videos Positive self-talk (audio tapes) Team talks Action movies
Prematch routine	Morning before to minutes before	Food and drink Physical warm-up (1 hour: stretching, aerobic, strength, drills, plays, specific situations) Mental warm-up (mental rehearsal: kicks, plays, success, relaxation and breathing, positive self-talk, music, audio tapes, aggression, focusing/refocusing cues)
Match routine	During breaks in action and halftime	Focusing/refocusing cues (breaks in play: mistakes, poor start, strategy changes) Confidence building (positive self-talk, ignoring or reframing mistakes) Mental rehearsal (throws, passes, kicks, plays, roles, success) Motivation cues (offensive and defensive strategies, positive feedback, communication)
Postmatch routine	Immediately after game to end of day	Physical and mental cooldown (stretching and discussion) Fluid and food intake Postmatch evluation (focus on good execution, analyse mistakes, mentally correct, put behind you, set new goals, sandwich approach to feedback, socialize)

breakfast and travel plans choreographed within the team structure. Once the team arrives at the playing venue, the routine takes precedent. Some players even have a superstitious dressing routine, and if these strange minor routines provide a sense of order and control, they certainly can't hurt.

Once ready to warm up on the pitch, players should begin their well-organized warm-up routine to get them mentally and physically ready for kickoff (use the example in table 9.2 to create your own routine). The warm-up should include physical activities such as familiar stretching routines, aerobic warm-ups (sprints, strength work and aggressive hitting, for example), and team drills and play simulations. Mental routines can include mental rehearsal of plays, kicks and successful moves, which can be done during stretching routines and breaks. Relaxation and deep breathing exercises can be used to fine-tune arousal level. Repetition of positive self-affirmations enhance their confidence levels, and a review of focusing/refocusing cues helps players turn on their automatic pilots. Often players use rousing rock music or national anthems that combine imagery, relaxation or positive self-talk to get totally focused and mentally ready before stepping on the pitch. To feel in control, each player simply needs to devise an individual routine that is comfortable, comprehensive and performed in the same order before game time.

Match Routine

Match routines are quick reminders and mental cues that players can use during breaks in the action to refocus, reintensify, and reverse negative thoughts and actions. Focus cue words help players rehearse their roles and bring their minds back to the upcoming task. Positive self-talk boosts confidence when it's lagging, and it reinforces a well-executed play. Mental imagery can be used for rehearsing upcoming roles in lineouts, pack or back moves and kicking schemes. Refocusing routines help identify task cues—such as the ball, an opponent or teammate—that help players return to the task at hand after a disastrous mistake, periods of poor play, a bad start in a match or for changes in offensive or defensive strategy. Finally, effective match routines contain communication cues and phrases that are frequently used by team leaders among teammates to ensure team coherence and success. These cues or routines should be written down and rehearsed both individually and in team practices.

Postmatch Routine

Every player needs a way to quickly elicit a physical and mental cooldown after a match. These immediate postgame periods usually involve stretching routines with fluid and nutrient replacement. Short, open team meetings led by a coach or team leader allow for initial analysis, open discussion of good and bad events, reinforcement of effective strategies and preliminary goal setting for next week's workouts.

When possible, the emphasis should be on good performance and execution, nonemotional analysis of errors and immediate mental correction for proper execution. Players shouldn't dwell on mistakes; once stated and corrected, they need to set them aside until they can be corrected in training. Good coaching should involve the "sandwich" method of feedback, where leaders first identify positive aspects of effort or play to an individual, then offer technical corrections about a specific decision or action and finally encourage the player to spend extra effort in training to improve this aspect of his game. And a bit of advice: enjoy the postmatch social. Winning the party may not be the ultimate goal, but forming friendships with opponents and learning from the opposition is an enjoyable culmination to the day.

Team Mental Preparation Routines

If the goal is to reduce uncertainty and raise team confidence, then the team must develop and regularly use physical and mental routines that give players a sense that they are optimally ready to succeed. As table 9.3 shows, good teams structure pregame preparation beginning several days before the match and organize specific activities to deal with the opposition and the environment. A team can modify the individual mental preparation routines (table 9.2, p. 226) for the team to use before, during and after the match.

Preparing for the Environment

Many teams ignore this side of preparation at their peril. Field conditions and weather often call for a severe change of tactics. One of the first things that many coaches do upon arrival at the pitch is to step off the yardage for length and width to see if

TABLE 9.3 TEAM MENTAL MATCH PREPARATION

	Areas to consider	Interventions
Preparing for the environment: creating the psycho-logical mindset	Pitch: grass, size, slope, posts Atmosphere: crowd, stands, noise, family, friends Referee: typical penalties, allowable fouls, accessibility, game length Weather: wind, rain, cold, snow, heat, altitude	Mental rehearsal Scouting reports Videotapes Simulated noise Prior practice on the pitch Simulation in same conditions
Preparing for the opposition: psychological domination	Attack their weaknesses: defense, scrum, lineout, rucks/mauls Attack with your strengths: kicking, running plays, rucks/mauls, scrums, lineouts Defend their strengths: back-row attacks, kicking, rolling mauls Rehearse specific tactics to start the game: long kickoff, receiving kick Specific situational attacks for a psychological edge: tapped ball, kicking, recycling rucks/mauls, score in match (ahead, behind, time left), score before or after the half, score back-to-back, defend after being scored upon	Videotape Mentally rehearse strategies Communication during the match for back and forward calls Cues for psyching up (challenge call) Focusing/refocusing cues Positive feedback at breaks Simulated scrimmages under match conditions (score, time left, field position)

reduced size will affect the game plan. Condition of the grass, slope of the field and goal post size should also be checked.

Next, teams should be aware of the atmosphere at the pitch. Will there be a large crowd with lots of noise that could negatively affect the team, which is used to playing in front of sparse crowds and silence? Are the stands very close to the touchline? Will there be many friends and family in the stands that may cloud players' attentional focus?

A veteran side knows what to expect from the referee. Does he allow play to continue with small infractions or is he a whistle freak? Are many penalties called on set plays? Does the referee allow fringing on off-sides in rucks and mauls? Does the referee allow team representatives, including the coach, to talk to him? How much time is typically added to the half? If players don't know the answers to these questions ahead of the match, they may be spending time in the sin bin or even be sent off!

Finally, it is important to be aware of the coming weather conditions and how they affect the pitch. Does the wind tend to blow from one end constantly (this is especially important for kickers to know)? Can players expect to have a hard time handling a greasy ball in rain, mud or even snow? Is fatigue due to high temperature likely to be a concern? Will altitude affect the visiting team more than the home team? A good team may lose because their preplanned match strategy is not effective under certain environmental conditions.

How can teams mentally prepare for a certain pitch or weather conditions? Probably the most effective means, other than experience, is to imagine how the playing venue will look and what it will seem like under certain conditions. A coach or player who has been there before can describe the layout in detail, and the rest of the squad can visualize the venue. Of course, a videotape of the pitch would be very helpful.

If the transfer-of-training principle suggests that teams should practice under the same conditions as they play, then the team should train on the same pitch under the same weather and crowd conditions as during the match. If an especially noisy crowd may disrupt on-field communications and jeopardize effective concentration, then teams may want to practice with noisy crowd noise piped in over the public address system. Always try to get on the pitch the day or morning before to learn about its idiosyncrasies and adjust strategies if necessary. Try to make the pitch seem familiar to reduce home field advantage and increase certainty and confidence.

Preparing for the Opposition

Much of today's coaching science and team training involves preparation for specific opponents, but more effective preparation should include a means of psychological attack. An obvious rule of thumb is to attack the opponent's weaknesses—their defense, scrum, lineouts, rucks and mauls, kick coverage and so on. For example, if they commit too many bodies to the ruck or maul, then quickly move the ball outside to an overlap. If the flyhalf despises tackling, run the back row at him repeatedly. Scouting reports, prior opponents and videotapes provide many potential areas for attack.

Another no-brainer is to attack with your team's strengths, whether by kicking, running, handling, rucks and mauls, lineouts or scrums. For example, if your side has a relatively large, immobile pack, you may want to keep the ball in their hands on set plays from the scrum or lineout, or you could use rolling mauls or pounding fringe runs from the rucks. It may be foolish to try

A prepared team will be able to take advantage of the opponent's weaknesses.

to run the ball wide repeatedly where your lack of support will be quickly exploited.

Finally, from a defensive point of view, teams should defend against their opponent's strengths in training. For instance, if you know the opposition attacks frequently from the #8 player off scrums, then make sure your backrow and scrumhalf are automatic in their defensive cover. If the flyhalf kicks often, train your fullback and wings in catching high balls, support and counterattacking.

Although rugby is a fluid sport, many teams attempt to control play and tempo by scripting several plays or tactics at certain times during a match. For example, let's presume that you are the kick-off side. A well-placed, deep kickoff can often force the receiving team to kick to touch for your next planned lineout call, or it can force them to mishandle the ball resulting in a turnover in possession deep in their own end. Even many teams that are receiving the kickoff plan several set plays to retain possession, maintain recycling confidence and quickly get into the flow of the match. Specific positions on the pitch at certain times and in certain situations allow for preplanned attacks that can be rehearsed in training.

Many tactics in rugby can be used to swing momentum and quickly enable one side to gain a psychological edge. Quickly tapped penalties are an easy way to gain field advantage and put the opposition on its heels. Often a kick-and-cover strategy can disrupt a wide open offensive-style opponent and create offensive opportunities through effective Garryowens or chip kicks to the opposition's backfield. The oft forgotten rolling maul has made a comeback lately because it is difficult to defend and so effective from offensive lineouts in the opponent's territory. On the defensive side, you must know what the opponent is likely to try when ahead on points, behind in score or with little time remaining. Tactics to incur a change of possession are critical on defense in these situations.

Complete psychological domination of the opposition can occur if your team scores or shows great success at various junctures in the match. Scoring tries immediately before or after the half can finish off many a wilting opponent. Back-to-back tries can occur when the opposition is still focused on a past mistake. If a team hits them before they regroup, they will often fold. For your side, make sure you have a means to quickly regroup your defense after a score against you. Learn to quickly change possession or take an offensive role when the opposition is overextending itself on offense. Ultimately the team that wins dominates the psychological momentum, not just the field position and ball possession.

Chapters 7 and 8 discussed some mental ploys for optimal preparation for the opposition. In this technological age, videotape analysis is a necessity for every serious club. Players can also mentally rehearse their offensive and defensive roles and plays during physical training on and off the pitch. Communication on the pitch between team members is essential for team success. Backs and forwards need cue words and strategy calls so that players can anticipate their roles in ever-changing attacks or defense. Team leaders should also regularly call cues to rally down sides and psych them up, refocus team concentration and reinforce good play. Scrimmages should simulate every expected game situation—the score, time in the match, field position—and allow rehearsal of every practical option to enhance player certainty. Good teams psychologically prepare for plan B in case plan A fails.

Summary

We hope the new ideas introduced here are useful to players and coaches. Sport psychology abounds with techniques to maintain or regain focus, the other obvious component of mental sharpness. The major problem with such approaches, however, is that it is often unclear as to exactly what the focus should be on. An emphasis on coherence and the DWeb enables players to know what to focus on. The capacity of players and teams to use and modify plans rapidly in the face of dynamic situations typifies the modern game.

This text has introduced many psychological skills for players and how to incorporate them into team training and competition. While good coaches can teach many of these strategies, players who want to be sharp for every match must take responsibility to create and rehearse their own prematch and match routines. Elite players have learned that a fully prepared mind is the most powerful weapon they possess and the difference between success and failure. We wish you success in this mental challenge.

references

Chapter 1

Butler, R. 1996. *Profiling for better performance.* Leeds, UK: National Coaching Foundation.

Jenkins, N., and Rees, P. 1998. *Life at number 10: An autobiography.* Edinburgh, UK: Mainstream.

Chapter 2

Hodge, K. 1994. *Sport motivation: Training your mind for peak performance.* Auckland, NZ: Reed.

Hodge, K. 2000. *Sports thoughts: Inspiration and motivation for sport.* Auckland, NZ: Reed.

Hodge, K., and McKenzie, A. 1999. *Thinking rugby: Training your mind for peak performance.* Auckland, NZ: Reed.

Hodge, K., Sleivert, G., and McKenzie, A. 1996. *Smart training for peak performance: A complete sports training guide for athletes.* Auckland, NZ: Reed.

McKenzie, A., Hodge, K., and Sleivert, G. 2000. *Smart training for rugby: A complete rugby training guide for players and coaches.* Auckland, NZ: Reed.

Chapter 3

Hale, B.D. 1998. *Imagery training: A guide for sportspeople.* Leeds, UK: National Coaching Foundation.

Chapter 4

Hodge, K., and McKenzie, A. 1999. *Thinking rugby.* Auckland, NZ: Reed.

Moran, A.P. 1996. *The psychology of concentration in sport performers: A cognitive analysis.* Hove, UK: Psychology Press.

Nideffer, R. 1976. *The inner athlete.* New York: Crowell.

Pienaar, F. 1998. *Rainbow warrior.* London: CollinsWillow.

Summers, J.J., and Ford, S. 1995. Attention in sport. In *Sport psychology: Theory, applications and issues.* Ed. T. Morris and J.J. Summers, 63–89. Chichester, UK: Wiley.

Chapter 5

Jones, G. (in press). Performance Excellence: A personal perspective on the link between sport and business. *Journal of Applied Sport Psychology.*

Chapter 7

Andrew, R. 1994. *A game and a half.* London: Hodder & Stoughton.

Brown, V. 2001. The trying adventures of Captain Hook. *The Irish Times,* 8 March.

Dwyer, R. 1992. *The winning way.* Auckland, NZ: Rugby Press Limited.

McConnell, R. 1998. *Inside the All Blacks.* Auckland, NZ: Harper Collins (New Zealand) Limited.

McConnell, R. 2000. *The successful coach.* Auckland, NZ: Harper Collins (New Zealand) Limited.

Chapter 8

McConnell, R. 1998. *Inside the All Blacks.* Auckland, NZ: Harper Collins (New Zealand) Limited.

Chapter 9

Bacon, T.A. 1988. The planning and integration of mental training programs. *Science Periodical on Research and Technology in Sport* 10:1-8.

Bompa, T.O. 1983. *Theory and methodology of training: The key to athletic performance.* Dubuque, IA: Kendall and Hunt.

Orlick, T. 1986. *Psyching for sport.* Champaign, IL: Human Kinetics.

Royce, J. 1994. How do you coach decision-making? *Coaching Focus* 26:20-22.

index

contributors

Angela Abbott, Department of Physical Education, Sport and Leisure Studies, University of Edinburgh

Kirsten Barnes, England Women's Rugby sport psychologist, British sport psychologist.

Albert Carron, sport psychologist, University of Western Ontario

Steven Christensen, Australian sport psychologist, University of Southern Queensland

David J. Collins, England RFU sport psychologist, RFU Full Badge rugby coach

Bob Easson, Rugby Coach, Scottish Institute of Sport

Bruce D. Hale, USA Rugby sport psychologist; RFC coach at Penn State University, RFC coach at University of Maine

Ken Hodge, sport psychologist at the University of Otago (New Zealand), New Zealand RFU sport psychologist, RFC coach at University of Otago

Bruce Howe, Canada RFU sport psychologist; University of Victoria RFC coach, dean of faculty of education, University of Victoria

Alex McKenzie, Highlanders Super 12 Rugby Team—Professional Development Manager, RFC coach at University of Otago

Patrick Mortimer, Sale RFC coach, Heriot's RFC coach, University of Edinburgh sport psychologist

Krista Munroe, sport psychology professor, University of Windsor

Eddie O'Sullivan, national coach, Irish Rugby Football Union

Dean Richards, England Rugby, Leicester FC director of rugby, Leicester Football Club PLC

Hugh Richards, sport psychologist, University of Edinburgh

Paul Sheath, Australian sport psychologist, St. Peters Lutheran College

P.J. Smyth, sport psychologist, University of Limerick

Jeff Summers, sport psychologist, University of Tasmania

Austin Swain, Lane 4 Management Group Ltd.

Peter Terry, Wales RFU sport psychologist, Brunel University RFC Coach, University of Southern Queensland

about the editors

Bruce D. Hale possesses firsthand experience and in-depth knowledge of rugby as both a player and coach. He played as a fullback at Penn State University. He then coached for one of the top U.S. collegiate rugby programs at Penn State University. During that time, he led two men's rugby teams to the U.S. Collegiate Final Four.

Hale is also a certified sport psychology consultant for the Association for the Advancement of Applied Sport Psychology (AAASP) and has served as a consultant for the U.S. rugby team. He has specialized in rugby consulting for the U.S. Eagles, the Under 19s, the Cardiff Rugby Football Club, and the Wales Elite 2000 program. Hale is currently the director of academic support services at the University of Maine at Orono. He lives with his wife, Sandra, in Glenburn, Maine.

David J. Collins played rugby at prop for several top-level clubs in England (Bedford, Saracens) and holds an RFU full coaching badge. He served as the sport psychologist for the English RFU and also helped coach Penn State to the collegiate final four in the United States. Collins is currently the head of the department of physical education, sport, and leisure studies at the University of Edinburgh.

Collins is also a sport psychologist accredited by the British Association of Sport and Exercise Sciences (BASES) and has consulted with many elite athletes. For BASES, he serves as the president of the psychology section. Collins resides in Edinburgh, Scotland.